YOUR

FACE

TOMORROW

JAVIER MARÍAS

YOUR

FACE

TOMORROW

Volume One
Fever and Spear

Translated from the Spanish by Margaret Jull Costa

A NEW DIRECTIONS BOOK

The translator would like to thank Javier Marías, Annella McDermott, Palmira Sullivan,
Antonio Martín, and Ben Sherriff for all their help and advice.

Grateful acknowledgment is made to Ian Fleming Publications Ltd. for permission
to reproduce the extract from *From Russia With Love*, copyright © 1957 by Gildrose
Productions Ltd.

Manufactured in the United States of America
New Directions Books are printed on acid-free paper.
Published simultaneously in Canada by Penguin Books Canada, Ltd.
First published clothbound in 2005 and as a paperbook (NDP1081) in 2007
Design by Semadar Megged

Library of Congress Cataloging-in-Publication Data

Marías, Javier.
[Tu rostro mañana. English]
Your face tomorrow : fever and spear/Javier Marías ; translated from the Spanish by
Margaret Jull Costa.
p. cm.
Volume I, Fever and Spear ISBN: 978-0-8112-1612-8
Volume II, Dance and Dream ISBN: 978-0-8112-1656-2
Volume III, Poison, Shadow and Farewell ISBN: 978-0-8112-1812-2

(alk. paper)
I. Costa, Margaret Jull.   II. Title.
PQ6663.A7218T8313 2005
863'.64—dc22
2005000992

5 7 9 10 8 6

New Directions Books are published for James Laughlin
by New Directions Publishing Corporation
80 Eighth Avenue, New York 10011

For Carmen López M,
who will, I hope, want
to go on listening to me

And for Sir Peter Russell,
to whom this book is indebted
for his long shadow,
and the author,
for his far-reaching friendship

1
Fever

One should never tell anyone anything or give information or pass on stories or make people remember beings who have never existed or trodden the earth or traversed the world, or who, having done so, are now almost safe in uncertain, one-eyed oblivion. Telling is almost always done as a gift, even when the story contains and injects some poison, it is also a bond, a granting of trust, and rare is the trust or confidence that is not sooner or later betrayed, rare is the close bond that does not grow twisted or knotted and, in the end, become so tangled that a razor or knife is needed to cut it. How many of my confidences remain intact, of all those I have offered up, I, who have always laid such store by my own instinct and yet have still sometimes failed to listen to it, I, who have been ingenuous for far too long? (Less so now, less, but these things are very slow to fade.) The confidences I shared with two friends remain preserved and intact, unlike those granted to another ten who lost or destroyed them; the meagre confidences shared with my father, and the chaste ones vouchsafed to my mother, which were very similar, if not the same, although those granted to her did not last very long, and she can no longer break them or, at least, only posthumously, if, one day, I were to make some unfortunate discovery, and something that was hidden ceased to be hidden; gone are the confidences given to sister, girlfriend, lover or wife, past, present or imaginary (the sister is usually the first wife, the child wife), for in such relationships it seems almost obligatory that one should, in the end, use what one knows or has seen against the beloved or the spouse – or the person who turns out to have been only momentary warmth and flesh – against whoever it was who proffered revelations and allowed a witness to their weaknesses and sorrows and was ready to confide, or against the person who absent-mindedly reminisced out loud on the pillow not even aware of the dangers, of the arbitrary eye always watching or the selective, biased ear always listening (often it's nothing very serious, for domestic use only, when cornered or on the defensive, to prove a point if caught in a tight dialectical spot during a prolonged discussion, then it has a purely argumentative application).

The violation of a confidence is also this: not just being indiscreet and thereby causing harm or ruin, not just resorting to that illicit weapon when the wind changes and the tide turns on the person who did the telling and the revealing – and who now regrets having done so and denies it and grows confused and sombre, wishing he could wipe the slate clean, and who now says nothing – it is also profiting from the knowledge obtained through another's weakness or carelessness or generosity, and not respecting or remembering the route by which we came to know the information that we are now manipulating or twisting – sometimes it's enough just to say something out loud for the air to grasp and distort it: be it the confession of a night of love or of one desperate day, or of a guilty evening or a desolate awakening, or the drunken loquacity of an insomniac: a night or a day when the person talking talked as if there were no future beyond that night or that day and as if their loose tongue would die with them, not knowing that there is always more to come, that there is always a little more, one minute, the spear, one second, fever, another second, sleep and dreams – spear, fever, my pain, words, sleep and dreams – and then, of course, there is interminable time that does not even pause or slow its pace after our final end, but continues to make additions and to speak, to murmur, to ask questions and to tell tales, even though we can no longer hear and have fallen silent. To fall silent, yes, silent, is the great ambition that no one achieves not even after death, and I least of all, for I have often told tales and even written reports, more than that, I look and I listen, although now I almost never ask questions. No, I should not tell or hear anything, because I will never be able to prevent it from being repeated or used against me, to ruin me or – worse still – from being repeated and used against those I love, to condemn them.

And then there is distrust, of which there has been no shortage in my life either.

It's interesting how the law takes this into account and, even odder, takes the trouble to warn us: when someone is arrested, at least in films, he is allowed to remain silent, because, as he is immediately informed, 'anything you say can be used against you'. There is in this warning a strange – or indecisive and contradictory – desire not to play entirely dirty. That is, the prisoner is told that the rules will, from now on, be dirty, he is informed and reminded that, somehow or other, they are going to catch him out and will make the most of any blunders, lapses and mistakes he might make – he is no longer a suspect, but an accused man whose guilt they are going to try to prove, whose alibis they will try to destroy, he has no right to impartiality, not between now and the day he appears in court – all their efforts will be channelled into gathering the evidence that will condemn him, all their vigilance and monitoring and investigation and research into collecting the clues that will incriminate him and support their decision to arrest him. And yet they offer him the opportunity to remain silent, indeed, almost urge it upon him; they tell him about this right which he may have known nothing about, and therefore, sometimes, actually put the idea in his head: not to open his mouth, not even to deny what he is being accused of, not to run the risk of having to defend himself alone; remaining silent appears or is presented as being clearly the most sensible option, one that could save us even if we know ourselves to be and are guilty, as the only way in which this self-declared dirty game can be rendered ineffectual or barely practicable, or at least not with the involuntary and ingenuous collaboration of the prisoner: 'You have the right to remain silent'; in America, they call it the Miranda law and I'm not even sure if its equivalent exists in our countries, they used it on me once, a long time ago, well, not that long ago, but the policeman got it wrong, left out a bit, he forgot to say 'in court' when he rattled off the famous phrase, 'anything you say can be used against you', there were witnesses to this omission and the arrest was invalidated. The same strange spirit imbues that other right of the accused, not to testify against himself, not to prejudice himself verbally with his story or his answers, with his contradictions or stumblings. Not to harm himself by his own narrative (which can, indeed, cause great harm), in other words, to lie.

The game is, in fact, so dirty and so biased that, on such a basis, no justice system can possibly presume to be just, and perhaps, therefore, there is no possible justice, ever, anywhere, perhaps justice is a phantasmagoria, a false concept. Because what the accused is told boils down to this: 'If you say something that suits us and is favourable to our aims, we will believe you and accept it and use it against you. If, on the other hand, you allege something to your advantage or in your defence, something that proves exculpatory for you and inconvenient for us, we won't believe you at all, they will be like words in the wind, given that you have the right to lie and that we simply assume that everyone – that is, all criminals – will avail themselves of that right. If you let slip an incriminating statement or fall into a flagrant contradiction or openly confess, those words will carry weight and will be used against you: we will have heard them, recorded them, noted them down, taken them as said, there will be written evidence of them, we will add them to the report, and they will be used against you. Any phrase, however, that might help to exonerate you will be considered frivolous and will be rejected, we will turn a deaf ear, ignore it, discount it, it will be so much air, smoke, vapour, and will not work in your favour at all. If you declare yourself guilty, we will judge it to be true and take your declaration very seriously indeed; if innocent, we will take it as a joke, and, as such, undeserving of serious consideration.' It is thus taken for granted that both the innocent and the guilty will proclaim themselves to be the former, and so, if they speak, there will be no difference between them, they will be made equal, on a level. And it is then that these words are spoken: 'You have the right to remain silent', although this won't help to distinguish between the innocent and the guilty either. (To remain silent, yes, silent, the great ambition that no one achieves not even after death, and yet, at critical moments, we are advised and urged to do just that: 'Keep quiet and don't say a word, not even to save yourself. Put your voice away, hide it, swallow it even if it chokes you, pretend the cat's got your tongue. Keep quiet, and save yourself.')

In our dealings with others, in ordinary, unsurprising life, no such warnings are given and we should perhaps never forget that absence or lack of warning, or, which comes to the same thing, never forget the always implicit and threatened repetition, be it accurate or distorted, of whatever we say and speak. People cannot help but go and tell what they hear, and they tell everything sooner or later, the interesting and the trivial, the private and the public, the intimate and the superfluous, what should remain hidden and what will one day inevitably be broadcast, the sorrows and the joys and the resentments, the grievances and the flattery and the plans for revenge, what fills us with pride and what shames us utterly, what appeared to be a secret and what begged to remain so, the normal and the unconfessable and the horrific and the obvious, the substantial – falling in love – and the insignificant – falling in love. Without even giving it a second thought. People are ceaselessly relating and narrating without even realising that they are, and quite unaware of the uncontrollable mechanisms of treachery, misunderstanding and chaos they are setting in motion and which could prove disastrous, they talk unceasingly about others and about themselves, about others when they talk about themselves and about themselves when they talk about others. This constant telling and retelling is perceived sometimes as a transaction, although it always successfully disguises itself as a gift (because it does have something of the gift about it) and is more often than not a bribe, or the repayment of some debt, or a curse that one hurls at a particular person or perhaps at chance itself, for chance to turn it, willy-nilly, into fortune or misfortune, or else it is the coin that buys social relations and favours and trust and even friendships and, of course, sex. And love too, when what the other person says becomes indispensable to us, becomes our air. Some of us have been paid to do just that, to tell and to hear, to put in order and to recount. To retain and observe and select. To wheedle, to embellish, to remember. To interpret and translate and incite. To draw out and persuade and distort. (I have been paid for talking about what did not exist and had not yet happened, the future and the probable or the merely possible – the hypothetical – that is, to intuit and imagine and invent; and to convince.)

Besides, most people forget how or from whom they learned what they know, and there are even people who believe that they were the first to discover whatever it might be, a story, an idea, an opinion, a piece of gossip, an anecdote, a lie, a joke, a pun, a maxim, a title, a story, an aphorism, a slogan, a speech, a quotation or an entire text, which they proudly appropriate, convinced that they are its progenitors, or perhaps they do, in fact, know they are stealing, but push the idea far from their thoughts and thus manage to conceal it. It happens more and more nowadays, as if the times we live in were impatient for everything to pass into the public domain and for an end to all notions of authorship, or, put less prosaically, were impatient to convert everything into rumour and proverb and legend that can be passed from mouth to mouth and from pen to pen and from screen to screen, all un-constrained by fixity, origin, permanence or ownership, all headlong, unchecked and unbridled.

I, on the other hand, always do my best to remember my sources, perhaps because of the work I've done in the past which remains always present because it never leaves me (I had to train my memory to distinguish what was true from what was imagined, what really happened from what was assumed to have happened, what was said from what was understood); and depending on who those sources are, I try not to make use of that information or that knowledge, indeed I even prohibit myself from doing so, now that I only work in that area very occasionally, when it can't be helped or avoided or when asked to by friends who don't pay me, at least not with money, only with their gratitude and a vague sense of indebtedness. A most inadequate recompense, by the way, for sometimes, indeed, not so very rarely, they try to transfer that feeling to me so that I am the one who suffers, and if I don't agree to that swapping of roles and don't make that feeling mine and don't behave as if I owed them my life, they end up considering me an ungrateful pig and shy away from me: there are many people who regret having asked for favours and having explained what those favours were and having, therefore, explained too much about themselves.

A while ago, a woman friend of mine didn't ask me a favour exactly, but she did oblige me to listen and informed me – not so much dramatically as fearfully – of her recently inaugurated adultery, even though I was more her husband's friend than hers or, at least, had known him longer. She did me a very poor service indeed, for I spent months tormented by that knowledge – which she theatrically and egotistically expanded on and updated, ever more in thrall to narcissism – knowing that with my friend, her husband, I had to remain silent: not because I didn't feel I had the right to tell him something about which he might – although how was I to know – have preferred to remain in ignorance; not just because I didn't want to take responsibility for unleashing with my words other people's actions and decisions, but also because I was very conscious of the manner in which that embarrassing story had reached me. I am not free to dispose of something I did not find out about by chance or by my own means, or in response to a commission or a request, I told myself. If I had spotted my friend's wife and her lover boarding a plane bound for Buenos Aires, I could perhaps have considered finding some neutral way of revealing that involuntary sighting, that interpretable, but not incontrovertible fact (I would, after all, have had no knowledge of her relationship with the man, and it would have fallen to my friend and not to me to feel suspicious), although I would probably still have felt like a traitor and a busybody and very much doubt I would have dared to say anything in either case. But, I told myself, I would at least have had the option. Having found out what I knew from her, however, there was no way I could use this against her or pass it on without her consent, not even if I believed that doing so would be to my friend's advantage, and I was sorely tempted by this belief on certain extremely awkward occasions, for example, when I was with them both or the four of us were having supper together (my wife being the fourth guest, not the lover) and she would shoot me a look that combined complicity and a shudder of pleasurable fear (and I would hold my breath), or he would blithely mention the well-known case of the well-known lover of someone or other whose spouse, however, knew nothing at all about it. (And I would hold my breath.) And so I remained silent for several months, hearing about and almost witnessing something I found both dull and highly distasteful, and all for what, I used to ask myself in my darker moments, probably to be denounced one day – when the unpleasant facts are revealed or the truth is told or flaunted and exhibited – as a collaborator or an accomplice, or co-conspirator if you like, by the very person whose secret I am keeping and whose exclusive authority on the subject I have always acknowledged and respected and never breathed a word about to anyone else. Her authority and her authorship, even though at least two other people are involved in her story, one knowingly and the other entirely unwittingly, or perhaps, despite all, my friend is still not yet involved and would only become involved were I to tell him. Maybe I am the one who is already involved because of what I know, and because I listened and interpreted – I used to think – that is what my long experience and my long list of responsibilities tell me and confirm to me daily, with each day that passes, making them grow ever dimmer and more distant, so that it seems to me sometimes that I must have read them or seen them on the screen or imagined them, that it is not so easy to disentangle oneself or even to forget. Or that it isn't possible at all.

No, I should never tell anyone anything, nor hear anything either.

I did, for some time, listen and notice and interpret and tell, and I was paid to do so during that time, but it was something I had always done and that I continue to do, passively and involuntarily, without effort and without reward, I probably can't help it now, it's just my way of being in the world, it will go with me to my death, and only then will I rest from it. More than once I was told it was a gift, and Peter Wheeler was the one who pointed this out to me, alerting me to its existence by explaining and describing it to me, for, as everyone knows or, at least, senses, things only exist once they have been named. Sometimes, though, this gift seems more like a curse, even though I now tend to stick to the first three activities, which are silent and internal and take place solely in my mind, and therefore need affect no one but me, and I only tell anyone anything when I have no alternative or if someone insists. For during my professional or, shall we say, remunerated life in London, I learned that what merely happens to us barely affects us or, at least, no more than what does not happen, but it is the story (the story of what does not happen too), which, however imprecise, treacherous, approximate and downright useless, is nevertheless almost the only thing that counts, is the decisive factor, it is what troubles our soul and diverts and poisons our footsteps, it is doubtless also what keeps the weak, lazy wheel of the world turning.

It is not mere chance or fancy that in espionage, conspiracies, or criminal activities, what is known by the various participants in a mission or a plot or a coup – clandestinely, secretly – is always diffuse, partial, fragmentary, oblique, with each person knowing only about his or her particular task, but not about the whole, not the final aim. We've all seen this in films, the way the partisan, realising that he won't survive the next ambush or the next inevitable attempt on his life, tells his girlfriend when they say their farewells: 'It's best if you know nothing; then, if they interrogate you, you'll be telling the truth when you say you know nothing, the truth is easy, it has more force, it's more believable, the truth persuades.' (For lying does require certain imaginative and improvisational abilities, it requires inventiveness, a cast-iron memory, complex architectures, everyone does it, but few with any skill.) Or the way the mastermind behind the big robbery, the one who plans and directs it, informs his flunky or henchman: 'If you know only about your part of the job, even if they catch you or you fail, the plan can still go ahead.' (And it's true that you can always allow for one link to break or for some mistake to be made, total failure is not something that is achieved quickly or simply, every enterprise, every action resists and struggles for some time before it stops altogether and collapses.) Or the way the head of Secret Services whispers to the agent about whom he has his suspicions and whom he no longer trusts: 'Your ignorance will be your protection, so don't ask any more questions, don't ask, it will be your salvation and your guarantee of safety.' (And the best way to avoid betrayals is to provide no fuel for them, or only rumours, valueless and weightless, mere husks, a disappointment to those who pay for them.) Or the way someone who commissions a crime or threatens to commit one, or someone who confesses to vile deeds thus exposing himself to blackmail, or someone who buys something secretly – keep your collar turned up, your face always in the shadows, never light a cigarette – warns the hired assassin or the person under threat or the potential blackmailer or the commutable woman once desired and already forgotten, but still a source of shame to us:

'You know the score, you've never seen me, from now on you don't know me, I've never spoken to you or said anything, as far as you're concerned I have no face, no voice, no breath, no name, no back. This conversation and this meeting never took place, what's happening now before your eyes didn't happen, isn't happening, you haven't even heard these words because I didn't say them. And even though you can hear the words now, I'm not saying them.'

(Keeping silent, erasing, suppressing, cancelling and having, in the past, remained silent too: that is the world's great, unachievable ambition, which is why anything else, any substitute, falls short, and why it is pure childishness to withdraw what has been said and why retraction is so futile; and that is also why – because, unlikely though it may seem, it is sometimes the only thing that can effectively inject a little doubt – out-and-out denial is so irritating, denying that one said what was said and heard and denying that one did what was done and endured, it's exasperating that the action announced by those earlier words can be carried out unwaveringly and to the letter, words that could be spoken by so many and by such very different people, the mouth of the instigator and the threatener, of the person living in fear of blackmail and the one who furtively pays for his pleasures or profits, as well as in the mouth of a lover or a friend, and that those words can then, equally exasperatingly, be denied.)

All the words we have seen uttered in the cinema I myself have said or have had said to me or have heard others say throughout my whole existence, that is, in real life, which bears a closer relation to films and literature than is normally recognised and believed. It isn't, as people say, that the former imitates the latter or the latter the former, but that our infinite imaginings belong to life too and help make it broader and more complex, make it murkier and, at the same time, more acceptable, although not more explicable (or only very rarely). A very thin line separates facts from imaginings, even desires from their fulfilment, and the fictitious from what actually happened, because imaginings are already facts, and desires are their own fulfilment, and the fictitious does happen, although not in the eyes of common sense and of the law, which, for example, makes a vast distinction between the intention and the crime, or between the commission of a crime and its attempt. But consciousness knows nothing of the law, and common sense neither interests nor concerns it, each consciousness has its own sense, and that very thin line is, in my experience, often blurred and, once it has disappeared, separates nothing, which is why I have learned to fear anything that passes through the mind and even what the mind does not as yet know, because I have noticed that, in almost every case, everything was already there, somewhere, before it even reached or penetrated the mind. I have therefore learned to fear not only what is thought, the idea, but also what precedes it and comes before. For I am myself my own fever and pain.

This gift or curse of mine is nothing very extraordinary, by which I mean it is nothing supernatural, preternatural, unnatural or *contra natura*, nor does it involve any unusual abilities, not divination, say, although something rather similar to that was what came to be expected of me by my temporary boss, the man who contracted me to work for him during a period that seemed to go on for a long time, more or less the same period of time as my separation from my wife, Luisa, when I came back to England so as not to be near her while she was slowly distancing herself from me. People behave idiotically with remarkable frequency, given their tendency to believe in the repetition of what pleases them: if something good happens once, then it should happen again, or at least tend in that direction. And it was all because I chanced to make a correct interpretation of a relationship that was of (momentary) importance to Señor Tupra, that Mr Tupra – as I always called him until he urged me to replace this with Bertram and later, much to my distaste, with Bertie – wanted to hire my services, initially on an ad hoc basis and subsequently full-time, with theoretical duties as vague as they were varied, including acting as liaison or occasional interpreter on his Spanish or Latin-American incursions. But in reality or, rather, in practice, I was of interest to him and was taken on as an interpreter of lives, to use his own grandiose expression and exaggerated expectations. It would be best just to say translator or interpreter of people: of their behaviour and reactions, of their inclinations and characters and powers of endurance; of their malleability and their submissiveness, of their faint or firm wills, their inconstancies, their limits, their innocence, their lack of scruples and their resistance; their possible degrees of loyalty or baseness and their calculable prices and their poisons and their temptations; and also their deducible histories, not past but future, those that had not yet happened and could therefore be prevented. Or, indeed, created.

I had met him at the home of Professor Peter Wheeler, of Oxford, an eminent and now retired Hispanist and Lusitanist, the man who knows more than anyone else in the world about Prince Henry the Navigator and one of those who knows most about Cervantes, and who is now Sir Peter Wheeler and the first winner of the Premio Nebrija de Salamanca, awarded to the most brilliant members of a particular speciality or field and – rather surprisingly in the university world, which is either miserly or impoverished depending on the institution – worth a not insignificant amount of money, which meant that the narrowed eyes of his greedy or needy international colleagues rested enviously upon him on that penultimate occasion. I used to travel down from London to see him now and then (an hour on the train there, another hour back), having met and got to know him slightly many years before, when, for two years, I held the post of Spanish *lector* at Oxford University – I was single at the time, and now I was separated; I seem always to be alone in England. Wheeler and I had liked each other from the start, perhaps out of deference to the person who had first introduced us, Toby Rylands, Professor of English Literature, and a great friend of his since youth and with whom he shared a number of characteristics, as well as the age and status of the reluctantly retired. Although I often visited Rylands, I did not meet Wheeler until the end of my stay there, since he was teaching as emeritus professor in Texas during term time, and I went back to Madrid or went travelling during the vacation, and we did not, therefore, coincide. But when Rylands died, after I had left, Wheeler and I continued that deference which will, I suppose, since it became, from then on, deference to a memory or to a defenceless ghost, now last indefinitely: we used occasionally to write or phone, and, if I was going to be in London for a few days, I always tried to make time to visit him, alone or with Luisa. (Wheeler as substitute for or successor to Rylands, or as his inheritance: it's shocking how easily we replace the people we lose in our lives, how we rush to cover any vacancies, how we can never resign ourselves to any reduction in the cast of characters without whom we can barely go on or survive, and how, at the same time, we all offer ourselves up to fill vicariously the empty places assigned to us, because we understand and partake of that continuous universal mechanism of substitution, which affects everyone and therefore us too, and so we accept our role as poor imitations and find ourselves surrounded by more and more of them.)

He amused me and taught me a great deal with his intelligent though never cruel brand of mischief, and with his astonishing perspicacity, so subtle and unostentatious that one often had to presume or decipher it from his remarks and questions, apparently innocuous, rhetorical or trivial, sometimes almost hieroglyphic if you were alert enough to spot them; you had to listen 'between the words', as sometimes you have to read between the lines of what he writes, although this predominantly indirect manner did not prevent him, if he suddenly grew bored with hints and judged them to be burdensome, from being franker and more ruthless – with third parties or with life or himself, although not usually with his immediate interlocutor – than anyone else I have ever known, with the possible exception of Rylands and, perhaps, myself, but only as disciple and pupil of both. And I – well, I didn't dare think anything else – doubtless amused him, and even flattered him by my ready affection, my easy delight and my celebratory laughter, which never takes much coaxing in the presence of people who have earned my respect and admiration, and Wheeler deserves both.

(I was, in his case, a replacement for or a successor to no one, or to no one known to me, possibly someone from his ancient past, the long-delayed or, who knows, long-since-ruled-out replacement of some remote figure whose echo or mere shadow or reflection he had already relinquished.)

So during my time in London, working for BBC radio, until Mr Tupra took me away, I used to go and see him where he lived in Oxford, by the River Cherwell, like Rylands, whose neighbour he had been, either on my own initiative or occasionally on his, when, for whatever reason, he required witnesses to his verbal interventions or to his disguised *mises-en-scène*, or if he had visitors whom he wanted to provide with a little variety – for example, with a Latin who had nothing to do now with the all-too-familiar university world – or visitors he was looking forward to discussing with me afterwards, the next day when we were alone. I had that feeling on two or three occasions: it was as if Wheeler, well into his eighties, was always preparing conversations that might entertain or stimulate him in the near, or, to him, still foreseeable future. And if he foresaw that he would find it amusing later on to talk to me about Tupra, or to recount his indiscretions, his vices and enigmas and funny ways, it would be a good idea for me to meet Tupra first, or at least be able to put a voice and a face to him and have formed some impression, however superficial, which he, Wheeler, could then confirm or deny, or even argue about with unnecessary zeal, and only then would we get any real enjoyment out of the conversation. He needed a counterpoint to his perorations.

I wonder if this is what the enigmatic and fragmented time of the old is like, the paradoxical discovery – for those who manage to get that far and become part of it – that you have such a superfluity of that dwindling time that you can afford to devote no small part of it to the preparation or composition of prized moments; or, so to speak, to guiding the numerous empty or dead moments towards a few pre-planned and carefully considered dialogues, in which you have, of course, memorised your own part: it is as if the old took great care of their time – at once brief and slow, limited and abundant, the time of an astute old man – and planned and channelled and directed it as much as they could, and were no longer willing to accept – enough, no more: no more fever or pain; no word or spear, not even sleep and dreams – that it was a mere consequence of chance, of the unexpected or of something beyond them, but tried to convert it into a work of their own making, of their own dramaturgy and design. Or, which comes to the same thing, as if they took great pains to anticipate and configure it and to shape its content as much as possible; and that this was what they wanted, as being the only sure way of truly making the most of their remaining time, which seems to move so very slowly, but is, in fact, sliding from their shoulders like snow, slippery and docile. And the snow always stops.

I definitely had that feeling as regards Tupra, that Wheeler wanted me to meet him or see him, because he could easily just have phoned and said: 'A few friends and acquaintances are coming here for a buffet supper two weeks from Saturday; why don't you come too, I know how alone you are in London.' He didn't know if I was a little or very much alone or even suffering from an excess of company, but he tended to attribute to others his own situation, needs and even neglect, a trick of his, because if he spoke first, no one was likely to point out the same thing in him or to return the favour, for it would have shown a lack of originality on their part – or mere childishness. But although that is more or less what he said, he remained on the line for a few seconds more, even when I had already accepted the invitation with pleasure and made a note of the date and the hour, and then he added with feigned hesitancy (but without concealing the fact that it was feigned): 'Anyway, that fellow Bertram Tupra will be there, a former pupil of Toby's.' (He used the word 'fellow', which is perhaps less disparaging than the Spanish '*individuo*': for we were speaking in both Spanish and English, or sometimes each of us in our own language.) And before I could make any comment on that unlikely surname, he anticipated me and spelled it out, agreeing: 'Yes, I know, it sounds like an invented name, doesn't it, and it might well be, though it's more likely that the Bertram is false and not the Tupra, a name like that has to be genuine, Russian or Czech in origin, I don't know, or Finnish perhaps, or maybe that's just because it sounds a bit like "tundra" . . . Anyway, it's glaringly obvious that he isn't English, but all too frankly foreign, possibly Armenian or Turkish, so the man must have thought it prudent to compensate with a first name worthy of our English theatres, you know the sort of thing, Cyril, Basil, Reginald, Eustace, Bertram, they turn up in all the old comedies. Perhaps that's why he changed it, he couldn't have gone around here without arousing suspicion if he was called, oh, I don't know, Vladimir Tupra or Vaslav Tupra or Pirkka Tupra, can you imagine how unfortunate that would have been up until a few years ago, the only job he could have got then would have been in the ballet or the circus, certainly not in his present line of work . . .' Wheeler gave a short, scornful laugh, as if he had had a sudden vision of Tupra, whose appearance he was familiar with, got up in dark tights and a top with a low or plunging neckline, leaping about on stage, displaying his sturdy thighs and bulging, veiny calves; or in the leotard and brief, phosphorescent cape of a trapeze artiste. He even paused before continuing, as if he were expecting some kind of encouragement from me or was wondering whether to explain exactly what Tupra's 'line of work' was. I said nothing, and he hesitated further, I noticed that he wasn't really paying attention to what he went on to say, it seemed to me he was just playing for time and was merely improvising until he came to some decision: 'I wonder if perhaps he drew his inspiration from that legendary bookseller near Covent Garden, Bertram Rota, you know the shop, I think his full name was Cyril Bertram Rota, I hadn't realised until now what an unusual surname he had for someone with a business in Long Acre or wherever, it's probably Spanish in origin, I should think. Do you know any other Rotas in Spain, apart from the venal ecclesiastical tribunal of course? Then again, Bertram could well be his real name, Tupra's I mean, and it was perhaps his father, assuming he was the one who emigrated here from the tundra or the steppe, who had the idea of Britishising his son at birth in order to mitigate the barbarous, almost accusatory effect of Tupra, in Spain he would have had to drop it entirely, don't you think, it sounds far too much like "*estupro*", and he would doubtless have been the butt of endless cruel puns about rape. And these silly tricks work, Rota is a case in point, the penny hadn't dropped until now, after all these years of frittering my fortune on expensive books from his catalogue; I'll have to ask his son Anthony, who is still alive I think . . .' Wheeler stopped again, he was weighing up the situation while he talked, did he or did he not want to tell me or forewarn me or ask me about something. 'Besides,' he went on, 'being called Bertram would mean that he, Tupra, could be called Bertie in private, which would make him feel as if he had stepped straight out of a P. G. Wodehouse story, when he's amongst friends or with his girlfriend, I mean, oh, by the way, she'll be coming too, a new girlfriend whom he insists on introducing to us, though it's bound to be her physique he's proud of rather than her probable wisdom . . .' He paused one last time, but since I was either not in a very communicative mood or had nothing to add, he resorted to another digression in order to conclude in style, a digression that proved far more intriguing to me than all the others: 'Of course, he speaks English like a native, a half-educated South Londoner, I'd say. In fact, when I think about it, he's possibly more English than I am, after all, I was born in New Zealand and didn't come here until I was sixteen, and I'd changed my surname too, for different reasons obviously, nothing to do with patriotic euphony or with the steppes. But then you know all that, and it's hardly relevant, besides I'm taking up far too much of your time. I'll expect you on that Saturday, then.' And he said goodbye in his fondest tones, which rendered imperceptible his ever-present irony: 'I await your arrival with the greatest impatience. You're so alone in London. Don't let me down now.' That last phrase he said in my language: '*No te me rajes.*'

That is how Sir Peter Wheeler was and still is – that simulacrum of an old man, by which I mean that his venerable, docile appearance often conceals certain energetic, almost acrobatic machinations, and his absent-minded digressions an observant, analytical, anticipatory, interpretative mind, which is constantly judging. For several interminable minutes he had directed my attention towards Bertram Tupra, on whom I would find myself obliged to focus during the buffet supper, which had doubtless been Wheeler's main aim, that I should focus on him I mean. But he had not, in the end, explained why, nor had he actually uttered a single descriptive or informative word about the individual or fellow in question, only that he had been a pupil of Toby Rylands's and that he had a new girlfriend, the rest had been nothing but idle disquisitions on and conjectures about his absurd name. He had not even been able to bring himself, after all those unexpressed vacillations, to specify what his 'line of work' was, the one in which he would never have prospered had he been called Pavel or Mikka or Jukka. Finally, he had even diverted me from any possible interest I might have had about that by referring for the first time in my presence to his own New Zealand roots, to his rather late transplantation to England and to his changed or apocryphal surname, and had, at the same time, prevented me from asking him about this by adding immediately 'But then you know all that, and it's hardly relevant', when the truth was that I had known nothing at all about it until that very moment.

'Something else he has in common with Toby,' I thought

after I'd put down the phone, 'it was rumoured, among other things, that he was originally from South Africa; yet another reason for them to become friends when they were young, both of them British foreigners or British by virtue of citizenship alone, both of them bogus Englishmen.' Rylands had never thrown any light on these rumours and I had never asked him about them, as he didn't much like talking about the past, at least so people said and so it was with me; and it seemed to me disrespectful to make my own investigations after his death, it would have been like going against his own wishes when he was no longer there to maintain or revoke them ('Strange to no longer desire one's desires,' I quoted to myself from memory, 'strange to have to abandon even one's own name'). I wondered whether I should dial Wheeler's number immediately, so that he could flesh out these new facts about himself, about his past, and explain to me why the devil he had talked so much about Tupra, almost to the point of exasperation on my part. Just before he called I had been trying the number in Madrid that was still listed under my name, but was now no longer mine but the children's and Luisa's, and which had remained so insistently engaged that I wanted to try it again as soon as possible, if only to gauge the length of time it took me not to get through. That's why I didn't phone Wheeler back at once, as soon as I'd hung up, because I was in a hurry to continue dialling that now-lost number of mine, the number I'd had to abandon, and which I often used to answer when I was at home. Now I never answered it because I wasn't at home any more nor could I go back there to sleep, I was in another country, and although not as alone as Wheeler believed me to be, I was sometimes a little alone, or perhaps I merely found it hard not to be always in company or occupied, and then time weighed heavy on me or I hampered its passing, which is perhaps why it was no hardship for me to listen attentively, first, to Wheeler, at his house, and then to accept Tupra's proposition, which, if nothing else, would at least afford me constant company, even if, sometimes, it was only auditory or visual, as well as keeping me fully occupied.

Luisa's phone in Madrid was still busy, there was no problem with the line the phone company told me, and neither of us owned one of those snooping devices, a cell phone. Perhaps she was on the Internet, I'd begged her to get another line installed so as not to block the telephone, but she hadn't got around to it, even though I'd offered to pay for it, true, she only used the Net now and then, so that was unlikely to be the reason the phone was busy for such a long time on a Thursday night, which was one of the days we had agreed on in principle as a time when I could talk to our son and daughter before they went to bed, it was too late now, an hour later in Spain, past ten o'clock there and past nine o'clock here, the three of them would have had supper with the TV on or a video, it wasn't easy for them to agree on what to watch, the age difference was too great, fortunately, the boy was patient and protective towards his sister and often gave in, I was beginning to fear for him, he was even protective about his mother and, who knows, possibly even about me, now that I was far away, exiled, an orphan in his eyes and understanding, those who act as a shield suffer greatly in life, as do the vigilant, their ears and eyes always alert. They would have gone to bed by now, although they would still have had the light on for a few minutes longer, which was what Luisa and I allowed them by way of extra time so that they could read something – a comic book, a few lines, a story – while sleep circled over them, it's wretched knowing the precise habits of a house from which you are suddenly absent and to which you return now only as a visitor and always with prior warning or like a close relative and only occasionally, yet remain caught in the web of settings and rhythms that you established and which sheltered you and seemed impossible without your contribution and without your existence, the long-term prisoner of what was seen and done so many times, and you are incapable of imagining any changes, although you know there is nothing to prevent them and that they might well occur and might even be wanted, and you learn, in an abstract fashion, to suspect them, what could they be, those changes that will happen in your absence and behind your back, you cease to be present, you are no longer a participant or even a witness, and it's as if you had been expelled from advancing time, which, seen from the disadvantage of distance, is transformed for you into a frozen painting or a frozen memory.

I foolishly believe that they will wait faithfully for me to return, not in essence, but at least symbolically, as if it were not infinitely easier to lay waste to symbols than to actual past events, when these are suppressed or erased with no effort at all, one has only to be resolute and to subdue one's memories. I cannot believe that Luisa will not soon have a new love or lover, I cannot believe that she isn't waiting for one now without knowing that she is, or maybe even looking for one, neck straining, eyes alert, without even knowing that she's looking, nor that she isn't passively anticipating the foreseeable appearance of someone who as yet lacks a face and a name and therefore contains all faces and all names, the possible and the impossible, the bearable and the repugnant. And yet, illogically, I believe that Luisa will not take this new love or lover back to the apartment where she lives with our children or into our bed which is now hers alone, but that she will meet him almost secretly, as if respect for my still recent memory imposed this on her or implored it of her – a whisper, a fever, a scratch – as if she were a widow and I a dead man deserving to be mourned and who cannot be replaced too quickly, not yet, my love, wait, wait, your hour has not yet come, don't spoil it for me, give me time and give him time too, the dead man whose time no longer advances, give him time to fade, let him change into a ghost before you take his place and dismiss his flesh, let him be changed into nothing, wait until there is no trace of his smell on the sheets or on my body, let it be as if what was had never happened. I cannot believe that Luisa will admit that man into our habits and into our picture just like that, that she will allow him suddenly to be the one helping her to prepare supper – it's all right, I'll make the omelette – and who sits down with her and the children to watch a video – has anyone got any objections to Tom and Jerry – nor that he should be the one to tiptoe in afterwards – no, don't you move, you're exhausted, I'll go – to turn out the lights in their two bedrooms, having first checked that my children have fallen asleep holding a Tintin book that has now slipped quietly to the floor or with a doll on the pillow that will be smothered by the tiny embrace of innocent dreams.

But we must get used to the idea that there is no mourning and no respect for our memory nor for whatever we belatedly decide now to erect as symbols, apart from anything else because Luisa is not a widow and we have not died and I have not died, we were simply not attentive enough, and no one owes us anything, and above all because her time, the time that wraps around and steals away the children, is already very different from ours, hers advances but without including us, and I don't quite know what to do with mine, which advances without including me, or perhaps it is just that I have still not worked out how to climb aboard, perhaps I will never catch up and will always follow along behind alone in the wake of my own time. There will soon be someone by her side cooking omelettes and always on his best behaviour with her and the children, for months he will conceal the irritation he feels at not having her all to himself and whenever he wants, he will play the patient, understanding, supportive partner, and through hints and solicitous questions and retrospectively pitying smiles he will dig my grave still deeper, the grave in which I am already buried. That is one possibility, but who knows . . . He might be a jolly, laid-back fellow who will take her out on the town every night and won't even want to know about the children or to step over the threshold of our apartment, where he'll stand dressed and ready to party, drumming his fingers impatiently on the door frame; who will force her to distance herself from them and to neglect them, who will expose her to dangers and lure her into the kind of cheerful excesses I quite often indulge in here . . . Or he might be the poisonous, despotic sort, who subjugates and isolates her and, little by little, quietly feeds her his demands and prohibitions, disguised as infatuation and weakness and jealousy and flattery and supplication, a devious sort who, one rainy night, when they're stuck at home, will close his large hands around her throat while the children – my children – watch from a corner, pressing themselves into the wall as if wishing the wall would give way and disappear and, with it, this awful sight, and the choked-back tears that long to burst forth, but cannot, the bad dream, and the strange, long-drawn-out noise their mother makes as she dies. But no, that won't happen, that doesn't happen, I won't have that luck or that misfortune (luck as long as it remains in the imagination, misfortune were it to become reality) . . . Who knows who will replace us, all we know is that we will be replaced, on all occasions and in all circumstances and in whatever we do, in love and friendship, as regards work, influence, domination, even hatred, which also wearies of us in the end; in the houses we live in and in the cities that receive us, in the telephones that persuade or patiently listen to us, laughing into our ear or murmuring agreement, at play and at work, in shops and offices, in the childhood landscape we thought was ours alone and in the streets exhausted from seeing so much decay, in restaurants and along avenues and in our armchairs and between our sheets, until no trace of our smell remains, and they are torn up to make strips or rags, even our kisses are replaced, and they close their eyes as they kiss, in memories and in thoughts and in daydreams and everywhere, I am like the snow on someone's shoulders, slippery and docile, and the snow always stops . . .

I look out of the window of an apartment, ingenuously furnished by an Englishwoman I have never seen, while I put down the phone, then pick it up again, dial and hang up, I look out at the lazy London night across the square that is emptying of active beings and their resolute steps, to be filled for a while – an interregnum – by the inactive and their erratic steps, which lead them now to the trash bins and garbage cans into which they plunge their ash-grey arms, rummaging for treasures invisible to us or for the fortuitous wages of another day survived, when it is still not yet night but certainly not day either, or when it is still today for those going home or getting dressed up to go out again, but is already yesterday for those who come and go and never find their bearings. I look up to seek out and to continue seeing the living world that knows where it's going and to which I imagine I still belong, which finds shelter in its illuminated interiors from the crepuscular ash of the air, so as to distance myself from and not be assimilated by the disoriented world of these ghosts who plunge in among the garbage and become one with it; I look out across the traffic that is growing quieter now and beyond the shadowy beggars and the stragglers – they run five or six steps and leap on to the back of the double-decker bus just pulling away, the women's high heels scrape on the ground, they're taking a real risk – I look up and past the trees and the statue on the other side of the square, at the smart hotel and the vast offices and the private houses that are homes to families, but not always, just as I was not always part of a family, but sometimes still am – 'I'll be more myself,' I murmur. 'I'll be more myself now,' I say, by being and living alone; I sometimes see people who look like me, people who don't live with anyone and receive, at most, visitors, some of whom occasionally stay the night, as also happens in my apartment, should anyone be watching me from some observatory.

A man lives opposite, beyond the trees whose tops crown the centre of this square and on exactly the same level as me, the third floor, English houses don't have blinds, or only rarely, sometimes lace curtains or shutters which are not usually closed until sleep begins its wild circling, and I often see this man dancing, sometimes with a partner, but nearly always alone and with great enthusiasm, using, as he dances or, should I say, bops, the whole length of his sitting-room which is long enough to accommodate four large windows. He is definitely not a professional dancer busy rehearsing, that much is clear: he's usually wearing street clothes, sometimes even a tie and everything, as if he'd just walked in through the front door after a day's work and was too impatient to take off his jacket and roll up his sleeves (although he normally wears an elegant sweater or a long- or short-sleeved polo shirt), and his dance steps are spontaneous, improvised, not without a certain harmony and grace, but without, I would say, much control or rhythm or thought, he makes whatever movements he's inspired to make by the music I cannot hear and which perhaps only he can hear; I've seen him through my horse-racing binoculars putting on some sort of headphones or other such contraption – or so I believe: I occasionally use them at home myself – obviously cordless, otherwise he wouldn't be able to leap about and move as freely as he does. That would explain how it is that on some nights he begins these sessions quite late, especially for England, where no neighbourhood would put up with loud music after eleven o'clock at night, or even an hour earlier, though I don't know what he does to dampen the sound of his dancing feet. Perhaps, when he begins so late, he's trying to summon up sleep: to wear himself out, to numb or stun himself, to distract the desires of his conscious mind. He's about thirty-five, thin, with bony features – jaw and nose and forehead – and has an agile, athletic build, with fairly broad shoulders and a flat stomach, all of which seems perfectly natural rather than the product of working out at a gym. He has a thick but well-groomed moustache, like that of a boxer from the early days, except that it's cut straight with no nineteenth-century curlicues, and he wears his hair combed back with a middle parting, as if he had a ponytail, although I've never seen it, perhaps one day he'll reveal it. It's odd seeing him moving about to different rhythms without my ever hearing the music that guides him, I amuse myself trying to guess what it is, to supply it mentally, in order – how can I put it – to save him from the ridiculous fate of dancing in silence, dancing before me in silence that is, it's an incomprehensible, illogical, almost crazy sight if you don't supply the music with your own musical memory – or even get out the record you think he's playing and put it on, if you have it to hand – the tune controlling or guiding this man, but which is never heard, sometimes I think, 'Judging by the frantic way he's moving his upper body, he might be dancing to Chubby Checker's "Hucklebuck" or perhaps something by Elvis Presley, "Burning Love" for example, with all those fast head movements, like a puppet nodding, and those short steps, or it could be something more recent, maybe Lynyrd Skynyrd, and that famous song of theirs, the one about Alabama, he lifts his thighs up a lot like the actress Nicole Kidman did when she unexpectedly danced to it once in a film; and now perhaps it's a calypso, he has a certain sway to his hips, absurdly West Indian or something, he's even picked up some maracas, I'd better look away at once or else immediately put "I Learn a Merengue, Mama" or "Barrel of Rum" on the record-player, the guy's mad, but so happy, so oblivious to everything that wears the rest of us down and consumes us, immersed in his dances danced for no one, he'd be surprised if he knew that I sometimes watch him when I'm waiting or have nothing to do, and I might not be the only person watching from my building, it's fun and even rather cheering to watch, and mysterious too, I can't imagine who he is or what he does, he eludes – and this doesn't happen very often – my interpretative or deductive faculties, which may or may not be right, but which never hold back, springing immediately into action to compose a brief, improvised portrait, a stereotype, a flash, a plausible supposition, a sketch or snippet of life however imaginary and basic or arbitrary these might be, it's my alert, detective mind, the idiotic mind that Clare Bayes criticised and reproached me for in this same country years ago now, before I met Luisa, and which I had to suppress with Luisa so as not to irritate her or fill her with fear, the superstitious fear that always does the most damage and yet serves so little purpose, there is nothing to be done to protect ourselves from what we already know and most fear (perhaps because we are fatalistically drawn to it, and we seek it out so as to avoid disappointment), and we usually know how things will end, how they will evolve and what awaits us, where things are going and what their conclusion will be; everything is there on view, in fact, everything is visible very early on in a relationship just as it is in all honest, straightforward stories, you just have to look to see it, one single moment encapsulates the germ of many years to come, of almost our whole history – one grave, pregnant moment – and if we want to we can see it and, in broad terms, read it, there are not that many possible variations, the signs rarely deceive if we know how to read their meanings, if you are prepared to do so – but it is so difficult and can prove catastrophic; one day you spot an unmistakable gesture, see an unequivocal reaction, hear a tone of voice that says much and presages still more, although you also hear the sound of someone biting their tongue – too late; you feel on the back of your neck the nature or propensity of a look when that look knows itself to be invisible and protected and safe, so many are involuntary; you notice sweetness and impatience, you detect hidden intentions that are never entirely hidden, or unconscious intentions before they become conscious to the person who should be concealing them, sometimes you foresee what someone will do before that person has foreseen or known or even become aware of what this will be, and you can sense the betrayal as yet unformulated and the scorn as yet unfelt; and the feelings of irritation you provoke, the weariness you cause or the loathing you inspire, or perhaps the opposite, which is not necessarily any better: the unconditional love they feel for us, the other person's ridiculously high hopes, their devotion, their eagerness to please and to prove themselves essential to us in order to supplant us later on and thus become who we are; and the need to possess, the illusions built up, the determination of someone to be or to stay by your side, or to win your heart, the crazed, irrational loyalty; you notice when there is real enthusiasm and when there is only flattery and when it is mixed (because nothing is pure), you know who isn't trustworthy and who is ambitious and who has no scruples and who would walk over your dead body having first run you down, you know who has a candid soul and what will happen to these last when you meet them, the fate that awaits them if they don't mend their ways, but grow still worse and even if they do mend their ways: you know if they will be your victims. When you are introduced to a couple, married or not, you see who will one day abandon whom and you see this at once, as soon as you say hello, or, at least, by the end of the evening. You detect too when something is going wrong or falling apart, or flips right over and the tables are turned, when everything is collapsing, at what moment we stop loving as we once did or they stop loving us, who will or will not go to bed with us, and when a friend will discover his own envy, or, rather, decide to give in to it and allow himself to be led and guided from that moment on by envy alone; when it starts to ooze out or grow heavy with resentment; we know what it is about us that exasperates and infuriates and what condemns us, what we should have said, but did not, or what we should have kept silent about, but did not, why it is that suddenly one day they look at us with different eyes – dark or angry eyes: they already bear a grudge – when we disappoint or when we irritate because we do not as yet disappoint and so do not provide the desired excuse for our dismissal; we know the kind gesture that is suddenly no longer bearable and that signals the precise hour when we will become utterly and irredeemably unbearable; and we know, too, who is going to love us, until death and beyond and, much to our regret sometimes, beyond their death or mine or both . . .

against our will sometimes . . . But no one wants to see anything and so hardly anyone ever sees what is there before them, what awaits us or will befall us sooner or later, no one refrains from striking up a conversation or a friendship with someone who will bring them only remorse and discord and poison and lamentations, or with someone to whom we will bring all those things, however clearly we perceive this at the very first moment, or however obvious it is made to us. We try to make things different from the way they are and from how they appear, we foolishly insist that we like someone we never liked much to begin with, and insist on trusting someone who inspires our intense distrust, it is as if we often went against our own knowledge, because that is how we tend to experience it, as knowledge rather than intuition or impression or hunch, this has nothing to do with premonitions, there is nothing supernatural or mysterious about it, what's mysterious is that we pay no heed to it. And the explanation must be a simple one, since it is something shared by so many: it is simply that we know, but hate knowing; we cannot bear to see; we hate knowledge and certainty and conviction; and no one wants to be transformed into their own fever and their own pain . . .'

Sometimes, as I have said – although I only saw this on a couple of occasions – this man whom I have failed to interpret or sum up, about whom I cannot form a clear or even a vague idea, danced with a partner, contrary to his custom, and he did so with two different women, one white and the other black or mulatto (I couldn't really tell which, the lights were low); but even then he seemed less intent on his partners than on himself and his own enjoyment, although he doubtless liked dancing with them just for a change and so that he could swing them around and hold them and brush lightly past them in that large uncluttered room, a whole long zone or area bare of furniture, of all obstacles, as if he kept it like that on purpose to facilitate his cavortings. The white woman wore trousers, which was a pity; the black woman, on the other hand, wore a skirt that swirled about and up, and sometimes did not immediately subside, but remained caught for a few seconds on her stockings (or, rather, tights or whatever they're called, that come up to the waist) until a wiggle of her hips or a distracted movement with her hand freed the fabric and returned it to the censorious laws of gravity. I enjoyed seeing her thighs and, fleetingly, her buttocks, which is why I stopped using my binoculars, spying isn't really my style, at least not intentionally, as was the case here. The white woman left after the dance session and got on her bike (perhaps that's why she wore trousers, not that one needs to find a reason); the black or mulatto woman stayed the night I think; the two of them stopped after they had been dancing for a while and immediately turned out the lights, and I didn't see her leave for a long time afterwards, it was late and had grown still later by the time I decided to go to bed in order to forget all about her. Women have occasionally stayed in this apartment too, especially during my first few months of settling in and reconnaissance and taking stock: one of them has been back since, another one wanted to, but I wouldn't let her, the third didn't even suggest it, she washed her hands of the affair before it was even over – yes, there had been three thus far; I knew nothing about her then and have heard nothing since, not since she had breakfast in my kitchen, not so much hurriedly as mechanically and swiftly, as if being there so early in the morning had nothing to do with her, a mere coincidence of accommodation, she was engaged to some VIP's son and got a thrill out of announcing her imminent marriage to him and yet was terrified by its very imminence, perhaps he had been phoning her since the previous night or since early that morning, dialling and hanging up, then picking up the phone again and dialling, that nervous fiancé getting no reply or only her answer machine or voice mail, which is unbearable, calling and calling in vain, I couldn't stand this constant trying to get through to Luisa, what could she be doing, perhaps she'd taken the phone off the hook because she had a visitor, perhaps someone was going to stay the night with her, and the only way of ensuring that my distant voice did not interrupt or disturb anything – she must have suddenly realised that it was Thursday, when it became clear that the visit would last longer than expected: spear, fever, my pain, sleep, dreams, the substantial or the insignificant – was to put the children to bed slightly earlier than usual and to leave the phone off the hook all night, she could always claim tomorrow that it had been an accident.

But only the flattering, diligent man stays, at least at this stage, only the one doing his best to move in and occupy the empty space in the warm bed without aspiring to introduce any changes, since his predecessor's way of doing things seems just fine and he yearns only to be him, even though he does not yet know it; the jolly, smiling one leaves or does not even come in, he's not interested in sharing a pillow except during active waking hours; and the despotic, possessive one puts on an act at first, takes great care not to appear intrusive, waits to be encouraged and even when he is, declines the first invitations ('I don't want to complicate your life, I'd be putting you to a lot of trouble, and maybe you're not sure yet that you want to see me tomorrow, perhaps you should give it a bit of thought'), he appears deferential, respectful, even cautious, he tries not to reveal any invasive or expansionist tendencies, and he does not linger or dawdle in alien territory until a much later phase, precisely because he is planning to take the whole place over and cannot run the risk of arousing suspicion. He does not spend the night, even if begged to do so, not at first: he puts all his clothes back on despite the lateness of the hour, the exhaustion and the cold, and overcomes all inertia – having to put his socks back on – and postpones all eagerness, all haste – he does not mind if eagerness and haste are condensed into one; he gets in his car or calls a taxi and leaves noiselessly at dawn, in order that he can begin to be missed more quickly, as soon as he closes the door behind him and enters the elevator and leaves the dishevelled, still-warm woman to return to her rumpled, unwelcoming bed, to her wrinkled sheets and to the still lingering smell. If that man is there, that devious guy who, later on, will not give her so much as a moment's breathing space and will isolate her totally, and who will not even have to bury me or dig me in any deeper because he will have suppressed my memory with the first terror and the first supplication and the first order; if he is her visitor tonight, then Luisa might put the phone back on the hook again once he has gone, as smartly dressed as when he arrived and even with his gloves on, and perhaps she will replace the phone when she hears the downstairs door bang and hears his steps in the street, noisy and confident and firm now, his progress towards it steady and sustained. So maybe I should keep ringing, or try again later, when I finally decide to go to bed in order to forget about her, it's almost eleven o'clock in Madrid and what am I doing here so far away, unable to go home to sleep, what am I doing in another country behaving like a nervous fiancé or, worse, like an insignificant lover or, worse, like a pathetic suitor who refuses to accept what he already knows, that he will always be rejected? That time is no more, it is not my time now, or, rather, my time has passed, I have had two children for a long while now and the person I am phoning is their mother, long enough for my thoughts never to forget about them and for them to be for me eternally children, why has my time been overturned or why has it been left hanging, what is the point of getting anxious on the pretext of fearing for the possible future that awaits all three of them depending on who replaces me, as far as I know there is no one on the way or travelling along that route, although if there was, Luisa would not necessarily tell me, still less about her occasional encounters that as yet have led to no inauguration, about who she sees or who she goes out with, not to mention who she goes to bed with and who she sees off at the front door, a dressing-gown thrown over her warm and, until only a moment ago, naked body, to whom she says goodbye with a long kiss as if storing it up until the next time, or perhaps she is pale after a long day, without a trace of makeup, all dishevelled, her hair grown childlike with the commotion of the day and the night, her tiredness apparent in the dark circles under her eyes and in her dull skin, when not even the momentary contentment of what has just happened can beautify a face that asks for and tolerates only repose and sleep, more sleep, and an end, at last, to thought. Neither have I told her about the three women who have spent the night here, not even one, which one, why would I, not even about the one who has been here twice.

The beggars have withdrawn after devouring their booty – they are a mere interregnum of ash and shadow – and the square is almost empty, someone crosses it now and again, no one is ever the last person anywhere, there is always someone who crosses later on. Lights are on in the smart hotel and in a few of the houses, but in my field of vision no one, at that moment, appears. The unfathomable dancer opposite has stopped and turned out the lights, he started at too late an hour to be able to withstand much prancing about. So here I am, all alone like a boyfriend or a lover, substantial and insignificant, here I am still awake.

'¿Sí?'

I picked up the phone almost before it had rung, it was so close. I spoke in Spanish, having been thinking in my own language for some time.

'Deza.' Luisa sometimes called me by my surname, when she wanted to be forgiven or to get something out of me, but also when she was in a very bad mood, because of something I had done. 'Hi, you've probably been trying to get through, I'm sorry, my sister has had me on the phone for an hour playing psychiatrist, she's going through a really rough patch with her husband and she considers me to be an expert on the subject now. Honestly. And the children are asleep now, I'm really sorry, I put them to bed at the usual time, the fact is that I'd completely forgotten it was Thursday until this very moment, when I put the phone down, you know what it's like when what's perfectly clear to you isn't at all clear to the other person, so you repeat yourself about ten times and end up getting more and more exasperated, and my sister's the same, I mean, she only really wants to hear what she's telling herself and not what I might think about the matter or advise her to do. Anyway, how are you?'

She sounded very tired and slightly absent, as if talking to me was a final, additional night-time chore she hadn't counted on, and as if she were still in conversation with her sister and not with me, always assuming that the conversation did take place. It's always the same, every day and with anyone, constantly, in any exchange of words, trivial or grave, we can believe or not believe what we're told, there aren't that many options, too few and too simple, and so we believe almost everything we're told, or, if we don't, we usually keep quiet about it, because otherwise everything becomes so tangled and difficult, staggering forwards in fits and starts, and nothing flows. And so everything that's said is taken, in principle, as the truth, the true and the false, unless the latter is obvious, that is, obviously false. This wasn't the case with Luisa now, what she was telling me could be what had really happened or it could be a mask for something else – a different phone call, a supper out under the protection of a talkative babysitter, a prolonged visit from someone and then a prolonged goodbye, it wasn't my business, and what did it matter – I had to accept it, in fact, I shouldn't even be thinking about it. Besides, there is another option, everything is full of half-truths, and we all take our inspiration from the truth in order to formulate or improvise lies, so there is always a pinch of truth in every lie, a basis, the starting-point, the source. I usually know, even if they don't concern me or there is no possible way of checking (and often I couldn't care less, it doesn't really matter). I detect them without any need of proof, but, generally speaking, I say nothing, unless I am being paid to point them out, as was the case when I was working in London.

'Fine,' I said, and even that one word was false. I didn't really feel like talking at all. Not even to ask about the children, there probably wouldn't be anything new to report. Nevertheless, she gave me a rapid summary as if to compensate me for not having heard their voices that night: perhaps that is why she had called me Deza, so that I would forgive the oversight with which I was not reproaching her, after all, those few minutes with my son and daughter on the phone were always very routine and rather silly, the same questions from me and similar responses from them, who never asked me anything apart from when I would be coming to see them and what presents I would bring, then a few affectionate words, the odd joke, all very stilted, the sadness came afterwards in the silence, at least in mine, but it was bearable.

'I'm absolutely done in,' said Luisa in conclusion. 'I've had enough of phones for one night, I'm going straight to bed.'

'Good night, then. I'll try and phone on Sunday. Sleep well.'

I hung up or we both did, I too felt exhausted and I had a lot of work to do the following morning at the BBC, I was still working there at the time and had no idea then that I would do so for only a short while longer. While I was getting undressed to go to bed, I remembered a foolish question I had asked Luisa while she was getting undressed to go to bed about a thousand years ago, shortly after our son was born, when I had still not quite got used to his existence, to his omnipresence. I had asked Luisa if she thought he would always live with us, while he was a child or very young. And she had responded with surprise and a touch of impatience: 'Of course he will, what nonsense, who else would he live with?' And then she had immediately added: 'As long as nothing happens to us.' 'What do you mean?' I asked, slightly distracted and disconcerted, as I often was at the time. She was almost naked. And her answer was: 'If nothing bad happens, I mean.' Our son was still only a child and he did not live with us, but with her alone, and with our daughter, who should also always have lived like that, with us. Something bad must have happened, or perhaps not to both of us, but only to me. Or to her.

In the first instance and at a party, Tupra turned out to be a cordial man, smiling and openly friendly, despite being a native of the British Isles, a man whose bland, ingenuous form of vanity not only proved inoffensive, but caused one to view him slightly ironically and with an almost instinctive fondness. He was unmistakably English despite his odd name, much more Bertram than Tupra: his gestures, intonation, his alternating high and low notes when he spoke, the way he had of standing, swaying gently back and forth on his heels with his hands behind his back, his initial assumed timidity, which is often used in England as a sign of politeness, or as a preliminary declaration of one's renunciation of all attempts at verbal domination – although *his* timidity was very much initial, since it lasted no further than the introductions – and yet something of his remote or traceable foreign origins survived in him – perhaps they were only paternal – possibly learned unintentionally and quite naturally at home and not entirely erased by the area where he'd been brought up and gone to school, not even by the University of Oxford where he had studied and which brings with it so many affectations and turns of phrase and so many exclusive and distinctive attitudes – almost like passwords or codes – a large degree of arrogance and even a few facial tics amongst those who have become most thoroughly assimilated into the place – although it is more akin to being assimilated into some ancient legend. That 'something' was related to a certain hardness of character or to a kind of permanent state of tension, or was it a postponed, subterranean, captive vehemence, impatiently waiting for there to be no witnesses – or only those who could be trusted – in order to emerge and show itself. I don't know, but it wouldn't have surprised me to learn that Tupra, when he was alone or had nothing to do, danced like a mad thing around his room, with or without a partner, but probably with a woman to hand, for he was obviously immoderately fond of them (such a predilection always stands out a mile in England, in marked contrast to the prevailing affectation of indifference), not just the woman he was with, but almost any woman, even one of mature years, it was as if he were able to see them in their previous state, when they were young women or, who knows, young girls, to be able to read them retrospectively and, with those eyes of his that probed the past, to make the past once more present during the time that he chose to reclaim and study it, and to cause women, who were in the process of shrinking or fading or withdrawing, to recover, in his presence, lust and vigour (or was it just a flash: the mad, ephemeral spluttering, more ephemeral even than the flame of a match newly struck). The most remarkable thing was that he made this happen not only in his own eyes, but in those of others, as if, when he talked about it, his vision became contagious, or, put another way, as if he persuaded and taught us all to see what he was seeing at that precise moment and which we would never have perceived without his help and his words and without his index finger pointing it out to us.

I observed this at the buffet supper at Sir Peter Wheeler's house and, of course, later on, when I knew more about him. Later, I realised, in fact, that his perspicacity as regards half-written biographies and half-travelled trajectories applied to everyone, women and men, although he found the former more stimulating and more interesting. At Wheeler's party, he arrived accompanied by the woman whom he had announced to Wheeler as his new girlfriend, a woman ten or twelve years younger than him and who appeared to find no novelty either in Tupra or in the situation: she lavished smiles on the wealthier-looking guests and half-heartedly rubbed shoulders with them, struggling to pay attention to their conversations as if she were playing an all-too-familiar role and kept mentally consulting her watch (she did look at it a couple of times without any apparent mental co-operation). She was tall, almost unusually so, in her well-trained high heels, and had the strong, solid legs of an American and a rather horse-like beauty of face, with attractive features, but a threatening jaw and such compact, excessively rectangular teeth that when she laughed, her upper lip curled back so far it almost disappeared – she was best when she wasn't laughing. She smelled good, of her own smell, one of those women whose pleasant, sour smell – a very sexual, physical smell – prevails over any other, this would doubtless be what most excited her boyfriend (that and her much-flaunted thighs).

Tupra was about fifty and shorter than she was, as were most of the other men present; he looked like a well-travelled diplomat who still did a lot of extempore dashing about, or else a high-ranking civil servant who spent more time out of the office than in, that is, someone not particularly important as a name but indispensable when it came to practical matters, more accustomed to putting out major conflagrations and covering up large holes, to sorting out messy pre-bellum situations and calming down or hoodwinking insurrectionists, rather than organising strategies from a desk. He looked like a man with his feet firmly on the ground, not lost somewhere in the upper echelons or bedazzled by protocol: whatever it was that he did ('his present line of work'), he probably spent more time padding streets not carpets, although now, perhaps, any streets he padded down would all be very elegant and well-to-do. His bulging cranium was softened by a head of hair considerably darker, thicker and curlier than one normally finds in Britain (with the exception of Wales), and which, particularly at the temples where the curls were almost ringlets, was probably dyed, revealing a premature but deferred greyness. His eyes were blue or grey depending on the light and he had long eyelashes, dense enough to be the envy of any woman and to be considered highly suspect by any man. His pale eyes had a mocking quality, even if this was not his intention – and his eyes were, therefore, expressive even when no expression was required – they were also rather warm or should I say appreciative, eyes that are never indifferent to what is there before them and which make anyone upon whom they fall feel worthy of curiosity, eyes whose very liveliness gave the immediate impression that they were going to get to the bottom of whatever being or object or landscape or scene they alighted upon. It is the kind of gaze that barely exists now in our societies, it is disapproved of and is being driven out. It is, of course, rare in England, where ancient tradition requires the gaze to be veiled or opaque or absent; but it's just as rare in Spain, where it used to be commonplace, and yet now no one sees anything or anyone or has the slightest interest in seeing, and where a kind of visual meanness leads people to behave as if others did not exist, or only as shapes or obstacles to be avoided or as mere supports to keep one upright or to be clambered up, and if you trample them in the process, so much the better, and where the disinterested observation of one's fellow man is seen as giving him an entirely unmerited importance which, moreover, diminishes that of the observer.

And yet, I thought, those who do still look at people in the way Bertram Tupra does, those who focus clearly and at the right height, which is the height of a man; those who catch or capture or, rather, absorb the image before them gain a great deal, especially as regards knowledge and the things that knowledge permits: to persuade and to influence, to make yourself indispensable and to be missed when you step aside or leave or even pretend to, to dissuade and convince and appropriate, to insinuate and to conquer. Tupra had that in common with Toby Rylands, whose student he had been, that warm, enveloping attention; and he had something in common with Wheeler too, except that Wheeler's gaze was wary, watchful, and his eyes seemed to be forming opinions even when they were merely reflective or distracted or sleepy, thinking on their own without the intervention of the brain, judging when there was no need to form a judgement, not even for his own purposes. Tupra, on the other hand, was not initially intimidating, he did not give that impression, and you did not, therefore, feel it necessary to be on your guard, rather, he invited you to lower your shield and take off your helmet, to allow him to get a better look at you. They all had something in common, and he, as nexus, made me aware of more similarities between the two older men, the dead friend and the living friend: links of character, no, links of ability. Or perhaps it was a gift that all three of them shared.

Tupra, I thought, would prove irresistible to women (I thought this often, I saw it) regardless of class, profession, experience, degree of conceit or age, even though he was getting on for fifty and not exactly handsome, but he was attractive in himself, despite the odd feature that might prove repellent to the objective eye: not so much his rather coarse nose which looked as if it had been broken by a blow once or by several more since; not so much his skin, disturbingly lustrous and firm for a man of his years and which was the lovely golden colour of beer (not a wrinkle in sight, and without recourse to artificial aids); not so much his eyebrows like black smudges and with a tendency to grow together (he probably plucked the space between them with tweezers now and then); it was more his overly soft and fleshy mouth, as lacking in consistency as it was over-endowed in breadth, lips that were rather African or perhaps Hindu or Slavic, and which, when they kissed, would give and spread like pliable, well-kneaded plasticine, at least that is how they would feel, with a touch like a sucker, a touch of always renewed and inextinguishable dampness. And yet, I told myself, he would still captivate whoever he chose to captivate, because nothing is so short-lived as the objective eye, and then almost nothing repels, once it has gone or once you have perhaps got rid of it in order to be able to live. Besides, there would be no shortage of people whom that mouth would please and inflame. As an adult, and even as my younger, more uncertain self, only very rarely have I felt convinced, in the presence of another man, that, whatever the situation, I would not stand a chance against him; and that if that fellow or individual looked at the woman beside me, there would be no way of keeping her there. But I had no woman beside me, not at Wheeler's buffet supper nor during most of the time I was under contract to Tupra as his assistant. Thank heavens Luisa isn't with me, I thought; she isn't here and so I have nothing to fear (I thought this often, I saw it). This man would amuse and flatter and understand her, he would take her out on the town every night and expose her to the most appropriate and most fruitful of dangers, he would be solicitous and supportive and would listen to her story from start to finish, and he would isolate her too and quietly feed her his demands and his prohibitions, all at once or within a very brief space of time, and he would not have to dig an inch deeper to send me down to the very depths of hell, nor have to make the slightest move to despatch me to limbo, me and my memory, as well as any occasional, improbable nostalgia she might feel for me.

This conviction made his new girlfriend's attitude towards him even stranger in my eyes, for she seemed more like someone who had made the whole journey with him some time ago, indeed, had done so long enough to grow weary of their shared trajectory and weary too, therefore, of Tupra, who, one would have said, she treated with familiar affection and in a conciliatory – and perhaps adulatory – spirit, rather than pursuing him enthusiastically about the large living-room or clinging to him like the brand-new lover who can still not believe his or her good fortune (this man loves me, this woman loves me, what a blessing) and confuses it with predestination or some other such uplifting nonsense. Not that she did not seem dependent on Tupra, but this was more because he was her companion and the person who had dragged or led her to Wheeler's house to be with these people, half university types and half diplomatic or financial or political or business types, or perhaps literary or professional – it's harder to distinguish amongst smartly dressed people in another country with an archaic etiquette, even when one has lived there; also present was a vast, drunken nobleman, Lord Rymer, an old Oxford acquaintance of mine and now the retired warden of All Souls – than out of inclination or submission or desire or love, or out of the natural impatience for novelties which conceal for the moment the inevitable end of their condition, and which, deep down, we all want to accelerate (the new is so tiring, for it has to be tamed and has no established course to follow). Peter had introduced her to me as just plain Beryl. 'Mr Deza, an old Spanish friend of mine,' he had said in English when they arrived and I was already there, thus giving them natural pre-eminence by mentioning my name first, it may simply have been deference to the lady's presence or there may have been more to it; and then: 'Mr Tupra, whose friendship goes back even further. And this is Beryl.' And that was all.

If Wheeler wanted me to observe Tupra and to pay closer attention to him than to anyone else during the evening, he made a grave miscalculation in inviting another Spaniard, a certain De la Garza, I wasn't clear whether he was cultural attaché or press attaché at the Spanish embassy, or something of an even vaguer and more parasitic nature, although given some of his language I could not entirely dismiss the idea that he was merely the officer in charge of improper relations, a *sommelier*, a suborner *in petto* or a gentleman-in-waiting. He was immaculately dressed, arrogant and insolent and, as tends to be the norm amongst my compatriots whenever and wherever they happen to meet up with foreigners, whether in Spain as hosts or abroad as guests of honour, whether they are in the absolute majority or in a minority of one, he could not bear to have to socialise with foreigners or to find himself in the tiresome situation of having to express a little polite curiosity, and so, consequently, as soon as he spotted a fellow Spaniard, he scarcely left my side and dispensed altogether with having any truck with the natives (we, after all, were the dagos), apart from with the two or three or perhaps four sexually attractive women amongst the fifteen or so guests (cold like the buffet and occasionally seated, but with no fixed place, or wandering about or standing in one spot), although this consisted mainly in ogling these women with his all too diaphanous eyes, in making crude remarks, in pointing them out to me with his ungovernable chin and even, occasionally, dealing me a knowing, mortifying, entirely unforgivable dig in the ribs, rather than going over to them himself to strike up an acquaintance or a conversation, that is, giving them the come-on more than just visually, which would not have been at all easy for him to do in English. I noticed at once his contentment and relief when we were introduced: with a Spaniard on hand, he would be saved the tension and fatigue of the onerous use of the local language which he thought he spoke, for his appalling accent transformed the most ordinary of words into harsh utterances unrecognisable to anyone but me, although this was more torment than privilege, since my familiarity with his implacable phonetics meant that I had to decipher, much against my will, a lot of presumptuous nonsense; he could also give free rein to his criticisms and slanders of those present without them understanding a word, although he did sometimes forget Sir Peter Wheeler's perfect command of Spanish, and when he remembered this and saw that Wheeler was within earshot, he would resort to obscene or criminal jargon, even more than he did when Wheeler was out of range; he felt at liberty to bring up absurd Spanish topics, whether justified or not, given that I know almost nothing about bullfighting or about the nonsense published in the tabloid press or about members of the royal family, not that I have anything against the first and very little against the third; and with me he could also swear and be as crude as he liked, which is very difficult to do in another language (easily and convincingly) and which you miss terribly if you're used to it, as I've often had occasion to observe when abroad, where I have known ministers, aristocrats, ambassadors, tycoons and professors, and even their respective beautifully dressed wives and daughters and even mothers and mothers-in-law of varying backgrounds, education and age, take advantage of my momentary presence to unburden themselves with oaths and diabolical blasphemies in Spanish (or Catalan). I was a blessing and a boon to De la Garza, and he sought me out and followed me all over the room and the garden, despite the cool of the night, mingling coarseness with pedantry and generally revelling in Spanish.

He shadowed me all evening, and even if I was talking to other people, in English naturally, he would sidle up to me every few minutes (as soon as someone gave him the slip, having had enough of his phonetic idiocies and barbarisms) and interrupt in his hideous English, only to slide immediately into our common language, given the evident struggle it represented for my interlocutors to understand him, with the apparent, initial intention of using me as simultaneous interpreter ('Go on, translate the joke I just made to this stupid cow, will you, she obviously didn't get it'), but with the real and determined intention of scaring them all away and thus monopolising my attention and my conversation. I tried not to pay him the former or allow him the latter and continued to do as I pleased, barely bothering to listen to him, or only when he spoke more loudly than normal, when I would catch ambiguous fragments or odd phrases which he interposed whenever there was a pause or even when there wasn't, though more often than not I didn't even understand the context, since the attaché De la Garza attached himself to me at every moment, and at no moment did he cease to hold forth to me, whether I answered him or listened to him or not.

This began to happen after our first bout together, which

caught me unawares, and from which I escaped feeling alarmed and battered and during which he interrogated me about my duties and my influence at the BBC and went on to propose six or seven ideas for radio programmes which ranged from the imperial to the downright stupid, often both at once, and which would purportedly prove beneficial to his embassy and our country and doubtless to him and his prospects, for, he told me, he was an expert on the writers of our poor Generation of '27 (poor in the sense of over-exploited and stale), on those of our poor Golden Age (poor because hackneyed and over-exposed), and on our not at all poor fascist writers from the pre-Civil War, post-Civil War and intra-Civil War periods, who were, in any case, one and the same (they suffered few losses during the fighting unfortunately), and to whom he did not, of course, apply that epithet, for this band of out-and-out traitors and pimps seemed to him honourable, altruistic people.

'I mean most of them were marvellous stylists, and who, confronted by such poetry and such prose, could be so mean-spirited as to mention their ideology? It's high time we separated politics and literature.' And to ram the point home: 'High bloody time.' He displayed that mixture of sentiment and coarseness, soppiness and vulgarity, mawkishness and brutality so common amongst my compatriots, a real plague and a grave threat (it's gaining support, with writers leading the way), foreigners will soon conclude that it is our main national characteristic. He had addressed me as '*tú*' from the moment he saw me, on principle: he was one of those Spaniards who reserve what used to be the more formal '*usted*' for subalterns and artisans.

I was about to throw a gauntlet at his slick, gelled hair (it would have stuck fast, no problem), but I didn't have one to hand, only a napkin and, despite the general cheapening of the age, it would not have been the same, and so I merely answered him, more curtly than scornfully, so as to lessen the tension:

'There is some prose and poetry whose very style is fascist, even though it's all about the sun and the moon and is signed by self-proclaimed left-wingers, our newspapers and bookshops are full of them. The same thing happens with people's minds or characters: some are, by their nature, fascist, even if they inhabit bodies that have a tendency to raise the clenched fist and do the right thing at marches and demonstrations with hordes of photographers pushing their way through and, of course, immortalising them. The last thing we need now is a rehabilitation of the mind and style of those who not only *were* fascists, but were proud to call themselves fascists, just in case you didn't recognise them by what they wrote, by every page they published and every person they denounced to the police. They've left enough of a mark on present-day writers without the need for that, although most keep quiet about it and look for rather less sullied antecedents, poor old Quevedo is usually the first in line, and some may not even be aware of their much more immediate legacy, which they carry in their blood and which boils inside them.'

'Dammit, man, how can you say that?' De la Garza protested, more out of confusion than genuine disagreement, for I hadn't given him time for that. 'How can you possibly tell that someone's style is, in itself, fascist? Or someone's mind. You're just showing off.'

I was tempted to reply by imitating his way of speaking: 'If you can't spot it four paragraphs into a book or after talking to someone for half an hour, then you know fuck-all about literature or people.' But I stood there thinking a little, thinking superficially. It really wasn't that easy to explain how, nor even in what that mind or style with all its many faces consisted, but I was able to recognise them at once, or so I thought then, or perhaps I was just showing off. I had been doing so, of course – although only to myself – when I spoke of four paragraphs and half an hour, I should have said or thought 'a few hours', and even that would have been pushing it. It takes perhaps days and weeks or months and years, sometimes you see something clearly in that first half-hour only to feel it fade, to lose sight of it and to recapture it, perhaps, a decade or half a lifetime later, if it ever comes back. Sometimes it's best not simply to let time pass, or to allow ourselves to become entangled in the time we grant to others or to become confused by the time we ourselves are granted. It's best not to be dazzled, which is what time always tries to do, all the while slipping past. It isn't easy any more to define what fascist meant, it's becoming an old-fashioned adjective and is often used incorrectly or, of course, imprecisely, although I tend to use it in a colloquial and doubtless analogical sense, and in that sense and usage I know exactly what it means and know that I'm using it properly. But with De la Garza I had used it more than anything in order to annoy him and to put the dreadful fascist writers he so admired firmly in their place, I had taken an instant dislike to the man, I've seen so many of his sort from childhood on, and they never die, they just disguise themselves and adapt: they're snobbish and vain and extremely pleasant, they're cheerful and even, in form at least, affectionate, they're ambitious and rather false (no, they're not even entirely false), they try to appear refined and, at the same time, pretend to be one of the guys, even common (a very poor imitation, they don't fool anyone, their deep aversion to what they are imitating soon unmasks them), that's why they're so free with their language, thinking that this makes them seem more down-to-earth and will win round the reluctant, which is why they combine stiff refinement with the manners of the barracks and the vocabulary of the prison, military service served them perfectly to complete the picture; the final effect is that of a perfumed boor. De la Garza's mind did not strike me as fascist, even by analogy. He was merely a flatterer, the kind who cannot bear anyone to dislike them, not even people they detest, they aspire to be loved even by those they hurt. He was not the sort who would, on his own initiative, stick the knife in, or only if he needed to earn a few brownie points or to ingratiate himself or if he were given a special assignment, then he would have no scruples at all, because people like him are very adroit with their own consciences.

But I postponed these thoughts for later, and merely cocked my head and raised my eyebrows in response, as if agreeing or saying: 'What more can I say?' and let the matter drop, and he didn't press it, indeed he took advantage of my silence to tell me that he also knew a hell of a lot – purely as an amateur, he explained, not this time as an expert – about literary fantasy, medieval stuff too (that's what he said, he said 'a hell of a lot' and 'medieval stuff too'). From the way he said this, it was clear that he considered literary fantasy to be chic. I thought he would one day be Minister of Culture, or at the very least Secretary of State of said branch, to use the old expression, although I've never known exactly what 'branch' meant in the bureaucratic rather than the botanical sense.

Those few seconds of political-cum-literary tension proved no impediment, as I said, to the attaché who remained glued to my side or hard on my heels with scarcely a break once that initial encounter of ours was over and despite the fact that I overtly and frequently turned my back on him and talked to some of the other guests in the most obscure, affected and, for him, off-putting English I could muster. Thus, for example, the brief opportunity I had to speak to Tupra was marred by De la Garza's occasional and entirely inappropriate interpolations in Spanish. This was not until some time later, when the two of us were standing up drinking coffee by the sofas which, at that moment, were occupied by Wheeler, Beryl the girlfriend, the Dean of York's very buxom widow, and two or three others, there is always a constant coming and going and changing of positions at these nomadic, informal buffet suppers.

The fact is that Wheeler had done nothing to bring us together, Tupra and me, and I began to think that his telephonic lecture about this fellow or, rather, about his surname and his first name had been pure chance and without any hidden agenda, however difficult I found it to imagine Peter restricting himself to a plain and boringly open agenda, let alone to the absolute absence of any agenda at all. He had been equally attentive to almost all his guests, assisted by Mrs Berry (more smartly dressed than usual), the housekeeper he had inherited from Toby Rylands when the latter had died years before, and by three waiters hired for the evening along with the viands and whose shift ended at midnight exactly, as Peter had slightly anxiously informed me (he was hoping that, by then, there wouldn't be many guests still hanging around). He and I had barely spoken, knowing that we would have time to talk the next day: I would stay the night at his house, as I sometimes did, so that I could spend the following morning with him and have Sunday lunch there. Studying him from afar, I hadn't noticed him paying particular attention to any one person, like the good host he was, nor bringing particular people together, at least not in my case, because I couldn't believe that he would deliberately have thrown me together with De la Garza, who had soured my soul and hampered my every conversation with his attempts at chit-chat and his comments that had nothing at all to do with what was being discussed; and although he understood English better than he spoke it, the large quantity of alcohol with which he had filled his unintended soliloquies – he wanted to be part of things and wasn't at all happy being his own audience – brought about a rapid deterioration in his intellectual faculties (if you can call them that) and coarsened the nature of his remarks.

While I spoke briefly to Beryl, for example, fairly early on in the evening (she replied reluctantly and purely out of duty, I obviously didn't strike her as being sufficiently well-heeled), he prowled tirelessly around us, coming out with crass comments about her which, fortunately, no one else could understand ('Fucking hell, have you seen the legs on this woman? You could practically toboggan down them. What do you reckon, eh? Do you think we could steal her from that gypsy she arrived with? She doesn't take the least bit of notice of him; but then again, he never takes his eyes off her and he could turn out to be the sort who would knife you, however British he might be'). And while I was conducting a soporific conversation about terrorism with an Irish historian called Fahy, his wife and the Labour mayor of some unfortunate town in Oxfordshire, the attaché, when he heard a few Basque names fall from my lips, tried to butt in with a little folklore ('Hey, tell them that San Sebastián is only the city it is because of us *madrileños*, dammit, because us people from Madrid used to go and spend our summer holidays there and wrapped it all up for them with a nice pink ribbon, otherwise it would be a complete dump; go on, tell 'em, I mean they may have been to university this lot, but they don't know shit about anything.' By then he had mixed sherry and whisky and three different kinds of wine.) He liked the Dean of York's well-upholstered widow even more than he did Beryl the girlfriend, and while I chatted to her for a few minutes, De la Garza kept muttering to me: 'Shit, get a load of that, God, she's fucking gorgeous', apparently too bowled over to make a proper breakdown of the whole, to analyse in detail, to notice subtleties or, for that matter, anything else (by now he had drunk some port as well). His excitement was as puerile as the expression 'get a load of that', more suited to someone with little experience of women than to a natural and expert womaniser. It occurred to me that De la Garza would know many nights on which he would succumb to women whom a combination of over-eagerness and alcohol would make him think desirable, only to clutch his head in the morning on discovering that he had got into bed with some vast relative of Oliver Hardy's or with some flighty Bela Lugosi look-alike. This wasn't the case with the widowed deaness, with her placid pink face and her voluminous upper body set off by a vast necklace made of what appeared to me to be Ceylonese jacinths or zircons made to resemble orange segments, but she was nevertheless old enough to be the mother (albeit a young one) of her callow, foul-mouthed admirer.

Tupra, with a cup of coffee in his hand, had asked me what my field was, following the Oxonian norm according to which it is taken for granted that everyone in that city has their specific field of teaching or research, or some field worthy of boasting about.

'I've never been very constant in my professional interests,' I replied, 'and I've only been at the university here intermittently, almost by chance really. I taught for a couple of years a long time ago, contemporary Spanish literature and translation, that's when I first met Sir Peter, although I saw less of him at the time than I did of Professor Toby Rylands, under whom, I understand, you studied.' I could have stopped there; it was enough for a first reply, and I had even given him the opportunity to continue the conversation seamlessly by mentioning Toby, whom he could easily have started reminiscing about, and I would gladly have joined in. But Tupra allowed a second or two to pass without saying anything, and would probably have continued to say nothing for a third or fourth or fifth (one, two, three and four; and five), but I wasn't sure, he was one of those rare men who knows how to withstand silence, who can remain silent, but without making you feel nervous, rather, encouraging you and making it clear that he is ready to hear more, if you have more to say. That receptive manner combined with his courteous or affectionately mocking eyes invited one to talk. And so I did, perhaps also because my superfluous explanations would give me all the more right to ask him in turn about *his* field, his 'line of work' to use Wheeler's expression, it was high time I found out, and it was strange that the word 'right' should have crossed my mind in relation to something so innocuous and normal, we all ask other people what they do, it's almost our first question. Or perhaps it's because with Tupra one always felt under an obligation to speak even if he didn't open his mouth, as if he were our tacit creditor. And so I added: 'Then I spent some time in the United

States, but I hardly did any teaching at all when I went back to my own country, I've had various occupations, I worked for a while on a very influential magazine, I've done a bit of translation, I've set up a couple of businesses, I even had my own tiny publishing house, then I got fed up and sold it.'

'For a profit, I hope,' he said, smiling.

'For a large and entirely unmerited profit, to tell you the truth.' And I too smiled. 'Now I'm working for BBC Radio in London, on the Spanish-language broadcasts, well, sometimes in English too, of course, when they touch on Spanish or Latin-American matters. It's always the same old thing, there are so few Spanish topics that are of interest in England, just terrorism and tourism really, a lethal combination.' My tongue had wanted me to say not 'it's always the same old thing', but '*es siempre sota, caballo y rey*', but I wasn't sure what the equivalent idiom in English might be, or even if there was one, and a straight translation – 'it's always knave, queen and king' – would have made no sense at all, and for a moment I understood De la Garza and his longing for his own language and his resistance to this other language, sometimes other languages overwhelm and weary us, even though we're accustomed to them and can speak them fluently, and at other times what we long for are precisely those other languages that we know and now almost never use. *Sota, caballo y rey*. It was literally only a moment, because I was infuriated suddenly to hear one of De la Garza's absurd, extemporaneous phrases addressed to me, belonging to who knows what arbitrary argument that he alone was following:

'*Las mujeres son todas putas, y las más guapas las españolas*', reached my ears. 'Women are all sluts, but for looks you can't beat the Spanish.' By then he was probably awash with port, for I had seen him making two or three toasts one after the other with Lord Rymer (bottoms up, cheerio) during the few minutes in which the latter claimed him as a drinking companion, thus keeping him entertained and giving me a breather. Lord Rymer, I remembered then, had been known in Oxford from time immemorial by a malicious nickname, The Flask, which, with semantic inexactitude but intentional, phonetic proximity, I would be inclined to translate simply as '*La Frasca*', or The Carafe.

'I see,' said Tupra pleasantly, when he had got over his surprise. Fortunately, as I found out later, he knew only a few words of Spanish, although amongst them, as might have been feared and as I also found out later, were '*mujeres*', '*putas*', '*españolas*' and '*guapas*', that careless brute De la Garza hadn't even had the decency to be obscure in his choice of vocabulary. 'So am I right in thinking that, at the moment, you would find almost any other kind of work attractive? Not, of course, that there's anything wrong, objectively speaking, with the BBC, but it probably gets a bit repetitive. But, then, if you like variety and if you've had it up to here with the job already, who the hell cares about objectivity?' Tupra had a fairly deep, rather mournful voice (here my tongue might have chosen another word from the language I was speaking, 'ailing' perhaps), and had the same tonality as a string, by which I mean that it seemed to emerge from the movement of a bow over strings or to be caused by or to respond to that, if a viola da gamba or a cello can emit feeling (but perhaps I was wrong and it wasn't so much 'mournful' as 'affecting', and 'ailing' would not therefore be the right word: for the gentle, almost pleasant feeling, that eased all affliction, was felt not by him, but by the person listening to him). 'Tell me, Mr Deza, how many languages do you speak or understand? You said you had worked as a translator. I mean, apart from the obvious ones, your English, for example, is superb, if I hadn't known what nationality you were, I would never have thought you were Spanish. Canadian perhaps.'

'Thank you, I take that as a compliment.'

'Oh, you should, believe me, that was my intention. I mean it. The cultivated Canadian accent is the one that most closely resembles ours, especially, as the name suggests, the English spoken in British Columbia. So what other languages do you know?' Tupra did not allow himself to be distracted by the to-ing and fro-ing that make conversations so erratic and undefined, until tiredness and time put an end to them, he always returned to where he wanted to be.

He had drunk his coffee down in one (that large mouth) and, with real urgency, had immediately placed the empty cup and saucer on the low table next to the sofas, as if what had already been used and therefore served no further function made him impatient or troubled him. As he bent down to do so, he shot a rapid glance at his girlfriend Beryl, whose minuscule skirt barely covered her legs which were now uncrossed (and this was perhaps the reason behind the glance), so that from lower down than we were you might have been able to see, how can I put it, the crotch of her underpants, if she was wearing any, I noticed that De la Garza was sitting on a pouffe at just the right height, and it seemed highly unlikely that this was pure chance. Beryl was talking and laughing with a very fat young man, slouched on the sofa, who had been introduced to me as Judge Hood and about whom I knew nothing except that, despite his plumpness and his youth, he was presumably a judge, and she continued to pay scant attention to Tupra, as if he were the dull husband who no longer represents for her diversion or fun and is just part of the house, not quite part of the furniture, more perhaps like a portrait, which, even though it is generally ignored, still has eyes to see and to watch what we get up to. Tupra also exchanged a glance with Wheeler, who was concentrating on applying a very long match to a cigar that was already very much alight (if not positively ablaze) and was speaking to no one while thus engaged, by his side the ecclesiastical widow of York appeared sleepy and rather less pneumatic, she probably rarely stayed up late or wine perhaps diminished her. I noticed no gesture or signal pass between Wheeler and Tupra, but the eyes of the former permitted themselves a moment of elevation and fixity, through the flames and the smoke, which seemed to me to suggest some implied meaning and recommendation, as if with that unblinking look he were advising him: 'Fine, but don't delay much longer', and as if the message were referring to me. Just as Peter had singled out Tupra for my attention, so he must have told Tupra something about me, although I didn't know what or why. But the fact was that Tupra had said 'and if you've had it up to here with the job already', and I hadn't mentioned how long I had been at the BBC or back in England – how could I possibly be back, my previous stay belonged to the remote past that can never be re-created, or, indeed, to the past from which no one returns – so he must have found out from Wheeler that it was only three months. Yes, only three months ago I had still been in Madrid and had normal access to my home or our home, since I still lived and slept there, although Luisa's increasing remoteness from me had already begun and was advancing with frightening speed, an advance that was troubling, disturbing, and daily – if not hourly – it's astonishing how swiftly what is and has endured suddenly ceases to be, and becomes null and void, once the last line of light has been crossed and the processes of darkness and ambiguity begin. You lose the trust of the person with whom you have shared years of continuous narrative, that person no longer tells you things or asks or even responds and you yourself don't dare to ask or tell, you grow gradually more and more silent and there comes a time when you don't talk at all, you try to pass unnoticed or to make yourself invisible in the home you share in common, and once you know and it has been agreed that it will soon cease to be the common home and which one of you will have to leave, you have the feeling that you're living there on sufferance until you find somewhere else to seek refuge, like an impertinent guest who sees and hears things that should not concern him, goings-out and comings-in that are not commented on before or talked about afterwards, enigmatic phone calls that remain unexplained, and which are possibly no different from those which, a short time before, you didn't even listen to or register, nor, of course, did you retain them in your memory as you do – every one of them – now, because then you weren't alert, you didn't wonder about them or think they concerned you or constituted an implied threat. You know all too well that the phone calls do not concern you now and yet you jump every time the phone rings or you hear her dial a number. But you say nothing and listen fearfully and say nothing, and there comes a point when your only means of communication or contact are the children whom you often tell things purely so that she will hear you in the next room, or so that they'll reach her ears eventually, or in order to make amends, although this will never now be perceived as that, just as feelings will be disregarded too, and, besides, no child in the world can be entirely trusted as an emissary. And the day that you finally leave you feel a touch of relief as well as sadness and despair – or is it shame – but even that meagre sense of mingled relief will not last, it disappears at once, the moment you realise that your relief is as nothing compared with that felt by the other person, the one who stays and does not move and breathes easily at last to see you leaving, disappearing. Everything is so unbearably ridiculous and subjective, because everything contains its opposite: the same people in the same place love each other and cannot stand each other, what was once long-established habit becomes slowly or suddenly unacceptable and inadmissible – it doesn't matter which, that's the least of it, the person who built a home finds himself barred from entering it, the merest contact, a touch so taken for granted it was barely conscious, becomes an affront or an insult and it is as if one had to ask permission to touch oneself, what once gave pleasure or amusement becomes hateful, repellent, accursed and vile, words once longed-for would now poison the air or provoke nausea, they must on no account be heard, and those spoken a thousand times before are made to seem unimportant (erase, suppress, cancel, better never to have said anything, that is the world's ambition); the reverse is true too: what was once mocked is taken seriously, and the person once deemed repugnant is told: 'I was so wrong about you, come here.' 'Sit down here beside me, somehow I just couldn't see you clearly before.' That is why one must always ask for a postponement: 'Kill me tomorrow; let me live tonight!' I quoted to myself. Tomorrow you might want me alive, even for only half an hour, and I won't be there to grant your wish, and your desire will be as nothing. It is nothing, nothing is nothing, the same things, the same actions and the same people are themselves as well as their opposite, today and yesterday, tomorrow, afterwards, long ago. And in between there is only time that takes such pains to dazzle us, which is all it wants and seeks, which is why none of us is to be trusted, we who are still travelling through time, all of us foolish and insubstantial and unfinished, foolish me, insubstantial and unfinished me, no one should trust me either . . . Of course I had had it up to here already and even before it began, I'd never been interested in that job with the BBC, it had merely been the one reasonable way of ceasing to be irrelevant and phantasmagoric and so very silent, the one way of leaving there and disappearing.

'I've only ever dared translate from English and I didn't do it for very long. I have no problem speaking and understanding French and Italian, but I don't have a good enough command of them to be able to translate literary texts from those languages into Spanish. I can understand Catalan pretty well, but I would never even attempt to speak it.'

'Catalan?' It was as if Tupra had heard the name for the first time.

'Yes, it's the language spoken in Catalonia, as much or more, well, much more nowadays than Spanish or *castellano*, as we often call it. Catalonia, Barcelona, the Costa Brava, you know.' But Tupra did not respond at once (perhaps he was trying to remember), so I added as further orientation: 'The artists Dalí and Miró.'

'Mention Montserrat Caballé, the soprano,' De la Garza suggested, almost breathing down my neck. 'The silly fool is bound to like opera.' He could clearly understand more than he could speak and was drawn like a magnet by any Spanish names he happened to catch. He had got up from the pouffe in order to pester me again (Beryl had crossed her legs now, that was probably the real reason). I assumed he had meant to use the word 'gypsy' again about Tupra (because of his curly hair, I assumed, those ringlets), but that, after all the outrageous toasts he had drunk, he could now only manage to say 'fool'.

'Gaudí, the architect,' I suggested, I had no intention of taking any notice of De la Garza, that would have been tantamount to giving him permission to join in the dialogue.

'Yes, yes, of course, George Orwell and all that,' said Tupra at last, finally placing the name. 'Sorry, I was remembering . . . I've forgotten most of what I read about the Spanish Civil War, things I read in my youth, you know, you tend to read about that romantic war when you're nineteen or twenty, perhaps because of all those idealistic young British volunteers who died there, some of them poets, you identify easily with other people at that age. Well, I don't know about nowadays, I'm talking about my day, of course, although I would say it was still the same, for restless young people that is: they still read Emily Brontë and Salinger, *Ten Days that Shook the World* and books about the Spanish Civil War, things haven't changed that much. I remember being particularly impressed by what happened to Nin, I mean, how utterly ridiculous to accuse him of spying. And the complete farce of those German members of the International Brigade passing themselves off as Nazis come to liberate him, it just goes to show how even the craziest, most unlikely things have their moment to be believed. Sometimes the moment lasts only a matter of days, sometimes it lasts for ever. The truth is that, initially, everything tends to be believed. It's very odd, but that's how it is.'

'Nin, the Trotskyite leader?' I asked, surprised. I couldn't believe that Tupra knew nothing about Dalí and Miró, Caballé and Gaudí (or so I deduced from his silence), and yet knew so much about the slandered Andrés Nin, probably more than I did. Perhaps he didn't know about art and didn't like opera, and his field was politics or history.

'Yes, who else? Although, of course, he did break with Trotsky in the end.'

'Well, there was a musician called Nin, and, of course, that awful woman writer,' I began, but stopped myself. Things he had read in his youth, he had said. Something as real to me and still so close was, in another not so distant country, just like *Wuthering Heights* had been for years: that is, a fiction, a romantic fiction, read by the surlier, angrier university students in order, in their imaginings, to feel defeated, pure and perhaps heroic. It's probably the fate of all horrors and all wars, I thought, to end up abstract and embellished by dint of sheer repetition and, ultimately, to feed both youthful and adult fantasies, more quickly if the war happens abroad, perhaps for many foreigners our war seems as literary and remote as the French Revolution and the Napoleonic campaigns or perhaps even the sieges of Numantia or Troy. And yet my father had nearly died in that war, wearing the uniform of the Republic in our besieged city, and, when it was over, had endured a mock trial and imprisonment under Franco, and an uncle of mine aged seventeen had been killed in Madrid and in cold blood by those on the other side – that side split into so many factions, and so full of calumnies and purges – by the militiamen who wore no uniform and were subject to no control and who would bump off anyone, they had killed him for no reason at an age when almost all one does is fantasise and when there are only imaginings, and his older sister, my mother, had searched that same besieged city for his body without finding it, only the tiny, bureaucratic photograph of his corpse, which I've seen and which is now in my possession. Perhaps in my country, too, without my realising it, this was all turning into fiction, everything moves ever faster, is less enduring, more quickly cancelled out and filed away, and our past grows ever denser and fuller and more crowded because it has been decreed – and even accepted as true – that yesterday is passé, the day before yesterday mere history, and what happened a year ago remote and immemorial. (Perhaps what happened three months ago too.) I thought that the time had come to find out at last what his 'line of work' was, I had earned enough brownie points, always assuming I needed them. In my thoughts I didn't believe this to be so, yet I had the distinct feeling that it was. 'Tell me, Mr Tupra, what is your field, if you don't mind my asking? It's not, by any chance, the history of my country, is it?' I realised that I was still awaiting permission to ask the easiest and most harmless of questions asked in our societies.

'No, no, of course not, you can be quite sure of that,' he replied, laughing loudly and with genuine mirth, his teeth were small but very bright, his long eyelashes danced. When you had got used to it, his was the sort of face to which you warmed more and more with each minute, objectivity would not last long with him, and suspicion would quickly dissolve. You noticed at once the generosity of the interest he took in you, as if at every moment he was concerned only with the person he was with and as if, behind you, the lights of the world had gone out and the world had been transformed into a mere backdrop designed to set you off. He also knew how to hold the attention of the person he was talking to, in my case that mention of Andrés Nin had been enough to intrigue me, and not merely because of what he knew, for I was filled now with a desire to plunge into Orwell's *Homage to Catalonia* or into Hugh Thomas's summary and to brush up on the story of the slandered Andrés Nin, of which I could barely remember a thing. One also noticed in Tupra that strange tension – a sort of postponed vehemence – but I took it at first as simply part of his natural alertness. He was well dressed, but not extravagantly so, discreet fabrics and colours (the cloth was always of extraordinarily high quality, his superb ties always pinned with a tie-pin), his vanity evident only – unless it was a remnant of past bad taste – in the perennial vests he wore under his jacket, and one of which he was wearing at Wheeler's buffet supper. 'No, my activities have been as diverse as yours, but my real talent has always been for negotiating, in different fields and circumstances. Even serving my country, one should if one can, don't you think, even if the service one renders is indirect and done mainly to benefit oneself.'

He had evaded the question, this was all very vague, he hadn't even said what he had studied at Oxford, although Toby Rylands, one of his teachers, had been Professor of English Literature. Not that this meant anything. In that university it doesn't really matter what you study, what counts is to have been there and to have submitted to its method and its spirit, and no course of study, however eccentric or ornamental, prevents its graduates and postgraduates from going on to do whatever they choose to do afterwards, however different that may be: you can spend years analysing Cervantes and end up in the world of finance, or studying the traces left by the ancient Persians and convert that afterwards into the extravagant preamble to a career in politics or diplomacy, doubtless the latter for Tupra, I thought again, basing this now not only on my intuition or on his appearance, but on that verb 'negotiate' and that expression, 'serving my country'. He was lucky – in a way – that there is no one-word English equivalent for the unequivocal '*patria*' of my own language (or only highly recondite, rhetorical ones): the word he had used, 'country', means different things depending on the context, but is less emotive and less pompous and should almost always be translated as '*país*'. Otherwise, I might perhaps have thought – that is, if he had used the Spanish word '*patria*', which was impossible; and yet the shadow of that mad idea did cross my mind, though without taking proper shape – that he had a fascist mind, in the analogical sense, despite the evident solidarity and sympathy with which he had referred to the fate of Nin,

Trotsky's former secretary, for in the colloquial or analogical sense the word is compatible with all ideologies, one's ideology isn't necessarily relevant, which is why it has become such a vague term, I've known official champions of the old Left, the apparently incontrovertible Left, who were intrinsically fascist by nature (and in their writing style too, if they were writers). In that idea of serving one's country I had noticed a hint of coquetry and a touch of arrogance. The coquetry of someone who enjoys appearing mysterious, the arrogance of someone who sees or conceives of himself as a granter of favours, even to his own country. A third foreign Briton, perhaps, a third bogus Englishman, I thought, like Toby, according to all the rumours, and like Peter, as he himself had confessed a few weeks ago. I had still not had a chance to ask him about that. Bogus at least to judge by the surname, that strange name Tupra, though perhaps not by birth in his case, the newly arrived and those with suspicious names are always and everywhere the most patriotic, the readiest to render a service, noble or base, clean or dirty, they feel grateful and volunteer, or perhaps it is their way of believing themselves to be indispensable to the country that one day allowed them to stay and continues to do so, as it would even if they had changed their name, like that poor Anatolian Hohanness who went on to be Joe Arness in America, or the fabulously wealthy Battenburg, who was transformed into Mountbatten for his English existence. It was strange that Tupra should have kept his name, perhaps it seemed excessive or too risky, 'strange to abandon even one's own name'.

'Hey, Deza,' I heard De la Garza's voice in Spanish beside me again, he never tired of his prowling, 'if you keep nattering on to this gypsy, we're going to miss all the pussy. The rate we're going, Miss Longlegs here will end up going off with the fat guy, look at the way the great tub of lard is sweet-talking her. Fucking shameless.'

Not even Wheeler would have understood a word this time,

for all his impeccable bookish Spanish. It was true that young Judge Hood was whispering in Beryl's ear and was being rewarded by peals of laughter, the neglectful girlfriend's upper lip had been hidden for some time now; they were inevitably sitting very close to each other on the sofa, the judge being extremely large and voluminous. I did not respond to the attaché, not yet, as if he did not exist, he seemed to have forgotten who Miss Longlegs had come with. But Tupra himself alluded to him, he had, like me, been observing him out of the corner of his eye, or else guessed what was going on despite not knowing our language, still less De la Garza's slang, which tended to the artificial or wilful, and sounded affected, put on. His sleek hair was becoming soft and unruly, no one in Oxford escapes unscathed from sharing a few drinks with The Flask.

'You'd better deal with your compatriot or friend,' Tupra said in a tone of fatherly amusement, 'he's getting in a real state about the ladies, and his English isn't helping him in the enterprise. You should lend him a hand. I don't think he'll get anywhere with Mrs Wadman, the dowager deaness,' he used the legal or ironic term 'dowager' rather than the more usual 'widow', 'I paid her a few compliments earlier on which have not only given her a glow that has lasted all evening, but have made her feel, how can I put it, inaccessible, I doubt that tonight she would feel herself worthy of any living being, look at her, so above all earthly passions, so lovely in the September of her life, so placid in the face of the encroaching autumn. He would be better off trying Beryl, although she's rather distracted at the moment and, besides, we'll have to leave soon, we've got to drive back to London. Or Harriet Buckley, she's a medical doctor and got divorced a few days ago, her new state might inspire her to start making some investigations.'

There was not only humour in these remarks, they breathed a kind of ingenuous, almost literary satisfaction; and the usual look of natural and unaffected mockery in his pale eyes was intensified by his own enjoyment, any mockery this time was quite intentional. It was then that I realised how aware he was of his power to persuade women and to make them feel either like goddesses – albeit minor ones – or mere cast-offs. Or, rather, I thought at that moment, he believed that he did or, if not, that it was all a joke, because he had still not realised the true extent of his powers. He had made the widowed deaness glow with his compliments, no less, and he must have been very confident about Beryl's devotion or the unconditional nature of her feelings to speak of her like that, like an old buddy or even an old flame, in theory free to succumb to weaknesses brought on by a few last-minute drinks or by one last laugh.

'I didn't know the Dean of York's widow was called Mrs Wadman,' was all I managed to say.

Tupra smiled broadly again, his wide lips seemed less so when he did, they seemed less moist.

'Well, that must, I assume, be her name, since she's a widow and the widow of York.' He glanced around him then, as if mention of his imminent departure had filled him with haste. He looked at his watch, which he wore on his right wrist. 'I'm afraid you must excuse me now, I'll leave you with your compatriot. I must talk to Judge Hood before I leave. It's been a pleasure to meet you, Mr Deza.'

'It's been a pleasure for me too, Mr Tupra.'

As proof of his Englishness, he did not shake my hand when he left, normally in England this is done only once between serious-minded people, and only on being introduced and never again, even if months and years pass before those two individuals next meet. I always forgot this, and my hand hung there empty for a second.

'Just one thing, Mr Deza,' he added, swaying on his heels, having moved only a step away, 'I hope you won't think me a busybody, but if you really have had enough of the BBC and fancy a change of scene, we could have a chat about it and see what we can do. With all your useful knowledge . . . Anyway, talk to Peter, ask him what he thinks, consult him, if you like.

He knows where to find me. Good night.'

He looked across at Wheeler as he mentioned his name, and I did the same, out of pure imitation. Wheeler was greedily smoking his cigar and trying to prop up the widow Wadman with a discreet but firm elbow in the ribs, drowsiness was making her slump to one side and if someone did not rouse her – for she was clearly ready to dream the dreams of the just – she was likely to succumb altogether at any moment, and end up with her head resting on her host's shoulder, or even more awkwardly, soft bosom upon soft bosom, her necklace might become unclasped, and orange segments disappear down her *décolletage*. Again I saw a reciprocating look in Peter's eyes, I mean in response to Tupra's, a slightly reproving look, though only slightly, with the lack of emphasis with which one alludes to a rash action which has turned out to be not so very grave: 'You've overdone it, but there we are. You wouldn't be told,' that is what the message seemed to say, if there was a message. Then Tupra walked round behind the sofa, bent over and rested his forearms on the back of it in order to say something quickly – one phrase – in the ear of young Judge Hood, or, rather, a phrase addressed to the back of his neck, it was not, I assume, confidential. Hood and Beryl stopped laughing, they turned to listen to him, she again looked mechanically at her watch, like someone waiting only to be rescued or perhaps relieved, she uncrossed her very bare long legs. 'They're going to leave together, they're all going to leave at once,' I said to myself. 'Tupra will drive the fat guy home. Or Beryl will, if she's driving.'

'I'm going to have one of these sluts tonight or my name's not Rafael de la Garza. I didn't come here in order to go away empty-handed, damn it. I'm going to dip my wick if it kills me.'

De la Garza did not let up for a second, barely had I left Tupra's side than he returned to the attack. Prompted no doubt by his name, which, in Spanish, means 'heron', I suddenly recalled a proverb, as incomprehensible as most proverbs.

'No matter how high the heron flies, the falcon will pounce.'
I said the words without thinking, just as they came into my head.

'What? What the fuck did you say?'

'Nothing.'

De la Garza did go away empty-handed, damn it, or, rather, he left accompanied only by the glum mayor of that Oxfordshire town and the woman I took to be the mayor's wife, neither of whom seemed likely candidates for interminglings of any kind (I hadn't even noticed the wife until then, she would clearly do little to alleviate the miseries of the place over which they presided), especially not at their age, the attaché was caught off guard, and it fell to him to drive them to wherever it was they lived, Eynsham, Bruern, Bloxham, Wroxton, or perhaps to what has been the most ill-famed of places since Elizabethan times, Hog's Norton, I've no idea. He was in no fit state to drive (especially with the steering wheel on the right), but he obviously didn't care a fig about getting a ticket and was so vain it would never even occur to him that he might cause a car crash. It did occur to Wheeler and he expressed his concern, wondering if he shouldn't put all three of them up for the night. I dissuaded him from the mere idea, despite the evident unease of the Labour mayor and his Labour mayoress wife, who talked of getting a taxi to Ewelme or Rycote or Ascot, or wherever. It wasn't very far, I said, and De la Garza was a young man, doubtless endowed with marvellous reflexes, a very leopard. The last thing I wanted was to find myself at breakfast with that fan of or expert in chic universal medieval fantastic literature, the Lord of the Sluts, and, anyway, I didn't care two figs if he crashed.

The three people I had expected to leave together also left, indeed, they were the first to go. Fortunately for Sir Peter Wheeler, the only guest who lingered until gone midnight was Lord Rymer, The Flask, not because he was very animated or not as yet sleepy, but due to his complete inability to put one foot in front of the other. Since The Receptacle lived in Oxford, this did not pose such a problem. Mrs Berry called a taxi, and between the two of us we managed to detach the heavy, alcoholic Flask from the armchair in which he had installed himself half-way through the evening, and with a few discreet heaves (it was impossible to perform this task quickly) we got him as far as the front door under the supervision and guidance of Peter's walking-stick; we gladly accepted the help of the driver in squeezing him into the taxi, although the poor man would have a tough time prising him out of there on his own when they reached their destination. The hired waiters could not leave without first collecting the more substantial leftovers from plates and serving dishes, and then I helped Mrs Berry with the cups and glasses and the remaining ashtrays, so that everything was pretty much cleared away, Wheeler hated coming down the following morning to the debris of the previous night, well, almost everyone does, including me. When Peter's housekeeper had gone up to bed, Peter took a seat slowly and carefully at the foot of the stairs, holding on to the banister rail until he had touched down (I did not dare offer him a hand), and took another cigar out of his cigar case.

'Are you going to smoke another cigar now?' I asked, surprised, knowing that this would take him a while.

I had assumed that his sudden decision to take up such an inappropriate seat for a man well into his eighties had been due to a momentary weariness or that it was his usual way of pausing and gathering a little strength before going on up to the second floor where he had his bedroom, perhaps he always stopped there before the ascent. He was still very mobile, but that daily, continual tussle with those shallow, rather steep, wooden steps – thirteen to the first floor, twenty-five to the second – seemed ill-advised at his age. He had laid his walking-stick across his knees, like the carbine or spear of a soldier at rest, I watched him preparing his Havana cigar, sitting on the third stair, his gleaming shoes poised on the first, the central part of the stairs was covered by a carpet or perhaps it was a runner carefully fitted and fixed or invisibly stapled in place. His posture was that of a young man, as was his still thick hair, although this was now completely white and slightly wavy as if it were made of pastry, neatly combed with the parting on the left, which gave one a sense of the far-off little boy, for the parting must have been there, unchanged, ever since early childhood, doubtless predating the surname Wheeler. He had got dressed up for his buffet supper and was not the sort to reach the end of a party in a state of semi-disarray, like Lord Rymer or the widow Wadman or, to some extent too, De la Garza (his tie loose and somewhat askew, his shirt growing unruly at the waist): everything remained intact and in its place, even the water with which he had combed his hair seemed not entirely to have dried (I ruled out the use of brilliantine). And as he sat there apparently untroubled it was still easy to see him, to imagine him as a young heart-throb of the '30s or perhaps '40s – years that were inevitably more austere in Europe – not perhaps in a film, but in real life, or perhaps in an advertisement or poster of the period, there was nothing of the unreal about him. He was obviously pleased with the way his banquet had gone and, even though we had the following morning to talk, he perhaps wanted to discuss it a little now, not to declare the evening quite over yet, he probably felt livelier – or perhaps simply less alone – than he did on other nights, which usually ended early for him. Even though I was the one who was supposed to be all alone in London, not him here in Oxford.

'Oh, only half of it or less. I'm not really that tired. And it's not such an extravagance,' he said. 'Anyway, did you have a good time?'

He asked this with just a hint of condescension and pride, he clearly considered that he had done me a great favour with his idea and his invitation, allowing me to leave my supposed isolation, to see and to meet other people. So I took advantage of this slight display of arrogance to lodge my only justifiable complaint:

'Yes, an excellent time, Peter, thank you. I would have had a much better time, though, if you hadn't invited that idiot from the embassy, what on earth made you do it? Who the hell is he? Wherever did you dig that idiot up? Oh, he's got a future in politics, that's for sure, even in the diplomatic service. And if that's the idea and you're hoping to squeeze some funding out of him for symposia or publications or something, then I won't say a word, although it still seems a little unfair that I should end up acting as his interpreter, and very nearly procurer and nursemaid as well. He'll be a minister in Spain some day, or, at the very least, ambassador to Washington, he's exactly the kind of pretentious fool with just a thin veneer of cordiality that the Right in my country produces by the dozen and which the Left reproduces and imitates whenever they're in power, as if they were the victims of some form of contagion. When I say "the Left", of course, that's just a manner of speaking, as it is everywhere nowadays. De la Garza is a safe investment, I agree, and, in the short term, he'll get on well in any political party. The only problem is that he did not leave here a happy man. Still, that's some consolation, at least, since he ruined most of my evening.' I had said my piece.

Wheeler lit his cigar with another of his long matches, although he did so less singlemindedly this time. He looked up then and fixed his eyes on me in fond commiseration, I was standing at the bottom of the stairs, a short distance from him, leaning on the frame of the sliding door that led from the main living-room to his office and which he usually kept open (there were always two lecterns on view in the study, on one a dictionary of his own language lay open, along with a magnifying glass, on the other an atlas, sometimes the Blaeu, sometimes the magnificent Stieler, also open, with another magnifying glass), I had my arms crossed and my right foot crossed, too, over my left, with only the toes of the former resting on the ground. Whereas the eyes of his colleague, friend and fellow scholar, Rylands, had had a more liquid quality and, most strikingly, had each been of a different colour – one eye was the colour of olive oil, the other pale ashes, one was cruel like the eye of an eagle or a cat, the other bespoke rectitude, the eye of a dog or a horse – Wheeler's eyes had a mineral appearance and were rather too identical in design and shape, like two marbles almost violet in colour, but flecked and very translucent, or even mauve, but veined and not at all opaque or even, almost, the colour of garnets, or possibly amethysts or morganites or the bluer varieties of chalcedony, they varied according to the light, according to whether it was day or night, according to the season and the clouds and whether it was morning or evening and according to the mood of the person doing the looking, and, when narrowed, resembled the seeds of pomegranates, the early autumn fruit of my childhood. They would once have been very bright, and frightening when in angry or punitive mood, now they preserved only the embers and a touch of fleeting irritation in their otherwise mild appearance, they usually looked with a calm and a patience that were not innate, but learned, honed by the will over time; but there had been no attenuation of their mischievousness or their irony or their all-embracing, earthy sarcasm, of which they were clearly capable at any moment, given the chance; nor of the assured penetration of one who has spent his entire life observing and comparing, and seeing in the new what he has seen before, and making links and associations, and tracking things down in his visual memory and thus foreseeing what is yet to be seen or what has not yet happened, and venturing judgements. And when they appeared to take pity – which was not infrequent – that spontaneous expression of pity was immediately tempered by a sort of jaded recognition or weary acceptance, as if in the depths of his pupils lay the conviction that in the end and in some measure, however infinitesimal, we all brought our own misfortunes upon ourselves, or created them or allowed ourselves to suffer them, or perhaps acquiesced to them. 'Unhappiness is an invention,' I sometimes quote to myself.

'The Left has always been a manner of speaking everywhere, I mean, the Left that you Spaniards, Italians, French and Latin Americans refer to, as if it existed or ever had existed outside the realms of the imaginary and the speculative. You should have seen it in the '30s, or even before. A mere collective fantasy. Disguises, rhetoric, the more austere the uniform, the more fraudulent, all pompous facets or forms of the same thing, always hateful and always unjust, and invulnerable too. I prefer being able to tell that someone's a bastard from his face, right from the start, at least you know where you are and don't have to waste energy convincing anyone else. They're all oppressors, it's amazing that people don't realise this *ab ovo*, it makes little difference what cause they're fighting for, what public cause, or what their propaganda motives are. Frauds and transcendental innocents alike all describe these motives as historical or ideological, I would never call them that, it's too ridiculous. It's amazing that some people still believe there are exceptions, because there aren't any, not in the long run, and there never have been. Well, can you think of any? The Left as the exception, how absurd. What a waste.' He exhaled a large puff of smoke as if indicating a paragraph break, and as if to move on to another subject, which is what he did: 'As for Rafita, as his poor father calls him, I don't think you should complain about him or bear him a grudge, that would be pure viciousness having just sent him off to his certain death on the roads (who knows, it may already have happened)' – and he made to look at his watch, without even getting as far as pushing back his sleeve – 'possibly condemning in passing Mayor Pennick and his submissive wife, not, I suppose, that they would be any great loss to anyone either, in public or in private life. Rafa's the son of an old friend of mine, quite a bit younger than me, in fact, by at least ten years. He was in London during the war, he helped when things got difficult. Later on, he joined the diplomatic corps and applied unsuccessfully for the embassy. I mean the embassy here, he spent half his life wandering around Africa and part of Oceania until they retired him. He's asked me to keep Rafita amused now and then, to give him a bit of guidance and lend him a hand when he needs it. You know what parents are like, they never see their children as grown-ups nor as the unpleasant people they can sometimes turn into, always assuming they weren't clearly so from the cradle on and the parents have simply chosen not to notice.' – 'Much less the utter morons they can turn into,' I thought, without interrupting Peter. – 'You may think I'm not the best person to amuse, guide or help anyone, but if I give a supper . . . To be honest, I didn't think he'd come. As far as I know, he has plenty of company in London. I'm sorry you got stuck with him for so much of the time, and Lord Rymer wasn't much help either, I was relying on their shared interests to bring them together. And, of course, I'd assumed Rafita would be more self-sufficient in English than he is, he's been living here for nearly two years now, and I would have sworn that he learned it when he was a child, his father's English is very good, true he has a slight accent, but nothing like his offspring's, which is diabolical. Pablo, the father, hardly drinks at all, whereas Rafita is like a hip-flask only with more capacity, terrible, a kind of refillable bottle. His father's a wonderful man, but he's got an imbecile for a son. It happens, doesn't it, as frequently or as infrequently as the other way round. And yet that idiot will go far.' – 'He's got a complete moron for a son,' I thought, again without saying it, 'and he'll doubtless end up a minister.' – Wheeler exhaled more smoke, slowly this time, the time it took to blow two or three smoke-rings, as if this topic were not of much interest to him either and as if his explanations should have been more than enough to settle the matter once and for all. I took out my cigarettes, he rattled his large box of expensive matches at me, offering me one, I showed him my lighter to indicate that I already had a light, and lit my cigarette. The manner in which he asked his next question led me to believe that he was, for some reason, driven to ask it or that it had been on the tip of his tongue for a while, it clearly wasn't just a way of passing the time nor did it belong to the chance to-and-fro of conversation, to the post-prandial comments that arise or assert themselves at the end of a supper or a party, when everyone has gone or when you are one of those to have left the party along with other guests. Tupra and the fat judge and Beryl, who were probably approaching London by now, would perhaps be talking about us or about the Fahys and the widow Wadman. To the lady mayoress's great embarrassment, De la Garza and the mayor of Thame or Bicester, or wherever it was, would possibly be mulling over the topic of elusive sluts, assuming they had not yet perished on a bend in the road and that De la Garza was managing to make himself understood in English for more than two consecutive words (he could always resort to mime and, in doing so, take his hands off the wheel, thus increasing the risk of an accident). And even Mrs Berry would be going over it all in her head, unable to sleep, she too had received guests and been an ancillary hostess, she wouldn't want this long night to finish just yet either. 'Tell me, what did you think of Beryl? How did she strike you? What impression did she make?'

'Beryl?' I said, caught slightly offguard, I hadn't imagined he would ask me about her, but rather about his friend Bertram, if he was a friend, and about whom he had forewarned me. 'Well, we barely spoke really, she seemed to take very little notice of anyone else, and she didn't appear to be enjoying herself much either, as if she was here out of duty. But she's got very good legs, and she knows she has and makes the most of them. She's got rather too many teeth and too big a jaw, but she's still rather pretty. Her smell is the most attractive thing about her, her best feature: an unusual, pleasant, very sexual smell.'

Wheeler shot me a glance that was a mixture of reproof and mockery, although his eyes seemed amused. He fiddled with his walking-stick, but without picking it up, he merely gripped the handle. Sometimes he treated me as if I were one of his students, and although I never had been, in a sense I was. I was a pupil, an apprentice to his vision and style, as I had been to Toby in his day. But with Wheeler I was jokier. Or perhaps not, perhaps it is just that what fades and returns only in memories becomes greatly attenuated and diminished, I had joked with both men, as I had with Cromer-Blake, another colleague from my time in Oxford, more my own age and outstandingly intelligent, not that this got him very far, he died of AIDS four months after the end of my stay there and my departure, and no one in the Oxford community said then (or afterwards, these are people who gossip about trivia, but are discreet when it comes to anything really serious) what his illness was. I visited him when he was ill and when he had recovered and when he was even worse, and never once asked him the origin of his *malaise*. And I had always joked a lot with Luisa, perhaps that is my principal and unsatisfactory way of showing affection. Problems arise, I think, when there is more than affection.

'As I've told you before, you're far too alone down there in London. That isn't what I meant at all. I would never have dared even to ask myself if you had or hadn't found Beryl's animal humours stimulating, you'll have to forgive my lack of curiosity about your proclivities in that area. I meant regarding Tupra, what impression did you have about her in relation to him, in her relation to him now. That's what I want to know, not if you were aroused by her . . .', he paused for a moment, 'by her secretions. What do you take me for?'

And having said this, he stretched out his arm and pointed with his index finger at some imprecise place in the living-room, doubtless indicating to me that I should fetch something for him. Since I needed an ashtray for my cigarette, I did not hesitate and fetched one for me and another for him and his cigar, the ash of which was growing perilously long. He took it and placed it on the stair beside him, but he still failed to make long overdue use of it, instead, he shook his head and continued pointing in the same vague direction with his now tremulous finger. His lips were pressed tight shut, as if they had suddenly become glued together and he could not open them. His face, however, remained unchanged.

'A port? Do you fancy a last glass of port, Peter?' I suggested, the various bottles with their little chains and medals were still there. He again shook his head, as if the word in question eluded him, a slip, a blockage, perhaps old age however well borne (old age mocked) occasionally plays these tricks. 'A chocolate? A truffle?' The respective trays had not been removed from the living-room. He again shook his head, but kept his finger outstretched, moving it up and down. 'Do you want me to bring you a scarf? Are you cold?' – No, that wasn't it, he shook his head, his elegant tie was keeping his neck perfectly warm. 'A cushion?' – He nodded at last with relief and then raised his middle finger too, he wanted two cushions.

'Of course, "cushion", honestly, I don't know what's wrong with me, but sometimes the most stupid words just get stuck, and then I can't get another word out until I've said the one I can't remember, like a kind of momentary aphasia.'

'Have you seen a doctor about it?'

'No, no, it's not a physiological thing, I know that. It only lasts a moment, it's like a sudden withdrawal of my will. It's like a warning, a kind of prescience . . .' He did not go on. 'Yes, get them for me, will you, they would greatly ease my lower back.'

I took two from one of the sofas and gave them to him, he positioned them behind his back, I asked if he would prefer us to go and sit in the living-room, but he made a negative gesture with the hand holding the cigar (the ash fell at last on to the carpet), as if to indicate that it wasn't worth it, that he wouldn't delay me much longer (with the side of his hand he rolled the still intact ash safely into the ashtray, which he had placed at the foot of the stained stair), I returned to my place, but first fetched a small ladder of five or six steps that was kept in the study for getting books down from the higher shelves, placed it in the doorway and sat down on that at the same distance from him as before.

Wheeler had said the last few words in English, we spoke more in that language because it was the language of the country we were in and the one we heard and used with other people all day, but we alternated it with Spanish when we were alone, and passed from one to the other according to necessity, convenience or caprice, all it took was for one of us to slip in a couple of words from one or other language for us to shift automatically into the language thus introduced, his Spanish was excellent, accented, but only slightly, fluent and quite fast – although, naturally, much slower than my rapid-fire native Spanish, full of strings of crude elisions which he avoided – too precise in his choice of words, too careful perhaps to be a native speaker. He had used the word 'prescience', a literary word in English, but not as uncommon as *'presciencia'* is in Spanish, Spaniards never say it and almost no one writes it and very few even know it, we tend to prefer *'premonición'* or *'presentimiento'* or even *'corazonada'*, all of which have more to do with the senses, a feeling, *'un pálpito'* – we use that too in colloquial speech – more to do with the emotions than with the intelligence and with certainty, none of them implies a *knowledge* of future events, which is what 'prescience' and, indeed, *'presciencia'* mean, a knowledge of what does not yet exist and has not yet happened (though it has nothing to do with prophecies or auguries or divinations or predictions, still less with what modern-day quacks call 'clairvoyance', all of which are incompatible with the very notion of 'science'). 'It's like a warning, a kind of prescience, a foreknowledge of that withdrawal of the will,' I thought Wheeler had been about to say, had he completed the sentence. Or perhaps he would have been still clearer in his thought, which he would have completed by saying: 'It's like a warning, a kind of prescience, a foreknowledge of what it's like to be dead.' I remembered something that Rylands had said to me about Cromer-Blake once, when we were both very worried about that unmentionable illness of his. 'To whom does the will of a sick man belong?' he had said beside the same river, the Cherwell, that could be heard now nearby in the darkness during the silences, when we were trying to understand the way our sick friend had been behaving. 'To the patient? To the illness, to the doctors, to the medicines, to the sense of unease, to pain, to fear? To old age, to times past? To the person we no longer are and who carried off our will when he left?' ('How strange not to go on wanting,' I paraphrased to myself, 'and, even stranger, not to want to want. Or perhaps not,' I immediately corrected myself, 'perhaps that isn't so very strange.') But Wheeler wasn't ill, he was just old, and almost all his times were now past, and he had had ample opportunity not to be the person he had been, or any of the various possible selves he might have gone on to be. (He had even, early on, abandoned his own name.) He had not even said 'prefiguration', he was used to that, to the prior representation of all the things and scenes and dialogues in which he intervened, he had probably prefigured and even planned the conversation we were having, the two of us sitting on our respective steps after the party, when everyone else had gone and Mrs Berry was upstairs, tossing and turning in her sheets, unable, unusually for her, to get to sleep, going over all her tasks and preparations, tormented perhaps by some mistake that only she would have noticed. This conversation was probably evolving according to Wheeler's criterion and design, doubtless he was directing it, but that didn't really matter to me in principle, it intrigued and amused me, and I never begrudged him these pleasures. Peter had used the word 'prescience', a Latin word that has reached our languages almost unchanged from the original *praescientia*, a rare, unusual word and, therefore, a difficult concept to grasp.

'Like a warning of what, Peter? What kind of prescience?

You didn't finish what you were saying.'

Neither he nor I was the sort to allow ourselves to be distracted or tricked or to lose sight of our objective or of what interested us. We were not the sort to let go of our prey. I knew this about him and he about me, though I was still unsure as to the extent of his knowledge, I would have a clearer idea the following day. Perhaps that is why he laughed quietly, as if he had caught me out, and the smoke escaped from between his teeth, not this time indicating a paragraph break.

'Don't ask a question to which you already know the answer, Jacobo, it's not your style,' he replied, still smiling. He was also not the sort to allow himself to be easily cornered or trapped, he was the kind who would say only what he had set out to communicate or confess. He was the kind who called me Jacobo; others, like Luisa, called me Jaime, it's the same name, but neither of them was mine exactly (perhaps, aware of this, my own wife would sometimes call me by my surname). I was the one who introduced myself using one or the other or the more authentic name, depending on people, place and what seemed appropriate, depending on which country I was in and which language was being spoken. Wheeler liked what was possibly the most pretentious form, or the most artificially historical, being familiar with the old Spanish tradition of translating the names of the Stuart King Jameses in this way.

'How long has this been going on? As far as I can recall, it's never happened before when I've been with you.'

'Oh, it must have started about six months ago, possibly more. But it doesn't happen often, just now and then, otherwise it would be grotesque. And, as you saw, it only lasts a moment, it's not really surprising that you haven't seen it before, it would be odd or sheer bad luck if you had. But let's not waste any more time on that, you still haven't told me what you thought of Beryl, apart from her thighs and her jaw: as regards Tupra, what impression did they make on you as a couple?' He would not let go of his prey, he was forcing me to answer the question he wanted to have answered. And when he was insistent about something, I never resisted.

I noticed that his socks, knee rather than ankle socks, were beginning to slide down, due perhaps to his youthful posture on the stairs, his legs more bent than they would be if he were sitting in an armchair or a kitchen chair, his knees higher. They looked wrinkled, suddenly loose, in contrast now with his spotless, gleaming shoes with their too-smooth soles (an accident waiting to happen, Mrs Berry had been rather inattentive there), if his socks continued on their downward path, his shins would be left uncovered. And if that happened, I might have to point it out to him, he would be displeased at this unnoticed fault, he who was always so particular, so impeccably dressed, even though I was the sole witness and the only one who could point it out.

'Well, if you must know, I wouldn't hold out any hope for that couple at all, things seem distinctly unpromising for your friend Tupra. The last thing she looks like is someone's latest girlfriend. On the contrary, it's as if she was with him out of laziness or routine or because she had nothing better or worse to do, which seems a very strange attitude to take if theirs is a new relationship. The impression I had was precisely one of over-familiarity and lassitude, as if they were old flames,' I said, 'who are still on good terms, but who know everything there is to know about each other and very soon reach saturation point, although they put up with each other and still feel a flicker of reciprocal nostalgia, which has more to do with their roles as representatives of their respective past lives. It was as if, how can I put it, Tupra had turned to her so as not to have to come to the party alone, you know the kind of arrangement. And that strikes me as odd in someone of his appearance and style, you wouldn't think he was a man who would have difficulty finding company, and very beautiful company at that. And if he was the one doing her a favour by taking her out, it still doesn't make sense, since, as I said, Beryl was clearly bored, almost as if she had been obliged to come, as part of an agreement, perhaps, yes, almost as if she had been forced to be here. She didn't even seem bothered about making a good impression on his friends, assuming those people are his friends. In the early stages of a relationship, you seek the approval of the other person's cat, or their canary, or their chiropodist, even the milkman. You make a continual effort to get on with your beloved's entire circle of friends, however repugnant her world might be. And I didn't see her making the slightest effort. She wasn't even trying.'

Wheeler studied the lit end of his cigar, holding it very close to his eyes, whose metallic gleam was brighter than the burning ember; he blew on it to stir it into life, his cigar wasn't drawing well or so he pretended; and without looking at me, feigning an indifference he doubtless did not feel, he urged me to continue. But although he kept his eyes from me, I saw his very white, smooth eyebrows pucker with pleasure, and in his voice I noticed a contained excitement and disquiet, the feelings of someone putting another person to the test and who can see, as the test proceeds, that the person is likely to acquit themselves well (though he still waits with fingers crossed, not yet daring to claim victory).

'Really,' he said, not quite making that word into a question. 'Like old flames, eh? And she came here *velis nolis*, you think.' He really liked those Latin tags. 'Go on, tell me what else you noticed.'

'I don't know that I can tell you much more, Peter, I didn't talk much to either of them, and I spoke to both of them separately, just the usual formalities with her and a few minutes spent talking to him, I didn't see them together. Why all this interest? Actually I have a few questions of my own to ask about Tupra, you still haven't explained why you talked to me about him for so long on the phone the other day. Did you know that he's offered me a job if I get fed up with the BBC? I don't even know what he does. He suggested I talk to you, by the way. That I consult with you. I assume you know about it. And presumably you'll tell me when you're ready to, Peter. At first sight, though, he seems a very pleasant fellow. With the ability to . . .' I hesitated: it wasn't an ability to seduce, or to intimidate, or to proselytise, although he was capable of doing all those things, 'to dominate, don't you think? What does he do, what's his field?'

'We'll talk about Tupra tomorrow over breakfast. And possibly about that job.' Wheeler wasn't being bossy, but his tone of voice did not really allow for objection or protest. 'Tell me more about Beryl, about her and Tupra. Go on.' And he indicated the idea on which I should focus. 'Old flames, well, well . . .' We were talking in English and he was pointing the way ahead, as if urging me on ('you're getting warmer') in the middle of deciphering a riddle. 'Representatives of their respective past lives, you say. Of their respective pasts.'

I was sure now that Wheeler was putting me through a test, but I had no idea why, or what the test was, I didn't know either if I wanted to pass the test, whatever it was. Confronted by that feeling of being examined, however, we all instinctively feel a need to pass, simply because it's a challenge, and still more if the person assessing and judging us is someone we admire. But I felt uneasy working in the dark. It obviously had to do with Tupra and with Beryl, and probably with the informal or hypothetical offer of work that Tupra had made me when he said goodbye, I had taken the offer as a kindness on his part or as a last-minute desire to make himself seem important, although such vain boasts didn't really fit with Tupra, he didn't seem to need them, that was more in De la Garza's line. In the mouth of Rafita the attaché – the great dolt, the great dunderhead, the jerk – they would doubtless have been mere empty words. I couldn't fathom Wheeler's ins and outs and meanderings, unless they were simply intended to amuse him and to intrigue me, he could, after all, speak openly to me. I understood that he was going to do so the following morning during breakfast, to each thing its chosen or allotted time, he would make a decision based on the crumbling, dwindling time of his old age, but then again whose time is not dwindling? So I obliged him, I let myself be drawn out, although I really didn't have much else to add: I invented a little, embellishing and elaborating on what I had already said, dragging things out, I possibly invented too much. I noticed that Wheeler's socks or knee socks (they had started out below the knee, like the socks I wear) had slid a little further down, from where I was sitting I could already see a narrow band of brown skin, now that I thought of it, his colour and complexion were more southern than English. He was holding his walking-stick with his two clenched fists one above the other, as if it were definitely a spear, he had placed his still smouldering cigar in the ashtray, and had it not been for the pleased expression on his face, I would have said he was on pins and needles, albeit rather blunt ones, which would never have inflicted much pain.

'Yes, well, I don't know, they both seemed to be too much into doing their own thing to be a new item, which wouldn't have surprised me if they'd been a battle-hardened couple, in a marriage where the excitement has become so faded and worn that it's basically well past its expiration date, except when the couple are left alone with nothing to keep them amused, and even then. You, of course, didn't have time to experience that, with your brief marriage all those years ago, but you must have noticed such things: there is a terrible moment, a moment of tacit grief, in almost every such marriage, in which all it takes is for a third person to be present, anyone will do, even a taxi driver with his back to them, for either the wife or the husband to pay the other not the slightest attention. Fun is no longer ever to be found in themselves, his in her or hers in him or that of either in either, it depends who loses interest first or whether the sense of boredom is simultaneous, but it almost always ends up enveloping or affecting both if they stay together, and then neither suffers too much or only from their own disappointment or withdrawal, but during periods when that balance is lacking, this saddens one partner and irritates the other beyond words. The sad one doesn't know what to do or how to behave, trying first one thing and then another and then the opposite of each, racking their brains for ways to make themselves interesting again or to be forgiven even though they don't know what fault it is they've committed, and nothing works because they are already condemned, they try being charming or unpleasant, gentle or surly, indulgent or critical, loving or belligerent, attentive or uncouth, flattering or intimidating, understanding or impenetrable, but the result is confusion and a lot of wasted time. And the irritated partner is occasionally aware of his or her partiality and unfairness, but can do nothing to avoid it, they just feel permanently irascible, and everything about the other person gets on their nerves, and this is the ultimate proof, in personal, day-to-day life, that nothing is ever objective and that everything can be misinterpreted and distorted, that no merit or value is worth anything in itself without the recognition of another person which, more often than not, is purely arbitrary, that actions and attitudes always depend on the intention attributed to them and on the interpretation someone chooses to give them, and that without that interpretation they are nothing, they do not exist, they are either merely neutral or can, without a moment's hesitation, be denied. The most obvious truths are denied, something that has just happened and been witnessed by two people can be immediately denied by one of them, one can deny what the other has just said or heard that very moment, not yesterday or some time ago, but just the minute before. It's as if nothing mattered, nothing accrued or had weight and was, simultaneously, being destroyed, out of sheer indifference, mere uncounted, unremembered air, and grubby air at that, and it's equally maddening for both, although in a different way for each of them and more intensely so for the sad one. Until everything breaks apart. Or doesn't, and then the whole thing drags on, it's assimilated internally, while on the outside all is calm and languor, or else it's stored away and quietly, secretly rots, like something buried. And even though it's all over, the two remain together, as it seemed to me, more or less, Tupra and Beryl have stayed together.'

Wheeler clearly didn't want to lose sight of them, and I had returned to them at last after my long digression, which I was, nevertheless, thinking of continuing. But instead of taking advantage of my return to the subject, he seemed to have momentarily forgotten about the couple and to be interested in what I was saying, even though he thus ran the risk that I might once again go off the subject. It was probably just curiosity, because he couldn't resist asking:

'Was that what happened with you and Luisa? Except that it didn't drag on and you didn't stay together.' He observed me for a second with that look of compassion which he immediately corrected or toned down. He didn't dismiss or reject or withdraw it, far from it, he merely adjusted it after its first appearance, which was entirely sincere and spontaneous. But it could never persist in him, that state of innocence or elementality, as he might have put it were he describing it.

'No, I or we didn't let it get that far. It was something else, something simpler perhaps and certainly faster. Less cloying. Cleaner perhaps.'

'Some day you'll have to tell me a little more about it. If you want to, of course, and if you can, sometimes it's impossible to explain the really important things, those that have affected us most deeply, and keeping silent is all that saves us in difficult times, because explanations almost always sound so lame with respect to the pain we have inflicted or that others have inflicted on us. They tend not to match up to the evil suffered or caused and so they break down. I don't understand what's happened between you two, although I can understand why I don't. I was very fond of you both. Well, it's absurd to talk about you in the past: I *am* very fond of you both. I suppose it's because as a couple you seem to belong to the past, for the moment. Because you never know with such bonds, do you, regardless of their actual nature. Bonds.' He stopped for a moment, as if weighing the word or remembering some particular bond of his own. 'I meant that I liked you together, and usually one tends to prefer people separately, on their own, without conjugal or family accretions. Although, now that I think of it, I don't know if I've ever seen Luisa without you, if I've ever seen her alone, can you remember? I have an idea that I have, but I'm not entirely sure.'

'I don't think so, Peter, I don't think you've seen her without me being there. Though obviously you've spoken on the phone.' I must have sounded reluctant to take up this final and, for me, unexpected tangent. But it did not escape me that if Wheeler and Luisa had *not* seen each other without me (I wasn't quite sure about this either, some vague, ungraspable memory was nagging at me), what he had just said was that he liked me more with Luisa than on my own, as I was when he had first met me. I was not offended by the inference: I was in no doubt that she had improved me, had made me happier and lighter, less given to brooding, less dangerous and much less opaque. 'My dear, my dear,' I thought, and I thought it in English because that was the language I was speaking and because some things are less embarrassing in a language not your own, even if you only think them. 'If I could only forget,' I thought now in Spanish. 'If you would only grant me your forgetting.'

But before getting back to the Tupras – or, rather, to Tupra and Beryl – Peter added something of his own to this detour, or as he would doubtless have called it, this *excursus*.

'I don't know if you realise,' he said, as he rekindled his cigar with another match, so that, as he spoke, he was enveloped in a cloud of smoke worthy of a steam engine, 'but everything you have described as happening in the conjugal or private world happens in every other sphere as well, at work, in public life, in politics. The denial of everything, of who you are and who you've been, of what you do and what you've done, of what you're trying or have tried to do, of your motives and intentions, of your professions of faith, your ideas, your greatest loyalties, your causes . . . Everything can be distorted, twisted, destroyed, erased, if, whether you know it or not, you've been sentenced already, and if you don't know, then you're utterly defenceless, lost. That's how it is with persecutions, purges, with the worst of intrigues and plots, you have no idea how frightening it is when someone with power and influence decides to deny you, or when many people band together in agreement, although agreement isn't always necessary, all that's needed is a malicious deed or word that takes and spreads like fire, and convinces others, it's like an epidemic. You don't know how dangerous persuasive people can be, never pit yourself against such people unless you are prepared to become even more despicable than they are and unless you're sure that your imagination, no, your capacity for invention is even greater than theirs, and that your outbreak of cholera will spread faster and in the right direction. You have to bear in mind that most people are stupid. Stupid and frivolous and credulous, you have no idea just how stupid, frivolous and credulous they are, they're a permanently blank sheet without a mark on it, without the least resistance, and though you may think you know this, you can never really know it, after all, you haven't lived through wars, and I hope you never will. The person doing the persuading relies on that stupidity, he may rely on it too much and yet he's never wrong, he relies on it to the utmost, to the point of exaggeration, and that reliance confers on him an almost limitless boldness. If he's good, he never makes a mistake.' He stopped talking for a moment and allowed the smoke, which seemed now to be emerging from his white, pastry-like hair, to subside, then he looked at me very hard, with a mixture of curiosity and confirmation, as if he were both seeing me for the first time and recognising me (perhaps as the subject of the last sentence he had uttered), or were comparing me with someone else or with himself, or as if he were perhaps blessing me. 'You have that quality, you're very persuasive. It would be most unwise of anyone to pit themselves against you.' The cigar was drawing well again, he observed its glowing red end with satisfaction and even blew on it for sheer pleasure, to see it blush redder still. 'Nowadays, people don't often use the expression "to fall from grace", do they? To fall from grace. It's interesting and rather odd that it should be so little used, when what it denotes, better than any other expression, is happening all the time, unstoppably and everywhere and possibly more than ever, although more quietly and more surreptitiously than in the past, and it often entails the destruction of the person who falls, who is literally one of the fallen, who is, how can I put it, a casualty, a non-person, a felled tree. I've seen it often, and more than that, I've even been a party to it myself, by which I mean that I've contributed to the fall from grace of a number of individuals, a horrible fall which no one ever recovers from. I've even brought it about myself. Or, rather, I've helped to bring about a fall from grace decreed by others. I've helped carry it out.'

'Here, at the university?'

'No. Well, yes, but not only here. On fronts where that fall was far more serious and brought with it far worse consequences than not being invited to high tables' – the dinners of which I had endured a good few in my time at Oxford – 'or becoming the object of gossip and criticism or finding oneself in a social or academic vacuum or being discredited professionally. But we'll talk about that tomorrow too, perhaps, a little, just enough. Or perhaps we won't, I don't know, we'll see. Tomorrow we'll see.'

I don't know quite how I looked at him, but I know that he did not like that look. Not so much because of what it revealed – surprise perhaps, curiosity, slight incredulity, a touch of suspicion, but not, I think, disapproval or censure, it was intuitively impossible for me to harbour such feelings towards him – but because of the mere fact that my look existed. It was as if it made him doubt his previous statement or comparison or recognition, when it was too late or was inappropriate.

'Have you spread any outbreaks of cholera?' That was the question that accompanied my look.

He rested the end of his walking-stick on the ground, grabbed hold of the banister and, with cigar and handle in the same hand, tried to get up, but couldn't. He remained like that, two arms raised, as if he were hanging from both supports or was caught in a gesture reminiscent of the one people make to proclaim their innocence or to announce that they are carrying no weapons: 'Frisk me, if you like.' Or: 'It wasn't me.'

'You're far too intelligent, Jacobo, for it even to occur to me to think that you could have understood that turn of phrase as anything but metaphorical. Of course I've spread them.' And that convoluted Jamesian gibe and the subsequent defiant affirmation were swiftly followed by the dilution of the latter, or its diminishment or an attempt at a nebulous, partial explanation, as if Wheeler did not want my vision of him to be muddied or spoiled by a misunderstanding or by an unpleasant metaphor. I don't know how he could possibly think that I would take him for a callous swine. 'That was a long time ago,' he said. 'Don't forget, I was born in 1913. Before, can you imagine it, the Great War. It doesn't seem possible, does it, that I should still be alive. Some evenings it doesn't seem possible to me either. In a life like mine there is time for too many things. Well, there's simultaneously not time for anything and, yes, time for too much. My memory is so full that sometimes I can't bear it. I'd like to lose more of it, I'd like to empty it a little. No, that's not true, I would rather it didn't fail me just yet. I just wish it wasn't quite so full. When you're young, as you know, you're in a hurry and always afraid that you're not living enough, that your experiences are not varied enough or rich enough, you feel impatient and try to accelerate events, if you can, and so you load yourself up with them, you stockpile them, the urgency of the young to accumulate scars and to forge a past, it's so odd that sense of urgency. No one should be troubled by that fear, the old should teach them that, although I don't know how, no one listens to the old any more. Because at the end of any reasonably long life, however monotonous it might have been, however anodyne and grey and uneventful, there will always be too many memories and too many contradictions, too many sacrifices and omissions and changes, a lot of retreats, a lot of flags lowered, and a lot of acts of disloyalty, that's for sure. And it's not easy to put all that in order, even to recount it to yourself. Too much accumulation. Too much vague material collected together and yet somehow dispersed as well, too much for one story, even for a story that is only ever thought. Not to mention the infinite number of things that fall within the eye's blind spot, every life is full of episodes that are literally invisible, we don't know what happened because we didn't see it, couldn't see it, much of what affects us and determines us is concealed or, how can I put it, not available for viewing, kept out of sight, out of shot. Life is not recountable, and it seems extraordinary that men have spent all the centuries we know anything about devoted to doing just that, determined to tell what cannot be told, be it in the form of myth, epic poem, chronicle, annals, minutes, legend or *chanson de geste*, ballad or folk-song, gospel, hagiography, history, biography, novel or funeral oration, film, confession, memoir, article, it makes no difference. It is a doomed enterprise, condemned to failure, and one that perhaps does us more harm than good. Sometimes I think it would be best to abandon the custom altogether and simply allow things to happen. And then just leave them be.' He stopped, as if he realised that he had moved a long way away from his planned conversation. But he had not lost sight of Tupra and Beryl, of that there was no doubt, he could allow himself digression upon digression upon digression and still come back to where he wanted to be. He grew defiant again and then immediately moderated that defiant tone: 'Of course I've spread outbreaks of cholera, malaria and plague too. I would remind you that we fought a long war against Germany far fewer years ago than I've been alive, I was already an adult by then. And before that, I was briefly involved in your war too. I was an adult then as well, you can do the calculations yourself.'

I rapidly did the calculations in my head. Wheeler's birthday was on October 24th, and so he wouldn't even have been twenty-three in July 1936, when the Civil War broke out, and in April 1939, when it ended, he would have been twenty-five. His involvement in the Civil War was a further revelation, he had never mentioned it. 'And before that, I was briefly involved in your war,' he had said, which must mean that he had taken part, had fought or perhaps spied or simply made propaganda, or perhaps he had been a correspondent, or a nurse with the Red Cross, or had driven ambulances. I couldn't believe it. Not the fact itself, but not knowing about it until that night, after we'd known each other all these years.

'You never told me you were involved in the Spanish War, Peter.' I used the expression 'the Spanish War', in excessive obedience to the language I was speaking, for that is how it is occasionally referred to in English. 'You've never even mentioned it.' I really couldn't believe it. 'How is that possible? You've never even so much as hinted at it.'

'No, I don't think I have,' Wheeler agreed gravely, as if he had no intention of adding anything further now either. And then his face lit up with a smile of undisguised delight which made him look still younger, he loved to get me all intrigued and then leave me dangling, I assume he did it with everyone if the opportunity arose, in that respect, too, he resembled Toby Rylands, who would often hint at deplorable events in his past, or remote, semi-clandestine activities, or unexpected or clearly inappropriate friendships for an academic, and yet never told a single one of those stories in its entirety. He would insinuate something and then fall silent, he would fire the imagination, but not stir or feed it, and if he did begin a story, it was as if it were only his memory and not his will – his memory talking out loud – that led him to do so, and he would immediately stop, pull himself up short, so that he never told the whole story of those possibly testing or adventurous times, he allowed only glimpses. They belonged to the same school and to the same past era, he and Wheeler, it wasn't surprising that they'd been friends for such a long time, he, the still-living, must miss his dead friend very much, immensely. 'But I didn't conceal it from you either,' Wheeler added with a broad grin, as he finally stubbed out his cigar, pressing it hard down in the ashtray, in one vertical movement, as if it were an undesirable insect to be crushed. 'If you'd ever asked me about it . . .' And, still more amused, he took great pleasure in saying to me reproachfully: 'But you've never shown the slightest interest in the subject. You've shown no curiosity at all about my peninsular adventures.'

Whenever I saw that he was playing a game, I would usually join in, just as, when I saw that he was enjoying himself, I would try to prolong his enjoyment. So I said what he wanted me to say, even though I knew what his reply would be or simply so that he could give me that reply:

'Well, I'm asking you now, Peter, urgently. I assure you that nothing in the world could ever be of more interest to me. Go on, tell me now about those mysterious adventures of yours in the Second Peninsular War.'

'Now don't exaggerate, we weren't, alas, quite as involved in it as we were in the First.' Needless to say, he had got the joke, for in England what we Spanish call the War of Independence is known as the Peninsular War, and the English, unlike us, have written numerous books about the campaign, a campaign they consider to be theirs. It's interesting how names vary according to the point of view, beginning with the names of conflicts. What is known everywhere as the First World War or the 1914–18 War or even the Great War is, for the Italians, officially known as *La Guerra del Quindici-Diciotto*, because it wasn't until 1915 that they entered the fray. 'No, it's too late,' Wheeler was still firmly in exasperating mode, 'and tomorrow we won't have time, we have various other matters to discuss. You should have made the most of past opportunities, you see. You have to plan ahead, to anticipate.' He was still smiling. He tried again to get up and this time managed it, leaning both on his walking-stick and on the banister. He really was very strong for his age, he got up almost without effort or difficulty, quickly, and his socks or knee socks finally succumbed completely, I watched as they slid synchronously down to his ankles. When we were both standing (I too got up from my library steps, I could hardly remain seated, my manners, too, are slightly outmoded), he leaned on the banister and brandished the walking-stick in his left hand, the tip uppermost, as if it were a whip rather than a spear, and suddenly he reminded me of a lion-tamer. 'But before we say good night,' he added, 'as regards Tupra and Beryl, I take it from your remarks, that is, I deduce,' he pronounced each word slowly now, perhaps he was choosing them with great care, or, more likely, savouring them, together and individually, with mocking cynicism, 'that I failed to mention that Tupra did not, in the end, come with his new girlfriend, as he had at first told me he would, but with his ex-wife, Beryl. Beryl is his most recent ex-wife, you didn't know that, did you? Didn't I tell you? But then, of course, it's obvious.'

Now I smiled too or perhaps even laughed, I lit another cigarette, more smoke, companionable, friendly smoke, I must admit that sometimes I find barefaced cheek extremely amusing. Of course, it depends entirely on who the perpetrator is, in such minor matters one must learn to be unfair.

'Come on, Peter, you know perfectly well you didn't tell me, besides, why on earth would you tell me about such a change, which was no concern of mine, although now I'm beginning to think that perhaps it should have been, for some reason which you know, but which I do not. You just casually mentioned his new girlfriend over the phone, that was all. What are you up to? There seems to me to be nothing very casual about any of this, am I right? What is this, a game, a test, a puzzle, a bet?' And then I remembered one tiny detail: so that was why Wheeler, always so proper in his introductions, had omitted Beryl's surname when he introduced us. It wasn't very improper if it was the same as that of her companion and could be deduced as such. 'Mr Tupra, whose friendship goes back even further. And this is Beryl,' he had said, and it was possible to assume that her name was 'Beryl Tupra', if that still was her name, and she had not replaced it with another by marrying someone else, for example. If she had been the new girlfriend, Peter would have made a point of finding out her whole name so that he could introduce her properly. He was not an imitator of namby-pamby innovations, indeed I had heard him rail against the current custom, more suited to adolescents, but ingrained now even amongst many silly adults, of depriving people of their surnames when introducing them for the first time, the equivalent of the near universal use of the informal '*tú*' in my own language.

Needless to say, he did not answer my question. It was late, his schedule had been drawn up, or he had arranged his timetable for that weekend, and he would deal with whatever he wanted to deal with when he wanted to.

'It's interesting, remarkable really, that despite not knowing all that, you were still able to discover the true nature of their relationship, and without having seen them together except at a distance,' he said, and raised his walking-stick to his shoulder, like the rifle of a soldier on parade or on guard, with the handle as the rifle butt, it was a meditative gesture. 'Tupra has serious doubts at the moment, or so he told me. They finally separated a year ago, after some big bust-up or after a long decline, then about six months ago, they applied for a divorce by mutual consent. The decree is about to be made absolute, so I don't think they are yet technically ex-spouses. And as often happens when a change is imminent, one of them, Beryl, has suggested that they get back together, stop the whole process and try again. Despite the new girlfriend (not that she'll prove crucial, lately Tupra has been getting through girlfriends rather too quickly), and Tupra doesn't know what to do. After all, he's a certain age, he's been married twice already and Beryl was very important to him, enough for him to miss that importance, I mean miss her being important to him, even when, in my view, she isn't any more. On the one hand, he's tempted by the thought of going back, but, on the other, he doesn't really trust it. He knows that she's not doing brilliantly either romantically or financially, even though she wouldn't do badly out of the divorce, since he's hardly opposed a single one of her requests. But Beryl is used to leading a more comfortable life, or used, shall we say, to the unexpected treats, to the pleasant surprises so frequent in Tupra's profession, to the little extras, paid in kind. And, of course, to not being alone. He's afraid, that is, he suspects, this is the only reason she wants to come back, out of fear and impatience, rather than out of genuine nostalgia or a stubborn fondness for him, not because she's reconsidered (let's not talk about love here), but because her situation hasn't improved in the last year, probably contrary to her expectations. It seems she hasn't even made a new life for herself, as they say, and since she's not as young as she was, she doesn't know how to wait or to trust, for she suddenly feels time pressing and has forgotten how, because women, you know, only stop being young when they think they're not young any more, it's not so much age as self-belief that makes them old, they're the ones who give up on themselves. So Tupra is testing her out at the moment, he's left the door ajar, he's not rejecting her, he ferries her around, gauges her behaviour, they even go out together occasionally. He wants to wait and see. But Tupra is worried that Beryl is just pretending. Playing for time and getting temporary backing until a better substitute, who has not yet appeared, comes along: someone who will take a fancy to her or love her, someone she likes.'

Tupra's profession. Again it did not escape my notice. But I put it to one side and could not help but be somewhat acerbic. None of this rang true of a man like Mr Tupra, that is, the man I thought I had glimpsed. Anything was possible, of course. It's a well-known fact that those with most choice almost always choose badly.

'He must have it really bad,' I said, 'he must be completely blind if he's only "worried". It stands out a mile that she's more interested in almost any other possible future than in a present existence spent by his side. Obviously I can't be sure, but, I don't know, it was as if from time to time she would suddenly remember that she was supposed to be trying to win back her husband, which, as you say, is her announced intention, and then she would try a bit harder for a while, or, rather, she would apply herself to routinely pleasing or even flattering him, I suppose. But she wasn't even capable of remembering that reminder or of making that impulse last, it must be too artificial, pure invention, it doesn't even exist in ghost form, and, as you know, the hardest part about fictions is not creating, but maintaining them, because, left to their own devices, they tend to fall apart. It takes a superhuman effort to keep them in the air.' I stopped, perhaps I'd gone too far, I sought solid, prosaic support. 'I mean, even De la Garza could see that Beryl *no le hacía ni puto caso*, that's what he saw and said, he didn't mince his words. And I think he was right, he had a good look at Beryl because he thought she was *pistonuda*, that's what he said, you know. Or perhaps that was what he said about the widowed deaness, but it doesn't matter: he barely took his eyes off Beryl, especially from the waist down and from the thighs up.'

I shifted into Spanish where I had to: '*no le hacía ni puto caso*' – she didn't take the least bit of notice of him – '*pistonuda*' – fucking gorgeous. Untranslatable really. Or perhaps not, there's a translation for everything, it's just a question of working at it, but I wasn't prepared to do that work then. The reappearance of my language made Wheeler move into it momentarily too.

'"*Pistonuda*"? "*Pistonuda*" did you say?' He asked this with a degree of confusion as well as annoyance, he didn't like to discover gaps in his knowledge. 'I don't know that term. Although I think I can grasp what it means. Is it the same as "*cojonuda*"?'

'Well, yes, pretty much. But don't worry, Peter. I can't really explain it to you now, but I'm sure you've understood it perfectly.'

Wheeler scratched himself just above one sideburn. Not that he wore them long or carefully sculpted, not at all, but he was, in his own way, elegant; he didn't lack sideburns either, certainly not, he wasn't one of those obscene men who do not frame their faces with hair, faces that look fat even when they're not. They are bad people in my experience (with, in my experience, one major exception, there's always one, which is awkward and disconcerting, it really throws you), almost as bad as someone who sports a chin-tuft, a newgate frill, an imperial. (Proper goatee beards are another matter.)

'I assume it has something to do with pistons,' he muttered, suddenly deep in thought. 'Although I can't really see the connection, unless it's like that other expression "*de traca*", which I do know, I learned it a few months ago. Do you use "*de traca*"? Or is it very vulgar?'

'It's the kind of thing young people say.'

'I really should visit Spain more often. I've visited so rarely in the last twenty years that I'll be incapable of reading and understanding a newspaper soon, colloquial language changes all the time. Don't do yourself down, though. Rafita may not be quite as imbecilic as we thought, and if so, I'd be very pleased for his good father's sake. But his perceptive powers are nothing in comparison with yours, you can be quite sure about that, so don't delude yourself.'

I noticed that he looked suddenly tired. A few minutes before he had been jolly, smiling vivaciously, now he seemed worn out, sunk in himself. And then I noticed my own tiredness too. For a man his age, such a long, busy day must have been utterly exhausting, with all the preparations, the fuss, the waiters, the party, the cigarette smoke and the clever comments, lots of drink and lots of talk. Perhaps the final surrender of his socks had been the limit, or the cause.

'Peter,' I said, perhaps out of superstition, and showing a definite lack of prudence, 'I don't know if you realise, but your socks have slipped down.' And I managed to point with one timid finger at his ankles.

He immediately pulled himself together, blinked away his fatigue and had sufficient presence of mind not to look down and check. Perhaps he'd already noticed, perhaps he knew and didn't care. His gaze had grown sombre or dull now, his eyes were two newly extinguished match-heads. He smiled again, but feebly this time, or with fatherly compassion. And he reverted to English, it was less of an effort for him, as it is for me to speak in my own language.

'Another time I would have been infinitely grateful to you for pointing that out, Jacobo. But it's of little importance now. I'm going to get straight into bed and I'll be sure to take them off first. We'd both better get some sleep if we're to be fresh in the morning, we have a lot of unfinished business to deal with. Thanks for telling me, though. Good night.' He turned and started up the stairs that lay between him and the second floor, where he had his bedroom, the guest room that I would occupy and had occupied on other occasions was on the third and penultimate floor. As he turned, Wheeler accidentally kicked the ashtray, which was still there along with the corpse of his cigar. It rolled away, without breaking, its fall cushioned by the carpeted area on which the ash fell like snow, I hurried to pick it up when it was still spinning. Wheeler heard and identified the noise, but did not turn round. Still with his back to me, he said, unconcernedly: 'Don't bother cleaning it up. Mrs Berry will restore order tomorrow. She can't stand dirt. Good night.' And with the aid of his walking-stick and the banister, he began the ascent, overwhelmed once more by exhaustion, as if a great wave had suddenly broken over him, leaving him soaked and shaken, a suddenly dislocated figure, slightly shrunken despite his great size, as if he were shivering, his steps hesitant, each stair a struggle, his lovely new shiny shoes seeming to weigh heavily, his walking-stick merely a stick now. I listened, I could hear very clearly the quiet or patient or languid murmur of the river. It seemed to be talking, calmly or indifferently, almost indolently, a thread. A thread of continuity, the River Cherwell, between the dead and the living with all their similarities, between the dead Rylands and the living Wheeler.

'Sorry, Peter, can I just delay you a second longer? I wanted to ask you . . .'

'Yes?' said Wheeler, stopping, but still not turning round.

'I don't think I'll be able to get to sleep straight away. I imagine you've got Orwell's *Homage to Catalonia* and Thomas's history of the Spanish Civil War somewhere. I'd like to have a quick look at them, to check something before I go to bed, if you don't mind, that is. If you wouldn't mind lending them to me, and if they're more or less to hand.'

Now he did turn round. He raised his walking-stick and with it indicated a place above my head, moving the stick gently from side to side to his left, that is, to my right, like a pointer. His muscles had slackened, his skin, like tree bark or damp earth, seemed suddenly terribly worn.

'Almost everything about the Spanish Civil War is in there, in the study, behind you. The west bookshelf.' Then, irritated, he said in scolding tones: '"I imagine", he says. "I imagine." Of course I've got them. I am a Hispanist, remember. And although I've written about centuries of greater interest and momentum, the twentieth century is still my period too, you know, the one I've lived through. And yours too, by the way. Even though you've got a lot of the next century to live through as well.'

'Yes, sorry, Peter, and thanks. I'll go and find them now, if that's all right. Sleep well. Good night.'

He turned his back on me again, he only had a few more stairs to climb. He knew I wouldn't take my eyes off him until I saw that he'd reached the top, safe and sound, I feared those too-smooth soles. And doubtless knowing this, he didn't even turn his head when he spoke to me again for the last time that night, but continued to present me with the back of his neck as the obscure origin of his words. With its wavy white hair, the back of his neck was the same as Rylands's, like a carved capital grown blurred over time. From behind they were even more alike, the two friends, the similarities even more marked. From behind they were identical.

'If you're thinking of looking me up in the index of names, to see if I appear and to find out what I did in the Civil War, don't lose a minute's sleep over it. I don't think Orwell's book even has that kind of index. Bear in mind, too, that in Spain my name wasn't Wheeler.'

I couldn't see his face, but I was sure that he'd recovered his vivacious smile while he was saying this. I didn't know whether to reply or not. I did:

'I see. So what did you call yourself then?'

I saw that he was tempted to turn round again, but each time he did so was something of an effort, at least it was that night, at that late hour.

'That's asking an awful lot, Jacobo. Tonight anyway. Perhaps another time. But as I say, don't waste your time, you'll never find me in those indices of names. Not in those of that period.'

'Don't worry, Peter, I won't,' I said. 'Actually, that isn't what I wanted to look up, honestly, it hadn't even occurred to me. I wanted to check something else.' I fell silent. He did not move. He did not speak. He still did not move. He still did not speak. I added quickly, anxious not to slight him, 'It's an excellent idea though.'

Wheeler had just climbed to the top of the stairs in silence. I breathed a sigh of relief when I saw him there. Then he again placed his walking-stick on his shoulder, he again turned it into a spear, and, flattered, he mumbled, without looking back at me, while he turned to the left and disappeared from view:

'An excellent idea, indeed!'

Books speak in the middle of the night just as the river speaks, quietly and reluctantly, or perhaps the reluctance stems from our own weariness or our own somnambulism and our own dreams, even though we are or believe ourselves to be wide awake. Our contribution is minimal, or so we think, we have the feeling of understanding almost effortlessly and without needing to pay much attention, the words slip by gently or indolently, and without the obstacle of the alert reader, or of vehemence, they are absorbed passively, as if they were a gift, and they resemble something easy and incalculable that brings no advantage, their murmur, too, is tranquil or patient or languid, those words are a connecting thread between the living and the dead, when the author being read is already deceased, or perhaps not, but who interprets or relates past events that show no sign of life and yet can be modified or denied, can be seen as vile deeds or heroic exploits, which is their way of remaining alive and continuing to trouble us, never allowing us to rest. And it is in the middle of the night that we ourselves most resemble those events and those times, which can no longer contradict what is said about them or the stories or analyses or speculations of which they are the object, just like the defenceless dead, even more defenceless than when they were alive and over a longer period of time too, for posterity lasts infinitely longer than the few, evil days of any one man. Even then, when they were still in the world, few could undo misunderstandings or refute calumnies, often they didn't have time, or didn't even have the chance to try because they knew nothing about them, because such things always happened behind their backs. 'Everything has its moment to be believed, even the craziest, most unlikely things,' Tupra had said casually. 'Sometimes that moment lasts only a matter of days, but sometimes it lasts forever.'

Andrés Nin certainly didn't have time to deny the slanders or to see them refuted by others later on, according to Hugh Thomas's summary, in which, with its index of names, it was easy to find the references, unlike in Orwell's book, it was astonishing that Wheeler should remember such a detail, or perhaps he had deduced it from the fact that *Homage to Catalonia* was published in 1938, while the war was still on, no one then would have been concerned about mere names. First, though, just in case, I looked up Wheeler's name in Hugh Thomas's book, Peter could so easily have lied to me about that to make sure I wouldn't find it, always assuming I believed him, of course, and didn't even bother to look. But it was true, he wasn't there, nor was Rylands – I checked for checking's sake, it wasn't hard. What name could Wheeler possibly have used in Spain, for he *had* now managed to prick my curiosity. Perhaps some exploit of his was recorded in that book or in Orwell's, or in one of the many other books about the Civil War on the west bookshelf in Peter's study (and over which I lingered far too long), and, if that were the case, I found it extremely irritating to be unable to find out about it even though the exploit was public knowledge. What wasn't public knowledge was his name, or alias, a lot of people used them during the War. I remembered who Nin was, but not the details of his tragic end, to which Tupra had presumably been referring. He had worked as Trotsky's secretary in Russia, where he had lived for most of the 1920s, until 1930; he had translated quite a bit from Russian into Catalan, and a certain amount into Spanish, from *The Lessons of October* and *The Permanent Revolution*, written by his protector and employer, to Tolstoy's *Anna Karenina* and

Chekhov's *The Shooting Party* and *The Volga Flows into the Caspian Sea* by Boris Pilniak, as well as some Dostoyevsky. When the War began, he was political secretary of the POUM or Partido Obrero de Unificación Marxista (the Workers' Marxist Unification Party), of which Moscow always took a dim view. That I did remember, as well as the 'shooting party' to which the Stalinists submitted POUM members in the spring of 1937, especially in Catalonia, where the party was more established. That was why Orwell left Spain in such a hurry, in order not to be imprisoned or, possibly, executed, for he had been very close to the POUM and may even have been a member – I was reading snippets here and there, skipping and dipping and passing from one volume to another (I'd made quite a pile of them on Peter's immaculate desk), looking in particular for that business about the German members of the International Brigade that had so impressed Tupra – and Orwell had, at any rate, fought with the Twenty-ninth Division, which was formed by the POUM militia, on the Aragon front, where he had been wounded. As with so many individuals, movements, organisations and even whole peoples, the party was more famous and most remembered for its brutal dissolution and persecution rather than for its constitution or its deeds, some endings leave a deep mark. In June 1937, as Orwell describes in great detail and (very much) at first hand, with Thomas and others providing a briefer and more distanced account, the POUM was declared illegal by the Republican government at the request of the Communists, not so much the Spanish Communists – although they were involved too – as the Russians, and, it seems, on the decision or personal insistence of Orlov, the head in Spain of the NKVD, the Soviet Secret Service or Security Service. To justify this measure and the detention of its main leaders (not just Nin, but also Julián Gorkin, Juan Andrade, Major José Rovira and others) as well as activists, sympathisers and militiamen, however loyally the latter had fought on the front, they trumped up false and somewhat grotesque bits of evidence, everything from a letter supposedly signed by Nin and addressed to Franco no less, to the incriminating contents of a suitcase (various secret documents bearing the stamp of the POUM military committee, in which the latter revealed themselves to be fifth columnists, traitors and spies in the service of Franco, Mussolini and Hitler, paid by the Gestapo itself) which was found, conveniently enough, in a bookshop in Gerona, where it had been left for safekeeping shortly before by a well-dressed individual. The owner of the bookshop, a certain Roca, was a Falangist recently unmasked by the Catalan Communists, as was the probable writer of the forged letter, a certain Castilla, who had been picked up in Madrid along with other conspirators. Both were converted into *agents provocateurs* and forced to collaborate in the farce so as to give some shabby verisimilitude to the connection between the POUM and the fascists. It is possible that this saved their lives.

None of this interested me particularly, but it was mentioned by everyone, with a greater or lesser degree of attention and knowledge, with either sympathy or antipathy towards those who had been purged: Orwell, Thomas, Salas Larrazábal, Riesenfeld, Payne, Alcofar Nassaes, Tinker, Benet, Preston, Jackson, Tello-Trapp, Koestler, Jellinek, Lucas Phillips, Howson, Walsh, Wheeler's table was now heaped with open books, I didn't have enough fingers to keep all those places and hold a cigarette, luckily, though, most books had an index of names, Nin being referred to as Andreu or Andrés depending on the writer. Nin was arrested in Barcelona on June 16th and disappeared immediately (or, rather, was kidnapped), and as he was the best-known of the leaders, both in Spain and, above all, abroad, the fact that his whereabouts remained unknown became a brief scandal and, later, a long, possibly eternal, mystery which remains unsolved to this day, and which now, I imagine, not many people will be particularly bothered about resolving, although some foolish, dishonest novelist may yet turn up (unless he already has, and I don't know about it) and take it upon himself to reveal the answer: according to the bibliographies there has already been a film, half-English, half-Spanish, about those months and those events, I haven't seen it, but it appears, fortunately, not to be entirely foolish, unlike all those clichéd Spanish films made about our War, bland and fallacious, vaguely rural or provincial and very sentimental, and which are always applauded in my country by right-thinking people, the professionally compassionate and the career demagogues, who get a very good return on them.

Doubtless because of this mystery, historians or memorialists or reporters began to differ on this point. They all agreed, however, on the astonishing fact that not even the government, with those theoretically responsible for public order at its head – the Head of Security Ortega, the Minister of the Interior Zugazagoitia, the Prime Minister Negrín, least of all President Azaña – had the slightest idea what had happened to Nin. And when they were asked and they denied all knowledge of his whereabouts, no one, logically and ironically enough, believed them, even though they were, in effect, incapable of answering, according to Benet, 'because they knew nothing of the machinations of Orlov and his boys at the NKVD', who had acted entirely on their own account. Graffiti began to appear asking 'Where is Nin?', and often received the reply from the Stalinists 'In Burgos or in Berlin', implying that the revolutionary leader had fled and gone over to the enemy, that is, to his real friends Franco or Hitler. The accusations were so incredible and so crude (members of the POUM were described as 'Trotsko-fascists', exactly echoing the insults from Moscow) that, in order to defend them and make them acceptable, the socialist and Republican press found themselves having to support the Communist press: *Treball, El Socialista, Adelante, La Voz*, all of whom joined in the libel.

Certain historians in some collective work, I can't remember who they were now, maintained that Nin had been taken immediately to Madrid to be interrogated and that, shortly afterwards, 'he was kidnapped while being held in the Hotel de Alcalá de Henares' – despite being under police guard – by 'a group of armed and uniformed people who took him away by force'. According to these historians, during the supposed struggle between the police guarding him and the mysterious uniformed assailants (they didn't specify what kind of uniforms they were wearing), 'a wallet fell to the floor containing documents bearing a German name and various written texts in that language, as well as Nazi insignia and Spanish notes from the Franco side'. But the matter of the members of the International Brigade to which Tupra had referred was set out more clearly in Thomas and in Benet (it was probably the former's monumental *The Spanish Civil War* – I don't know why the devil I keep calling it a 'summary', it's over a thousand pages long – that Tupra would have read in his youth). According to Thomas, Nin was taken by car from Barcelona to 'Orlov's own prison' in Alcalá de Henares, Cervantes's birthplace very close to Madrid, but 'almost a Russian colony' at the time, to be interrogated personally by the nastiest and most devious of Stalin's representatives in Spain, using the customary Soviet methods deployed against 'traitors to the cause'. Nin's resistance to torture was apparently amazing, that is, appalling, bearing in mind that Howson mentions an unspecified – and one hopes unreliable – report according to which Nin was flayed alive. The fact is that he refused to sign any document admitting his guilt or that of his friends, nor did he reveal the names they asked him for, of lesser-known Trotskyites or of others entirely unknown. Orlov, enraged by his stubbornness, was at his wits' end; employed with him on this fruitless task were his comrades Bielov and Carlos Contreras (the latter was an alias, that of the Italian Vittorio Vidali, as Orlov was of Alexander Nikolski and Gorkin of Julián Gómez, everyone, it seems, had an alias), and all three of them feared the likely wrath that their persuasive incompetence would arouse in Yezhov, their superior in Moscow and the chief of the NKVD, so much so that Bielov and Contreras suggested staging 'a "Nazi" attack to liberate Nin' and to rid themselves in this picturesque way of their troublesome prisoner, who was also doubtless too broken and battered to be restored to the light, or even to the shadows, or even perhaps to the darkness. 'So, one dark night,' wrote Thomas as if he were the murmur of the river and the thread, 'probably June 22nd or 23rd, ten German members of the International Brigade assaulted the house in Alcalá where Nin was held. Ostentatiously, they spoke German during the pretended attack, and left behind some German train tickets. Nin was taken away and murdered, perhaps in El Pardo, the royal park just to the north of Madrid.' Benet, in his account – even more fluvial, or more intimately mingled with the river, a thicker thread of continuity, perhaps because he was speaking in my own language – said that Orlov had locked Nin 'in the cellar of the barracks in Alcalá de Henares to interrogate him personally'. (One imagines that during the interrogations in the cellar, house, barracks, hotel or prison – it was odd how the historians were unable to agree on the nature of the place – they would have spoken Russian, which the interrogated man doubtless knew better – Tolstoy, Chekhov, Dostoyevsky – than his interrogator knew Spanish.) Nin 'so exasperated Orlov that Orlov decided to kill him for fear of reprisals from his superior in Moscow, Yezhov. The only idea he could come up with was a "rescue" carried out by a German commando group from the International Brigade, supposedly Nazi, who killed him in a Madrid suburb and probably buried him in a little inner garden in the palace of El Pardo.' And Benet, unable to ignore the grim irony that the palace became Franco's official residence during his thirty-six years of dictatorship, added: '(The reader might consider the fate of those poor bones beneath the footsteps of that other staunch anti-Stalinist, when he strolled about there during his moments of leisure.)' And he went on: 'In the weeks that followed, as if under a curse – that of Nin's silence – Orlov's boys kept turning up in the gutters of Madrid, with a bullet in the neck or a whole clip of bullets in the belly.' That may have been the case with Bielov, but not with Vidali or Contreras (or, in the United States, Sormenti), who was, for a long time, leader of the Communists in Trieste, or with Orlov himself, who, no later than 1938, when he received the order to leave Spain and return to Moscow, had no illusions about the fate that awaited him there and so left, incognito, on a boat to reappear later on in Canada, going on to spend many years living a secret life as a respectable citizen of the United States, where he finally published a book in 1953, *The Secret History of Stalin's Crimes* (barely mentioning his own part in them, of course), and lending an occasional hand to the FBI in tricky espionage cases, like that of the Soble brothers or that of Marc Zbrowsky: how many useless things one learns during these unexpected nights of study. This, I have to say, led some rather simplistic, fanatical and frivolous exegete – I can't remember who, the books were still mounting up, I went to get some chocolates and truffles, I poured myself a glass of wine, I had wreaked havoc on Wheeler's west bookshelf, and his desk was in a terrible state – to conclude that Major Orlov had, from the outset, been an American mole and that most of the people he had executed in Spain as 'fifth columnists' were, in fact, pure, loyal reds, the victims of Roosevelt not Stalin. This particular Manichaean was certainly right as far as Nin was concerned, if not about the 'loyal' (if that meant being loyal to Stalin, he clearly wasn't), but certainly about being 'pure' and 'red'. And even if he wasn't an angel or a saint or merely harmless (who could have been in that war), his murder and that of his comrades (one historian puts in the hundreds and another in the thousands the number of POUM members and anarchists from the CNT who were sent to their graves by Orlov and his Spanish and Russian acolytes), these murders and the slander spread and believed by far too many – and which did not even cease after his physical annihilation and the crushing of his party – constituted, according to almost all the voices I heard in the pages of that silent night by the River Cherwell, the worst and most vicious of all the despicable deeds committed by one side against its own people during the War.

I remembered that Tupra had also said: 'The truth is that, initially, everything tends to be believed. It's very odd, but that's how it is,' I remembered his words while I continued to read snippets from one book and from another: to crown all these mad calumnies, a book was published in 1938 by a certain Max Rieger (surely a pseudonym, possibly of Wenceslao Roces, whose name I knew because, later on, he translated Hegel's *Phenomenology of Mind*), supposedly a Spanish version based on the French translation by Lucienne and Arturo Perucho (the latter was the editor of the Catalan Communist organ, *Treball*), and with a 'Preface' by the famous, more-or-less Catholic and more-or-less Communist writer José Bergamín – oh dear, these mixtures – which, under the title *Espionage in Spain*, collated all the tall tales, falsehoods and accusations hurled at Nin and at the POUM, presenting them as true and bona fide, sanctioning them, repeating them, elaborating on them, documenting them with fabricated proofs, embellishing them, adding to them and exaggerating them. I remembered once hearing my father talk about this prologue by Bergamín as an act of rank indecency, justifying as it did the persecution and slaughter of people from the POUM and denying its leaders the right to any defence (Bergamín was pushing at an open door there: for this had already been denied to quite a few people, tortured and imprisoned or executed without trial), one of many acts of indecency committed by various Spanish intellectuals and writers from both sides during the War, and even more afterwards by those on the winning side. I read one dishonest, incompetent commentator – it may have been Tello-Trapp, but it could have been someone else, I had begun rather randomly taking notes on bits of paper, poor Peter's study was rapidly becoming a complete dump – who tried to excuse Bergamín, because he had known him in person ('a charming, fascinating man', 'a worthy Don Quixote, a lover of truth') and because he loved his poetry, 'profound, pure and romantic' and 'the lamp-light glow of his voice' – I gulped down another chocolate and a truffle and some wine to recover, I wondered how he could possibly come out with such schmaltz and still go on writing – but the preface in question, which I found widely quoted elsewhere, left no room for its author's salvation: the POUM was 'a small treacherous party', which had not even turned out to be 'a party, but an organisation for spying and collaborating with the enemy; that is, not an organisation merely conniving with the enemy, but the enemy itself, part of the international fascist organisation in Spain . . . The Spanish Civil War revealed international Trotskyism at the service of Franco in its true colours as a Trojan horse . . .' The duplicitous commentator could only regret and condemn this prologue, but 'we do not know', he said, if its author 'wrote it while in the sway of the Communist Party, or in good faith', when the most likely and obvious answer is that he wrote it perfectly freely and in the worst possible faith; as the almost always considered and objective Hugh Thomas remarked: 'He could not possibly have believed what he wrote.' The text of that 'lover of the truth' makes a good pairing with the poster or vignette which, according to Orwell and others, circulated widely in Madrid and Barcelona in the spring of 1937, and which showed the POUM taking off a mask bearing the hammer and sickle to reveal a face stamped with a swastika. My father was not exaggerating when he spoke of rank indecency.

That was when I noticed that Wheeler also kept on his well-stocked shelves, in six large bound volumes, the installments brought out, under the title *Doble Diario de la Guerra Civil 1936–1939* ('Double Newspaper/Diary of the Civil War 1936–1939') by the newspaper *Abc* between 1978 and 1980, that is, between three and five years after Franco's death. Before that, such an initiative would have been impossible, for it consisted of a facsimile reproduction, in two colours, of whole pages, columns, editorials, news items, interviews, advertisements, gossip columns, articles, opinion pieces, reports, from the two *Abcs* in existence during the War, the Republican one in Madrid and the pro-Franco one in Seville, in accordance with whichever side had prevailed in those two cities at the start of the conflict. The one published by the Madrid office was printed in red ink, and the one in Seville in blue-grey, so it was easy to follow their vision or version of the same events – though they never seemed like the same events – according to the press on either side. I was tempted to look up the issue corresponding to the spring of 1937, although the incidents relating to the POUM would have taken place mainly in Barcelona. Rather tired now and rushed, I did not find much at first glance. But one of those few news items made me momentarily set aside the larger tomes – one book always leads to another and another and they all have something to say, there is something unhealthy about curiosity, not for the reasons usually given, but because it leads inexorably to exhaustion – and to ask myself foolishly about Ian Fleming, the creator of Agent 007 and author of the James Bond novels. The note in question appeared in the Madrid *Abc* of June 18, 1937, and was, as far as the newspaper was concerned, probably of secondary importance, for it took up only half a column. The headline read: 'Various important POUM members arrested'. I read it very quickly and then carelessly pushed various books on to the floor to make room on the table for the old electronic typewriter I had noticed lying covered up and dumped in a corner, and transcribed the whole article. I didn't even dare think about what would happen if Wheeler or Mrs Berry woke up and came downstairs to discover the chaos into which that clean, tidy study had been plunged, and in far too brief a period of time to justify such anarchy: dozens of books taken from their shelves and left wide open and scattered about the floor, even a disrespectful invasion of Wheeler's two decorative lecterns with their dictionary and their atlas and their respective magnifying glasses; the plates of chocolates and truffles strewn willy-nilly, with, as I noticed in some consternation, the consequent and inevitable chocolate crumbs and smudges left behind on a number of pages; the glass and the bottle of whisky and the can of Coca-Cola that I had brought from the fridge as a mixer, and a beaker containing a few half-melted ice cubes, one or two or even three drops spilled and doubtless rings left on the wooden surface, it hadn't occurred to me to get a coaster; both my ashtray and Peter's filled to overflowing and, who knows, an ugly, yellowing nicotine mark in some highly conspicuous place, or even the odd scorch mark on certain key pages; my cigarettes and my lighter and my matches and an empty pen cartridge floating around or half hidden, perhaps an ink stain made while I was replacing it; and now a typewriter with its cover off and sheets of papers, scrawled on or typewritten, in English or in Spanish depending on the quotes. I would have the devil's own job putting everything back in its place, in order to leave the room just as it had been before these ruinous, impromptu, nocturnal studies of mine.

'Barcelona 17, 4 p.m.,' said the first and briefest part of the report:

The Police have arrested various prominent members of the POUM, amongst them Jorge Arques, David Pérez, Andrade and Ortiz. Nin, who was arrested yesterday, has been moved to Valencia.

This was signed 'Febus', another obvious alias. The second part added:

Barcelona 17, 12 midnight. During the day the Police have continued their arrests of prominent members of the POUM. As readers will be aware, the best-known of the party's leaders, Andrés Nin, was arrested a few days ago and taken from the Delegación del Estado in Catalonia to Valencia and from there to Madrid. There were approximately fourteen subsequent arrests, amongst them, that of the editor of the newspaper *La*

Batalla, the organ of the POUM, and of some of that newspaper's journalists. The newspaper's printing works, editorial and administrative offices were seized by the authorities. Following statements made by those under arrest, further investigations ensued, which led to the arrest of another fifty people. They have all been taken to the Delegación del Estado in Catalonia. <u>Amongst those arrested are several singularly beautiful foreign women.</u> This work is being carried out by officers of the criminal and social brigades with the assistance of officers from the Public Order and Security divisions. All the organisation's offices in Barcelona have been seized and a specialist team of twenty-five officers have carried out a detailed study of documents found in the files there. A meticulous search is being made of a house in San Gervasio, which was the property of Beltrán y Musitu, where the POUM had set up a barracks, and where several thousand complete sets of equipment for soldiers, all of the latest design, were found.

Again this was signed by '*Febus*'.

The underlining had been added not by the pseudonymous writer or by me, but by Wheeler, and was quite a common feature in the many books of his I had now leafed through or even plundered, as were notes in the margin, which were very brief indeed and usually in some kind of code or so abbreviated as to be barely comprehensible to me or to anyone else who happened upon them. On this occasion, to the right of the half-column reproduced in red ink, he had written vertically (there was barely any space), in ink as always and in the unmistakable hand that I knew so well: 'Cf. *From Russia with Love*,' even in the margins he used Latin expressions, although the abbreviation 'Cf.' is a common way in English of referring in one text to another work, the equivalent of the Spanish '*Vide*' or '*Véase*'. *From Russia with Love*, the second James Bond adventure or installment if I remembered correctly, at most the third or fourth. And I went on to wonder if it referred to the film, which I had, of course, seen at the time (still with the great Sean Connery, of that I was sure), or to the novel by the ill-fated Ian

Fleming on which it was based. Gratuitous or motiveless curiosity (which is what afflicts the erudite) turns us into puppets, shakes us up and hurls us about, weakens our will and, worse, divides and disperses us, makes us wish that we had four eyes and two heads or, rather, several existences, each of them with four eyes and two heads. Nevertheless, I managed to keep my mind trained for a while longer on that *Doble Diario*, but it had little to say about the vicissitudes of Nin and the POUM, which, on the other hand – I realised – didn't interest me much in themselves, or at least hadn't interested me until I had opened those books, Orwell and Thomas to begin with. (It was all Tupra's fault, he had drawn me in, from the very first moment.)

In the same Republican *Abc* from the following day, June19, 1937, I found a whole page about the plenary meeting of the Communist Party Committee that had just opened in Valencia. In the first session, there had been a 'report' by Dolores Ibárruri, doubtless better known then and now and in the future by her alias, *La Pasionaria*, who, 'always addicted to Stalin' and possibly 'in an hysterical outburst', as Benet had murmured a short while before, dedicated a few furious, pitiless words to the purges taking place at the time: 'In the ceremony at the Monumental Cinema,' she said, 'we raise the flag of the Popular Front. The enemies of this union are certain left-wingers and Trotskyites. No measures taken to liquidate them can ever be too extreme.' I felt like underlining that last sentence, such an open invitation to the liquidations that did in fact follow, but I refrained from doing so, after all, the books belonged to Peter, and I was unlikely to consult them ever again, after that night of strange, unforeseen wakefulness.

I saw that, for its part, the pro-Franco *Abc* of Seville almost inaudibly echoed the Catalan purges in a succinct and dispassionate note written on June 25th, the indifferent tone of which hardly squared with the accusations that placed the POUM and its leaders at the service of Franco, Mussolini, Hitler, his Gestapo and even the Moroccan Guard: 'Following the loss of Bilbao,' read the headline, 'the Red Government shoots several leaders of the POUM. The situation in Catalonia.' The article said:

> Salamanca, 24th. French news reports state that following the loss of Bilbao, the Government of Valencia has gone on the offensive against the POUM and other dissident parties, in order to prevent the contrary happening.

(An almost unintelligible sentence, incidentally, the Right always was more stupid than the Left.)

> According to these reports, Andrés Nin, Gorkin and a third leader whose name we do not know, have been taken to Valencia and executed. All the Trotskyite leaders have been arrested by order of the Soviet consul, Ossenko, who has received orders from his Government to carry out a purge in Catalonia similar to that carried out in Russia against Tukachewsky and his friends.

Obviously the information was entirely wrong, and not just as regards Nin, for more than a month later, on July 29, 1937, the Republican *Abc* in Madrid, in another article again signed by *Febus*, reproduced without comment the note published by the Ministry of Justice 'about those accused of High Treason'. 'Statements have been handed to the Tribunal of Espionage and High Treason' (which had, in fact, been specially created on June 22nd, as proved by the fact that Summary No. 1 for that Special Court was the statement issued against the POUM) relating to eleven defendants, ten from the Partido Obrero de Unificación Marxista (POUM) and one from the Falange Española (Spanish Falangist Movement), and among the first to be mentioned are Juan Andrade and 'Julián Gómez Gorkin'. These statements were compiled from 'abundant documentation found in the POUM offices: ciphers, telegraphic codes, papers referring to arms trafficking, the smuggling of money and valuable goods, various newspapers from various capital cities, mainly from Barcelona;

communications from foreigners alluding to interviews held inside and outside loyalist territory, and to the participation of foreigners in the weeks prior to the espionage and subversive activity of last May'. The report ended with an eloquent warning to anyone who might intercede: 'Any steps other than those intended to bring about the strict and faithful application of the laws are, therefore, useless.' That bit about 'various newspapers from various capital cities' seemed to me the most indefensible and treacherous of all, and about them being 'mainly from Barcelona', the POUM offices being registered in precisely that city, an obvious aggravating factor and doubtless damning. The ten POUM defendants were all men and had Spanish names, so the various foreign women of singular beauty seem to have got off scot-free and to have vanished, as befitted women of their ilk.

As for 'the Soviet consul, Ossenko', according to the blue-grey ink – his name was in fact Antonov-Ovseenko – if the arrests had indeed been ordered by him, in response to orders from his own Russian government, it must have been *in extremis*, and his obedience certainly did not get him very far, since in June – in late June one assumes, so that he at least had time to issue the orders and to know that Nin had been executed – he was called back to Moscow to be appointed People's Commissar for Justice and to take up his post with immediate effect: 'a joke typical of Stalin', muttered Thomas in a footnote, for the old revolutionary Antonov-Ovseenko never reached his post and disappeared without trace, whether he died a slow death in some distant concentration camp or was promptly despatched underground as soon as he stepped out on to Russian soil is not known. His compatriot in Madrid, Orlov, clearly learned the fatal lesson taught him by the consul – a veteran of the storming of the Winter Palace in St Petersburg and formerly a personal friend of Lenin – when, a little later on, he, in turn, received the call from Russia with love.

For its part, that note of Wheeler's continued to call to me: 'Cf. *From Russia with Love*'. What the devil did that novel or film about long-since cold spies have to do with Nin, or with the POUM, or with those beautiful foreign women? And although the *Doble Diario* still drew my attention for a thousand other reasons and, however late it was, I was certainly not going to abandon my readings just yet – everything aroused my gratuitous curiosity, from incomprehensible headlines like this one from July 18, 1937, which said and I quote: 'Brooklyn-born Bullfighter Sidney Franklin Exposes Franco's Lies', to articles, which I kept stumbling across, written by my father when he was very young, in the Madrid *Abc* and therefore reproduced now in red ink, either signed with his own name, Juan Deza, or with the pseudonym he had sometimes used during the conflict – I suddenly remembered something that made me put the large volumes to one side and get hesitantly to my feet. In a small room next to the guest room where I had stayed on other occasions and which would already be prepared for that night, I had noticed some detective novels and mystery novels, to which Wheeler, like all people of a speculative or philosophical bent, was quietly addicted (not secretly, but he would never keep that part of his vast library in one of his living-rooms or in the study, in full view of any snooping, slanderous colleague who might visit him). I had occasionally wondered if he didn't write them himself under a pseudonym, like so many other Oxbridge dons who, in principle, do not wish to have such plebeian activities mixed up with their real names as savants, scholars or sages, but they nearly always end up unmasking themselves, especially if high praise and good sales accompany those novels, minor works or mere diversions to which they never give any importance, but which prove far more lucrative than the books they do consider valuable and serious and which, nevertheless, almost no one reads. There are many such cases: the Professor of Poetry at Oxford, Cecil Day-Lewis, was Nicholas Blake to fans of enigmas, the English scholar, J. I. M. Stewart, also at Oxford, was Michael Innes, and even one of my former colleagues, the Irishman Aidan Kavanagh, an expert on the Golden Age and head of the sub-faculty of Spanish where I taught, had published successful full-blown horror novels beneath the extravagant alias of Goliath Cherubim, no one would ever have a name like that.

On the occasional sleepless night spent in that house, I had browsed a little in that small room, and I remembered having seen works by classic detective novelists, Ellery Queen and Agatha Christie, Van Dine and Van Gulik, Woolrich, Highsmith and Dexter, and, of course, Conan Doyle, Simenon and Chesterton, names I knew from my father – who was of a much more speculative bent than me – although not their actual creations (with the exception of Sherlock Holmes and Maigret, who are part of basic general culture). Perhaps I would be in luck – curiosity is very pressing when it gets us in its grip – and Fleming would be there amongst them, although he wasn't, properly speaking, a detective novelist, I imagine all the above-named would have sneered at him, there are always plebeians for the plebeians, and pariahs for pariahs (just big-fish-eats-little-fish voracity, I suppose). I hesitated for a few seconds. If I went up those two flights of stairs now, I would run a greater risk of waking Wheeler and Mrs Berry, but I would have to go up them later anyway in order to go to bed (although I wouldn't then come down and go up them again), and the noise of the old typewriter I had been blithely using had already represented a considerable risk, I realised. I wasn't sure whether or not I should first impose some kind of order on the mess in the study; but I wanted to continue leafing through that *Doble Diario* with its ridiculous news items and unfamiliar articles written by my young, very young father, when he had no idea that the red-ink side would lose the War nor that, after the defeat, he would be betrayed by his best friend, in cahoots with another man whom he did not even know – possibly hired for the task, possibly happy to add his signature and thus get into the good books of the pro-Franco victors – nor that, because of this, his main vocations and aspirations, in the teaching and speculative lines, would all be dashed. So without so much as an attempt to put anything to rights, I left the trashed spare room into which the study had now been transformed and went slowly and cautiously up the stairs, like an intruder or a spy or a burglar (there is no specific word for this in my language, for the kind of thief who sneaks into houses), I held on to the banister as Peter had done, my balance wasn't perfect, I had, without even trying, had quite a lot to drink, by which I mean that with those last few solitary drinks I had unwittingly slid into the very early stages of Flask emulation.

Despite all my precautions, I nevertheless turned on various lights, it would have been a great deal worse to trip and roll down far more stairs than the ashtray had simply because I couldn't see clearly enough to make those inebriated, silent steps. Wheeler had a good collection of detective novels, larger than I remembered, he was clearly very keen, also represented were Stout, Gardner, and Dickson, MacDonald (Philip) and Macdonald (Ross), Iles and Tey and Buchan and Ambler, the last two belonged more to the spy sub-genre or so it seemed to me – again I knew all these names from my father – so I had high hopes of finding Fleming there, and these were fulfilled when I realised that the books were in alphabetical order, allowing me to focus my search: it didn't take me long to spot the spines of the complete collection containing the famous missions of Commander Bond, there was even a biography of his creator. I picked up *From Russia with Love*, it looked like a first edition, as did the other volumes, all of them in faded dust jackets, and when I looked for the copyright page to verify this, I saw that the book was dedicated to Wheeler in the author's own hand, so they must have known each other, Fleming's handwritten note did not allow one to infer any more than that, that they were perhaps friends: '*To Peter Wheeler, who may know better. Salud! from Ian Fleming 1957*', the year of publication. The very brevity of the phrase '*who may know better*' was highly ambiguous – that, at least, was partly the reason – which could be translated or even understood in various ways: 'Who may know more', 'Who may be better informed', 'Who may be more up to date', even 'Who may be wiser' (about something in particular in this case). But there was also a whole range of less literal interpretations, given the sense that the expressions 'to know better' or 'to know better than' often have, and in all those possible versions there would have been a touch of warning or reproach, something like, 'For Peter Wheeler, who would be advised not to . . .' or 'who should be careful not to . . .' follow whatever course of action he was referring to; or 'who would be better off'; or 'who presumably knows what he's doing'; or even 'who can make his own choices' or 'who can do what he likes', or some other such hint or suggestion. I looked at the other novels, from *Casino Royale*, 1953, to *Octopussy and The Living Daylights*, 1966, published post-humously. The five oldest all had written dedications, the one in *From Russia with Love* was, in fact, the last, and those published afterwards bore no dedication at all, and none of the four previous ones was any more expressive, on the contrary, they were either more anodyne or frankly laconic, '*To Peter Wheeler from Ian Fleming*', '*This is Peter Wheeler's copy from the Author*' and so on. Perhaps Wheeler and Fleming had stopped seeing each other around 1958. And Fleming – as I learned from the blurb on a book about his life – had died in 1964, at the age of fifty-six, at the height of his success or, rather, that of the Bond films starring Sean Connery, which were the real impetus behind the success of his novels. As for the Spanish word 'Salud!', I assumed there was nothing more mysterious behind this than the simple fact that the dedicatee was a Hispanist. That relationship or friendship between the eminent Oxonian and the inventor of 007 didn't match up at first, but then, lately, almost nothing did match up. And Wheeler had not, after all, been as eminent in the 1950s – not to speak of the 1930s, during the Spanish Civil War – as he was later on (the title of Sir had been given to him after we met, for example, he was still plain 'Professor Wheeler' when Rylands had introduced me to him).

I was getting tired standing up, I felt uncomfortable and was not a little unsteady on my feet, so I decided to take the copy of *From Russia with Love* downstairs with me so that I could read it quietly in the study – I carried it down, clutched to me as if it were a treasure – and it was as I was going down, and as I was turning out the lights I had switched on in order to go up the stairs without stumbling, that I discovered a large drop of blood at the top of the first flight of stairs. I mean it wasn't a small drop: it was on the wood, not the carpet, and was circular, about four or five centimetres in diameter or about an inch and a half or two, it was more like a stain than a drop (luckily it hadn't reached the dimensions of a pool), and I couldn't understand what it was doing there when I saw it initially or, perhaps, afterwards either. The first thing I thought, when I finally thought using my thinking faculties (which I hadn't initially), was that it belonged to me, that perhaps it had come from me without my noticing as I climbed the stairs; that I had hit or scratched myself or scraped against something and had not even noticed – it happens to everyone – absorbed as I was in my bookish snooping, not to mention being rather drunk. I looked back and up, at the next flight of stairs, where I once more turned on the light, I looked at the stairs below as well, but there were no other drops and that was odd, because when you drip blood, you always leave several drops, what's called a trail or a trace, unless you notice it as soon as the first drop falls and immediately staunch the wound – the gaping wound, but then there would be no staunching that – so as not to cause further stains. And in that case you always take care to clean up the drop you saw on the floor, once you have stopped the haemorrhage, of course. I felt myself, I looked at myself, I touched my hands, my arms, my elbows – I had taken off my jacket and rolled up my shirt-sleeves during my furious researches – I could see nothing, not on my fingers either, which bleed profusely at the slightest prick or scratch or cut, even a paper cut, I touched my nose with my thumb and index finger, sometimes your nose can bleed for no apparent reason, I remembered a friend whose nose had bled for a very good reason, he had taken rather too much cocaine over a number of years and had dealt in it as well, albeit in small quantities, and, once, having successfully smuggled a modest consignment through the Italian customs (the cocaine had been perfumed with cologne to put the dogs off the track, that is, the packaging had been perfumed) and just as he was about to leave the area, a slow dribble of blood began to emerge from one nostril, so slow that he didn't even feel it: there's nothing unusual about that, certainly not in a customs shed, but this small detail was enough for a keen-eyed border guard to stop him and carry out a thorough search with all the dogs on hand to help, that drop of blood cost him a long spell in a Palermo jail, until Spanish diplomacy managed to obtain his release, that particular slammer turned out to be a hellhole, a hornet's nest, it brought him suffering and scars, but it also furnished him with contacts and important alliances and a way of continuing his disreputable life indefinitely and, I suppose, of extending it, the last I heard he was leading a wealthy and respectable existence as a building magnate in New York and Miami, having started in the business in Havana, renovating hotels, although he had never done anything in that line before. It's amazing how a single drop of blood that didn't even fall – it only appeared – can betray someone and change his life, simply because of the place where it appeared, for no other reason, chance is never very discerning.

I looked at my shirt, at my trousers, from waist to ankle, it's terrifying to think how many places one can bleed from, any or all of them probably, this skin of ours is so unresisting, so useless, everything wounds it, even a fingernail can breach it, a knife can tear it and a spear can rip it open (it can also pierce the flesh). I even raised the back of my hand to my lips and spat on it, to see if the blood came from my gums or from further back or further down and the blood had been spat up by a cough I had forgotten about or simply failed to register, I stroked my throat and my face, I sometimes cut myself when I'm shaving and a nick which I thought had healed over could have reopened. But there was not a trace of blood on my body, it was apparently closed, without a single fissure, the drop of blood was not mine, therefore it was perhaps Peter's, he had turned to the left when he went up to bed, I looked over there but in the brief distance between the stairs and his bedroom door I saw no other stains, perhaps, then, it had come from a guest, someone who had come up to the first floor during the buffet supper in search of a second toilet, when the one downstairs was occupied, or else accompanied and in search of a handy room. It could also belong to Mrs Berry, I thought, to that utterly opaque and silent figure, of whom for years, on and off, I had caught glimpses, so discreet she was almost a ghost, serving first Toby Rylands and then Wheeler who had employed her or taken her on, I had never given her any thought at all, she was just taken for granted, reliable, ever since I had known her, she had attended satisfactorily to the provisioning and to the needs of those two single and already retired professors, first one and then the other, but I could know nothing about her needs, or her problems, or her health, her anxieties, any family she might have, her origins or her past, about a probable and probably late Mr Berry, that was the first time I had thought about that, about a Mr Berry by whom she had been widowed or perhaps divorced and with whom, who knows, she still remained in touch, there are people who we assume were always destined for their jobs, who were born for what they do or for what we now see them doing, when no one was born for anything, there is no such thing as destiny and nothing is assured, not even for those who were born princes or very rich, for they can lose everything, not even for the very poor or slaves, who can gain everything, although this rarely happens and almost never without recourse to plunder or larceny or fraud, without tricks or treachery or deceit, without conspiracy, deposition, usurpation or blood.

I thought that I should, anyway, clean it up, that stain at the top of the first flight of stairs, it's odd – irritating – how responsible we feel for whatever we find or discover, even though it's nothing to do with us, how we feel that we should concern ourselves with or remedy something which, at the time, exists only for us, and about which only we know, or so we believe, even though it's nothing to do with us and we have had no part in it: an accident, a difficult situation, an injustice, an abuse, an abandoned baby, and, of course, a dead body or someone who could easily become one, someone badly injured, something of the kind had happened to that friend of mine who dealt a bit in drugs – a schoolfriend, Comendador his name was and still is if he hasn't changed it to something else in America or wherever it is he has gone, he spent years and years sitting immediately in front of me when the register was called, if it was his turn to answer or to be punished, I knew that I was next, he was my straw in the wind throughout my childhood – and he had both run away and not run away: he had gone to pick up a package from the house of the dealer who usually supplied him and also sent him on the occasional assignment, like the one that got him banged up in that Palermo pen; he rang the doorbell several times without success, which was strange because he had told the man that he was coming round, then, at last, the door opened, but the man wasn't in, he had had to go out unexpectedly, at least that is what he gleaned from the woman who answered the door, the dealer's girlfriend of the moment, he, like Comendador, changed girlfriends every few weeks, he didn't want them to get suspicious, and sometimes they even swapped girlfriends, a form of amortisation. The young woman seemed completely out of it, she could barely speak and only just managed to recognise my friend ('Ah, yes, I've seen you at the *Joy*, haven't I?') and she staggered towards the bedroom where her partner of only a few days had left the package ready for her to hand over, she knowing nothing of its contents, but two seconds later and before she had even reached the bedroom, she and Comendador having exchanged only a few disconnected phrases ('What's wrong, what have you taken?' he asked, 'Ah, yes, now I recognise you,' she replied), he watched her trip and apparently rush headlong down the corridor, two or three running steps under the wild impetus of that stumble, and run straight into the wall, with a thump ('A sharp sound, like wood being chopped') then drop to the floor, unconscious. He immediately noticed a small gash, the young woman was dressed only in a long T-shirt that reached her thighs and which she had probably put on in response to the insistent ringing of the doorbell and a vague awareness of a duty to be performed, but she had nothing on underneath, as Comendador observed the moment after that fall, that death, that faint. He also saw a spot of blood on the floor, perhaps similar to the one I had before my eyes now, but fresher, as if it really had come from the girl, from between her legs, maybe she was menstruating and, in her dreamy, absent state, drugged perhaps, she had not noticed, or perhaps she had wounded herself on something pointed or sharp when she fell, something on the floor, a splinter, but that was unlikely. The most worrying thing was not that or the gash, but her air of derangement and confusion following her loss of consciousness, which had happened at the same time as the blow, but was clearly not due to that or, at least, not solely, but to whatever the girl had been taking shortly before or, who knows, for some hours already, she might well have combined a whole morning of excesses with a compulsory previous night of partying. Comendador crouched down and carefully sat her up, she appeared completely lifeless, he propped her against the wall, on the wooden floor, did his best to cover her bottom, the tail of her T-shirt was all spotted with red, tried to bring her round, slapped her face, shook her by the shoulders, saw that her eyes were half-closed or, rather, half-open, and yet as if frosted over, veiled, lacking focus, vision or life, she looked like a dead woman and he did, in fact, think she was dead, inexorably and permanently dead, right there in front of him, and he was the only one who knew. He stopped trying to revive her. He realised that the apartment door had been left open, he heard footsteps on the stairs and once they had gone, he walked back to the door and closed it, returned to the corridor, saw from there the small package he had come to pick up, it was on the bedside table in the adjacent bedroom, towards which the young woman had been heading in her somnambular state before she stumbled and slammed her head against the wall. The bed in that room was unmade, there was a bloodstain on the sheets too, not that big, perhaps her period had started while she was dozing or dying without realising what was happening, she had not noticed or had lacked the will or the strength to check the flow, although I'm not quite sure that is the right expression. Comendador pondered various possibilities, but not carefully, very quickly, slightly panic-stricken, it would be best to take the package anyway, because if, by some misfortune, nurses or policemen arrived before the dealer got back, it would be really bad news for him if they saw it. He didn't think twice, he stepped over the legs of the sullied, seated girl, went into the bedroom, grabbed the goods, stuffed the package in his pocket, stepped over her legs again and made his way to the front door without a backward glance. He opened the door, made sure there was no one around, discreetly closed it behind him and in four bounds and three strides he was down the stairs and out into the street.

He fled and did not flee, because it was precisely then that he realised that he had no way of going back to the apartment or of getting in if he wanted to, nor of helping the young woman if she was still alive, and that was when he raced madly to a phone booth and tried to get the dealer on his cell phone, to warn him about what had happened and to tell him what he knew. The dealer's voice-mail answered, so Comendador left a brief, confused message, then it occurred to him that the man must be at his shop, or that he would at least find the shop assistants, whom he knew, and who could then take action, the dealer owned a shop selling expensive designer-label Italian clothes, a franchise or whatever they're called, and was putting more and more of his energies into that, everyone tends towards respectability as soon as they see a chance and are allowed to or able to, both those who break the law and those who aspire to subvert order, both criminals and revolutionaries, the latter often only behind closed doors, they conceal the tendency when they have to live off their appearance. Comendador and I have known a few like that. Comendador didn't know the phone number of the shop, but it wasn't far away, so he started running, and he ran and ran and ran through the streets as he had not done since childhood, or since university perhaps, during the demonstrations that marked the end of the Franco era, fleeing the always much slower guards bundled up in their greatcoats. And as he ran, he went over in his mind what was still so very recently the past that he found it hard to believe it wasn't still the present and that he could do nothing to change it, and thinking: 'I didn't do anything, I didn't even try, I didn't even find out or make sure, I didn't take her pulse or try mouth-to-mouth resuscitation or heart massage, I've never done it and don't know how to, apart from having seen it done in ten thousand films, not that that's any use, but I could at least have tried, who knows, I might have saved her and now it's too late, every minute that passes is a minute later, a minute that condemns us, me and the girl, but especially her, perhaps she isn't dead yet, instead she'll die while I'm running or when I finally get to the boutique and talk to the assistants and tell them what's happened, or while they look for Cuesta, or for Navascués, his partner, who will probably have a key to the apartment and could then let them in, or let *us* in if I decide to go back there with them, although I'd better not, I've still got the stuff on me, but meanwhile that silly girl could well die because of all the time I'm wasting or, rather, have wasted, time I should have used taking whatever desperate measures I could take or else calling an ambulance, I could have moistened her temples, the back of her neck, her face, I could have given her a whiff of cognac or alcohol or cologne, I could at least have cleaned up the blood, I'm as selfish, mean and cowardly as I always thought I was, but knowing that is not the same as being brought face to face with it, and seeing that it has its consequences.' He entered the shop like a horse at full gallop and there they all were, the dealer Cuesta, Navascués his partner, and the shop assistants, Cuesta had turned off his cell phone, he was serving some customers, who looked quite taken aback, hadn't he got the message, Comendador asked, and gave a garbled account of what had happened, Cuesta took him into his office at the back of the shop, calmed him down, picked up the phone, quickly dialled his own number, but without any great panic, and a few seconds later, Comendador heard him speaking to his girlfriend in the apartment that he had just left like a shot, without so much as a backwards glance. 'What happened,' he heard him ask her, 'Comendador tells me that you hit your head and fainted. Ah, I see. It's just that when you didn't come round, he didn't know what to think. But don't you always have them with you? You should watch that, you know, you can't afford to skip one. Are you sure you're all right, you don't want me to come over? Sure? Fine. Dab some alcohol on that cut and put a plaster on it, there's nothing you can do about the bump, but you'd better disinfect it, don't just leave it, will you? OK. Fine. Yes, yes, you obviously frightened the life out of him, he came charging over here, he's in my office now all out of breath. Yes, he said you gave it to him before you passed out, yeah, well, you probably wouldn't remember. All right, I'll tell him. See you later, then. 'Bye, take care.' Cuesta explained briefly that the girl suffered from diabetes, and these episodes happened sometimes when she drank too much and then, to make matters worse, forgot to take her medication, the two things usually went together and happened, to be honest, far too often, she was silly about it, a child really. She had recovered now and was feeling better, she had taken her medication, and about time too, and the cut was nothing, a nasty bump and bit of blood. She was really sorry to have frightened Comendador like that, she sent him her love and hoped he would forgive her for having put him through it, and thanked him for having taken so much trouble over her, he was an angel, Comendador was an angel.

I remembered this episode as I was going to the bathroom on the ground floor, where I picked up a box of cotton balls and a bottle of alcohol and then returned to the top of the first flight of stairs to clean up that inexplicable stain that was not my responsibility, it was lucky it was on the wooden floor and not on the carpet. When he gave his rapid, flustered account in the shop, Comendador had not mentioned to Cuesta anything about the bloodstains that had clearly come from his girlfriend, about those on the floor and those on the sheets and the spots on her T-shirt, and she herself had not apparently mentioned them over the phone, after all, what was the point – it might, indeed, have seemed indiscreet, tactless. The girl might have felt embarrassed and preferred to pretend that they had never existed and that no one could, therefore, have seen them: perhaps – without actually saying so – she was asking his forgiveness for that. And so Comendador never knew for certain where they came from or what had caused them, but decided to content himself with the explanation of an unexpected period or one which, out of perfectly understandable carelessness, had not been intercepted in time, and, after a few days had passed, he even began to doubt he had seen them at all, those bloodstains, that's what happens sometimes with those things that we deny or keep silent about, that we hide away and bury, they inevitably start to fade and blur, and we come to believe that they never actually existed or happened, we tend to be incredibly distrustful of our own perceptions once they have passed and find no outside confirmation or ratification, we sometimes renounce our memory and end up telling ourselves inexact versions of what we witnessed, we do not trust ourselves as witnesses, indeed, we do not trust ourselves at all, we submit everything to a process of translation, we translate our own crystal-clear actions and those translations are not always faithful, thus our actions begin to grow unclear, and ultimately we surrender and give ourselves over to a process of perpetual interpretation, applied even to those things we know to be absolute fact, so that everything drifts, unstable, imprecise, and nothing is ever fixed or definite and everything oscillates before us until the end of time, perhaps it's because we cannot really stand certainty, not even certainties that suit us and comfort us, and certainly not those that displease or unsettle or hurt us, no one wants to be transformed into that, into their own fever and spear and pain. 'Perhaps I was frightened by the cut on the girl's forehead, I mean, she hit her head with such a thud, and, who knows, seeing a little blood appear possibly made me think that a dark stain on the wooden floorboards was also blood, it was pretty hard to see in that corridor,' Comendador had said to me when he told me about the incident some days later. 'And what about the stains on the sheets, the drops of blood?' I said. 'Oh, I don't know, they could have been something else, wine perhaps, or even brandy, she had probably been swigging it straight from the bottle in the corridor and in bed and then, when she felt ill, had spilled it and not even noticed, I mean, she was completely out of it, either that or feeling in a really bad way by the time she did finally manage to drag herself out of bed and come and open the door to me.' 'Are you telling me that while you're absolutely sure that you saw drops of blood in several places, at the same time you also think it's perfectly possible that you didn't see them or that they might not even have been there, that it was just a product of your imagination or your fear?' 'Yes, I suppose I am, I suppose that's possible,' replied Comendador, perplexed.

I was now cleaning up the stain in Wheeler's house with some cotton balls soaked in alcohol, the blood was not very fresh, but neither had it completely dried or hardened, and the varnished, waxed and polished wood made it fairly easy to remove or eliminate it, although not without some effort and by dint of rubbing repeatedly and using up more alcohol and cotton balls than I had expected, I placed them – the bloodstained ones – in Peter's ashtray, all the while taking care not to damage the floorboards or to replace one stain with another, you can never be too careful with alcohol. What is hardest to get rid of with bloodstains is the rim, the circle, the circumference, I don't know why that should stick to the floor so much more obstinately than the rest, or to the porcelain of the sink or the bath, where drops or stains tend to fall, in fact, it happens immediately, even when the blood is fresh, as soon as it's spilled, there's doubtless some physical law that explains it, although I don't know what it is. 'Perhaps,' I thought, 'perhaps it's a way of clinging on to the present, a reluctance to disappear that exists in objects and in the inanimate generally, and not just in people, perhaps it's an attempt by all things to leave their mark, to make it harder for them to be denied or glossed over or forgotten, it's their way of saying "I was here", or "I'm still here, therefore I must have been before", and to prevent others from saying "No, this was never here, never, it neither strode the world nor trod the earth, it did not exist and never happened." And now, while I continue with my cleaning, and the stubborn ring of blood starts to give and to fade, I wonder if, once it has gone completely and not a trace of it is left, I will begin to doubt I saw it, as Comendador did with his bloodstains, and to doubt that I was here on my knees like an old-fashioned cleaning-lady, although without the foam-rubber cushion they used to kneel on so as not to bruise their knees on the hard floor, it was bad enough that the poor women had to show us the backs of their thighs, by "us" I mean us children, the boys at least. And when there is not the slightest trace left, perhaps then I will start to think that this stain was just a figment of my imagination, caused by lack of sleep and too much reading and too much drink and too many contrary voices and by the indifferent, languid murmur of the river. And by Wheeler's sinuous conversation.' And for a few seconds I felt a desire – or perhaps it was only superstition – not to remove it entirely and for ever, but to leave a remnant that I could see again the following morning, a morning which, according to the clocks, had already begun, just a fragment of the circum-ference, a minimal curve that would remind me 'I'm still here, therefore I must have been here before: you saw me then and you can see me now.' Instead, I finished my task and the wood was left spotless, no one would ever know about the blood if I said nothing and asked neither Wheeler nor Mrs Berry about it. And I went back down the stairs, but did not throw the red or brown or used bits of cotton into the kitchen bin, instead I went to the bathroom to restore to their places the packet and the bottle and there I lifted the lid of the toilet and emptied the ashtray into it, then immediately pulled the chain – we still keep the expression, even though there are no chains and we no longer pull them – and thus did away with the last material proof.

'You're always such a lucky bastard,' I said to Comendador. 'You leave the poor girl lying there with her head cracked open and bleeding, you abandon her, believing her to be dead or not even wanting to know whether she is or not, and she ends up apologising to you for giving you such a fright and thanking you for having gone off without helping her. If the same thing had happened to me, and I had behaved the way you did, the girl would have died and it would have turned out later on that she could have been saved if only I hadn't wasted so much time. And then I'd have had her on my conscience for ever after.' Comendador looked at me with a mixture of superiority and resigned envy, I knew that look well, I've known it since childhood and have seen it subsequently in many other people throughout my life, although not directed at me: it is the look of someone who would prefer not to be the way he is – probably more for aesthetic, or perhaps narrative, reasons than moral ones – and at the same time knows that he has everything going for him and will always land on his feet by being precisely the way he is, unlike those he envies. 'Yes, but you wouldn't have done the same, Jaime, you wouldn't have behaved like that,' he replied. 'You would have stayed until you'd managed to bring her round somehow, and if you couldn't, then you would have immediately called a doctor or an ambulance, even though you still had the drugs in your pocket and even though there might have been God knows what else in the apartment or in the girl's body. Despite all the dangers. And if she had died, then it would have been because she was going to die anyway, and not because you ran away or didn't do what you should have done. I, as you know, have the luck of the coward, which is always far greater than the luck of the brave or the intrepid, despite what every story and every legend in the world may say. Nothing happened, and the girl doesn't bear me any ill will, nor does Cuesta. He doesn't even feel the tiniest bit suspicious or disappointed, which would have been a touch awkward just now. But that doesn't take away from the fact that I've found out precisely what I'm like. I mean I knew already, but now I've actually experienced it, in the flesh, so to speak, and although both the girl and Cuesta will soon have forgotten the whole episode, I'll never forget it, because, the way I see it, a girl died right in front of my eyes and lay there for several minutes, and I simply took off with my load of drugs safely stowed away and did absolutely nothing to help her.' 'Well, you did go and warn Cuesta, you did run all that way, you at least made sure that other people knew about it and could do something,' I said. Comendador was not one to deceive himself, or not much (he might do so more now that he has found respectability in New York or Miami or wherever). 'Yes, it could have been much worse, granted, but you and I know that what I did was nothing, and that it wasn't what I should have done. So although the girl is fine and nothing bad happened to her because of me and my selfishness, I still have it on my conscience.' Then he added with a half-smile, as if contradicting himself (the half-smile from school that he used on classmates and teachers alike, and which always got him out of the worst scrapes and the worst punishment, which always sowed a seed of doubt and contradicted both what he had said the moment before and what he was swearing to be the truth as he drew back his lips and unleashed that smile on us): 'Luckily, my conscience is tough enough to take it.' He did have a lot of luck, it was true, whether it was coward's luck or not. Even the slow drop of blood that trickled from his nose when in the presence of a highly deductive border guard in Palermo could, in the end, be seen as good luck. He had spent time behind some particularly sharp bars, but thanks to those cutting edges he had given up his life of small-time crime and ignominious dangers and was, when last I heard, a wealthy businessman, although I was rarely in touch with him, which, to be honest, is the way I preferred it, now that our contacts had grown cooler, less frequent, or perhaps had ended altogether: there are siblings and cousins, there are childhood friends with whom, as adults, one doesn't know what to do. Perhaps I am such a person for someone else or for some old flame. I was not persuaded, though, that I would have behaved any differently if placed in Comendador's position. I couldn't prove it, though, not having experienced it in the flesh, as they say. Who knows? No one knows until it happens to them, and not even then. The same person might react in different or contradictory ways depending on the day and the degree of fear and on mood, depending on what is at stake or on the importance he gives to his image or history at each stage of his life, depending on whether he is going to tell someone or keep silent about his behaviour afterwards, be it noble or petty, base or elevated. Or depending on how he hopes it will be seen subsequently, on how it will be told or recounted by others should he die and not be able to. No one knows about the next time, even if there has been a first, what happened before imposes no obligations, nor does it condemn us to a series of repetitions, and someone who was generous and brave yesterday may turn out to be treacherous and craven tomorrow, someone who, long ago, was a coward and a traitor may today be loyal and decent, and perhaps the future has more influence and imposes more obligations on us than the past, the unknown more than the already known, the as-yet-untried more than the tried and rejected, the still-to-come more than what has already happened, the possible more than what has already been. And yet. Not that anything that happened is ever completely erased, not even the bloodstain and that stubborn ring rubbed and scrubbed away, in time an analyst would have doubtless found some microscopic trace on the wood, and in the depths of our memory too – those rarely visited depths – there is an analyst waiting with his magnifying glass or his microscope (which is why oblivion is always blind in one eye). Or even worse, sometimes that analyst exists in other people's memories to which we have no access ('Will he remember, will he realise?' we wonder uneasily. 'Will it still rankle with him or will he have forgotten? Will he recollect meeting me before or will he treat me as a complete stranger? Will he know about it? Will his father have told him, or his mother, will he recognise me, will they have told anyone else? Or will he have no idea who I am, what I am, and know nothing at all? ["Keep quiet, say nothing, not even to save yourself. Keep quiet, and save yourself."] I'll know by the way he looks at me, but perhaps I won't, because he might want to deceive me with that look.'). There is much that both does and does not belong to me, in my own memory, to go no further. Who knew, who knows, no one knows. And probably Nin himself did not know that he would resist to the grave, when his political neighbours tortured him in the language he had learned and which he had served so well. There, right there, near my own city, Madrid, where I no longer live. There, in a cellar or in a barracks or a prison, in a hotel or a house in Alcalá de Henares. There, in the Russian colony, in the town where Cervantes was born.

And there was Nin in Fleming's novel, quite near the beginning, it didn't take me long to find him, Wheeler had marked
the paragraph as he had in the *Doble Diario* and in other books,
a meticulous, attentive and, at the same time, impulsive reader,
he wrote mocking interjections in the margins, or scornful
notes to the author (he never let a piece of false reasoning pass,
or a lie or ignorance or sheer stupidity, issuing terse, emphatic
judgements such as 'Silly' or 'Foolish'), or, now and then,
enthusiastic ones, as well as comments intended merely as
reminders to himself, and exclamation marks or question marks
when he did not believe something or thought it unintelligible,
and occasionally he had scribbled 'Bad' (deceitful and incompetent writers, Tello-Trapp or whoever, had incurred quite a few
of those), indicating with an arrow the statement condemned
by his shrewd mind and his exacting mineral eyes, or 'Excellent'
when a phrase seemed right to him or moved him, 'Quite
moving', I read once, in Orwell's *Homage to Catalonia* I think.
'Quite right', he sometimes wrote approvingly, in Benet's book
for example, and 'Quite true' occurred often in Thomas, whom
he must have known in person since the latter taught at a
university very near Oxford, Reading, a place famous for its old
prison and for the ballad written there by prisoner C.3.3., not
another alias exactly.

The paragraph came towards the end of Chapter 7, entitled
'The Wizard of Ice', which, in Spanish, would be an untranslatable pun on *The Wizard of Oz*. 'Of course', I read in that

paragraph:

> Rosa Klebb had a strong will to survive, or she would not have become one of the most powerful women in the State, and certainly the most feared. Her rise, Kronsteen remembered, had begun with the Spanish Civil War. Then, as a double agent inside POUM – that is, working for the OGPU in Moscow as well as for Communist Intelligence in Spain – she had been the right hand, and some sort of a mistress, they said, of her chief, the famous Andreas Nin. She had worked with him from 1935-37. Then, on the orders of Moscow, he was murdered and, it was rumoured, murdered by her. Whether this was true or not, from then on she had progressed slowly but straight up the ladder of power, surviving setbacks, surviving wars, surviving, because she forged no allegiances and joined no factions, all the purges, until, in 1953, with the death of Beria, the bloodstained hands grasped the rung, so few from the very top, that was Head of the Operations Department of SMERSH.

While I was at it, I decided I might as well type it out. I had seen OGPU mentioned in other books, and knew that it was the same as the NKVD or, indeed, as the later KGB, that is, the Soviet Secret Service. Beria was, of course, the notorious Lavrenti Beria, Commissar of Internal Affairs, chief of the secret police for many years, and, up until Stalin's death, Stalin's most astute and ruthless instrument in the organisation of plots, liquidations, purges, settlings of scores, forced recruitment, repression, blackmail, smear and terror campaigns, interrogations, torture and, needless to say, espionage. As for SMERSH, an acronym I did not know, Fleming explained in an author's note signed by him, that:

> SMERSH – a contraction of Smiert Spionam – Death to Spies – exists and remains today the most secret department of the Soviet government. At the beginning of 1956, when this book was written, the strength of SMERSH at home and abroad was about 40,000 and General Grubozaboyschikov was its chief. My description of his appearance is correct. Today the headquarters of SMERSH are where, in Chapter 4, I have placed them – at

No. 13 Sretenka Ulitsa, Moscow . . .

I had a quick look at Chapter 4, which, under the title 'The Moguls of Death', opened with the same or similar facts:

SMERSH is the official murder organization of the Soviet government. It operates both at home and abroad and, in 1955, it employed a total of 40,000 men and women. SMERSH is a contraction of 'Smiert Spionam', which means 'Death to Spies'. It is a name used only among its staff and among Soviet officials. No sane member of the public would dream of allowing the word to pass his lips.

When pedestrians walked past No. 13 of the wide, dull street in question, the narrator went on, they would keep their eyes on the ground and the hairs would prick on the back of their neck or, if they remembered in time and could do so inconspicuously, they would cross the street before they reached the ominous, inelegant, ugly building. But who knows, and I had no idea where to look in order to check if SMERSH really had or hadn't existed or if the whole thing – starting with that author's note – was a novelist's trick to support and confirm a false truth.

I returned to Rosa Klebb and Chapter 7. The truth is that, until then, I had never read a single line by Ian Fleming, but like nearly everyone else, I had seen the early Bond movies. In the cinematographic version, the character was, I seemed to remember, an older woman with short, straight, red hair, who was utterly lacking in charm or scruples, and who, in the end, confronted Connery in a way that proved unforgettable to the boy I must have been when I saw *From Russia with Love* in Madrid (I presumably had to sneak into one of the more accommodating cinemas: under the idiotic censorship laws of the Franco regime the Bond films were deemed suitable only for over-eighteens): she operated a mechanism that made terrifying knives appear horizontally out of the tip of one shoe (or possibly both), each blade being impregnated with a fast-acting and deadly poison, a mere scratch from one of those blades would ensure instantaneous and inevitable death, and so the woman kept aiming sharp-bladed kicks at Bond or Connery, who kept her at a distance with a chair, as animal tamers do at the circus with decrepit lions and tigers bored with such puerile tricks. In the film, as I also remembered, the role of the ruthless Klebb had been brilliantly played by the famous Austrian singer and theatre actress (who made only very rare screen appearances), Lotte Lenya, the greatest and most authentic interpreter of the songs and operas of Bertolt Brecht and Kurt Weill (*The Threepenny Opera* being the most famous) and, if my memory serves me right, the wife and widow of the latter, who had continued composing for her until his death, which occurred, of course, some time before the film adaptation of Ian Fleming's novel. And Fleming, let me say, and judging only by the few pages I read in Wheeler's study, seemed a better writer, more skilful and perceptive, than snooty Literary History has so far deigned to concede. The description that followed of Rosa Klebb, for example, contained some curious and rather valuable insights, I copied a few paragraphs:

> . . . much of her success was due to the peculiar nature of her next most important instinct, the sex instinct. For Rosa Klebb undoubtedly belonged to the rarest of all sexual types. She was a neuter . . . The stories of men and, yes, of women, were too circumstantial to be doubted. She might enjoy the act physically, but the instrument was of no importance. For her, sex was nothing more than an itch. And this psychological and physiological neutrality of hers at once relieved her of so many human emotions and sentiments and desires. Sexual neutrality was the essence of coldness in an individual. It was a great and wonderful thing to be born with. In her, the herd instinct would also be dead . . . And, of course, temperamentally, she would be a phlegmatic – imperturbable, tolerant of pain, sluggish. Laziness would be her besetting vice . . . She would be difficult to get out of her warm, hoggish bed in the morning. Her private habits

would be slovenly, even dirty. It would not be pleasant, thought Kronsteen, to look into the intimate side of her life, when she relaxed, out of uniform . . . Rosa Klebb would be in her late forties, he assumed, placing her by the date of the Spanish Civil War . . . The devil knows, thought Kronsteen, what her breasts were like, but the bulge of uniform that rested on the table-top looked like a badly packed sandbag . . .

('A bag of flour, a bag of meat,' I thought, 'that's what they use to practise sticking in bayonets and spears.')

The *tricoteuses* of the French Revolution must have had faces like hers, decided Kronsteen . . . of coldness and cruelty and strength as this, yes, he had to allow himself the emotive word, *dreadful* woman of SMERSH.

Fleming also seemed very well-informed (SMERSH aside; I would have to ask Wheeler about that, he would be sure to know whether the organisation was real or an invention), the mention of the POUM and Andrés Nin was an indication of that, even though he insisted on calling the latter 'Andreas'. According to his version, Nin might have been killed by a foreign woman – who may, who knows, have been 'singularly beautiful' in her youth in Spain – who had also been his collaborator and lover, to make the treachery and the bitterness still worse. Wheeler, at any rate, had made the link between the reference in the *Doble Diario* to 'several women' detained in Barcelona in June 1937 and the unkempt, sinister, neuter character in *From Russia with Love* (they would never have detained her), for he had marked the paragraph in Chapter 7 with two vertical lines and written in the margin 'Well, well, so many traitors'. So many indeed, in my own country then, and at other times, and, of course, at all other times since time immemorial, from the beginning of time itself and everywhere. How was it possible that there could have been and were so many betrayals, or so many successful betrayals, that is, ones that were never suspected or detected before they were carried out?

What is this strange proclivity we have for trust? Or perhaps it isn't that, perhaps it's a desire not to see or know, or a proclivity for optimism or for complaisant deceit, or perhaps it is pride that leads us to believe that what happens and has always happened to our peers will not happen to us, or that we will be respected by those who – before our very eyes – have already been disloyal to others, as if we were different, and perhaps pride makes us think for no good reason that we will be spared the misfortunes suffered by our ancestors and even the disappointments experienced by our contemporaries: all those who are not 'I', I suppose, who are not and will not be and never have been 'I'. We live, I suppose, in the unconfessed hope that the rules will at some point be broken, along with the normal course of things and custom and history, and that this will happen to us, that we will experience it, that we – that is, I alone – will be the ones to see it. We always aspire, I suppose, to being the chosen ones, and it is unlikely otherwise that we would be prepared to live out the entire course of an entire life, which, however short or long, gradually gets the better of us. In the *Doble Diario*, which I had picked up again, there were a few articles by my father, from the time when, despite the war, he was still trusting and confident: one dated July 2, 1937, on the occasion of the tercentenary of the publication of Descartes's *Discours de la Méthode* in 1637 in Leiden; another dated May 27th, deploring the craze for changing the names of streets and squares (and even cities) which was prevalent in both 'the rebel-controlled zone' and in 'the loyal zone' (his terms) and, in particular, in Madrid: 'It is highly regrettable,' he said, 'that we should thus imitate the rebels, because we should never imitate them in anything.' Or:

> The Prado, the Paseo de Recoletos and the Castellana have had their three names changed into one, the Avenida de la Unión Proletaria. In the first place, this proletarian union does not, alas, exist and it seems to us far more important to try to achieve this union rather than merely to write its name on street corners . . .

It is, in a sense, as if these new signwriters wanted to complete the work of the rebel bombardments in disfiguring our capital.

There were purely political articles too, some signed with the pseudonym he was using at the time, others with his real name, Juan Deza, it seemed so strange to me to see my surname on those ancient pages reproduced in red print. Here were the articles written in his youth and which, no doubt, formed part of the many charges made against him – most of them invented, imaginary, false – shortly after the war had ended and was lost, when he was betrayed and denounced to the victorious rebel authorities by his best friend of the time, a certain Del Real with whom he had shared classes and conversations, interests and cafés and friendships and debates and cinemas and doubtless many parties over the years, all the years during which they had studied together, and I imagine, too, the years of the War itself and the siege of Madrid with its disfiguring rebel bombardments and the rebel fire that came from the outskirts and the hills, the so-called *obuses* or mortar bombs that traced a parabola and fell on the Telefónica and, when their aim was poor, on the neighbouring square, which is why the square was called, with the blackest of humour, the *plaza del gua*, the square of surprises, almost three whole years of both their lives, of everyone's lives, besieged and running through those streets and squares with their shifting names, clutching hats and caps and berets, with skirts flapping and laddered stockings or no stockings at all, trying to choose pavements that weren't targeted by the mortars in order to walk or run down them towards a metro entrance or a shelter.

Along with a third colleague who later died very young, the two friends had even shared the publication in 1934 of a little book comprising what the Geographical Society had judged to be the three best travel diaries written by students who had taken part in what was, at the time, called the University Mediterranean Cruise, organised by the Madrid Arts Faculty of the Republic, and which took students and lecturers to Tunisia and Egypt, Palestine and Turkey, Greece, Italy and Malta, Crete, Rhodes and Mallorca, and lasted forty-five enthusiastic and optimistic days of the summer of 1933, on one of which the passengers were honoured with a visit by the great Valle-Inclán, who, quite where or why I don't know, boarded the ship to give a talk. The Compañía Trasmediterránea-owned ship on which they travelled was called the *Ciudad de Cádiz* ('City of Cádiz'), but its travels were brought to an end by the Italian submarine *Ferrari*, the pride of Mussolini, by which it was torpedoed and sunk in the waters of the Aegean Sea on August 15, 1937, at the height of the war, when, according to what my father had told me, the Republican merchant ship was returning from Odessa with food supplies and military equipment or possibly, as I happened to read in Hugh Thomas's book earlier on that interminable night, on August 14th, leaving the Dardanelles.

This publishing and travelling companion, this friend from university and even from school (as long a friendship, therefore, as mine and Comendador's), took it upon himself to promote and to lead the hunt for this person who was not as yet anyone's father. He carried out a smear campaign, sought 'witnesses for the prosecution' who would support any charges in a trial (or in a pretence of a trial, which was all there was during those days of triumph) and secured a signature of greater weight and authority than his own to place on the formal complaint that was lodged with the police one day in May, 1939. The signature belonged to a lecturer, Santa Olalla by name, from that same university, a man known for his fanaticism and with whom my father had had neither classes nor contact, although Santa Olalla had not apparently felt it necessary to deprive himself of a passage on that entirely unfanatical 1933 cruise. Many years later, when I was a student in those same lecture halls (which were Francoist then and seemed set to remain so eternally), Santa Olalla was still lecturing there in his role as veteran professor – he must have gained his chair swiftly and easily – and in my day, he was, in reality and by reputation, an out-and-out fascist, in all senses of the word, analogical, ideological, political and temperamental, that is, *sensu stricto*. I understand that the main betrayer, Del Real, also received a chair in some university in the north (La Coruña, Oviedo, Santander, Santiago, I'm not sure), doubtless as a reward for the immediate and spontaneous services he rendered to the new and hyperactive Francoist police of 1939. However, it seems that this other teacher-traitor still passed himself off as a 'semi-left-winger' to his rebellious students of the 1970s – nothing so very remarkable about that – and in those unruly times a few unwary and ignorant young women thought him 'charming'. So goes the world ('Talk, betray, denounce. Keep quiet about it afterwards, and save yourself'). The last my father knew of him on a more or less personal level was in May 1939, a month and a half after the War had ended, at the height of the repression and suppression and systematic purging of the defeated, and shortly after his detention and imprisonment on the feast day of San Isidro, patron saint of Madrid, when some mutual friend – or it may have been my mother who went to visit him and who was not, at the time, either my mother or his wife – mentioned to him that Del Real was going around boasting of his great achievement, saying more or less: 'I'm going to make sure Deza gets thirty years in prison, or worse.' At the time, that 'or worse' could easily befall any detainee, with or without reason, with or without evidence: if there was no evidence, then they would manufacture it, and even that wasn't usually necessary, all that was required in principle for someone to be condemned was the word of a concierge, a neighbour, a rival, a priest, a malcontent, a professional or paid traitor, a spurned suitor, a spiteful girlfriend, a colleague, a friend, anyone would do, it was better to go too far than not far enough when it came to completing the 'attrition' – the word is Hugh Thomas's – begun in 1936. And that 'or worse' was the firing squad.

All in all, compared with so many others, Juan Deza was lucky, and his betrayer did not manage to get him lined up against a white wall. During the War, my father had been a soldier in the Popular or Republican Army, as he preferred to call it (he was twenty-two when war broke out, a few months younger than Wheeler), but, consigned to administrative duties in the rearguard in Madrid, he was placed first in a regiment in the service corps, and was subsequently employed as an army translator, later on again, he worked as collaborator and assistant to Don Julián Besteiro until the capitulation, and he therefore never saw battle. And since he had never been obliged to fire a single bullet from his rifle, he could also be absolutely certain that he had never killed anyone, which, he said, was a source of infinite joy to him. He wrote articles for *Abc* and for a few other publications, he broadcast radio programmes for a time in 1937 when he was sent to Valencia, and was charged by the general staff with translating a vast English tome whose author he could not recall, but which was entitled, *Spy and Counterspy (A History of Modern Espionage)*, although his Spanish version, intended for the Ministry of War, probably never saw the light of day. The accusations made by his denouncers, though, included far more serious 'crimes' which – however fantastic – had been con-cocted with the very worst of intentions, lies that proved hard to rebut: these included having been a collaborator on the Moscow newspaper, *Pravda*, having worked as contact, interpreter and guide in Spain to the 'bandit Dean of Canterbury' (Dr Hewlett Johnson, known as 'the Red Dean', whom my father had never even seen), and having been privy to the whole web of 'red propaganda' throughout the conflict, which was tantamount to a direct invitation to prise such exceptional information out of him by any means available (as well as the usual one). Fortunately, none of this happened: he had some truthful witnesses, even amongst those hired for the purpose; miraculously, he came up in front of a remarkably decent second lieutenant, who, far from twisting his refutations during the hearing (as was normal in the judicial system of the time), proposed that they be taken down in writing for greater exactitude, fearing later imputations, and before returning my father to his cell, he said: 'I won't shake your hand because they can see us, but in spirit I'm on your side' ('Antonio Baena,' my father used to say, 'I'll never forget that name'); he was also lucky enough to get a blessedly lazy judge who mislaid his file and ended up dismissing the case due to confusion caused by the anomalous behaviour of one of the 'prosecution witnesses'. And so Juan Deza, my father, had a spell in prison, during which he taught illiterate fellow prisoners to read and write, to add, subtract and multiply (and taught the more educated a little French), and then he was released – he didn't get round to teaching them to divide – although he suffered reprisals for many years afterwards; he was, of course, banned from teaching at any level, unlike his enchaired accusers, and from printing a single line in his country's newspapers, the ink of which was now entirely blue. One of the 'prosecution witnesses', who found his own dark reflection in that role – another former fellow student whom the victim – my father – had visited and lent books to during the bombardments and who later enjoyed a little tawdry, commercial success as a novelist (Flórez was his name) – gave my mother, the victim's friend, this message for him: 'If Deza forgets that he ever had a career, he'll live; otherwise, we'll destroy him.' But that is another story. Sometimes I saw my father grieve in silence over his unfortunate situation, and I saw him suffer. But I never saw him bitter, he did not pass on to his children any feelings of resentment, and any such feelings we may have are of our own making. Nor did I ever hear him complain or mention out loud the names of his betrayers outside the circle of family and close friends, some of whom had known them well – those two names – and at first hand, ever since the feast day of San Isidro in 1939. Despite all these difficulties and obstacles, he managed to get by in life, and if he never complained not even during the harshest and most painful of times, I was not the one to do it for him. Or perhaps I was. Perhaps I was and the only one too, along with my two older brothers and my younger sister, who could carry out the inoffensive task of bemoaning the lot of others, on behalf of my mother now and of my father as well.

In exactly the same way, I have never shrunk from mentioning those names whenever the opportunity arose or whenever it seemed relevant, because I've known them since I was a child, Del Real and Santa Olalla, Santa Olalla and Del Real, and for me they have always been the names of treachery, and as such they do not deserve protection. And this was what I was thinking about during that long night beside the River Cherwell as I finally started collecting together all the books I had taken from Wheeler's west shelves, and which were now scattered around his office or study, and restoring some kind of order, clearing and cleaning the desk and removing trays and bottles and my glass and the ice, an arduous task given how tired and absorbed in thought I was and how late it was too, though I preferred not to know just how late and so deliberately did not look at my watch or at a clock. How was it possible that my father never suspected or detected anything? He was a quick, intelligent, cultivated man, certainly no fool, but he was also an irredeemable optimist, whose first instinct was to trust everyone. But even so. How could he have spent half his life with a colleague, a close friend – half his childhood, his schooldays, his youth – without having so much as an inkling of his true nature, or, at least, of his *possible* nature? (But perhaps any nature is possible in all of us.) How can someone not see, in the long term, that the person who does end up ruining us will indeed ruin us? How can you not sense or guess at their plotting, their machinations, their circular dance, not smell their hostility or breathe their despair, not notice their slow skulking, their leisurely, languishing waiting, and the inevitable impatience that they would have had to contain for who knows how many years? How can I not know today your face tomorrow, the face that is there already or is being forged beneath the face you show me or beneath the mask you are wearing, and which you will only show me when I am least expecting it? He must often have had to suppress his agitation and to bite his lips until they bled, and to cool his blood when it was already boiling, and to put off again and again its final, imperfect, fetid fermentation. All these things can be noticed, observed, smelled and even, on occasions, felt, the chill shock of condensing sweat. At the very least you sense them. You know or should know. Or perhaps once these things have happened, we do not realise that we knew they were going to happen and that this was precisely how it would turn out. And isn't it true that, deep down, we are not as surprised as we pretend to others and, above all, to ourselves, and that we then see the logic of it all and recognise and even remember the unheeded warnings that some layer of our unconscious mind did, nevertheless, pick up? Perhaps we want to convince ourselves of our own astonishment, as if we might find in it a specious consolation and various pointless excuses that really do not work: 'But I had no idea, how could I have imagined, let alone suspected this, it's the last thing I would have expected, why, it would never even have occurred to me, I would have given my word, I would have sworn an oath, I would have put my hand in the fire, I would have staked my life on it, I would have bet all my money and my honour too, how deceived and disappointed I am, how unbelievable, how unreal this betrayal seems.' Yet hardly anyone ever feels such astonishment. Not deep down, not in the knowledge that dares not speak or declare itself or even allow itself to be known or to become conscious, not in that knowledge which so fears itself that it hates and denies and hides from itself, or looks at itself only out of the corner of one eye and with its face half-hidden. That degree of astonishment does, however, exist in the uppermost layers, not just the superficial, epidermic ones, but all of them, the intermediate, the deep and the profound, even the obscure, the subterranean and the venous, those outside and inside, and those right at the very bottom, those of daily, external, superficial life – the point of the spear – and those of each solitary pause, the layers that are there in gaily laughing company and at the moment before each abyssmal plunge into sleep, when, just for a moment, we glimpse ourselves as a whole and glimpse, too, what story will be told when our ending ends. Yes, even that layer of surrender and anguish or premonition allows for such perplexity, such surprise. But not the most profound layer which we almost never reach, the one that lives on the other side of time and is never deceived or mistaken, and which is often confused with fear or adopts fear as a disguise, which is why we ignore it so as not to be controlled by fear or to allow it to dictate our steps and cause us to succumb to what we fear or, indeed, to bring it about. We dismiss the signs and refuse to interpret them ('Keep quiet, keep quiet, and then save me'), and so we relegate them to the realm of imaginings, and counter them with others which, basically, we know are not signs, but pretences and simulacra that seek our trust and our torpor or our drowsiness ('Sleep with one eye open when you slumber,' I quoted to myself). Because it would be impossible to deceive ourselves if that was what we really wanted – not to deceive ourselves, I mean – a vain and doomed endeavour. It isn't usually what we want. No, we don't usually want that, because protection and prevention and alertness all bore us, and we prefer to throw away our shield and march lightly ahead, brandishing our spear as if it were a decoration.

When I grew up, I asked my father about this, although I never liked to press him. He had told the story to my siblings and myself when we were children and adolescents, but only the bare bones, the minimum, as if he and my mother did not want us to find out too much about what awaits everyone to a greater or lesser extent and which does, in fact, begin in childhood – betrayal, tale-telling, treachery, back-stabbing, denunciation, calumny, defamation, accusation – even though, at the time, we were – through various channels – inevitably exposed to the founding example or ultimate instance of this as recounted in the Gospels, because other older examples, those of Jacob and David, Absalom, Adonijah, those of Delilah and Judith and even of unloved Cain, had a goal and adduced a cause, which was why their treacheries were less pure and disinterested, more expected and understandable, less gratuitous and less grave (the famous thirty pieces of silver were never the motive, merely a façade and a tangible symbol with which to clothe and represent the act). Juan Deza, however, had never said much about the subject, perhaps because the mere memory of it hurt him, perhaps so that he would not be tempted into expressions of rancour, or perhaps so as not to give importance – not even by talking about him – to someone who had deserved only scorn ever since the feast day of San Isidro in 1939, or possibly even before.

'But didn't you ever suspect anything?' I had asked, taking advantage of some occasion when he was recalling other episodes from that period.

'Before my detention, you mean? Well, yes, naturally, I'd heard that there was a smear campaign against me. Only indirectly, though, from the Nationalist zone, into which he crossed over without saying a word to anyone, we never knew exactly when or how he went (getting out of Madrid wasn't easy, in fact, it was pretty much impossible without outside help); and we found out too late, of course, when he'd already defected. I don't know why he went, I suppose he could see defeat looming and was already getting into position. It's not that I didn't realise how dangerous that could be, or how far-reaching. Someone who has been your friend for many years speaks with an authority that can prove lethal if used against you. People assume he knows what he's talking about. But in those days, convincing or persuading someone of something was hardly indispensable. A little vigour and vehemence were all you needed, and sometimes not even that.'

'No, I meant before, before you knew about the malicious

lies he was spreading. Didn't you ever suspect anything, didn't it ever occur to you that he might turn against you, that he had it in for you, that he was trying to destroy you?'

My father said nothing for a moment, but not like someone hesitating and pondering in order not to give an inexact response, it was more the silence of someone who wants to underline a truth or a certainty.

'No. I never imagined anything of the sort. When I found out, I didn't believe it at first, I thought it must be a mistake or a misunderstanding, or a lie being told by others, whose intention I couldn't quite grasp. Someone acting deceitfully, trying to spread discord. Then, when I had heard the same story from several sources and could no longer ignore it and had to resign myself to believing and accepting it, I simply found it incomprehensible, inexplicable.'

That was the word he always used, 'incomprehensible', I mean, on the few occasions when I had dared to try and get him to talk to me about it.

'But throughout all those years of knowing each other,' I had said, 'had you never had the slightest indication, the slightest moment of doubt, no inner warning, a pang, a presentiment, something?'

'No, nothing,' he had said, growing ever more laconic and more sombre, and so I changed the subject in order not to depress him further. I suppose it upset him to remember his own ingenuousness and good faith, not so much because he had had those feelings as because he had been unable to preserve them. Or so he must have thought. The truth is that he had preserved them, rather too well in my view (they brought him other heart-aches too, perhaps not so bitter and with the difference that now they only half surprised him), I have proved more cynical and sceptical, I think, although possibly not cynical or sceptical enough given the disloyal times in which we live. Perhaps it is simply that I've always kept my feet more firmly on the ground and have been more pessimistic, and sadder too.

My mother died when I was still too young to think deeply about these matters, and when I was properly grown-up (that is, fully aware that I was) I could no longer ask her: perhaps she, who'd had her feet more firmly on the ground, would at least have ventured some possible explanation – she had not been as close a friend of the traitor as my father, but she had, of course, known him. She had immediately taken action to try and get Juan Deza out of prison, even though they were not yet girlfriend and boyfriend, they had merely been inseparable companions since their university days. From what I know, she had also done a lot during the War to help and bring relief where she could. Some time before, in 1936, when the simultaneous military uprising and 'revolution' of July 18th transformed the days and weeks that followed into an absolute chaos of which both sides took full advantage (each in their respective territories) in order to carry out a rapid and irreversible settling of accounts and to kill whomever they chose, she, as the oldest of eight brothers and sisters, who ranged from adolescents to infants, had had to go in search of the seventeen- or eighteen-year-old brother who failed to return home one night. When such a thing happened during the first few months after the outbreak of war, the thought that immediately entered the minds of every family – before any other thought, such was the degree of terror – was that the missing relative could have been detained arbitrarily by militiamen on patrol, transferred to a *cheka*, or detention centre, and then, at dusk or later at night, and with no further legal proceedings, taken out and executed in some street or road on the outskirts. In the mornings, members of the Red Cross would scour the streets, picking up corpses from the gutters and from the outlying areas, then photograph and bury them, having first, if possible, identified them in order to note down on an index card the end of their life and their death. It was the same in both zones, a kind of crazy, sinister symmetry. In Madrid, after a certain date, so-called Popular Tribunals were set up, but although magistrates did preside over these (subject, however, to the parties' 'political commissars' and therefore shorn of any independence), the extremely brief and hasty methods they employed were all too like those that had preceded their establishment and so proved fairly powerless to stop or channel all that ferocious spleen.

My mother had trudged round the various police stations and *chekas* in search of her lost younger brother, in the contradictory hope of not finding any trace of him, not in those fateful places which were, nevertheless, the first places one always had to go to after any disappearance. She was, alas, unlucky, and found him, or found, rather, the last photo of him, dead, a dead young man, a dead brother. Who knows why he was detained by those who took him to the *cheka* in Calle Fomento along with a female friend who was with him and who met with the same swift, dark, premature fate. Perhaps because he had put on some silly tie that morning, one that the militiamen deemed to be insufficiently revolutionary (the famous blue boiler suits – I'd read about these in Hugh Thomas, I'd heard my parents mention them, and had seen endless photos too – became the almost obligatory civilian uniform of any proud, armed citizen of Madrid) or because they had not given the clenched fist salute, or because she was wearing an imprudent cross or medallion around her neck, such crimes were reason enough to receive a shot in the head or a bullet in the chest in those days when intense suspicion was

¡VIVA MADRID!

Primera Edición

¡VIVA MADRID!
¡Madrid...!
¡Que hermoso eres!
¡Como acarician las calles
los ojos negros
de tus mujeres
¡Como brilla en la mañana
la risa republicana
de tu gente jaranera!
¡Como ríes...!
¡Como embalsaman tu cielo
perfumes de primavera...
rosas, nardos, alelíes...!
¡Madrid...!
¡Como brilla la alegría
de tu noble corazón!
¡Como sale a borbotones
de tu pecho la riqueza,
remediando la tristeza
cuando tienes ocasión...!
¡Como prodiga tu mano
la limosna del cariño,
en la frente del anciano
y en las mejillas del niño...!
Das curso a tu «calderilla»
sin concederla valor,
derrochando con amor
lo que es una pesadilla
para más de un «gran señor»,
Eres noble, cual cordero,
que vá por donde le guía
la sanguinolenta arpía
disfrazada de carnero.
Sufres callado y humilde
la opresión de los tiranos,
siendo el blanco resignado
de sus tratos inhumanos
Pero un día, sonriente,
sin un gesto de desmayo,
demuestras que eres valiente,
que no necesitas ayo,
y elevas noble tu frente.
Y en esa tarde sublime
del día 13 de abril,
mientras un tirano gime,
tu gritas: ¡Viva Madrid!
Mientras, en Gobernación,
un gran corazón latía,
sin recibir todavía
los mandos de la nación,
que ostentaba aquel Borbón
trece de una dinastía.

Y tú en la calle agitando
tu bandera tricolor,
no veías el dolor
que su pecho iba minando,
por que sufría pensando
en el triunfo de tu honor.
. . . .
¡Ya triunfaste noble «gato»!
Solo corresponde ahora,
un recuerdo, dulce y grato,
al gran ALCALA ZAMORA
¡Modista republicana!
De estudiantes que acaudillas
con tu risa picaresca y cristalina
eres brava capitana
¡Como ríes...!
¡Como lanzas a tu paso
las saetas del amor!
¡Como esquivas ondulante
el intento de un «valiente»,
castigando sonriente
su «temerario valor»...!
¡Como llenan el ambiente
tus gorgeos cantarinos,
que van locos desde el «Puente»
hasta los Cuatro Caminos,
llenando de besos mil
tantos rincones divinos
del Barrio de Chamberí...!
¡Que hermosa eres mujer!
Contigo... ¡Viva Madrid!
¡Viva este Madrid castizo
pozo de tanta ilusión,
que en un día satisfizo
ansias de liberación,
sin derramar una sola
gota de su sangre brava,
enarbolando en la calle
la enseña republicana;
¡Sangre, trabajo y amor!
¡Cuanto te quiero salero
¡Con tu cielo me embeleso!
Recibe un profundo beso
del POETA CALLEJERO...!

Julio G. Miranda

Madrid, 7 de Junio de 1931

Precio 10 cts.

Canto a Madrid con motivo de los festejos organizados por el Exmo. Ayuntamiento en honor a la República Española
A los organizadores y al Ilustre Gobierno provisional, dedica éste humilde trabajo su autor

Registrado en el Registro de la propiedad intelectual.   Es propiedad

Imp. Sombrere, 11-Teléf. 71269

all that was needed as an alibi for an unnecessary murder, as, on the other side, was failing to give a fascist or Nazi salute or looking ostentatiously proletarian, or having been a reader of Republican newspapers and having acquired a reputation for walking straight past any of Spain's innumerable churches, those in the 'patriotic' zone, that is.

I never believed in the existence of that small bureaucratic photograph to which I had heard my parents allude. I mean, I never believed that it had been kept somewhere, put away or preserved by my mother, Elena, who was the one who had found it, or that she had asked the political commissars at the *cheka* if she could keep it and that they had given it to her, aged twenty-two, the eldest of eight siblings, but still very young. And when I happened upon it, many years after her death, wrapped in an odd little scrap of satin with two broad red stripes flanking another black stripe and placed in a small tin that had once contained almonds from Alcalá de Henares, along with another photo, unwrapped this time, of the same brother when he was still alive, as well as a library card from the Arts Faculty library and various bits of paper from the 1930s all neatly folded to fit (amongst them a naïve street poem addressed to Madrid, and crowned by the Republican flag with its purple stripe – the risks my mother had run to preserve it during the eternity of Franco's regime), my first impulse was not to look at it, at the photo, and not to linger over what had caught my eye like a flash or a bloodstain and which I recognised as soon as I removed the cloth, I recognised him at once even though I had never seen him and however far from my memory that remote, fatal episode was at that moment. My first impulse was to cover it up again with the little piece of satin, like someone protecting a living eye from seeing the face of a corpse, and as if I were suddenly aware that one is not responsible for what one sees, but for what one looks at, that the latter can always be avoided – you always have the choice – after the first inevitable glimpse, which is treacherous, involuntary, fleeting, and takes you by surprise, you can close your eyes or immediately cover them with your hands or turn away or choose to pass swiftly on to the next page without pausing ('Turn the page, turn the page, I don't want your horror or your suffering. Turn the page, and save yourself').

I stopped to think, heart pounding, and I thought that if my mother had asked for that photo of the atrocity and had taken it away with her and preserved it all her life, she had certainly not done so with any unhealthy intent nor in order to keep alive any rancorous feelings that would inevitably have lacked a precise target, because none of that was in keeping with her character. She probably wanted it as a form of confirmation, whenever it seemed to her impossible or merely a dream that her brother Alfonso had died in that wretched way and would not return home from that night, when she had trudged round streets and police stations and *chekas*, or from any other night. And so that the unreality that always wraps about any permanent loss did not also dominate her night-time imaginings. And perhaps, too, because to leave that photo in the file of administered deaths would have been rather like abandoning to the elements a body she never actually saw and whose final resting-place she never knew, tantamount to failing to give it a decent burial. And as for destroying it later on, I can understand why she didn't do that either, although I am equally convinced that she never looked at it again, and that she probably kept it wrapped in that scrap of red and black cloth so as not to put even herself at risk of seeing it, as a warning or as a dissuasive marker telling her: 'Remember I am here. Remember I still exist, and that this guarantees that I did once exist. Remember that you could see me and that you did see me.' She almost certainly never showed it to others, the photo I mean, at least I don't think so. Certainly not to her parents, not to her delicate and easily frightened mother, overwhelmed by all those children and by the continual demands of her husband, the father, who so much wanted her all to himself that he virtually kidnapped her; and not to him, to that father, as charming as he was authoritarian, who was French in origin, and because of whom my real name is not Jacobo or Jaime or Santiago or Diego or Yago, which are all forms of the same name, but Jacques, which is the French version of the name and by which only she, my mother, ever called me, apart, if I remember rightly, from a few friends in Paris. No, she wouldn't have shown it to them even though she was the one who had to give them the news and tell them of her discovery, nor to her other siblings, all of them younger and more impressionable, the only one who wasn't, the oldest of the boys and the next oldest after her, was in hiding somewhere in the city, constantly moving from house to house in the hope of finding refuge in some neutral or non-aligned embassy. She may have shown it, that photo, to my father, to her inseparable friend and perhaps, who knows, by then also her sweetheart, or maybe he himself found it at the police station and removed it from the file with a shudder and a muttered curse, and he was the one who had had to show it to her, the very last thing he would have wanted to do. For I believe he accompanied her all that night and that day, during her long, anguished and, ultimately, desolate pilgrimage.

Almost the worst thing about the photo are the numbers and labels placed around the neck and on the chest of this boy who was executed having committed no offence, no crime and having had no trial, and who was and wasn't my Uncle Alfonso, but who would have been. There is a 2, and underneath that, 3–20, God knows what those numbers mean, what improvised method was used to classify these unnecessary, nameless dead, so many over the years that no one has ever been able to count them, still less name them, so many throughout the peninsula, north and south and east and west. But, no, that is not the worst, how could it be when there are bloodstains on his young face, the largest on the ear, where it seems the blood may first have spurted forth, but on the nose too and the cheek and the forehead and there are spatters of blood on the closed left eyelid too, it barely looks like the same face as that of the living boy in the other photo not wrapped up in satin, the boy with the tie. The most recognisable features in both photos are the rather prominent front teeth and the left ear from which the dead boy had bled, and which looks just like the ear in the photo of the living boy. A friendly hand rests on his shoulder and its owner, whoever he was (his sleeve was rolled up just as mine was then, as I restored order to the study), had leaned forward to pose and to appear in the photo in which he did not, after all, appear, and he was perhaps another brother, the brother of my mother Elena and my uncle Alfonso, the latter, when alive, wore a handkerchief in his top pocket and parted his hair on the left above his widow's peak, in the prevailing fashion of the time which lasted into my childhood, I too wore my hair parted on that side as a child, when my mother still combed our hair with water, me and my two brothers, and my sister too, except that she lavished more care on hers, shorter or longer depending on her age (perhaps that same hand, a sister's hand, had been responsible for combing the living boy's hair too, when he was younger). I had re-wrapped the wrapped-up photo and put it away again after seeing it and not wanting to see it and then looking at it briefly, very briefly, because it is hard to look at it and even harder to resist doing so, I should never have looked at it and I must never show it to anyone else. But there are images that engrave themselves on the mind even if they last only an instant, and so it had been with that photo, so much so that I could draw it precisely from memory, which is what I suddenly did, when I had cleared Wheeler's desk, and everything had been more or less put back in place, thus saving Peter and Mrs Berry any domestic displeasure when they came down in the morning, much earlier, of course, than I would: it must be terribly late, although I still preferred not to know just how late.

So, all in all, I think my father was lucky after the War, when many of the victors thought only of taking revenge, as in my uncle's case and other still worse cases, revenge for fears experienced or frustrations suffered or weaknesses shown or compassion received, or often for something purely imaginary or for nothing at all – the climate was so conducive to vengeance, usurpation, retaliation, and for the incredible fulfilment of the most fantastic dreams of spite and envy and rage – and when others with more brainpower harboured another broader, wider-reaching idea, less passionate and more abstract, but with equally bloody results once put into practice: that of the total elimination of the enemy, of the defeated and, later, of anyone who seemed suspicious, neutral, ambiguous, insufficiently fanatical or enthusiastic, and, later, those who were moderate or reluctant or lukewarm, and always, of course, those they simply did not like.

So on other occasions, allowing some time to pass in between, I had asked my father again and had tried to tighten the net, though never very much, I didn't want to distress or sadden him. I don't remember how the subject came up, but each time it had arisen of its own accord, for I certainly had no wish to force the matter. And I said to him:

'But with the Del Real business, did you really never know or is it just that you didn't want to tell us about it?'

He looked at me with his blue eyes, which I have not inherited, and with his usual honesty, which has not passed to me either, or, at least, not to the same degree, he said:

'No, I didn't know. And when I left prison I was filled with such loathing for him that there seemed no point in finding out whether or not it was true, whether through third parties or directly.'

'But there was nothing stopping you going to see him, or picking up the phone and saying: "What's going on here, have you gone mad, why are you trying to get me killed?"'

'That would have meant giving him an importance he didn't deserve, regardless of what explanation he gave me, and the chances are he wouldn't have had one or even attempted one. I simply got on with my life and tried not to think about him, not even when I was on the receiving end of reprisals and rejections which were all down to him and his great initiative. I erased him from my existence. And that, I'm sure, was the best thing I could have done. Not just for my peace of mind, but on the practical front too. I never saw him again and never had any contact with him, and when, all those years later, I found out he'd died, it must have been in the '80s I think, I can't even remember when it was now, I didn't feel a thing and didn't give it a second thought. As far as I was concerned, he'd been dead for decades, ever since that feast day of San Isidro in 1939. Surely you can understand that.'

'Yes, I understand it perfectly,' I said. 'What I don't understand and have never understood is that you didn't suspect anything, that you didn't see it coming when you were so close all those years, I mean, something like that is bred in the bone. I don't understand why he did it, why anyone would do something like that, especially when there was absolutely no need. There must have been some cause for resentment between you, some petty argument, I don't know, perhaps you both went after the same woman, or perhaps there was some unconscious insult on your part, or which wasn't an insult at all, but which he might have taken as such. Surely you thought about it, went over it in your mind, pondered it. I can't believe you didn't, at least while you were in prison, with no idea what was going to happen to you. Afterwards . . . yes, afterwards, I can believe that you didn't give it any further thought. That I find quite easy to believe.'

'I don't know,' my father replied, and he sat looking at me with interest, almost with curiosity, as if deferentially recipro-cating a little of the interest and curiosity I was showing in him. He used to look at me like that sometimes, as if he were trying to get a better understanding of the man I had become, so different from him, as if struggling to recognise himself in me despite the more obvious and perhaps rather superficial differences, and occasionally, it seemed to me that he managed to do so, to recognise me 'between the lines' so to speak. And after that pause, he added: 'Do you remember Lissarrague? Now what he did was extraordinary; I'm sure I've told you the story often enough.' And before I could say that, yes, I remembered perfectly, he refreshed my memory (this was one story he did like to recall and to recount): 'His intervention was absolutely crucial. His father, a soldier, had been murdered, and he had contacts with the Falange, and so, what with one thing and another, he was in the Francoists' good books at the time. My accusers asked him if he knew what I'd done during the War, and when he said that he did, they gave his name as a witness for the prosecution. But when he was questioned at the trial, he not only denied all the false accusations that had been made against me, he spoke very favourably of me. The captain in charge of the prosecution was getting more and more agitated and, astonished by Lissarrague's declarations, he finally blurted out: "You do know you were summoned as a witness for the prosecution, don't you?" To which Lissarrague replied: "I thought I'd been summoned to tell the truth." The judge, taken aback, asked why, if what he said was true, there were so many extremely grave accusations being levelled at me. And Lissarrague replied succinctly and without hesitation: "Envy." You see, he and other people saw it like that and thought no more about it. Myself, I'm not so sure that the explanation was quite that simple.'

'That just proves my point,' I put in. 'All the more reason why you should ask yourself the question, given that you weren't satisfied with the simpler explanation, the one that everyone but you found perfectly acceptable.'

'No, I wasn't satisfied,' my father replied with a hint of intellectual *amour propre*. 'But that doesn't mean that I ever came up with a more complicated explanation, or that trying to find one interested me enough for me to devote my time to it or to speak to the man again, to call him to account. There are some people whose motives don't deserve further investigation, even though these may have led them to commit the most terrible acts or precisely because they did. I know this goes completely against the current trend. Nowadays everyone wonders what leads a serial killer or mass murderer to kill or murder serially or *en masse*, or what makes a collector of rapes constantly add to his collection, what makes a terrorist, in the name of some primitive cause, despise all life and try to put an end to the lives of as many other people as possible, what makes a tyrant endlessly tyrannise or a torturer endlessly torture, be it in the name of bureaucracy or sadism. There's an obsession with understanding the loathsome, there's an unhealthy fascination with it, and it does the loathsome a huge favour. I don't share the modern world's infinite curiosity about something that can never be justified, however many different explanations you come up with, psychological, sociological, biographical, religious, historical, cultural, patriotic, political, idiosyncratic, economic, anthropological, it doesn't matter. I'm not going to waste my time on the bad and the pernicious, its interest, I can assure you, is minimal at best and usually nil, I've seen plenty of it. Evil tends to be simple, although not always that simple, if you know what I mean. But there are some investigations that sully the investigator, and even some that infect you without giving anything valuable back in return. There is a taste today for exposing oneself to the base and the vile, to the monstrous and the aberrant, for peering in at the infra-human and rubbing up against it as if it had some kind of prestige or charm and were more important than the hundred thousand other conflicts that besiege us without their ever plumbing quite those depths. There's an element of pride in all of this too: you plunge into the anomalous, the repugnant and the wretched as if the human norm were respect and generosity and rectitude, and we had to make a microscopic analysis of anything that deviated from that norm; as if bad faith and treachery, ill will and malice did not form part of that norm and were the exception, and therefore merited all our effort and attention. And that isn't true. It's all part of the norm, and there's no great mystery about it, no more than there is about good faith. This age, however, is devoted to the silly, the obvious and the superfluous, and that's the way it is. Things should be the other way around: there are actions so abominable and so despicable that their mere commission should cancel out any possible curiosity we might have in those who committed them, rather than creating curiosity and provoking it, as is the imbecilic way of things now. And that was the case with me, even though it was *my* case, my life. What that former friend had done to me was so unjustifiable, so inadmissible and so grave from the point of view of friendship, that everything about him instantly ceased to interest me: his present, his future and his past too, even though I existed in that past. I didn't need to know anything more, and I had no wish to delve deeper.'

He had stopped and was looking at me again, hard and expectantly, as if I were not one of his own familiar children, but a much younger friend, a new friend who had come to see him that morning in his bright, welcoming apartment in Madrid. And as if he could expect from me a novel reaction to what he had said.

'You're a better man than I am,' was my response. 'Or if it isn't a question of better or worse, you're certainly freer and more astute. I can't be sure, but I think I would have sought to avenge myself. After Franco died, or whenever it would have been feasible to do so.'

My father laughed, and this he did paternally, more or less as he had when we, as children, came out with some wildly ingenuous or tactless remark in the presence of visitors.

'Possibly,' he said, 'you do have a tendency to hang on to things, Jacobo, and it's sometimes hard for you to let go, you're not always good at leaving things behind. But that's mainly a sign that you still feel very young. You still think you have unlimited time, time enough to squander. It may be hard for you to understand this, but trying to avenge myself would simply have meant wasting more of my time because of him, and those months in prison were quite enough for me. Besides, it would have given him a sort of *a posteriori* justification, a false validation, an anachronistic motive for his action. Bear in mind that when you look at your life as a whole the chronological aspect gradually diminishes in importance, you make less of a distinction between what happened before and what happened afterwards, between actions and their consequences, between decisions and what they unleash. He might have thought that I had, in fact, done him some harm, it didn't matter when, and then he would have gone to his grave feeling more at peace with himself. And that wasn't and hasn't been the case. I never wronged him in any way, I didn't harm him and I never had, either before or afterwards or, needless to say, at the time. And that perhaps was what he could not bear, what hurt him. Some people can't forgive you for behaving decently towards them, for being loyal to them, for defending them and giving them your support, let alone doing them a favour or getting them out of some difficulty, that can, on occasions, sound the death knell for the benefactor, I'm quite sure you can come up with your own examples. It's as if they felt humiliated by being the object of someone's affection and good intentions, or thought that this implied a degree of contempt towards them, it's as if they could not stand to feel indebted, however imaginary the debt, or to be obliged to feel grateful. Not that they would want to be treated otherwise, of course, heavens, no, they're always terribly insecure. They would be even more unforgiving if you behaved badly or disloyally towards them, if you denied them favours and left them firmly stuck in their own mire. Some people are simply impossible, and the only sensible thing to do is to remove yourself from their presence and keep them at a distance, and not to let them near you for good or ill, or count on you for anything, quite simply, to cease to exist for them, not even in order to fight them. That, of course, is the ideal. Unfortunately, you can't make yourself invisible by sheer will-power or by choice. For example, when I was in prison, our friend Margarita came to visit me (there was a metal grille between us), and she became so passionately indignant about the things she had heard my betrayer saying about me that this attracted the attention of the prison guards. They asked her who she was talking about, fearing, no doubt, that it was Franco himself. She, being of a highly excitable nature, told them, and they made her go with them to Del Real's house to find out if what she had said was true. There they found his mother, who, of course, Margarita knew (we all knew her, we had been good friends for many years), and whom she attempted to persuade to get her son to see reason and to withdraw his unfair and incomprehensible accusations. His mother, who was very fond of Margarita, listened with a mixture of astonishment and discomfort. In the end, though, maternal faith outweighed everything else, but all she could say in her son's defence was: "*La patria es la patria*" – "One's country is one's country." To which Margarita replied: "Yes, and lies are lies."'

My father fell silent again, but this time he didn't look at me, but at the arm of his chair. He seemed suddenly tired, or perhaps distracted by something that had nothing to do with our conversation. I couldn't tell if he had become slightly lost amongst his memories and did not intend to add anything more, or if he was still going to connect the last story to the one before and offer me a conclusion. It seemed unlikely that I would find out because my sister had arrived (perhaps my father had heard the lift) and had just come into the living-room, but only, I imagine, in time to hear Margarita's quoted words, because she immediately asked us in a jovial, chiding tone:

'All right, what are you two arguing about?'

And I said:

'We're not, we were talking about the past.'

'What past? Was I there?'

My sister always had a particularly cheering effect on my father, even though she resembled my mother rather less than I did. Well, not exactly: she resembled her more in that she was also a woman, but less so in her actual features, which I reproduced in my male face with disquieting fidelity. He replied with an ironic, happy smile, his usual harmonious blend:

'No, you weren't, not even as the embryo of a plan of a hypothesis of a possibility.' Then he went on to conclude, addressing himself solely to me: 'Lies are lies, you see. There's not really any more to say or time to waste on such things.'

'No, not once you've emerged from them, more or less unscathed that is,' I said.

'Yes, of course, once you've emerged from them, scathed or unscathed. That's obvious, I mean if I hadn't emerged, we wouldn't be talking now, you and me, still less this young woman here.'

'Is this some deep dark secret you two are talking about?'

That is what my sister said then, I remember it well, and those were the memories that came to me as I finally climbed into the familiar bed prepared by Mrs Berry many hours before, but first I returned to its place in the next room the copy of *From Russia with Love* with its dedication. I had, I thought, left almost everything in order, and had even cleaned up a strange bloodstain that I had neither spilled nor provoked and which now, in the midst of my drunkenness and tiredness, and just as I had foreseen before erasing it for good and expunging its rim or last remnant, was already starting to seem unreal to me, a product of my imagination. Or perhaps of my readings. Without realising it, I had read a great deal about the days of blood in my own country. The blood of Nin, the blood of the uncle who never was my uncle, the blood of so many people without names or who had to abandon their name and who inhabit the earth no longer. And the blood of my father which they sought but did not manage to spill (blood of my blood which did not spurt forth or spatter me). '*La patria es la patria*', the traitor's poor, trapped mother. An inextricable phrase, meaningless like all tautologies, empty words, a rudimentary concept – that of fatherland, homeland, mother country – and fanatical in its application. Never trust anyone who used it or uses it, but how would you know someone was using it if they were speaking in English and said 'country', which usually translates as '*país*', as in 'What country do you come from?', or '*campo*' as in 'countryside', which are both entirely inoffensive in Spanish. From the top floor I could hear the murmur of the river even more clearly now, quiet and patient or indifferent and languid; sound rises, or was it just the part of the house I was in, lying in bed at last. I could already see a little light in the sky or so I thought, it was barely noticeable, my eyes might have been deceiving me. But there you can't help but notice, even at dead of night and at the hour we Latins used to call the *conticinio* – a word now forgotten by my own language – because of that strange English penchant for sleeping without blinds on the windows, something I never did grow accustomed to, there are no blinds, they don't have them, indeed, they don't always have curtains or shutters, often only transparent net curtains which neither shelter nor conceal nor calm, as if they always had to keep one eye open when they fall asleep, the inhabitants of that large island on which I have spent more time than is advisable and more than was foreseeable, if I add up the before and the after, the now and the then. 'Lies are lies', another meaningless tautology, although this time the word is not empty, nor the concept rudimentary, nor its application fanatical, but, rather, universal, effortless, routine, constant, almost mechanical and casual at times, and the more mechanical and casual, the more difficult it is to identify, to distinguish, and the truer the lie, for lies have their truth, the more defenceless we are. 'Lies are lies, but all lies have their moment to be believed.' Just as I might believe the river as I lay listening to its murmurings, and, thinking I understood, repeated what it said, as I drifted off to sleep, keeping one eye open, as is the custom in this country, which is also, for some, their *patria*, softly and languidly, with the open eye of my contagion and the non-existent lightness in the sky: 'I am the river, I am the river and, therefore, a connecting thread between the living and the dead, just like the stories that speak to us in the night, I take on the likeness of past times and past events too, I am the river. But the river is just the river. Nothing more.'

2
Spear

We never know when we have entirely won someone's trust, still less when we have lost it. I mean the trust of someone who would never speak of such things or make protestations of friendship or offer reproaches, or ever use those words – distrust, friendship, enmity, trust – or only as a mocking element in their normal representations and dialogues, as echoes or quotations of speeches and scenes from times past which always seem so ingenuous to us, just as today will seem tomorrow for whoever comes after, and only those who know this can save themselves the quickening pulse and the sharp intake of breath, and so not submit their veins to any unpleasant shocks. Yet it is hard to accept or to see this, and so hearts continue their somersaults, mouths their drynesses and inhalations, and legs their tremblings, how was I or how could I have been – men say to themselves – so stupid, so clever, so smug, so credulous, so dim, so sceptical, the trusting person is not necessarily more ingenuous than the wary, the cynic no less ingenuous than the person who surrenders unconditionally and places himself in our hands and offers us his neck for the last or the first blow, or his chest so that we can pierce it with our sharpest spear. Even the most suspicious and astute and the most cunning turn out to be slightly ingenuous when expelled from time, once they have passed and their story is known (it's on everyone's lips, which is how, ultimately, it takes shape). Perhaps that's all it is, the ending and knowing the ending, knowing what happened and how things turned out, who was in for a surprise and who was behind the deception, who came off well or badly or who came out even or who did not bet at all and so ran no risk, who – nevertheless – came out the loser because he was dragged along by the current of the broad, rushing river, which is always crowded with gamblers, so many that eventually they manage to get all the passengers involved, even the most passive, even the indifferent, the scornful and the disapproving, the hostile and the reluctant; as well as those who live along the banks of the river itself. It doesn't seem possible to remain apart, on the margins, to shut oneself up in one's house, knowing nothing and wanting nothing – not even wanting to want anything, that's not much use – never opening the mailbox, never answering the phone, never drawing back the bolt however loudly they knock, even if they seem about to break the door down, it doesn't seem possible to pretend that no one lives there or that the person who did has died and doesn't hear you, to be invisible at will and when one chooses, it isn't possible to be silent and to eternally hold your breath while still alive, it's not even entirely possible when you believe that you inhabit this earth no longer and have abandoned your name. It simply isn't that easy, it isn't that easy to erase everything and to erase yourself and for not a trace to remain, not even the last rim or the last remnant of a rim, it's not easy simply to *be* like the bloodstain that can be washed and scrubbed and suppressed and then . . . then one can begin to doubt that it ever existed. And each vestige always drags behind it the shadow of a story, perhaps not complete, doubtless incomplete, full of lacunae, ghostly, hieroglyphic, cadaverous or fragmentary, like bits of a gravestone or like ruined pediments with fractured inscriptions, and sometimes it's not even possible to know how a story really ended, as in the case of Andreu Nin and of my uncle Alfonso and his young friend with a bullet in her neck and no name at all, as in the case of so many others about whom I know nothing and about whom no one speaks. But the form is one thing and quite another the actual ending, which is always known: just as time is one thing and its content another, never repeated, infinitely variable, while time itself is homogeneous, unalterable. And it is that known ending which allows us to dub everyone ingenuous and futile, the clever and the stupid, the totally committed as well as the slippery and the evasive, the unwary, the cautious and those who hatched plots and set traps, the victims and the executioners and the fugitives, the innocuous and the malicious, from the position of false superiority – time will see it off, it will be time, time that will cure it – of those who have not yet reached their end and are still groping their way uncertainly forwards or walking lightly with shield and spear, or slowly and wearily with shield all battered and spear blunt and dull, without even realising that we will soon be with them, with those who have been expelled and those who have passed and then . . . then even our sharpest, most sympathetic judgements will be dubbed futile and ingenuous, why did she do that, they will say of you, why so much fuss and why the quickening pulse, why the trembling, why the somersaulting heart; and of me they will say: why did he speak or not speak, why did he wait so long and so faithfully, why that dizziness, those doubts, that torment, why did he take those particular steps and why so many? And of us both they will say: why all that conflict and struggle, why did they fight instead of just looking and staying still, why were they unable to meet or to go on seeing each other, and why so much sleep, so many dreams, and why that scratch, my fever, my word, your pain, and all those doubts, all that torment?

That's how it is and will always be, Tupra more or less said as much to me on one occasion, and Wheeler said so quite clearly the following morning and over lunch. And if Tupra said it less clearly it was doubtless because he would never talk about such things or use words like 'distrust', 'friendship', 'enmity' or 'trust', at least not seriously, not in relation to himself, as if none of those words could apply to him or touch him or have any place in his experiences. 'It's the way of the world,' he would say sometimes, as if that really was all one could say on the subject, and as if everything else were mere ornament and possibly unnecessary torment. I don't think he expected anything, either loyalty or treachery, and if he came across one or the other, he didn't seem particularly surprised, nor did he take any precautions other than sensible practical ones. He didn't expect admiration or affection, but neither did he expect ill will or malice, even though he knew full well that the earth is infested with both the former and the latter, and that sometimes individuals can avoid neither and, indeed, choose not to, because these are the fuse and the fuel for their own combustion, as well as their reason and their igniting spark. And they do not require a motive or a goal for any of this, neither aim nor cause, neither gratitude nor insult, or at least not always, according to Wheeler, who was more explicit: 'they carry their probabilities in their veins, and time, temptation and circumstance will lead them at last to their fulfilment'.

So I never knew if I ever did win Tupra's trust, nor if I lost it or when, perhaps there was no one moment for either of those two phases or changes of mind, or perhaps one could not have given it a name, or not those names, of winning or losing. He didn't talk about such things, in fact, there was almost nothing about which he did speak clearly and directly, and had it not been for Wheeler's preliminary explanations on that Sunday in Oxford, it is quite possible that I would have known nothing either precise or imprecise about my duties, and that I would not even have guessed at their sense or their object. Not, of course, that I ever knew or understood this entirely: what was done with my rulings or reports or impressions, for whom they were ultimately intended or what purpose they served exactly, what consequences they would bring or, indeed, if they had any consequences, or belonged, on the contrary, to that category of task and activity which certain organisations and institutions carry out simply because they always have, and because no one can remember why these things were done in the first place or cares to question why they should continue. Sometimes I thought perhaps they simply filed them away, just in case. A strange expression, but one which justifies everything: just in case. Even the most absurd things. I don't think it happens any more, but any traveller visiting the United States used to be asked whether he or she had any intention of making an attempt on the life of the American President. As you can imagine, no one ever replied in the affirmative – it was a declaration made under oath – unless they wanted to make a joke, which could prove very costly on that stern, uncompromising border – least of all the hypothetical assassin or jackal who had disembarked with precisely that aim or mission in mind. The thinking behind this absurd question was, it seems, that should a foreigner take it into his or her head to assassinate Eisenhower or Kennedy or Lyndon Johnson or Nixon, then perjury could be added to the main charge; in other words, they asked the question in order to catch people out – just in case. I never understood, however, the relevance or advantage of that extra aggravating factor when used against someone accused of bumping off or trying to bump off the highest-ranking person in the land, a crime which would, one imagines, be of a gravity difficult to surpass. But that is the way with things that are done just in case. They anticipate the most unlikely and improbable events and are drawn up on that basis, and almost always in vain, since those events almost never happen. They perform fruitless or superfluous tasks that probably never serve any purpose or are never even used, they are based on eventualities and imaginings and hypotheses, on nothing, on the non-existent, on what never happens and has never happened. Just in case.

Initially, I was summoned three times in the short space of about ten days to act as interpreter, although they doubtless could have used others paid by the hour or some semi-permanent member of staff like Pérez Nuix, the young woman whom I met later on. On two of those occasions I barely had to do anything, for the two Chileans and the three Mexicans with whom Tupra and his subordinate Mulryan shared two rapid lunches – all five were dull men engaged on dull business, vaguely diplomatic, vaguely legislative and parliamentary – spoke reasonable, utilitarian English, and my presence in the restaurant was only necessary to clear up the occasional lexical doubt and so that the final terms of the draft agreements they apparently reached were clear to both parties and left no room for subsequent misunderstandings, voluntary or involuntary. In fact, all I had to do was to summarise. I didn't understand much of what they were talking about, as happens in any language when I'm not really interested in what my ears are hearing. I mean that while I did, of course, understand the words and the phrases and had no problem converting them and reproducing them and transmitting them too, I understood neither the subjects discussed nor their respective backgrounds, they simply didn't interest me.

The third occasion was much odder and more amusing, and I had to do more to earn my money, because I was summoned to Tupra's office where I had to translate what seemed to me to be some sort of interrogation. Not that of a detainee or a prisoner or even a suspect, but possibly – shall we say – of an infiltrator or a turncoat or an informer whom Tupra and Mulryan did not as yet quite trust, both of them asked questions (but Mulryan more often, Tupra held back) which I repeated in Spanish to a tall, burly, middle-aged Venezuelan, dressed in civilian clothes and looking somewhat uncomfortable, or, rather, uneasy and unnatural, as if the clothes were borrowed and temporary and recently acquired, as if he felt insecure and a bit of a fraud without the more than probable uniform to which he was doubtless accustomed. With his stiff moustache and his broad, tanned face, his agile eyebrows separated only by two coppery brushstrokes that flanked the brief space between the eyebrows like two tiny tufts of hair transported from chin to forehead, with his convex chest perfect for showing off rows of medals and yet far too bulky to be contained by a simple white shirt, dark tie and pale double-breasted suit (an odd sight in London, he looked as if he was about to burst out of it, the three buttons firmly done up like a reminder of his army jacket), I had not the slightest difficulty in imagining him wearing the peaked cap of a Latin American military man, in fact, the thick, wiry, grizzled hair that grew too low down on his forehead cried out for a patent leather peak that would provide a focus of attention and would hide or disguise that overly invasive hairline.

Mulryan's questions, plus the occasional one from Tupra, were polite, but quick and very much to the point (both of them seemed always to go straight to the point, in their conversations with jurists and senators too, or with Chilean and Mexican diplomats, they weren't prepared to spend any longer than was necessary, they were clearly trained and experienced negotiators, and didn't mind if they seemed somewhat abrupt), and I realised that they expected the same from my translations, that I should exactly reproduce not just the words but also the sense of haste and the rather sharp tone, and when I hesitated a couple of times because such an absolute lack of preambles and circumlocutions does not always sit well in my language, Mulryan, on both occasions, made a gentle but unequivocal gesture with two fingers together, indicating that I should hurry up and not bother inventing my own formulations. The Venezuelan military man did not know a word of English, but he paid as much attention to the voices of the two British men while they were asking their questions as he did to mine when I was providing him with the meaning of their interrogations, although, inevitably, when he gave his replies, he looked at me and spoke to me, even though I was merely the messenger, all too aware that I was the only one who would immediately understand him. Not that I understood a great deal more of what was talked about, or understood with any great precision the background to the matters discussed, but my curiosity was definitely more aroused than during the two lunches, which were truly soporific and whose subject-matter had proved far more abstruse for a layman. I remember translating questions for that disguised, ill-at-ease military man about what forces could be rallied by him and his colleagues, whoever they were, the guaranteed and the probable numbers, and that he replied that nothing was ever guaranteed in Venezuela, that anything guaranteed was only ever probable, and that the probable was always a complete unknown. And I remember that this answer irritated Mulryan, who tended to the absolutely specific and precise, and provoked one of Tupra's interventions, Tupra being perhaps more used to vagueness and evasion from his years of possible adventures abroad, and his various jobs and missions in the field, and from agreements he had brokered with insurrectionists, or so I thought, having constructed this past for him the moment I met him at Wheeler's house. 'Tell me the probable numbers then,' he said, thus dealing with both the interrogatee's reservations and Mulryan's bad temper. He also asked about the logistical support guaranteed 'from abroad', which I translated as '*desde el extranjero*', adding '*exterior, de fuera*', just so that there would be no misunderstandings. He doubtless understood, as I did, that this was a euphemism referring to one specific source of support, the United States. He replied that this depended in large measure on the result and popularity of the first phase of operations, that 'people from outside' always waited until the last moment before taking part in any enterprise and committing themselves fully, 'lock, stock and barrel', that was the expression he used, perhaps here in both the literal and figurative sense. However, seeing Mulryan's visible and growing irritation, he added that '*el Ambásador*' – that's what he called him, in English but with a strong Spanish accent, thus clearing up any possible doubt as to who he meant – had promised them immediate official recognition if there were little opposition or if this remained, from the start, '*emburbujada*' – 'enbubbled' – I had never heard this ridiculous word in Spanish before, but I had no problem understanding it. The term struck me as distinctly unmartial, more suited to some foolish, smooth-talking politician or some equally foolish top executive, the modern equivalents of snake-oil salesmen.

'And do you think that's likely, that there will be no resistance or that it will be reduced to a few isolated pockets?' Mulryan asked (that is how I had translated the absurd word, faithfulness here would have been not only difficult but embarrassing). And he added: 'That hardly seems feasible with such a stubborn, argumentative leader, one who was idolised in his day, I mean, I imagine he still has a lot of loyal supporters. And if there's strong resistance, the people from outside won't lift a finger or recognise anyone until they see that the situation has gone one way or the other, and that could take time. They'll await events, but I imagine they've told you as much already.'

'Well, yes, that's possible, and that is, perhaps, how we should understand their advice. But if we don't touch the leader, don't harm him physically I mean, I doubt that many units would risk their lives defending his office, nor would many Venezuelan citizens. The current widespread discontent would work in our favour, and, as long as we promise early elections, the full support of the traditional political class is guaranteed.'

'You mean probable, don't you?' asked Tupra.

'Yes, highly probable,' said the soldier, correcting himself, embarrassed and without even a hint of a smile, he seemed very self-conscious, tense and fragile, as if he felt he was at fault or had conflicting loyalties.

It did not escape my notice that, during the interrogation, neither Mulryan nor Tupra addressed him by name, they did not call this ill-disguised civilian anything, not once did they say 'Mr So-and-So', nor, of course, 'General' or 'Colonel' or 'Commander', or whatever the man's rank was. I assumed they preferred me not to know whom they were talking to, since I knew everything they were talking about.

'Now let's get one important, indeed, vital thing straight,' Tupra went on. 'You would definitely not attack the leader himself, is that correct? According to what you've said, you're only after his post. But you would never, under any circumstance, compromise his physical integrity. Have I understood you correctly?'

The Venezuelan gentleman instinctively loosened his tie, or, rather, eased his anxieties by making that gesture; he fidgeted in his chair; he stretched his legs a little as if he had suddenly realised that the crease in his trousers was not quite straight, in fact he did discreetly straighten his two trouser legs, first one, then the other, his feet off the ground, and I noticed that he was wearing short boots, made of some very dark green leather, like crocodile skin, though whether they were imitation or not, I don't know, I can't tell the difference. It seemed to me that he was thinking and playing for time, that he wasn't quite sure what the best answer would be. It seemed to me that Tupra was more skilful than Mulryan, which is why he didn't ask many questions, so as not to reveal his hand or to wear himself out, so as to remain fresh, supervising things from a distance.

'That would be too much like tempting Fate, if you know

what I mean. It would be dangerous, it could prove counter-productive, lighting a flame that should never be lit, not even one the size of a match-flame. He mustn't be harmed in any way, we're all quite clear about that, we'll treat him with kid gloves, don't worry, he can't be touched. Otherwise, the support we're counting on would collapse. Not entirely, of course, but partially.'

I remember that Tupra affected a pitying smile and paused, and that Mulryan didn't dare start asking questions again until he was sure that his superior had once again withdrawn momentarily from the interrogation. And he was right to hold back, because Tupra had not yet moved aside.

'You don't seem very determined,' he said. 'And in ventures like this, a lack of resolve means that failure is not only probable but guaranteed. As does a lack of hatred, you should know that, sir, either from your studies or from personal experience. In my experience, at least, you always need to be prepared to go further than is necessary, even if you don't go that far in the end, or decide to rein yourself in when the moment comes, or if it simply proves unnecessary. That, however, must be the prevailing spirit, not its opposite. You would agree, would you not, that one cannot impose a limit beforehand, setting the bar below what might prove necessary? If your resolve and your mood are as you say they are, then in my view you should hold back. And I would, for the moment, advise against any support or financial help.'

This somewhat unconvincing soldier shook his head vehemently while he listened to my Spanish version of Tupra's words, perhaps like someone who cannot believe what he is hearing or despairs over some extremely expensive mis-understanding, but perhaps, also, like someone who realises too late that he has given the wrong answer and, by doing so, has brought about an irremediable disaster, because, depending on the nature of the blunder, any retraction or rectification or clarification will always sound insincere and self-interested – like backing down. That phoney civilian or phoney soldier could well have been thinking: 'Oh, shit, what they wanted to hear was that we wouldn't blink an eye if we had to kill him and not, as I thought, that we would save the bastard's skin however difficult he made things for us.' Yes, he could have been thinking that, or something else which I had neither time nor imagination to elaborate in my mind, because as soon as my Spanish stopped, he was quick to protest.

'No, *señores*, you've misunderstood me,' he said anxiously and with rather more feeling than he had shown up till then. Or perhaps he didn't, but that's how I remember it, the precise way different Latin Americans speak gets very confused in one's memory and in the retelling too. 'Of course we'd be prepared to get rid of him, if we had no alternative. We certainly don't lack resolve and, as for hatred, well, you can summon up hatred in no time at all, from one moment to the next, all you need is a spark, a few well-chosen phrases and the fire spreads, but it's best not to start out with the flames too high, the fire might burn itself out, better a cool head than hand-to-hand combat, don't you agree? All I meant was that we believe that harming the leader might not be necessary, that it would be most unlikely and preferable for all concerned if we didn't. But, believe me, if he made any difficulties, and we had to kill him in order to keep things on an even keel, then we certainly wouldn't shrink from that. I mean, it's just a matter of a single shot, isn't it, and that's that, it's quick and it's easy, we have a number of men who are used to that kind of thing. And if his supporters complain, too bad, the liberator's gone. They can say what they like, but there's nothing they can do about it, the tyrant's dead, kaput.'

'It's quick and it's easy,' I thought. 'Don't I know it, there have always been a number of men used to that kind of thing. In the temple, in the ear, in the back of the neck, a gush of blood, you can always clean that up later.' I translated his words with as much feeling as I could muster, Tupra and Mulryan weren't looking at me while I was doing this, but at him, at the

Venezuelan, this was something I was always very struck by, because, normally, people instinctively look at the person emitting the sounds, the person speaking, even though he's only translating, even if he's only the person reproducing and repeating and not the person speaking, but they, on the other hand, invariably fixed their attention on the person originally responsible for uttering the words, even though the latter had to remain silent while his words were transmitted. This, I noticed, tended to make interrogatees nervous, for they always looked at me despite only understanding me by deduction (a fairly easy deduction on their part).

The civilian or fake soldier was no exception when it came to nervousness (though this was, admittedly, only my first experience), but possibly what upset him most, more than the four eyes trained on him while I emulated his words, was Tupra's immediate response:

'You must realise that if you shoot him, you'll have to shoot quite a lot of your fellow countrymen too, whether you hate them or not, in the heat of the moment and in cold blood, in combat and, who knows, in executions, which are also quick but not so easy. And nobody's going to like that, least of all the people outside, including us. With such a high risk of carnage, and with no guarantee that it will have the desired result, my opinion is that you really shouldn't try it. And I'm afraid that, for now, I'll have to advise against any support or financial aid.'

The Venezuelan crumpled his agile eyebrows into a frown, took a long, deep breath so that his chest puffed out even more, like that of a frog or a toad, he made as if to undo his tie (not just loosen it this time), hid his green boots under the armchair like someone moving them smartly out of the reach of some biting creature, or, more symbolically, like someone beating an instinctive retreat, overcome by confusion. I thought he might be thinking: 'What are these sons-of-British-bitches playing at? They don't want this, they don't want that, what do they want me to say, the stupid bastards?'

'What is it you want?' he said after a few seconds, like someone who has grown tired of guessing and gives up, it didn't even sound like a question.

It was Tupra again who replied:

'Just tell us the truth, that's all, without trying to read our minds and without trying to please us.'

The soldier's response was instantaneous, and I translated it as precisely as I could, although it wasn't easy:

'Oh, the truth. The truth is what happens, the truth is when it happens, how can you expect me to tell you that now? Until it happens, nobody knows.'

Tupra seemed somewhat surprised and amused by this reply, half-philosophical, half-crass, or perhaps he was just confused by it. He did not waver in his demand though. Instead, he smiled, and made sure he had the final word:

'And often not even afterwards either. And sometimes it doesn't happen at all. It just doesn't. Nevertheless, that is what we want, you see: we're asking you for the impossible, according to you. And if, at the moment, you're not in a position to satisfy that demand, if you want to consult with your colleagues to see if that impossibility could become a possibility,' he paused, 'feel free. I understand that you will be staying a few more days in London. We will phone you before you leave, to see if you have achieved it – the great deed, the impossible. We have your number. Mulryan, would you be so kind as to show the gentleman out.' Then he turned to me, and without changing his tone and with barely a pause, said: 'Mr Deza, would you mind staying behind for a moment, please?'

The fake or real soldier got up, smoothed tie, jacket and trousers, made the unnecessary gesture of tucking in his shirt, picked up from the floor a briefcase he had placed next to his armchair and which he had not had the chance either to take up or open. He shook Tupra's hand and mine in a distracted, preoccupied, absent way (a soft, rather limp hand, perhaps because he was preoccupied). He said:

'I don't believe I have your number.'

'No, I don't believe you do,' was Tupra's response. 'Goodbye.'

'Sir?' murmured Mulryan before disappearing, while, with both hands, he drew shut the two leaves of the door of that very unbureaucratic office, it was more reminiscent of the rooms of the various Oxford dons I had known, Wheeler's, Cromer-Blake's, Clare Bayes's, full of shelves overflowing with books, with a globe that looked like a genuine antique, the whole room was dominated by wood and paper, I saw no base materials, not even metal, I saw no filing cabinets, no computer. Mulryan murmured the word as if he were asking, in the manner of a major-domo, 'Anything else, sir?', but he looked more as if he was standing to attention (there was, however, no click of the heels). He was clearly devoted to his superior.

And it was then, when we were alone, with Tupra seated behind his ample desk and me sitting opposite him, that, for the first time, he required of me something similar to what subsequently became my main task during the period that I remained in his employ, and which was related, too, in a way, to what Wheeler had half-explained to me on that Sunday in Oxford, in the morning and during lunch. Tupra ran a hand over his cheeks the colour of barley, always so close-shaven and smelling always of after-shave as if the lotion impregnated his skin or as if he were constantly, secretly, applying more, he smiled again, took out a cigarette which he placed loosely between his threatening lips (as if they were always pursed, ready to inhale), but he didn't light it for the moment, and so I didn't dare light mine either.

'Tell me what you thought of him.' And with a lift of his head, he gestured towards the double doors. 'What did you learn about him?' And when I hesitated (I wasn't sure what he meant, he hadn't asked me anything about the Chileans or the Mexicans), he added: 'Say anything, whatever comes into your head, go on.' He usually withstood silence very well, except when it went against his own wishes or decisions; then his permanent state of vehemence and tension seemed to demand that he keep the time filled up with things palpable, recognisable or countable. It was a different matter if the silence came from him.

'Well,' I said, 'I don't know quite what this Venezuelan gentleman wants from you. Support and financial help, I assume. I suppose he's preparing for, or considering the possibility of a coup against President Hugo Chávez, that much I gleaned. He was in plain clothes, but judging by his appearance and by what he said, he could be a military man. Or, rather, I assume he's presented himself to you as such.'

'What else? Anyone in your place and in your role could have deduced that, Mr Deza.'

'What do you mean "what else", Mr Tupra?'

'What makes you think he was a military man? Have you ever seen a Venezuelan military man?'

'No. Well, only on television, like everyone else. Chávez is a military man, he calls himself *Comandante*, or Major, doesn't he, or Sub-Lieutenant, or perhaps Parachutist-in-Chief, I don't know. But naturally I can't be sure that this gentleman was a military man. I'm just saying that he probably presented himself to you as that. Or so I imagine.'

'We'll come back to that later. What do you think of the plot, the threat of a coup against a government elected by a popular vote, more than that, by popular acclaim?'

'I think it's terrible, the worst possible thing that could happen. Remember that my country suffered for forty years because of just such a coup. Three years of romantic war perhaps (romantic at least to English eyes), followed by thirty-seven years of destruction and oppression. But leaving theory aside, that is, leaving aside principles, I wouldn't really care in this particular case. Chávez led an attempted coup once, if I remember rightly. He conspired with his troops and rose up against an elected civilian government. True, it may have been a corrupt and thieving government, but then what government isn't nowadays, they handle far too much money and are more like businesses than governments, and businessmen want their profits. So he couldn't really complain if he was ousted. The Venezuelan people are another matter. They might. Except that there seem to have been quite a few complaints already about this leader whom they elected by popular acclaim. Being elected doesn't immunise a leader against becoming a dictator.'

'You seem very well informed.'

'I read the newspapers, I watch television. That's all.'

'Tell me more. Tell me if the Venezuelan gentleman was telling the truth.'

'About what?'

'Generally. For example, as to whether, if it came to it, they would touch the *Comandante* or not.'

'He said two different things about that.'

Tupra looked slightly irritated, but only slightly. He gave me the impression that he was enjoying himself, that he liked this conversation and my quickness, once I had got over my initial hesitancy and once stimulated by his questioning, Tupra was a great one for asking questions, he never forgot what people had said in reply and so was able to return to that reply when the interrogatee least expected it and had forgotten about it, we forget what we say much more than what we hear, what we write much more than what we read, what we send much more than what we receive, that is why we barely count the insults we hand out to others, unlike those dealt out to us, which is why almost everyone harbours some grudge against someone.

'I know that, Mr Deza. I'm asking you if either of those two things is true. In your opinion. Please.'

That 'please' worried me. Later on, I learned that he always resorted to such formulae, 'if you would be so kind', 'if you wouldn't mind' when he was about to get really annoyed. On that occasion, I merely sensed this and so hastened to respond, without giving much thought to what I said and having given it no previous thought at all.

'In my opinion, one was not true at all. The other was, but the context in which it was given wasn't.'

'Explain that, will you?' He had still not lit the dangling cigarette, which, despite having a filter, would surely be getting soggy, I was familiar with the extravagant brand, Rameses II, Egyptian cigarettes made from slightly spicy-tasting Turkish tobacco, the lavish red packet on the desk looked like a drawing from *Tintin*, they would be very expensive nowadays, he must have bought them from Davidoff or Marcovitch or Smith & Sons (if the last two still exist), I didn't recall him smoking them at Wheeler's house, perhaps he only smoked them in private. I didn't apply a match to my more commonplace cigarette either, although mine was still dry, my lips are not moist.

I merely improvised, that's all. I had nothing to lose. Nor to gain either, I had been summoned to act as translator and had performed that role. Remaining there was a courtesy on my part, although Tupra did not make me feel this to be the case, rather, perhaps, the opposite, for he was one of those rare individuals who can ask for a loan and manage to make the person giving the loan feel that he is the debtor.

'It didn't ring true to me at all that they were prepared to shoot the Lord High Parachutist, even if the success or failure of the operation depended on it. I did, therefore, believe him when he said that they wouldn't cause him any physical harm, if it turned out they couldn't get rid of him.'

'And what was the untrue context for this truth?'

'Well, as I say, I don't know why this gentleman came to see you, or what he wants to get out of you . . .'

'Oh, nothing from me, or from us, we have nothing to give,' broke in Tupra. 'They sent him to us merely so that we could pass judgement, that is, give our opinion on how convincing or truthful he is. That's why I'm interested to know your views, you speak the same language, or perhaps it isn't the same any more. I mean, I can't understand half the dialogue in some American films, they'll have to start adding subtitles soon when they show them over here, maybe it's the same with Latin American Spanish. There are subtleties of vocabulary, expressions I can't recognise or appreciate in translation. Other sorts of subtlety I can, precisely because I can't understand what someone is saying, and that sometimes proves very useful. Words distract sometimes, you see, and hearing only the melody, the music, is often fundamental. Now tell me what you think.'

Armed with boldness and indifference, I decided to improvise some more. I could hold out no longer, though, and finally lit a cigarette, not mine, however, but an expensive Rameses II, to which I asked his permission to help myself (he agreed of course, and didn't seem at all put out, although each cigarette must have cost around fifty pence).

'My impression is that there are no serious plans for a *coup d'état*. Or if there are, then this man will play no part in it or will have very little say in the matter. I assume you've checked his identity. If he's a soldier in exile or no longer in the army, or retired, an opponent with contacts in the country, but who acts from outside, then it's likely that his task is to raise funds based on nothing or based only on the vaguest of plans and on very tenuous information. And his own pockets may be the final destination for whatever money he does collect, after all, people tend not to ask questions or provide answers about money spent on abortive clandestine operations. If, on the other hand, he still is a soldier and has some authority, and is living in the country, and presents himself to us as someone regretfully betraying his leader for the good of the nation, then it's not impossible that the *Comandante* himself has sent him, to put out some feelers, to get in early, to make some enquiries, to be forewarned, and, if the opportunity arises, to raise funds from abroad that will doubtless end up in Chávez's own pockets, quite a clever move really. I also think that he might be neither one nor the other, that is, that he may not be and may never have been a military man. Anyway, I don't think he's behind anything serious, anything that would actually happen. As he himself said, the truth is what happens, which is a rough-and-ready way of saying just that. I would guess that this plan of his is never going to come to anything, with or without support, with or without financial help, internal, external or interplanetary.' I had got carried away by my own boldness, I stopped. I wondered if Tupra would say something now, even if only about the title under which the Venezuelan had presented himself to him (I had deliberately said 'presents himself to us', seeing that I was now included). 'If he doesn't,' I thought, 'he's obviously one of those people who is impossible to draw out, and who only says what he really means or what he knows he can safely reveal.' 'All this is pure speculation, of course,' I added. 'Impressions, intuitions. You did ask me for my impressions.'

Now he too lit his cigarette, his precious, saliva-sodden Rameses II. He probably couldn't stand to see me enjoying mine, or, rather, his, fifty pence going up in smoke in someone else's mouth, in, what's more, a continental mouth. He coughed a little after the first puff of that piquant Egyptian blend, perhaps he only smoked two or three a day and never quite got used to it.

'Yes, I realise you can't know anything for sure,' he said. 'Don't worry. I don't either, or not much more. But, tell me, why do you think that?'

I continued to improvise, or so I thought.

'Well, the man definitely looks the part of the Latin American military man, I'm afraid they're not much different from their Spanish counterparts twenty or twenty-five years ago, they all have moustaches and they never smile. His appearance just cried out for a uniform, a cap, and a super-abundance of medals festooning his chest, as if they were cartridge belts. Yet there were some details that just didn't fit. They made me think that he wasn't a military man disguised as a civilian, as I at first thought, but a civilian disguised as a military man disguised as a civilian, if you see what I mean. They're really insignificant details,' I said apologetically. 'And it's not as if I've had many dealings with the military, I'm hardly an expert.' I broke off, my momentary boldness was fading.

'That doesn't matter. And I do see what you mean. Tell me, what details?'

'Well, they're really tiny things. He used, how can I put it, inappropriate language. Either soldiers nowadays aren't what they used to be, and have been infected by the ridiculous pedantry of politicians and television newscasters, or the man simply isn't a military man; or he was, but hasn't seen active service for a long time. And that gesture of tucking in his shirt was too spontaneous, like someone used to civilian clothes. I know it's silly, and soldiers do sometimes wear a suit and tie, or a shirt if it's hot, and it is hot in Venezuela. I just felt that he wasn't a soldier, or else had been out of the army and hadn't worn an army jacket for some time, or had been removed from his post, I don't know. Or hadn't worn even a *guayabera* or a *liki-liki* or whatever they call them over there, they're always worn outside the trousers. And I felt, too, he was overly preoccupied with the crease in his trousers, and with creases in general, but then you get vain, dapper officers everywhere.'

'You can say that again,' said Tupra. '*Liki-liki*,' he said, but didn't ask any more. 'Go on.'

'Well, perhaps you noticed his boots. Short boots. They may have looked black from a distance or in a bad light, but they were bottle-green in colour and looked like crocodile, or possibly alligator. I can't imagine any high-ranking officer wearing footwear like that, not even on his days of absolute leisure or total abandon. They seemed more suited to a drug-dealer or a ranch-hand on the loose in the big city or something.' I felt like a minor Sherlock or, rather, a fake Holmes. I leaned back my chair a little in the sudden hope of catching sight of Tupra's feet. I hadn't noticed what he was wearing, and it had suddenly occurred to me that he might be wearing similar boots and that I might be making a grave mistake. He was an Englishman: it was unlikely, but one never knows and he did have a strange surname. And he always wore a vest, a bad sign that. As it turned out, I was unlucky, I couldn't get far enough back, the desk prevented me from seeing his feet. I went on – although if he was himself sporting some rather eccentric footwear, I was only making matters worse: 'Of course, in a country where the Commander-in-Chief appears in public dressed to look like the national flag and wearing a beret that's a shade of brothel red, as he did recently on television, it's not impossible that his generals and colonels do wear boots like that, or sabots or even ballet shoes, in these histrionic times and with a role model like him, anything's possible.'

'Sabots?' asked Tupra, perhaps more out of amusement than because he hadn't understood me. 'Sabots?' he said, since that was the term I had used: thanks to the translation classes I taught in Oxford and to my time spent toiling for various slave-drivers, I know the most absurd words in English.

'Yes, you know, those wooden shoes with pointed tips like onions. Nurses wear them and the Flemish, of course, at least they do in their paintings. I think geishas do as well, don't they, with socks?'

Tupra gave a short laugh, and so did I. Perhaps he had had a sudden image of the Venezuelan gentleman wearing clogs. Or perhaps Chávez himself, in thick-soled clogs and white socks. On a first meeting and at a party, Tupra struck one as a nice man. He did on a second meeting too and in his office, although there he let it be understood that he could never entirely forget the serious nature of his work, nor be entirely contained by it either.

'Did you say he dresses to look like the national flag? You presumably meant draped in the flag, did you?' he added.

'No,' I said. 'The print on his shirt or army jacket, I can't remember quite what he was wearing, was the flag itself, complete with stars.'

'Stars? I can't remember the Venezuelan flag at the moment. Stars?' To my relief, he did not appear to have taken my comments about the shoes personally.

'It's striped, I think. A red stripe and a yellow one, I seem to recall, and possibly a blue one too. And there's a sprinkling of stars on it somewhere. The President was definitely adorned with stars, of that I'm sure, and broad stripes, an army jacket or a shirt with horizontal stripes in those colours or similar. And stars. It was probably a *liki-liki*, which is a shirt they wear for special occasions, I think, well, they do in Colombia, I'm not sure about Venezuela.'

'Stars indeed,' he said. He gave another short laugh, and I did too. Laughter creates a kind of disinterested bond between men, and between women, and the bond it establishes between women and men can prove an even stronger, tighter link, a profounder, more complex, more dangerous and more lasting link, or one, at least, with more hope of enduring. Such lasting, disinterested bonds can become strained after a while, they can sometimes become ugly and difficult to bear, in the long term, someone has to be the debtor, that's the only way things can work, one person must always be slightly more indebted to the other, and commitment and abnegation and worthiness can provide a sure way of making off with the position of creditor. I've often laughed with Luisa like that, briefly and unexpectedly, both of us seeing the funny side of something quite independently, both us laughing briefly at the same time. With other women too, with my sister first of all; and with a few others. The quality of that laughter, its spontaneity (its simultaneity with mine perhaps) has led me, on occasions, to meet a woman and approach her or even to dismiss her at once, and with some women it's as if I've seen them in their entirety before even meeting them, without even talking, without them having looked at me and with me barely having looked at them. On the other hand, even a slight delay or the faintest suspicion of mimetism, of an indulgent response to my stimulus or my lead, the merest suggestion of a polite or sycophantic laugh – a laugh that is not entirely disinterested, but is egged on by the will, the laugh that does not laugh as much as it would like to or as much as it allows itself or yearns or even condescends to laugh – is enough for me promptly to remove myself from its presence or to relegate it immediately to second place, to that of mere accompaniment, or even, in times of weakness and a consequent slide in standards, to that of cortège. But the other kind of laughter – Luisa's, which almost anticipates our own laughter, my sister's, which wraps around us, young Pérez Nuix's, which fuses with our own and about which there is no hint of deliberation and in which we two are almost forgotten (although there is also detachment and arbitrariness and equality) – I have tended to give that a prime role which has subsequently turned out to be lasting or not, even dangerous at times, and, in the long run (when it has lasted that long), difficult to sustain without the appearance or intervention of some small debt, whether real or symbolic. However, the absence or diminution of that laughter is even harder to bear, and always brings with it the day when one of the two is obliged to get a little deeper into debt. Luisa had withdrawn her laughter from me some time ago, or else was rationing it out, I couldn't believe she had lost it entirely, she would still, surely, offer it to others, but when someone withdraws their laughter from us, that is a sign that there is nothing more to be done. It is a disarming laugh. It disarms women and, in a different way, men too. I have desired women – intensely – for their laughter alone, and they have usually seen that this was so. And sometimes I have known who someone was simply by hearing their laugh or by never hearing it, the brief, unexpected laugh, and even what would happen between that person and me, whether friendship or conflict or irritation or nothing, and I haven't been far wrong either, it might have taken some time to happen, but it always has, and, besides, there's always time as long as you don't die or as long as neither that other person nor I should die. That was Tupra's laugh and mine too, and so I had to ask myself for a moment whether, in the future, he or I would be disarmed, or if, perhaps, both of us would. '*Liki-liki,*' he said again. It's impossible not to repeat such a word, irresistible. 'Yes, but it's true, is it not, that one cannot judge the customs of another place from outside?' he added drily or only half-seriously.

'True, true,' I replied, knowing that what he had said was not (true, I mean) for either of us.

'Anything else?' he asked. He had given nothing away, not about the man's identity (I wasn't expecting him to), but not even about the supposed status or position of the Venezuelan to whom I had served as interpreter twice over. I had another go:

'Could you give the gentleman a name? Just in case we have to refer to him again.'

Tupra did not hesitate. As if he had an answer already prepared for any attempt at probing, rather than for my curiosity.

'That seems unlikely. As far as you're concerned, Mr Deza, his name is Bonanza,' he said, again mock-seriously.

'Bonanza?' He must have noticed my amazement, I couldn't help pronouncing the 'z' as it is pronounced in my own country, or at least in part of it and, of course, in Madrid. To his English ears it would sound something like 'Bonantha', just as Deza would sound something like 'Daytha'.

'Yes, isn't that a Spanish name? Like Ponderosa?' he said. 'Anyway, he'll be Bonanza to you and me. Did you notice anything else?'

'Only to confirm my initial impression, Mr Tupra: General Bonanza or Mr Bonanza, whoever he really is, would never make an attempt on Chávez's life. Of that you can be sure, whether it suits your interests or not. He admires him too much, even if he is his enemy, which I don't think he is.'

Tupra picked up the striking red packet with its pharaohs and gods and offered me a second Rameses II, an uncommon gesture in the British Isles, clearly no expense was being spared, Turkish tobacco, a piquant Egyptian blend, and I accepted. But it turned out to be one for the road, not to be smoked immediately, for at the same time as he was giving it to me, he stood up and walked around the desk to show me out, indicating the door with a slight gesture. I took the opportunity to glance down at his shoes, they were sober brown lace-ups, I needn't have worried. He noticed, he noticed almost everything, all the time.

'Is something wrong with my shoes?' he asked.

'No, no, they're very nice. And very clean too. Splendid, enviable,' I said. Unlike my black pair, also lace-ups. The truth was that, in London, I just didn't have the discipline to clean them every day. There are some things one gets lazy about when away from home and living abroad. Except that I *was* at home, that is, as I kept forgetting, I had no other home for the moment, sometimes force of habit insisted on my feeling the impossible, that I could still go back.

'I'll tell you where to buy them another day.' He was about to open the door for me, he had still not done so, he remained for a matter of seconds with a hand on each of the handles of the double door. He turned his head, looked at me out of the corner of his eye but did not see me, he couldn't, I was immediately behind him. It was the first time during the whole of that session that his active, friendly, unwittingly mocking eyes had not met mine. I could see only his long lashes, in profile. They would be even more the envy of the ladies in profile. 'Earlier on, if I remember rightly, you said something about "leaving aside principles". Or perhaps "leaving theory aside".'

'Yes, I think I did say something like that.'

'I was wondering.' He still had his hands on the door handles. 'Allow me to ask you a question: up to what point would you be capable of leaving aside your principles? I mean up to what point do you usually? That is, disregard it, theory I mean? It's something we all do now and then; we couldn't live otherwise, whether out of convenience, fear or need. Or out of a sense of sacrifice or generosity. Out of love, out of hate. To what extent do you?' he repeated. 'Do you understand?'

That was when I realised that not only did he notice everything all the time, he recorded and stored it away too. I didn't like the word 'sacrifice', it had a similar effect on me to the expression he had used in Wheeler's house, 'serving my country'. He had even added: 'one should if one can, don't you think?' Although he had immediately diluted this with: 'even if the service one does is indirect and done mainly to benefit oneself'. I too recorded and stored things away, more than is normal.

'It depends on the reason,' I replied, and then went on to use a plural since it was, as I understood it, only my principles he was asking me about. 'I can leave them aside almost completely if it's just a matter of conversation, less so if I'm called on to make a judgement. Still less if I'm judging friends, because then I'm partial. When it comes to taking action, hardly at all.'

'Mr Deza, thank you for your co-operation. I hope to be in touch with you again.' He said this in an appreciative, almost affectionate tone. And this time he did open the door, both leaves at once. I saw his eyes again, more blue than grey in the morning light, but still pale, and always seemingly amused by whatever the dialogue or situation happened to be, attentive and always absorbing, as if they honoured what they were looking at, or at which they did not even need to be looking: whatever entered his field of vision. 'Please be quite clear, however, that here we have no interests,' he went on to say, even though he was referring to something from further back in the conversation. Most people would not have returned to it, they would not have retrieved that extremely marginal comment of mine ('whether it suits your interests or not'), it's incredible how quickly words, pronounced and written, frivolous and serious, all of them, insignificant or significant, get lost, become distant and are left behind. That's why it's necessary to repeat, eternally and absurdly to repeat, from the first human babble of sound and even from the first index finger silently pointing. Again and again and again and, vainly, again. Words did not slip quite so easily from our grasp, his and mine, but this was doubtless an anomaly, a curse. 'We merely give our opinion and only when asked, of course. As you so kindly did now, when I asked you.' And he again gave that brief laugh, revealing small, bright teeth. It sounded to me like a polite or possibly impatient laugh, and this time, mine did not accompany his.

I was never told directly whether or not I had been right in any way about Colonel Bonanza from Caracas or, should I say, from exile and abroad, I was never told the results, and certainly not directly: they were not my concern, or, possibly, anyone else's. Probably sometimes there were no results, and the statements or reports would simply be filed away, just in case. And if decisions had to be taken about something (the support and financial backing for a coup, for example), they would doubtless be taken by the various people in charge – by those who had commissioned each report or requested our opinions – with no possibility of verification or certainty and purely at their own risk, that is, trusting or not trusting, accepting or rejecting what Tupra and his people had seen and thought, or perhaps recommended.

At first, though, I innocently assumed that I must have got something right, because not many days after that morning of dual interpretation, of language and intentions – the latter imprecise, but let's call it interpretation anyway – it was suggested that I abandon my post with BBC Radio and work exclusively (or principally) for Tupra, alongside the devoted Mulryan, young Pérez Nuix and the others, with, in theory, very flexible working hours and a considerably larger salary, I had no complaints on that score, on the contrary, I would be able to send more money home. The feeling of having success-fully passed an exam was unavoidable, as was my joining whatever that organisation was, I didn't ask myself much about it then or later or now, because it was always very vague (and lack of definition was its essence), and because Sir Peter Wheeler had warned me about it in a way, or given me enough of a warning: 'You won't find anything about this in any books, none of them, not even the oldest or the most modern, not even the most exhaustive accounts being published now, Knightley, Cecil, Dorril, Davies, or Stafford, Miller, Bennett, I don't know, there are so many of them, but you won't find so much as a cryptic reference in the books that were, in their day, and which continue to be, the most cryptic of all, Rowan, Denham. Don't even bother consulting them. You won't find so much as an allusion. It'll be a waste of your time and your patience.' Throughout that Sunday in Oxford, he always spoke to me not in half-truths exactly, but at most in three-quarter-truths, never in whole truths. Perhaps he didn't know what they were, the whole truths, that is, perhaps no one did, not even Tupra, or Rylands when he was alive. Perhaps there were no truths.

The work got off to a gradual start, by which I mean that once the contract had been agreed, they began giving me or asking me to undertake various tasks, which then increased in number, at a brisk but steady rate, and, after only a month, possibly less, I was a full-time employee, or so it seemed to me. These tasks took various forms, although their essence varied little or not at all, since this consisted in listening and noticing and interpreting and reporting back, in deciphering behaviours, attitudes, characters and scruples, indifferences and beliefs, egotisms, ambitions, loyalties, weaknesses, strengths, truths and contradictions; indecisiveness. What I interpreted were – in just three words – stories, people, lives. Often stories that had not yet happened. People who did not know themselves and who could not have said about themselves even a tenth of what I saw in them, or was urged to see in them and to put into words, that was my job. Lives that could even come to an early end and not even last long enough to be called lives, unknown lives and lives still to be lived. Sometimes they asked me to be present and to help in asking questions, if any occurred to me, at interviews or meetings (or perhaps polite interrogations, with nothing intimidating about them), even though there was no problem of comprehension, no language to translate, and everything was in English and amongst fellow Britons. At other times, they did use me as an interpreter of language, Spanish and even Italian, but over the whole range of talks and supervisions (which is what my silent activities were called), that was what I did least of, and anyway now I never merely translated words, at the end, I was always asked for my opinion, almost, sometimes, for my prognosis, or, how can I put it, my wager. On other occasions, they preferred me to be an absent presence, and I would witness the conversations held by Tupra or Mulryan or young Nuix or Rendel with their visitors from a kind of booth next to Tupra's office, from which one could see and hear what was going on without being seen, just like in a police station. The elongated oval mirror in Tupra's office corresponded in the booth to a window of identical size and shape: clear glass from one side, from the other a mirrored surface that did not arouse the slightest suspicion amongst all those books and in what looked more like a club or a private drawing-room than an office. The booth was an older, home-made version of the invisible hiding-places from which the victim of a mugging or the witnesses of a crime view a line-up of suspects, or from which the superior officers secretly oversee the interrogations of detainees and make sure that the police don't overdo the slaps or the flicks with a wet towel. It must have been a pioneering booth, perhaps adapted or made in the 1940s or even the 1930s: it seemed to have been conceived as a small-scale imitation of a train compartment from that period or even earlier, all in wood, with two narrow benches facing each other and placed at right angles to the oval window, with a fixed table between the benches on which to take notes or lean one's elbows. One was thus obliged to supervise from a somewhat oblique angle, sideways on, with the inevitable feeling that one was looking out of a train window while travelling along, or, rather, while permanently stopped at a station, a strange station-studio, far more welcoming than any real station, where the landscape was an unvarying interior in which only the people changed, the visitors and the hosts, although the latter had only limited permutations, usually two or, at most, three, Tupra and Mulryan, or them plus me (as at the meeting with Comandante Bonanza), or Tupra and young Nuix and Rendel if they needed someone who spoke German or Russian or Dutch or Ukrainian (it was said that Rendel was originally from Austria, and that his surname had initially been Rendl or Randl or Redl or Reinl or even Handl, and that he had half-anglicised it, Randall or Rendell or Rendall or Randell would have been more usual, but not Haendel), or Mulryan and me and some other less assiduous assistant, or young Nuix, Tupra and me . . . He and Mulryan (or more likely one of the two) were always there. And given that I sometimes had to occupy the booth, I could only suppose that when I was on the other side, in the station-studio, one of those not present would be posted in the booth to watch us, although I wasn't entirely sure of this at first; and I could only imagine that on that first occasion with Captain Bonanza, Rendel and young Nuix ('I hope it was her,' I thought) would have been in the reserved carriage, eyes trained on the lieutenant, but almost certainly on me as well, and that afterwards they would have given their objective report on me as well as on the sergeant (he was gradually being demoted in my memory), the report of someone invisible is always more objective and dispassionate and reliable, that of someone who sits unseen and at ease, observing with impunity, is always more objective than that of someone who is looked at by his inter-locutors and intervenes and speaks, and can never observe for very long in silence without creating enormous tensions, an embarrassing situation.

That is doubtless why television is such a success, because

you can see and watch people as you never can in real life unless you hide, and even then, in real life, you only have one angle and one distance, or two if you're using binoculars, I sometimes put them in my pocket when I leave the house, and at home I always keep them handy. Whereas the screen gives you the opportunity to spy at your leisure and to see more and therefore know more, because you're not worrying about making eye contact or exposed in turn to being judged, nor do you have to divide your concentration or attention between a dialogue (or its simulacrum) in which you are taking part and the cold study of a face, of gestures and vocal inflections, even certain pores, of tics and hesitations, of pauses and dry mouths, of vehemence and falsehoods. And inevitably you pass judgement, you immediately utter some kind of verdict (or you don't utter it, but say it to yourself), it only takes a matter of seconds and there's nothing you can do about it, even if it's only rudimentary and takes the least elaborate of forms, which is liking or disliking (which are nevertheless judgements or their possible anticipation, what usually precedes them, although many people never take that step or cross that line, and so never go beyond a simple and inexplicable feeling of attraction or repulsion: inexplicable to them, since they never take that step and so remain for ever on the surface). And you surprise yourself by saying, almost involuntarily, sitting alone before the screen: 'I really like him,' 'I can't stand that guy,' 'I could eat her up,' 'He's such a pain,' 'I'd do anything he asked,' 'She deserves a good slap on the face,' 'Fathead,' 'He's lying,' 'She's just pretending to feel pity,' 'He's going to find life really tough,' 'What a schmuck,' 'She's an angel,' 'He's so conceited, so proud,' 'They're such phonies, those two,' 'Poor thing, poor thing,' 'I'd shoot him this minute, without batting an eye,' 'I feel so sorry for her,' 'He drives me absolutely crazy,' 'She's pretending,' 'How can he be so naïve,' 'What nerve,' 'She's such an intelligent woman,' 'He disgusts me,' 'He really tickles me.' The register is infinite, there's room for everything. And that instant verdict is spot-on, or so it feels when it comes (less so a second later). It carries a weight of conviction without having been subjected to a single argument. Without a single reason to sustain it.

That is why they also gave me videos. I would sometimes watch them right there, in that building with no name, just a number, with no sign or notice or any obvious function, alone or accompanied by young Nuix or by Mulryan or Rendel; and sometimes I would take them home, to look at them more closely, to unpick them and later present my report, which was, almost always, purely oral, they rarely asked me for anything in writing, at least not so much later on, because I do seem to have written quite a few.

There were all kinds of things on those videos, they contained the most heterogeneous subject-matter imaginable, often all jumbled up, almost crammed together on some tapes, while the content of others was more carefully grouped, and organised with more discernment, some were almost monographs: fragments of programmes or news bulletins that had been broadcast publicly, recorded from the television, and edited and put together later on (sometimes I had to sit through whole programmes, new and old, even programmes about people who were already dead, such as Lady Diana Spencer with her awful, mistake-ridden English and the writer Graham Greene with his impeccable English); parliamentary speeches, talks or press conferences given by prominent or obscure politicians, British or foreign, and by diplomats too; interrogations of prisoners in police cells and their subsequent testimony in the relevant court; as well as the sentences or warnings handed out by bewigged judges, yes, there were quite a lot of videos of severe judges, I don't know why; interviews with celebrities which did not always appear to have been made by journalists or intended to be shown, some had the air of informal or more or less private conversations, perhaps with hangers-on or people pretending to be fans (I remember seeing a priceless one with a buoyant Elton John, another nice one with the actor Sean Connery, the real James Bond who was kicked by Rosa Klebb in *From Russia with Love*, those deadly blades, and another equally funny one with the ex-footballer and drinker George Best; a terrible one with the businessman Rupert Murdoch and a rather pompous and comic one with Lord Archer, the ex-politician – he had, by then, been sent to prison for lying about something or other, I can't remember what – and author of a few somewhat contrived action novels); at other times, the names rang a bell, but they weren't famous enough for me to be able to identify them, perhaps they were very local luminaries (there wasn't always any indication of who was speaking, sometimes none at all, just a few letters and numbers next to each face deemed to be of interest or a valid subject for interpretation – A2, BH13, Gm9 and so on – to which I could refer subsequently in my reports); there were also interviews or scenes with anonymous people in various circumstances, often filmed, I think, without their knowledge and without, therefore, their consent: someone looking for work or offering to do something, anything, some were really desperate; a granite-faced functionary (rolling his eyes) listening to some member of the public telling him his problems, doubtless in the former's municipal or ministerial office; a couple arguing in a hotel room; a man in a bank asking for a loan at a highly disadvantageous interest rate; four Chelsea fans in a pub, preparing to crush Liverpool by virtue of vast quantities of booze and vociferous enthusiasm; a business lunch put on by some company or other, with twenty or so guests (not the whole thing, fortunately, just highlights and a speech at the end); a university don giving an appalling seminar; the occasional lecture (not the whole thing, unfortunately, I saw a very interesting one by a lecturer at Cambridge, about literature that has never existed); the sermon (the whole thing this time) by an Anglican bishop who seemed slightly inebriated; the oral exams for students wanting to enter a particular university; a doctor giving a smug, detailed, verbose diagnosis; girls answering strange questions at casting sessions, perhaps for an advertisement or something far worse, all too monosyllabic for me to find out. Sometimes, the videos were obviously home-made or very personal, and consequently more mysterious (I couldn't help wondering how they had reached us and consequently me, unless we had private clients too): the patriarchal Christmas greeting of some absentee who clearly thought he was much missed and needed; the message of a rich man (presumably posthumous or intended to be) explaining to heirs and dispossessed alike the reasoning behind his arbitrary, capricious, disappointing and deliberately unfair will; the declaration of love by a sick man of self-confessed (or more likely alleged) timidity, who claimed he could not bear to experience 'live' the intended recipient's refusal, which he said he knew was inevitable, but which he clearly didn't think was inevitable at all, you could tell by the way he spoke. And this was just the British material, as the greater part of it was, of course. I became aware of the number of occasions and places where people are or can be recorded or filmed: to begin with, in nearly every situation in which we are submitted to a test or an exam, shall we say, and in which we are asking for something, a job, a loan, a chance, a favour, a subsidy, a reference, an alibi. And, of course, clemency. I saw that whenever we ask for something, we are exposed, defenceless, at the almost absolute mercy of the person giving or refusing. And nowadays we are recorded, immortalised, often when we are at our most humble, or, if you prefer, humiliated. But also in any public or semi-public place, the most obvious and flagrant ones being hotel rooms, it seems normal now that we will be filmed at a bank, a shop, a gas station, a casino, a sports arena, a parking lot, a government building.

I was rarely told in advance what I should look out for, what character traits, what degree of sincerity, or what specific intentions I should try to decipher in each indicated person or face, when, that is, I took work home. The following day, or a few days later, I would have a session with Mulryan or Tupra or with both, and they would ask me then whatever they wanted to know, sometimes one small detail and sometimes a great deal, it all depended, referring to the people in the videos by their respective names if these appeared in the films or were so well known as to be unmistakable, or, if not, by their assigned letters and numbers: 'Do you think that, despite his words of contrition, Mr Stewart is defrauding the tax office again? He got caught five years ago, but he came to an agreement and paid more than he owed to avoid any problems, so might he, therefore, believe that he is now free of suspicion?' 'Do you think FH6 intended to repay the loan when he applied to Barclays for it? Or did he never intend paying it back at all? He was given the loan three months ago, you see, and hasn't been seen since.' I would say what I thought or what I could, and then we would pass on to the next one, in the briefer, more practical and prosaic cases, that is. Most cases, however, were not like that at all, they were elusive and complex, often vague and even ethereal, always tricky to respond to, more like those that Wheeler had dealt with in his day and which he had forecast for my day too, or, rather, which he had suggested would come my way, even though there was no war on; that, sooner or later, they would be brought to me for my opinion. And for that majority of cases one needed in effect what he had distractedly called – as if to play down the solemnity of those two expressions, which appeared, at least initially or, indeed, not even then, to be contradictory – 'the courage to see' and 'the irresponsibility of seeing'. For a long time, I was far more conscious of the latter, until I got used to it and, when I did, stopped worrying. And then . . . Ah, then, it's true, came the great irresponsibility.

The process of getting used to it, however, had been started by Wheeler on that Sunday in Oxford when he also talked to me about myself. Or perhaps by Toby Rylands, who had, at some point, already spoken to Wheeler about me, and had singled me out as someone of like mind, made of the same clay from which they had been shaped. But, no, it wasn't Rylands, because it isn't what is said of us behind our backs which changes things – which transforms things inside ourselves – it is what someone with authority or armed with mere insistence tells us about ourselves to our face that reveals and explains and tempts us to believe. It is the danger that stalks every artist or politician, or anyone whose work is subject to people's opinions and interpretations. If a film director, writer or musician begins to be described as a genius, a prodigy, a reinventor, a giant, they can all too easily end up thinking that it might be true. They then become conscious of their own worth, and become afraid of disappointing or – which is even more ridiculous and nonsensical, but it can't be put in any other way – of not living up to themselves, that is, to the people it turns out they were – or so others tell them, and as they now realise they are – in their previous exalted creations. 'So it wasn't just a product of chance or intuition or even of my own freedom,' they might think, 'there was coherence and purpose in everything I was doing, what an honour to discover this, but what a curse too. Because now I have no option but to abide by that and to reach the same wretched heights in order not to let myself down, how awful, what an effort, and what a disaster for my work.' And this can happen to anyone, even if neither their work nor their personality is public, they have only to hear a plausible explanation of their inclinations or behaviour, an incantatory description of their actions or an analysis of their character, an evaluation of their methods – and to know that such a thing exists, or is attributed to them – for them to lose their blessedly mutable course, unforeseeable and uncertain, and with it their freedom. We tend to think that there is some hidden order unknown to us and also a plot of which we would like to form a conscious part, and if we glimpse a single episode of that plot in which there seems to be room for us, if we sense that we are caught up in its weak wheel even for an instant, then it is hard for us ever again to be able to imagine ourselves torn from that half-glimpsed, partial, intuited plot – a mere figment of the imagination. There is nothing worse than looking for a meaning or believing there is one. Or if there is one, even worse: believing that the meaning of something, even of the most trivial detail, could depend on us and on our actions, on our intention or our function, believing that there is such a thing as the will or fate, and even some complicated combination of the two. Believing that we do not owe ourselves entirely to the most erratic and forgetful, rambling and crazy of chances, and that we should be expected to be consistent with what we said or did, yesterday or the day before. Believing that we might contain in ourselves coherence and deliberation, as the artist believes is true of his work or the potentate of his decisions, but only once someone has persuaded them that this is so.

Wheeler had, in the end, begun at the beginning, if anything ever really has a beginning. Anyway, that Sunday morning, when I woke up much later than I would have wanted to and, of course, much later than he was expecting me to, he allowed himself no further preambles or postponements or circumlocutions, in so far as it was possible for him entirely to renounce such long-established characteristics of thought and conversation. The incomplete words he had at his disposal to tell me what he was going to tell me were, I suppose, mystery and limitation enough. As soon as he saw me come downstairs looking sleepy and ill-shaven (just a quick once-over with the razor so as to appear presentable or not, at least, too thuggish), he urged me to take a seat opposite him and to the right of Mrs Berry, who occupied one end of the table at which they both just had breakfast. He waited until she had very kindly poured me some coffee, but not until I had drunk it or woken up a bit. On the half of the table unoccupied by table-cloth and plates and cups and jams and fruit lay open a large, bulky volume, there were always books everywhere. I had only to glance at it (the attraction of the printed word) for Peter to say in urgent tones, doubtless because he had not counted on such a late awakening on my part:

'Pick it up, go on. I got it out to show you.'

I drew the volume to me, but before reading a single line, I half-closed it – with one finger keeping the place – to have a look at the spine and see what the book was.

'*Who's Who?*' It was a rhetorical question, because it clearly was *Who's Who*, with its rich red cover, the guide to the more or less illustrious, that year's United Kingdom edition.

'Yes, *Who's Who*, Jacobo. I bet you've never thought of looking me up in that, have you? My name is on that page, where it's open. Read what it says, will you, go on.'

I looked, I searched, there were quite a few Wheelers, Sir Mark and Sir Mervyn, a certain Muir Wheeler and the Honourable Sir Patrick and the Very Reverend Philip Welsford Richmond Wheeler, and there he was, between the two last names: 'Wheeler, Prof. Sir Peter', which was followed by a parenthesis, which I did not, at first, understand, which said: '(Edward Lionel Wheeler)'. It only took me two seconds, though, to remember that Peter used to sign his writings 'P. E. Wheeler', and that the E was for Edward, so the parenthesis was only there to record his name in its official entirety.

'Lionel?' I asked. Another rhetorical question, although less so this time. I was surprised by that third name, which had always seemed so actorly, doubtless because of Lionel Barrymore, and because of Lionel Atwill, who played arch-enemy Professor Moriarty to the great Basil Rathbone's Sherlock Holmes, and because of Lionel Stander who was persecuted in America by Senator McCarthy and had to go into exile in England in order to continue working (and become a bogus Englishman). And then there was Lionel Johnson, but he was a poet friend of Wilde and Yeats, a man from whom John Gawsworth claimed descendance (John Gawsworth, the literary pseudonym of the man who was in real life Terence Ian Fytton Armstrong, that secretive writer, beggar and king, with whom I had been rather obsessed during my time teaching in Oxford all those years ago: his fanciful ancestry also included Jacobite nobles, namely, the Stuarts, the dramatist Ben Jonson, Shakespeare's contemporary, and the supposed 'Dark Lady' of the sonnets, Mary Fitton, the courtesan). 'Lionel?' I said again with just a hint of mockery, which did not escape Wheeler.

'Yes, Lionel. I never use it, though, but there's nothing wrong with it, is there? Anyway, don't get distracted by trivia, that's not what matters, that isn't what I want you to see. Read on.'

I returned to the biographical note, but I had to stop almost at once and look up again, after reading the facts about his birth, which said: 'Born 24 October 1913, in Christchurch, New Zealand. Eldest son of Hugh Bernard Rylands and of the late Rita Muriel, *née* Wheeler. Adopted the surname Wheeler by deed poll in 1929.'

'Rylands?' This time there was nothing rhetorical about the question, just spontaneous, sincere astonishment. 'Rylands?' I repeated. There must have been a look of distrust in my eyes, and perhaps a suggestion of reproach. 'It's not, it can't be, can it? It can't just be coincidence.'

The look that Wheeler gave me reflected a mixture of patience and impatience, or of annoyance and paternalism, as if he had known I would stop there, at his father's unexpected surname, Rylands, and as if he accepted and understood my reaction, but also as if the matter bored him, or he saw it merely as a tiresome stage that had to be gone through before he could focus on whatever it was he really wanted to get to grips with. To judge by his expression, he could easily have said: 'No, that's not what matters either, Jacobo. Read on.' And he almost did, although not immediately, he showed me some consideration; but not without first making a vague attempt to avoid my reproaches:

'Oh, come on, you're not going to tell me you didn't know.'

'Peter.' My tone was one of clear warning and overt reproach, like the one I used with my children sometimes when they insisted on ignoring me so they wouldn't have to do as they were told.

'Well, I thought you knew, I could have sworn you did. In fact, I find it very odd that you don't.'

'Please, Peter. No one knows, not in Oxford. Or if they do, they keep very quiet about it, in fact, they've been unusually discreet. Do you think that if Aidan Kavanagh or Cromer-Blake had known about it, or Dewar or Rook or Carr, or Crowther-Hunt, or even Clare Bayes, do you think they wouldn't have told me?' They were old friends or colleagues from my time in Oxford, some less prone to gossip than others. Clare Bayes had been my lover too, I hadn't seen her or heard anything about her in ages, nor about her little boy Eric, who would no longer be a little boy, not now, he would have grown up. Perhaps I wouldn't even like her any more, my distant lover, if I saw her. Perhaps she wouldn't like me. Best not to see each other, best not. 'Did *you* know, Mrs Berry?'

Mrs Berry started a little, but did not hesitate to say:

'Oh, yes, I knew. But bear in mind, Jack, that I've worked for both brothers. And I tend to keep things to myself.' She, like all English people who had difficulty in pronouncing the name Jacques and who did not know that the name could be converted into Spanish as Jaime or Jacobo or Diego, always called me Jack (a phonetic approximation), the diminutive of John or Juan, but not of James. When they stopped addressing me as 'Mr Deza' (as happened quite quickly), Tupra and Mulryan also called me Jack. Not Rendel though, he wasn't on such familiar terms with anyone, at least not in the building with no name and no obvious function. And young Nuix, like Luisa, inclined to Jaime, or sometimes to my surname only, plain Deza, as Luisa did too.

'Brothers,' I murmured, and on this occasion, I managed not

to turn my repetition into a question. 'Brothers, eh? You know perfectly well, Peter, that I knew nothing about it. I didn't even know you were born in New Zealand until you mentioned it to me for the first time a few days ago, on the phone.' As I was speaking, memories of Rylands came rushing in on me, sometimes memories surface with such terrible speed. 'So Toby . . .' I said, rousing myself, '. . . but, he was supposed to have been born in South Africa, and I thought it must be true because once I heard him mention in passing that he didn't leave that continent, Africa, I mean, until he was sixteen. The same age that you were when you arrived here, which you also mentioned in passing for the first time during that phone conversation of a matter of days ago. You're not going to tell me now that you were twins, are you?'

Wheeler turned to look at me, but without speaking, his eyes said that he wasn't up to the labour of listening to reproaches or half-ironies, not that morning, he had other things on his mind, or on the repertoire drawn up for that performance.

'Well, if you really didn't know . . . I suppose you simply never asked me,' he replied. 'I've never concealed the fact. Toby might have preferred to, he may have concealed it from you, but I didn't. And I don't really know why I should have told you anyway.' He said these words in the same impassive, almost self-exculpatory tone, but I picked up on it, recognised it: it was intended to bring me up short. 'No, we weren't twins. I was nearly a year older. And now I'm considerably older still.'

I knew what Wheeler was like when something made him feel uncomfortable or when he became evasive, it was a waste of time insisting, you merely risked irritating him, he always decided the topic of conversation.

'All right, Peter. If you would be kind enough to explain, I'm all ears, curiosity and interest. I assume that's what you wanted me to see in *Who's Who*, and I trust you'll tell me why. Why now, I mean.'

'No, not at all,' he replied. 'I genuinely thought you knew all about that, otherwise I would never have risked us running aground here. No. There's something else I want to talk to you about, although it does indirectly have to do with Toby, in a way. Last night, if you recall, I put off telling you something until today. Read on, please, you haven't finished yet.' And with an imperative forefinger which moved up and down as if it had a life of its own (it now dropped almost vertically), he touched the large volume open before me.

'Peter, you can't just leave me dangling like that,' I ventured to protest.

'It will all become clear later on, Jacobo, don't worry, you'll find out. It's a trivial story, though; you'll be disappointed. Anyway, carry on. And read it out loud, will you. I don't want you to read the whole thing, that would be a terrible bore. So I'll tell you when to stop.'

I returned to the biographical note, to the next section, which was 'Education'. And I read out loud and in English, omitting all the incomprehensible abbreviations and acronyms:

'Cheltenham College; Queen's College, Oxford; Lecturer of St John's College, 1937–53, and Queen's College, 1938–45. Enlisted, 1940.' And I could not help but stop again, even though he had not yet told me to. I looked up. 'I didn't know you enlisted in 1940,' I said. 'And I see there's no mention anywhere of 1936. Was that perhaps when you were in Spain? A lot of the British people who went there left at the beginning or towards the middle of 1937, terrified or else wounded, they didn't last, well, George Orwell was one of them.' Then I remembered that, just in case and without success, I had also looked for the surname Rylands in the indices of names in the books I had consulted during the night, so his possible first or real name, Peter Rylands, had not been the one he had used in my country's war either. Or perhaps it had, but he had done nothing so outstanding there that he would merit a mention in the history books, and I had only allowed myself to imagine otherwise for my own amusement.

Wheeler seemed to read my thoughts, as well as my inopportune question.

'Many never left, there they still are, terrified and wounded. Wounded unto death,' he replied. 'But please, let's not talk about the Spanish Civil War now, however immersed you were in it last night. Almost no one used their real name there, nor did a lot of people in the Second World War. Not even Orwell was called George Orwell, if you remember.' I didn't remember, and seeing that I had forgotten, he added: 'His real name was Blair, Eric Blair, I knew him slightly during the war, he was in the BBC's India Section. Eric Arthur Blair. He was born in Bengal and had lived in Burma in his youth, he knew the East well. He was ten years older than me. Now I'm infinitely older. He died young, as you know, didn't even make it to fifty.' – 'Another one,' I thought, 'another foreign Britisher or bogus Englishman.' – 'Anyway, carry on reading, otherwise we'll never get to what I want to talk about.'

'Sorry, Peter.' And I read: 'Commissioned Intelligence Corps, December 1940; Temporary Lieutenant-Colonel, 1945; specially employed in Caribbean, West Africa and South-East Asia, 1942–46. Fellow of Queen's College, 1946–53 . . .'

'That's enough,' he said in English, which was the language we were speaking, to do otherwise would have been a discourtesy to Mrs Berry, although I found it slightly odd that she had not left the table, as she usually did, even during more conventional conversations or ones that had no clear direction, not that I knew yet which direction this one was heading in. So this was what Wheeler wanted to show me: 'Commissioned Intelligence Corps, December 1940 (*'Cuerpo de Información'* in Spanish, not *'Cuerpo de Inteligencia'* as a bad translator might render it, not that it matters, both refer to the Secret Service, MI5 and MI6, the initials mean Military Intelligence, a contradiction in terms some might say, the British equivalent of the Soviets' GPU, OGPU, NKVD, MGD, KGB, it has been called so many things over the years: MI5 for internal matters and MI6 for external ones, the first focused on the national and the second on the international); 'Temporary Lieutenant-Colonel, 1945; specially employed in Caribbean, West Africa and South-East Asia, 1942–46'. That was what I had just read. 'The rest doesn't concern us now,' he added, 'it's all about awards and publications and jobs, blah-blah-blah.'

'Toby worked for MI5 too, or so people said when I was teaching here,' I said. 'And he did actually confirm that to me once.'

'He talked to you about it?' asked Wheeler. 'That's strange. That's very strange indeed, you must be one of the few people he did talk to. He was in MI6 actually, we both were during the war, as was nearly everyone in Oxford and Cambridge, I mean those of us with enough training and confidence and who knew languages; besides, we would have been much less use at the front, although some of us did spend time there too. Being recruited or summoned by MI6 or SOE soon ceased to be anything very special, in fact, they started appointing us to responsible positions and tasks.' He realised that I was not familiar with the last acronym he had mentioned, so he explained: 'Special Operations Executive, it only existed during the war, between 1940 and 1945. No, I lie, it was officially dismantled in 1946. Fully and completely, well, I suppose that nothing that exists is ever fully and completely dismantled. They were executioners, and fairly inept ones too: MI6 was devoted to research and intelligence, well, call it espionage and premeditated deceit; the SOE to sabotage, subversion, murder, destruction and terror.'

'Murder?' I'm afraid that when confronted by this word, no one can possibly restrain themselves and keep quiet, even less when confronted by its companion 'terror'.

'Yes, of course. They bumped off Heydrich, for example, the Reich Protector in Bohemia and Moravia, in 1942, it was one of their major successes, they were so proud of it. Two Czech resisters actually hurled the grenades at his car and machine-gunned it, but the operation was masterminded by Colonel Spooner, one of the SOE's top men. With, as it happens, little foresight, poor judgement and only average implementation, you may have heard about this episode or seen it in films, I don't know how much you know about the Second World War. Heydrich wasn't in fact mortally wounded; people thought he would pull through, and one hundred hostages were shot at dusk each day of his convalescence (although it turned out to be his death agony). He took a whole week to die, imagine, and they say he only died in the end because the poison in the bullets was so slow to take effect. That was the German story anyway: they said the bullets had been impregnated with botulin brought from America by the SOE, I don't know though, maybe the Nazi doctors messed things up and invented the story to save their own necks. If the story is true, though, and Frank Spooner did poison the ammunition, he could have smeared it with something a bit deadlier and faster-acting, don't you think, curare perhaps, like the Indians use on their arrows and spears.' And Wheeler laughed a brief, mirthless laugh: for the first time his laugh reminded me of Rylands's laugh, which was short and dry and slightly diabolical and not aspirated (ha, ha, ha), but plosive, with a clear alveolar t, as the t always is in English: Ta, ta, ta, he said. Ta, ta, ta. 'Of course the same thing would have happened if it had been quick. When Heydrich did finally die, the Nazis exterminated the entire population of Lidice, the village the SOE's agents had parachuted into in order to direct the assassination *in situ*. Not a soul was left alive, but that wasn't enough for the Nazis, they reduced the place to rubble, they levelled it, erased it from the map, it was so odd that strong spatial sense of theirs, unhealthy, the malice they felt towards places, as if they believed in the *genius loci*, a kind of spatial hatred.' – 'Franco was the same,' I thought, 'and above all he hated my city, Madrid, because it had rejected him and refused to surrender to him until the bitter end.' – 'They were a pretty inept bunch, the men from the SOE, they often acted without establishing first whether the action was worth the consequences. Some soldiers hated them, despised them even. A few months ago I read in a book by Knightley that the Commander-in-Chief of Bomber Command, Sir Arthur Harris, dubbed them amateurish, ignorant, irresponsible and mendacious. Others said still worse things. In fact, their most beneficial effect was psychological, which was not without importance: knowing of their existence and their exploits (which were more legend than truth) raised the morale of the occupied countries, where they credited them with powers they lacked, and with far more intelligence, infallibility and cunning than they ever had. They made a lot of mistakes. But, as we know, people believe what they need to believe, and everything has its moment to be believed. Where were we? Why were we talking about that?'

'You were telling me about the people in Oxford and Cambridge who entered MI6 and the SOE.' Someone simply has to mention or explain a name for one to start using it almost with familiarity. Wheeler had used the same words Tupra had used, 'everything has its moment to be believed', I wondered if it was a motto, known to both. While Wheeler was talking I had been glancing over the rest of his biographical note which no longer concerned us: a man laden with distinctions and honours, Spanish, Portuguese, British, American, Commander of the Order of Isabel the Catholic, of the Order of the Infante Don Henrique. Amongst his writings, I noticed this title from 1955: *The English Intervention in Spain and Portugal in the Time of Edward III and Richard II.* – 'He's spent his entire life studying his country's interference abroad,' I thought, 'from the fourteenth century, from the Black Prince on, perhaps he got interested after his time in MI6.' – 'You said Toby belonged to the former.'

'Ah, yes, that's right. Well, you know our privileged reputation: they think of us as prepared and qualified in principle for any activity, regardless of whether it bears any relation to our studies or our particular disciplines. And this university has spent too many centuries intervening, via its offspring, in the government of this country for us to refuse to collaborate when it most needed us. Not that we had any choice, it wasn't like in peacetime. Although there were people who did, who refused, and they paid for it, paid very dearly. All their lives. There were double agents and traitors too, you'll have heard of Philby, Burgess, Maclean and Blunt, the scandal gradually dribbled out during the '50s and '60s, and even into the '70s, because no one knew anything about Blunt until 1979, when Mrs Thatcher decided to break the pact she had inherited and to make public what he had confessed in secret fifteen years before, thus completely destroying him and stripping him of everything, starting, ridiculously enough, with his title. Anyway, there were so many people involved, it's hardly surprising that four traitors should have emerged from our universities, fortunately the four came from the other place, not ours, and that's worked silently in our favour for the last half-century.' – 'Here too,' I thought, 'that spatial malice, the punishment of place.' – 'Well, I say four: the Four of Fame from the Ring of Five, but there must have been many more.' – I didn't understand what he was referring to, but this time I gave no sign of my ignorance, not even by my expression, I didn't want to have to interrupt again. 'Ring' in English can also mean the kind of ring you wear on your finger. – 'I joined, Toby joined, as did so many others, and it's remained quite common practice, even after the war, they've always needed all kinds of expertise and have sought it out in the best and most appropriate places. They've always needed linguists, decoders, people who knew languages: I don't think there's anyone in the sub-faculty of Slavonic Languages who hasn't done some work for them at some time. Not in the field, of course, they haven't gone on missions, anyone working in Slavonic languages was already too marked out by his profession to be useful to them there, it would have been tantamount to sending a spy with a sign on his forehead saying "Spy". But they have used them to do translations, to act as interpreters, to break codes, authenticate recordings or polish accents, to carry out phone taps and interrogations, in Vauxhall Cross or in Baker Street. Before the fall of the Berlin Wall, of course, now they don't need them so much, it's the turn of Arabists and Islamic scholars, they have no idea yet just what's hit them, they won't get a moment's peace.' – I thought of Rook with his massive head, the eternal translator of Tolstoy and the alleged and unlikely friend of Vladimir Nabokov, and about Dewar, a.k.a. the Ripper, the Butcher, the Hammer and the Inquisitor (poor Dewar and his insomnia, and how unfair all those nicknames were), a Hispanist who, as I discovered, could also read Pushkin in Russian, delighting in those iambic stanzas, either read out loud or to himself. Old acquaintances from the city of Oxford in which I had lived for two years – although I was only ever passing through – and with almost all of whom I had had no further contact once I returned to Madrid. Cromer-Blake and Rylands, with whom I had been friendliest, were both dead. Clare Bayes was back with her husband, Edward Bayes, or else with a new lover, but there would definitely be no room for me as a friend, there would be no reason, our affair had been entirely secret. I was in sporadic contact with Kavanagh, the head of my sub-faculty, an amusing man and a great hypochondriac, which is perhaps why he wrote his horror novels under that pseudonym, two different forms of an addiction to fear. And Wheeler. Except that he really dated from after my time there, he was more like an inheritance from Rylands, his successor, his substitute or replacement in my life, I realised now the family nature of it, of that inheritance and that succession I mean. Wheeler remained thinking for a moment (perhaps he was feeling sorry for some Arabist acquaintance of his, and of his imminent fate under siege from MI6), and then returned to something from earlier in the conversation, saying: 'It's very odd that Toby should have told you about that. He didn't like anyone to know, he didn't even like thinking about it. Nor do I actually, so don't go imagining that I'm going to regale you with stories of my adventures in the Caribbean or in West Africa or in South-East Asia, according to *Who's Who*'s rather imprecise accusations. What did he tell you? Can you remember how it came up?'

Yes, I did remember, almost word for word, on no other occasion had Rylands spoken to me with such intensity, so immersed in his own memory and with such disregard for his own will. It was true: he didn't like sharing his memories with others, and disliked revealing anything.

'We were talking about death,' I said. ('The worst thing about the approach of death isn't death itself and what it may or may not bring, it's the fact that one can no longer fantasise about things still to come,' Rylands had said, sitting in a chair in his garden next to the same slow river that we could see now, the River Cherwell with its muddy waters, except that Rylands's house gave on to a wilder, more magical, and far less soothing stretch of water. Occasionally swans would appear, and he would throw them bits of bread.)

'About death? That's odd too,' remarked Wheeler. 'It's odd that Toby should talk about that, odd that anyone should, especially once it's inevitable, because of infirmity or old age. Or, indeed, character.' ('Wheeler is talking about it now,' I thought, 'but more because he's an intelligent man than because of his age.')

'Cromer-Blake was already very ill, and we were worried then about what did, in the end, happen. Talking about that and about how little time there was left led Toby to speak of the past.' ('I've had what is commonly referred to as a full life, at least that's how I regard it,' Rylands had said. 'I haven't had a wife or children, but I've had a life spent in the acquisition of knowledge and that was what mattered to me. I've always gone on finding out more than I knew before, and it doesn't matter where you put that "before", even if it's only today or tomorrow.')

'And is that when he told you what he had done, about his adventures?' asked Wheeler, and I thought I noticed a touch of apprehension in his voice, as if he were referring to something more specific than having collaborated with MI6 which, in Oxford, was, after all, something trivial, commonplace.

'He wanted to explain to me that he'd had a full life, that he hadn't, as it might seem, devoted himself solely to study and knowledge and teaching,' I replied. ('But I've had a full life, too, in the sense that my life's been crammed with action and the unexpected,' Rylands had said.) 'And that was when he confirmed the rumours I'd heard, that he'd been a spy, that was the word he used. And I assumed that he'd belonged to MI5, it didn't occur to me to think of MI6, perhaps because it's less familiar to us Spaniards.'

'That's what he told you.' There was no interrogative tone. 'He used that word. H'm,' murmured Wheeler, as so many people in Oxford did, including Rylands. 'H'm.' Seeing Peter so thoughtful and full of curiosity, it seemed to me selfish and unkind not to fill in the context, which I remembered so well, and not to quote to him verbatim his younger brother's words. 'H'm,' he said again.

'"As you'll no doubt have heard," he said, "I was a spy, like so many of us here, because that, too, can form part of our duties; but I was never just a pen-pusher like that fellow Dewar in your department, indeed like most of them. I worked in the field."' I could tell by the look in Wheeler's eyes that he had noticed that his brother had used some of the same expressions he had just used.

'Did he say anything else?' he asked.

'Yes, he did: he talked for quite a long time, almost as if I wasn't there, and he added a few other things too. For example: "I've been in India and in the Caribbean and in Russia and I've done things I could never tell anyone about now, because they would seem so ridiculous that no one would believe me, I know only too well that what one can and cannot tell depends very much on timing, because I've dedicated my life to identifying just that in literature and I've learned to identify it in life too.'"

'Toby was right about that, there are things that can't be told now – or only with great difficulty – even though they really happened. The facts of war sound puerile in times of relative peace, and just because something happened doesn't mean it can be talked about, just because it's true, doesn't mean it's plausible. With the passing of time, the truth can seem unlikely; it fades into the background, and then seems more like a fable or simply not true at all. Even some of my own experiences seem like fiction to me. They were important experiences, but the times that follow begin to doubt them, perhaps not one's own time, but the entirely new eras, and it's those new eras that make what came before and what they didn't see seem unimportant, almost as if they were somehow jealous of them. Often the present infantilises the past, it tends to transform it into something invented and childish, and renders it useless to us, spoils it for us.' He paused, nodded at the cigarette I had hesitantly raised to my lips after drinking my coffee (I was afraid the smoke might bother them at that hour). He looked out of the window at the river, at his stretch of the river, more civilised and harmonious than Toby Rylands's. He had momentarily lost all his previous haste and impatience, which is what usually happens when one remembers the dead. 'Who knows, maybe that's partly why we die: because everything we've experienced is reduced to nothing, and then even our memories languish and fade. First, it's our personal experiences. Then it's our memories.'

'So everything also has its moment *not* to be believed.'

Wheeler smiled vaguely, almost regretfully. He had picked up on my inversion of the words he had used a short while before, of the possible motto that he shared with Tupra, if it was a motto and not just a coincidence of ideas, yet another affinity between them.

'But nevertheless he told you,' Wheeler murmured, and what I sensed now in his voice was, I thought, not so much apprehension as fatalism or defeat or resignation, in short, surrender.

'Don't be so sure, Peter. He did and he didn't. He may have dropped his guard sometimes, but he never entirely lost his will, I don't think, nor did he say more than he was aware he wanted to say. Even if that awareness was distant or hidden, or muffled. Just like you.'

'What else did he tell and not tell you, then?' He ignored my last comment, or kept it for later on.

'He didn't really tell me anything, he just talked. He said: "I shouldn't be telling you any of this now, but the fact is that in my lifetime I've run mortal risks and betrayed men whom I had nothing against personally. I've saved a few people's lives too, but sent others to the firing squad or the gallows. I've lived in Africa, in the most unlikely places, in other times, and was even a witness to the suicide of the person I loved."'

'He said that, "I was even a witness to the suicide . . ."' Wheeler didn't complete the phrase. He was astonished, or possibly annoyed. 'And was that all? Did he say who or what happened?'

'No. I remember that he stopped short then, as if his will or his conscious mind had sent a warning to his memory, to stop him overstepping the mark; then he added: "Oh, and battles, I've been a witness to those too," I remember it clearly. Then he went on talking, but about the present. He said no more about his past, or only in very general terms. Even more general, that is.'

'May I ask what those terms were?' Wheeler's question sounded not forceful, but timid, as if he were asking my permission; it was almost a plea.

'Of course, Peter,' I replied, and there was no reserve or

insincerity in my voice. 'He said that his head was full of bright, shining memories, frightening and thrilling, and that anyone seeing all of them together, as he could, would think they were more than enough, that the simple remembering of so many fascinating facts and people would fill one's old age more intensely than most people's present.' I paused for a moment to give him time to listen to the words inside him. 'Those, pretty much, were the terms he used or what he said. And he added that it wasn't, in fact, like that. That it wasn't like that for him. He did still want more, he said. He still wanted everything, he said.'

Wheeler now seemed at once relieved and saddened and uneasy, or perhaps he was none of those things, perhaps he was simply moved. It probably wasn't like that for him either, however many bright, shining memories he had. Probably nothing was enough to fill the days of his old age, despite all his efforts and his machinations.

'And you believed all that,' he said.

'I had no reason not to,' I replied. 'Besides, he was telling me the truth, sometimes you just know, without a shadow of a doubt, that someone is telling you the truth. Not often, it's true,' I added. 'But there are occasions when you have not the slightest doubt about it.'

'Do you remember when this took place, this conversation?'

'Yes, it was in Hilary term during my second year here, towards the end of March.'

'So a couple of years before he died, is that right?'

'More or less, or perhaps a bit more. I think he may not have even introduced us yet, you and me. You and I must have met for the first time in Trinity term of that year, shortly before I returned to Madrid for good.'

'We were already quite old then, Toby and I, well into our emeritus years both of us. I never thought I would be so much older, I don't know how he would have coped with all the additional time that I've had and he hasn't. Badly I suspect, worse than me. He complained more because he was more optimistic than me, and therefore more passive too, don't you agree, Estelle?'

I was surprised that he should suddenly address Mrs Berry by her first name, I had never heard him do so before, and yet he and I had often been alone together, but he had always addressed her as 'Mrs Berry'. I wondered if the nature of the conversation had something to do with it. As if he were opening up for me one door or several (I didn't yet know which one or how many), amongst them that of his unseen daily life. She always called him 'Professor', which in Oxford does not mean 'lecturer' or 'teacher' as it does in Spanish, but chair or head of department, and there is only one professor in each sub-faculty, the others being merely 'dons'. And this time Mrs Berry responded by calling him 'Peter'. That's what they must call each other when they're alone, Peter and Estelle, I thought. It was, however, impossible to know if they addressed each other as '*tú*', since in present-day English only 'you' exists, and there is no distinction made between '*tú*' and '*usted*'.

'Yes, Peter, you're right.' I decided to imagine that had they been speaking in Spanish, they would have used '*usted*', as I always did mentally when speaking to Wheeler in his language. 'He always assumed that people would come to him and that things would happen of their own accord, and so he tended perhaps to feel more let down. I don't know quite whether he was more optimistic or simply prouder. But he never went after people and things himself. He didn't seek them out the way you do.' Mrs Berry spoke in her usual calm, discreet tone, I could not detect the slightest variation.

'Pride and optimism are not necessarily mutually exclusive characteristics, Estelle,' replied Wheeler in slightly professorial mode. 'He was the one who told me about you,' he went on to say, looking at me, and then I did notice a distinct change from the tone of voice he had used before: the fog had lifted (the apprehension or irritation or sense of doom), as if, after a few moments of alarm, he had been reassured to learn that I did not know too much about Rylands, despite the latter's unexpected confidences to me that day in Hilary term during my second year in Oxford. That his reminiscences had not entailed a complete surrender of his will when I was present, and perhaps, therefore, not while anyone else was present either. That I knew about his past as a spy and a few imprecise facts without date or place or names, but nothing more. He felt once more in control of the situation after a brief moment of disequilibrium, I could see it in his eyes, I could hear it in the slight hint of didacticism in his voice. It doubtless made him feel uneasy to discover that he was not in possession of all the facts, always assuming he had believed he was, and he once more took it for granted that he had them all, those he needed or that afforded him a sense of ease and comfort. In the now rather late morning light his eyes looked very transparent, less mineral than they usually did and much more liquid, like Toby Rylands's eyes, or like his right eye at least, the one that was the colour of sherry or the colour of olive oil depending on how the sun caught it, and which predominated and assimilated his other eye when seen from a distance: or perhaps it is simply that one dares to see more similarities between people when you know there is a blood relationship to back you up. Wheeler had still not explained to me about their hitherto unknown kinship, but it had taken barely any effort on my part to apply that correction to my thought and to see them no longer as friends, but as brothers. Or as brothers as well as friends, for that is what they must have been. Wheeler's eyes seemed to me now more like two large drops of rosé wine. 'It was Toby who suggested to me that you might perhaps be like us,' he added.

'What do you mean "like us"? What do you mean? What did he mean?'

Wheeler did not reply directly. The truth is he rarely did.

'There are hardly any such people left, Jacobo. There were never many, very few in fact, which is why the group was always so small and so scattered. But nowadays there's a real dearth, it's no cliché or exaggeration to describe us now as an endangered species. The times have made people insipid, finicky, prudish. No one wants to see anything of what there is to see, they don't even dare to look, still less take the risk of making a wager; being forewarned, foreseeing, judging, or, heaven forbid, prejudging, that's a capital offence, it smacks of *lèse-humanité*, an attack on the dignity of the prejudged, of the prejudger, of everyone. No one dares any more to say or to acknowledge that they see what they see, what is quite simply there, perhaps unspoken or almost unsaid, but nevertheless there. No one wants to know; and the idea of knowing something beforehand, well, it simply fills people with horror, with a kind of biographical, moral horror. They require proof and verification of everything; the benefit of the doubt, as they call it, has invaded everything, leaving not a single sphere uncolonised, and it has ended up paralysing us, making us, formally speaking, impartial, scrupulous and ingenuous, but, in practice, making fools of us all, utter *necios*.' That last word he said in Spanish, doubtless because there is no English word that resembles it phonetically or etymologically: 'utter *necios*,' he said, mixing the two languages. '*Necios* in the strict sense of the word, in the Latin sense of *nescius*, one who knows nothing, who lacks knowledge, or as the dictionary of the Real Academia Española puts it, do you know the definition it gives? "Ignorant and knowing neither what could or should be known." Isn't that extraordinary? That is, a person who deliberately and willingly chooses not to know, a person who shies away from finding things out and who abhors learning. *Un satisfecho insipiente.*' He resorted to Spanish for both the quote and for the last few words, which, more or less, 'nincompoop'; in other languages one always remembers terms that are no longer in use or are unknown to native speakers. 'And that's how it is in our pusillanimous countries, people are educated from childhood on to be *necios*, fools. It isn't a natural evolution or degeneration, it doesn't happen by chance, it's conscious, calculated, institutional. It's a programme for the formation of minds, or for their annihilation (the annihilation of character, *ça va sans dire*!). People hate certainty; and that hatred began as a fashion, it was deemed trendy to reject certainties, simpletons put them in the same bag as dogmas and doctrines, the dolts (and there were a few intellectuals amongst them too), as if they were synonymous. But the idea has proved a tremendous success, it's taken root with a vengeance. Now people hate anything definite or sure, and, consequently, anything that is fixed in time; and that is partly why people detest the past, unless they can manage to contaminate it with their own hesitancy, or infect it with the present's lack of definition, which they try to do all the time. Nowadays people cannot bear to know that something existed; that it existed and in a particular way. What they cannot bear is not so much knowing that, as the mere fact of its existence. Just that: that it did exist. Without our intervention, without our considered opinion, how can I put it, without our infinite indecision or our scrupulous acquiescence. Without our much-loved uncertainty as impartial witness. This era is so proud, Jacobo, far prouder than any other, certainly since I've been in the world or before that either, I should think (it makes Hitler look tame). Bear in mind that when I get up each morning, I have to make a real effort and to resort to the help of much younger friends like you in order to forget that I can actually remember the First World War, or what you young people call, to my great disgust and displeasure, the 14–18 War. Bear in mind that one of the first words I learned and retained, from hearing it so often, was "Gallipoli", it seems incredible that I was already alive when that massacre took place. The present era is so proud that it has produced a phenomenon which I imagine to be unprecedented: the present's resentment of the past, resentment because the past had the audacity to happen without us being there, without our cautious opinion and our hesitant consent, and even worse, without our gaining any advantage from it. Most extraordinary of all is that this resentment has nothing to do, apparently, with feelings of envy for past splendours that vanished without including us, or feelings of distaste for an excellence of which we were aware, but to which we did not contribute, one that we missed and failed to experience, that scorned us and which we did not ourselves witness, because the arrogance of our times has reached such proportions that it cannot admit the idea, not even the shadow or mist or breath of an idea, that things were better before. No, it's just pure resentment for anything that presumed to happen beyond our boundaries and owed no debt to us, for anything that is over and has, therefore, escaped us. It has escaped our control and our manoeuvrings and our decisions, despite all these leaders going around apologising for the outrages committed by their ancestors, even seeking to make amends by offering offensive gifts of money to the descendants of the aggrieved, regardless of how gladly those descendants may pocket those gifts and even demand them, for they, too, are opportunists, an eye on the main chance. Have you ever seen anything more stupid or farcical: cynicism on the part of those who give, cynicism on the part of those who receive. It's just another act of pride: how can a pope, a king or a prime minister assume the right to attribute to his Church, to his Crown or to his country, to those who are alive now, the crimes of their predecessors, crimes which those same predecessors did not see or recognise as such all those centuries ago? Who do our representatives and our governments think they are, asking forgiveness in the name of those who were free to do what they did and who are now dead? What right have they to make amends for them, to contradict the dead? If it was purely symbolic, it would be mere oafish affectation or propaganda. However, symbolism is out of the question as long as there are offers of "compensation", grotesquely retrospective monetary ones to boot. A person is a person and does not continue to exist through his remote descendants, not even his immediate ones, who often prove unfaithful; and these transactions and gestures do nothing for those who suffered, for those who really were persecuted and tortured, enslaved and murdered in their one, real life: they are lost for ever in the night of time and in the night of infamy, which is doubtless no less long. To offer or accept apologies now, vicariously, to demand them or proffer them for the evil done to victims who are now formless and abstract, is an outright mockery of their scorched flesh and their severed heads, of their pierced breasts, of their broken bones and slit throats. Of the real and unknown names of which they were stripped or which they renounced. A mockery of the past. No, the past is simply not to be borne; we cannot bear not being able to do anything about it, not being able to influence it, to direct it; to avoid it. And so, if possible, it is twisted or tampered with or altered, or falsified, or else made into a liturgy, a ceremony, an emblem and, finally, a spectacle, or simply shuffled around and changed so that, despite everything, it at least looks as if we were intervening, even though the past is utterly fixed, a fact we choose to ignore. And if it isn't, if that proves impossible, then it's erased, suppressed, exiled or expelled, or else buried. And it happens, Jacobo, one or the other of those things happens all too often because the past doesn't defend itself, it can't. And so now no one wants to think about what they see or what is going on or what, deep down, they know, about what they already sense to be unstable and mutable, what might even be nothing, or what, in a sense, will not have been at all. No one is prepared, therefore, to know anything with certainty, because certainties have been eradicated, as if they were contagious diseases. And so it goes, and so the world goes.'

Wheeler's gaze had grown denser and brighter as he spoke, his eyes looked to me like two drops of muscatel now. It wasn't just that he enjoyed holding forth, as does any former lecturer or teacher. It was also because the nature of those thoughts illuminated him from within and from without, too, just a little, as if the burning head of a match sparked and sputtered in each pupil. He himself realised, when he stopped, that he was somewhat agitated, and so I had no qualms about cooling him down with my response, or disappointing him, the anxious look on Mrs Berry's face – of which we each could see one half – reminded me that too much dialectical excitement was bad for him.

'Forgive me, Peter, but I'm afraid I don't entirely understand what you're saying,' I replied, taking advantage of a pause (which was perhaps merely a pause for breath). 'I haven't had much sleep and I'm probably a bit slow on the uptake, but I really don't know what you're talking about.'

'Give me a cigarette, will you,' he said. He didn't usually smoke cigarettes. I handed him my pack. He took one, lit it, held it rather awkwardly between his fingers, took two puffs and this, as I saw, had an immediate calming effect, tobacco sometimes does that, whatever the doctors say. 'I know, I know. I may appear to be rambling, but I'm not really, Jacobo. I was talking to you about what we've been talking about all along, so, please, don't give up on me just yet. I haven't forgotten your question. You wanted to know what I meant and what Toby meant when he said that you might be like us, that was it, wasn't it?'

'Exactly. What did he mean? You still haven't explained.'

'But I *am* explaining. Just wait.' The ash on his cigarette was already beginning to grow long. I handed him the ashtray, but he didn't notice. 'Although we were apart for many years and knew nothing about each other's lives, I nevertheless knew Toby well, and in some matters I put a great deal of trust in his judgement (not everything, of course, I had little confidence in his literary tastes). But I knew him pretty well, both the boy who, like me, was also in the world when they sent the older boys to be slaughtered in Gallipoli along with the Australians . . . like pigs, the lot of them, some of them equipped with only their bayonets and no bullets . . . and the retired university colleague and riverside neighbour that he was in his latter years; once I moved here, of course. When we met up again.' He made a brief reiterative, historical digression, perhaps the one he had postponed in order to complete his previous sentence; another pause: '("Anzac", they were called, I don't know if you know: that's the acronym for the Australian and New Zealand Army Corps; and the Anzacs, in the plural, was the now glorious name of all those men who were so pointlessly sacrificed, in Chunuk Bair, in Suvla . . . There have been so many in my time, so many sacrificed for the same reason, because they couldn't see what was there before them and didn't know what was known already, so many in the course of one life. Mine has been a long life, it's true, but it's still only one life. It's frightening to think how many have been sacrificed and will continue to be sacrificed because of that, because they didn't dare or didn't want to . . . What a waste.) We led surprisingly parallel lives, Toby and I, given that we had said goodbye to each other in pre-adolescence, and that he had changed country and continent. I mean as regards our careers, the odd coincidence of our both in the end getting chairs at the same English university (and not just any university either). It was less of a coincidence that we both formed part of the same group, well, I recruited him, I suppose. The story of our surnames is, as I warned you, a trivial matter, no great mystery. Our parents got divorced when we were eight and nine years old respectively, around 1922 or thereabouts, he was a year younger, as I said. We stayed with my mother, amongst other things because my father was in a hurry to leave, I think because he didn't want to see my mother getting together with another man, which he was sure would happen sooner or later (well, that's what I think now and have for some time). He moved to South Africa and hardly seemed to miss us at all. So much so, that for many years I took this as certain and unquestionable, and resentment came easily to me. Our maternal grandfather, Grandfather Wheeler, decided to take charge of his two grandchildren, financially speaking. And since he only had two grandchildren, both, of course, bearing the surname Rylands, my mother, doubtless knowing little about pre-adolescent psychology, changed her name and ours, that is, she reclaimed her maiden name and gave it to us as well: a way of perpetuating the grandfather, I imagine, through his name; perhaps he made her do it. Anyway, it was made official in 1929, by deed poll' – I had read this English expression earlier in *Who's Who* – 'although we'd been using the surname Wheeler since shortly after the divorce. That was the name under which we were enrolled at school, and that was how we were known in Christchurch, where we were born. Poor Rita, my mother, probably did it as a show of gratitude or as a reward to my grandfather, her father, and more probably still, as a childish act of revenge on our father, her ex-husband Hugh. Almost from one day to the next, we went from feeling ourselves to be Peter and Toby Rylands to being the Wheeler brothers, with no father and no patronymic *sensu stricto*. But whereas I made no protest (later on, I realised what an upheaval it was, how messy, I mean, you can't with impunity change the label on an identity), Toby rebelled from the start. He continued answering "Toby Rylands" when asked his name and that was how he signed himself at school and even in exams. And after two or three years of these struggles and of evident unhappiness, at eleven, he expressed his strident desire not only to preserve his old surname, but to go and live with his father. He felt more affection for him than I did, more admiration, more comradeship and more dependence; he was more sentimental, and although, in the medium and long term, it must have been very painful to him to lose both me and my mother, he never said as much, he was too proud really; but he missed his father even more, immensely; and the bitterness I nurtured towards my father, Toby directed more and more at our mother. And (by assimilation or intuition) at Grandfather Wheeler, whom he could only ever see as a supplanter of or rival to his father, perhaps our grandfather was not that paternal towards his daughter. And I wasn't exempt either, no Wheeler was. In the end, Toby's misery and hostility became so intolerable, for him and for us, that my mother finally agreed to his moving out, as long as our father was prepared to take him and look after him, which seemed unlikely. The fact that my father took him in, contrary to all our predictions (or contrary to mine, which, I realised later, were more a desideratum than anything else) contributed in no small measure to my desire to eliminate him entirely from my consciousness, as if he had never existed, and then, very nearly, by assimilation and out of spite, to suppress all memory of my brother, because he had chosen my father and had gone away. As you know, that kind of thing is always happening, in adult life and even, I can assure you, in old age: but in childhood, that feeling of abandonment and despair (and of betrayal, that is, of desertion) is even more acute in the one who stays behind, while others leave and disappear. The impression is much the same when others die, for me at least, I always feel slightly resentful towards my dead. He went to South Africa, and I stayed in New Zealand. Not that South Africa was necessarily a better place, I had no objective reason to think so, but it became for me an infinitely more attractive place, and I soon began to grow impatient and to long to reach an age when I could leave my own country – clouded and diminished, in my eyes, by these absences – and come here to university. I finally did so when I was sixteen – and, by then, officially called Wheeler – on a boat so painfully slow I thought it would never reach its destination. I don't remember or believe it to be true, because I do have a kind of delayed sense of grievance regarding my change of name, the *de facto* change rather than the *de jure* one, but my mother said that the change by deed poll was done in my interests, even to please me. It's true that in the 1920s and 1930s everything was easier and less problematic, and in many respects one was freer than one is nowadays: neither the state nor the justice system were as regulatory or as interventionist as they are now, they allowed people room to breathe and move around, but that's all over now, our tutelary obsession did not exist, would not have been allowed. So it's possible that, in the end, my name would have been Wheeler anyway with no need for any red tape, simply sanctioned by use and by custom, just as Toby could go off to be with his father with only the agreement of his two progenitors and my mother's approval, without, as far as I know, any authority or judge interfering in such a private matter. Whatever the case, that was when I also started calling myself Wheeler legally, and perfectly willingly too. Needless to say, the deed poll only affected me and not Toby (that would have been the last straw), and from whom, by then, I had barely heard for four years. He didn't keep in direct contact, well, neither he nor I sought it out. From time to time I would get some vague bits of news about him from my mother, who received it, I fear, mainly from our father. And he would have received some news of me by the same channel, only in reverse. So I was born "Peter Rylands" and that was who I was until I was nine or ten, or indeed *in partibus* until I was sixteen. But then Toby was "Toby Wheeler" for a while too, much against his will, of course: you have no idea how he suffered at school in Christchurch, for example, when they called the register. It doesn't usually happen with the name they give you at birth, but it can with justice be said of Toby that, as well as receiving it, he also conquered and won his name.' Wheeler's expression changed for a moment, and when I saw this new expression, I imagined that some ironic or humorous comment was about to follow. 'He was never very keen on his first name either, which was Grandfather Wheeler's first name too, it was just bad luck that he got stuck with it. If that had been the name to be changed, he would have accepted with pleasure, I'm sure. And, who knows, we would probably have continued living together. He said it reminded him of that tedious character in *Twelfth Night*, Sir Toby Belch, you know what "belch" means, I suppose? Then, as an adult, he became slightly reconciled to the name when he read *Tristram Shandy*, thanks to Uncle Toby.'

And Wheeler appeared to conclude here his explanations about Wheeler and Rylands, because he added by way of bringing the matter to a close, 'So you see, as I told you, a trivial story. A divorce. An attachment to a name. To a mother. To a father. A separation. An aversion to another name. To a mother. And to a grandfather. To a father.' He was mixing the two points of view, his own and that of his brother. 'No great mystery.' I had the impression then, given the slowness with which he spoke, that he was expecting me to refute these words, now that he had told me the story: but that isn't what happened, he didn't get his refutation. He must have known that it wasn't a trivial story at all (that drastic separation of the two sides; Rylands saying to me once 'when I left Africa for the first time', as if he had been born there and denying, therefore, his first ten or eleven years in New Zealand, on another continent, albeit an island one), and that it did contain a mystery, despite the casual manner in which he had set out to tell it. And he must have told it in part only: he had not told the mystery itself, but the part around it, that pointed to it like an arrow.

'And then?' I asked. 'When did you meet up again?'

'In England, years later. By then I really was Wheeler and he was Rylands. I think that I was already the person I am, if I am who I think I am. I sought him out, we didn't just meet. Not exactly. But that's another story.'

'I'm sure it is,' I replied, perhaps with an unintentional touch of impatience: my lack of sleep caught up with me now and then, and when something, even a chance remark, refers in some way to ourselves, waiting becomes very difficult. 'And I assume that the answer to my original question, which you provoked, is hidden in there somewhere: in what way could I, according to Toby, be like the two of you? You're not going to tell me it was because of my variable first name, as you know, you and others call me Jacobo, but Luisa and many others call me Jaime, and there are even those who know me as Diego or Yago. Not to mention Jack, as I'm often called here in

England.'

Wheeler noticed my slight impatience, such things never escaped him. I saw that he was amused, it didn't make him feel embarrassed at all, or pressured.

'I call you Jack,' said Mrs Berry shyly. 'I hope you don't mind . . . Jack.' And this time she hesitated before saying the name.

'Not at all, Mrs Berry.'

'And by which name do you know yourself?' Wheeler was quick to ask.

I didn't have to think about it even for a second.

'Jacques. That's the name I learned and made mine as a child. Even though my mother was almost the only one to call me that. Not even my father does.'

'There you are,' said Wheeler in an absurdly demonstrative tone. '*Ahí lo tienes*' is the only way I can think to translate it into Spanish. 'But, no, Toby didn't mean that, neither did I,' he added at once. 'He had told me quite a lot about you, before you and I met. In fact, that's partly why we did meet, he aroused my curiosity. He said that you might perhaps be like us . . . That's what he had given me to understand, and he confirmed it later when we happened to talk about the old group. Of course, by then you were no longer living here, and it was unlikely that you would ever come back here to stay. Don't worry, I don't mean that now you're going to stay here for good, I'm sure you'll go back to Madrid sooner or later, you Spaniards don't survive very long far from your country; even though you're from Madrid, and *madrileños* tend to suffer least from homesickness. But you have, for the moment, come back to stay indefinitely, if you'll forgive the relative contradiction, and that's enough of a return. And so, posthumously, Toby's opinion suddenly acquires, how can I put it, an added practical interest. Especially as I share his opinion (after all, he no longer wields any influence, nor can he be pressed on the matter), having spent quite a lot of time with you since his death.

251

Intermittently, of course, but it's been some years now. As I said, I didn't set great store by his literary judgements, but I did by his personal judgements, by his judgement of people, his interpretation and foresight, he could see straight through them, or, as you say in colloquial Spanish, *las calaba*. He could suss them out. He was rarely wrong, little short of infallible. Almost as infallible as me.' He gave a brief, studied laugh, to cancel out or mitigate his immodesty. 'More, possibly, than our friend Tupra, who is very good, or than that very competent girl of his, although you do, I suppose, live in less testing times: she's Spanish too, the girl, or half-Spanish at any rate, he's spoken to me about her several times, but I can never remember her name, he says that, with time, she'll be the best of the group, if he can hold on to her long enough, that's one of the difficulties, most of them get fed up and leave. Toby was almost as infallible as you must be, even given the less testing times you live in. According to him anyway. He believed that you would prove more infallible than him, that you might outdo him assuming that you first became conscious of your abilities and then immediately let go of that consciousness, or at least deferred it, as did those of us who had or have it still. Indefinitely, for the moment, if you'll again forgive that relative contradiction as regards the deferral of consciousnesses. But, to be honest, I don't know if you would ever reach those heights.'

'What group are you talking about, Peter? You've mentioned it several times now.' I tried a different question. But I no longer felt impatient, that had been just a reflex reaction, a moment. And if he had been in a hurry before, that had probably been due to my lateness in waking up and coming downstairs, which he had not counted upon, any failure to keep to his mental timetables and plans upset and bothered him. But now that I was there with him, he was enjoying intriguing me, enjoying my state of expectation: he wasn't going to ruin his performance, which he had planned and possibly dreamed about, by rushing things. As expected, he did not answer my new question, but he did, at last, answer my previous one. With only half-truths, of course, or, at most, three-quarter truths. As I have said, he probably didn't know any whole ones. They probably didn't even exist.

'Toby told me that he always admired, and, at the same time, feared, the special gift you had for capturing the distinctive and even essential characteristics, both external and internal, of friends and acquaintances, characteristics which they themselves had often not noticed or known about. Or even people you had only glimpsed or seen in passing, in a meeting or at high table, or whom you had passed a couple of times in the corridors or on the stairs of the Taylorian without exchanging a single word. I understand that, shortly before you left, you even wrote a few sketches of our colleagues for his amusement, is that right?'

I had a vague memory of this. It was so long ago that any trace of it had been erased. You forget much more of what you write than of what you read, assuming it's addressed to you; much more of what you send than of what you receive, of what you say than of what you hear, your own offences more than those committed against you. And although you may not think so, the process of erasure happens more quickly with those who are dead. A few vignettes, perhaps, yes, a few lines about my colleagues of the time in Oxford, those in the sub-faculty of Spanish, whom Rylands, recently retired Professor of English Literature, knew well, although not as well as Wheeler himself, who was, for years, and up until his retirement, the direct boss of most of them, especially those who were, by then, already veterans. I felt a sudden retrospective shame, I was struggling to remember; perhaps they had been amusing, affectionate sketches, with just a touch of mischief or irony. That is why I felt it best to deny it, at least initially.

'I don't remember that,' I said. 'No, I don't think I've ever written a sketch about anyone. Possibly in conversation, yes. We talked a lot about everything, about everyone.'

'Can you pass me that file, please, Estelle?' Wheeler asked

Mrs Berry, and she produced one and handed it to him, like a nurse promptly handing a doctor a medical instrument. She must have had it on her lap all that time, like a treasure. Wheeler put it under his arm, or, rather, under his armpit. He got up and said: 'Let's go out into the garden for a while, for a stroll on the lawn. I need the exercise and Mrs Berry will need to clear the table if we want to have lunch later on. It's not that cold now, but you'd better wrap up, that river is treacherous, it gets into your bones before you know it.' His eyes had resumed their mineral quality, and he added calmly and seriously (or, rather, carefully, as if he were holding on to me with his words, but did not want to frighten me off): 'Listen, Jacobo, according to Toby, you had the rare gift of being able to see in people what not even they were capable of seeing in themselves, at least not normally. Or if they do see or glimpse something, they immediately block it out; the flash leaves them with sight in only one eye and then they look ever afterwards through that blind eye. It's a very rare gift indeed nowadays, and becoming rarer, the gift of being able to see straight through people, clearly and without qualms, with neither good intentions nor bad, without effort, that is, without any fuss or squeamishness. That is the way, in which according to Toby, you might be like us, Jacobo, and now I think he was right. We could both see people like that, clearly and without qualms, with neither good intentions nor bad. Seeing was our gift, and we placed it at the service of others. And I can still see.'

One night in London, I thought I had merely frightened myself with the idea that someone was following me, possibly with threatening intent. It could have been the rain, I reasoned, when that first idea seemed convincing, for the rain always makes footsteps on pavements sound as if they were giving off sparks or polishing something, like the rapid brushing of old-fashioned shoe-shines; or it could have been my raincoat rubbing against my trousers as I walked briskly along (the sound of flapping, dancing coat-tails, my raincoat unbuttoned, buffeted in turn by the gusty wind); or the shadow of my own open umbrella, which I could feel all the time at my back like a lingering sense of unease, I was holding it at an angle, resting on one shoulder the way soldiers carry a rifle or a spear when they're on parade; or perhaps the slight creak of its tense ribs as they were shaken by the wind. I had the constant feeling that someone was following close behind, sometimes I could hear what sounded like the short, rapid steps of a dog, for dogs always look as if they are walking over hot coals and being drawn airwards, so lightly do they place their eighteen invisible toes on the ground, as if they were always just about to leap up or levitate. Tis, tis, tis, that was the sound accompanying me, that was what I kept hearing and what made me turn round every few steps, a rapid turn of the head without stopping or slackening my pace, because of the wind the umbrella was only half-doing its job, I was walking at a steady rate, in a hurry to get home, I was returning after far too long a day at the building with no name, and it was late for London, although not at all late for Madrid (but I wasn't in Madrid now); I had only eaten a sandwich or two for lunch, many hours and even more faces ago, some of which I had observed from the stationary train compartment or wood-panelled hiding-place, although most had been on video, and their voices heard or, rather, listened to, their various tones, sincere or presumptuous, timid or false, crafty or boastful, uncertain or shameless. The effort required of me in this picking up and tuning in never diminished, and I had the distinct impression that it would steadily increase: the more one satisfies people's expectations, the more inflated these become and the more subtlety and precision they demand. And although I had, from the start (perhaps from Corporal Bonanza onwards) merely invented out of my own intuitions, the degree of irresponsibility and fiction being required or induced in me now by Tupra, Mulryan, Rendel and Pérez Nuix created a tension in me, almost an anxiety sometimes, usually before or after, but not during my inventive duties, which were termed interpretations or reports. I was aware that, with each day that passed, I was losing more and more scruples or, as Sir Peter Wheeler had put it, deferring my consciousness, letting it grow dim, deferring it indefinitely; and that I was venturing without its company ever farther away and with ever fewer qualms.

It was not, I thought, strange that I should frighten myself on a rainy night with the streets almost empty of other pedestrians and not a taxi in sight, although I had already abandoned that as an idea; or that my nerves should be on edge so that the slightest thing startled me, my loud, wet shoes, the anarchic flapping of my coat-tails, the battered dome of my umbrella whose floating image, in the more brightly lit areas, was reflected back up at me from the asphalt, as I passed by the monuments, gloomy in the evening dark, that pepper the many squares, the metallic creak of crickets produced by my every movement and by the gusty night wind, perhaps the real and weightless footsteps of some stray dog I could not yet see, but who, given the lack of other candidates – for I passed whole blocks without seeing a soul – was clearly following me, perhaps surreptitiously, until someone spotted it out all alone and took it away. Tis tis tis. I was aware of my own smells, but it was as if they had all been passed through water: damp silk and damp leather and damp wool, and I might have been sweating too, with not a trace left of the cologne I had put on that morning. Tis tis tis, I looked round, but there was nothing and nobody, just the sense of unease at the back of my neck and the feeling of menace – or was it merely vigilance – accompanying every rhythmic, constant step – one, two, three and four – as if I were on some interminable march with my umbrella-rifle or my umbrella-spear, even though their real function was that of a frail, over-sized helmet or a rickety shield borne on an arm that trembles and dances. 'I am myself my own fever and pain,' I was thinking when I believed I was merely frightening myself. 'I must be.'

No, it wasn't strange. Anyone who spends his days passing judgement, prognosticating and even diagnosing (not to say predicting), giving what are often groundless opinions, insisting that he has seen something when he has, in fact, seen little or nothing – always assuming he isn't pretending – ears pricked for any unusual emphases or vacillations, for any stumblings or quaverings, alert to the choice of words when those being observed have sufficient vocabulary to choose between several (which is not very often, some cannot even find the one possible word and have to be guided towards it, to have the word suggested to them, which makes them easy to mani-pulate), eyes tuned to detect any wilfully opaque glances, any excessive blinking, the drawing back of a lip as someone prepares to lie or the twitching jaw of the wildly ambitious, scrutinising faces to the point where you no longer see them as living, moving faces, observing them instead as if they were paintings, or as you might observe someone asleep or dead, or as you might observe the past; anyone whose main task is to trust no one ends up viewing everything in that suspicious, wary, interpretative light, dissatisfied with appearances and with the obvious and the straightforward; or, rather, dissatisfied with what is there. And then one easily forgets that what is there on the surface or in the first instance might sometimes be all there is, with no duplicity and no deceit or secrecy either, in the case of someone who is not hiding anything because they don't know how, because they know nothing of the theory and practice of concealment.

I had been carrying out my duties for several months, almost on a daily basis, hardly a day went by without my being summoned to the building with no name, even if only briefly in order to report back on what I had analysed and picked up, or what I had decided earlier at home. I had travelled a fair way along the path typically followed by all audacities (if it wasn't, in fact, mere insolence). You begin by prefacing everything with 'I don't know', 'I'm not sure'; or by qualifying and modifying as much as possible: 'It could be,' 'I would say that . . .', 'I can't be sure, but . . .', 'It seems likely to me that . . .', 'Possibly,' 'Possibly not,' 'This may be going too far, but . . .', 'This is pure supposition, but nevertheless . . .', 'Perhaps,' 'It might well be,' the archaic 'Methinks,' the American 'I daresay,' there are all kinds of shadings in both languages. Yes, you avoid affirmations in your speech and banish certainties from your mind, knowing full well that the former brings with it the latter just as the latter brings with it the former, almost simultaneously, with no noticeable difference, it's alarming how easily thought and speech contaminate each other. That is how it is at the beginning. But you soon grow more confident: you sense a commendation or a reproach in an oblique look or a chance remark, directed apparently at no one in particular and uttered in a neutral tone which you know, none the less, is intended for you, that it applies to you. You notice that 'I don't know' does not please, that inhibition is little appreciated, and that ambiguities are met with disappointment and niceties fall on stony ground; that the overly uncertain and cautious does not count and is not taken up, that the doubtful does not even persuade that there might be some reason for doubt, and reservations are almost a let-down; that 'Perhaps' and 'Maybe' are tolerated for the good of the enterprise and of the group, who, for all their audacity, do not wish to commit suicide, but they never arouse enthusiasm or passion, or even approval, they come across as faint-hearted and meek. And the bolder you get, the more questions they ask and the more skills they attribute to you, the bounds of what is knowable are always within a hair's-breadth of being lost, and one day you find that they are expecting you to see the indiscernible and to know the un-verifiable, to have an answer not just for the probable and even the merely possible, but for the unknown and unfathomable.

The most striking and most dangerous thing about this whole business is that you, too, begin to believe yourself capable of seeing and fathoming, of finding out and knowing, and, therefore, of hazarding an answer. Boldness never rests, it waxes or wanes, it burgeons or shrivels, it slips away or subjugates, and may disappear altogether after some major setback. But boldness, if it exists, is always on the move, it is never stable and never satisfied, it is the very opposite of stationary. And its main tendency is towards limitless increase, unless kept in check or brought up brutally short, or else systematically forced to retreat. In its expansive phase, perceptions become excitable or intoxicated, and arbitrariness, for example, ceases to seem arbitrary to you, believing, as you do, that your judgements and insights, however subjective, are based on solid criteria (a lesser evil, but what can you do); and there comes a point when it doesn't much matter whether you get things right, especially since in my work this was rarely verifiable, or if it was, they certainly never told me. From my continuance there, from the fact that they continued to request my services – somewhat bureaucratically and absurdly – and did not get rid of me, I inferred that my success rate must be quite high, but I also wondered occasionally if such a thing could be determined, and if it was, if anyone would bother to do so. I gave my opinions and verdicts, my prejudices and judgements: they were read or listened to; they asked me concrete questions: I gave them my answers, expanding on them and making comments and observations, identifying and summarising, inevitably going too far. I didn't know what they did with it all afterwards, if it had any consequences, if it was useful and had any practical effect or was merely fodder for the files, if it ever actually worked for or against someone; normally nothing was said, they never said anything to me afterwards, everything – for me at least – came down to that first act dominated by my ideas and a brief interrogation or dialogue; and the fact that, as far as I could see, there was no second or third or fourth act meant that the whole business (in day-to-day life, which is what matters most) seemed to me a rather silly game, or a series of hypothetical wagers, exercises in invention and perspicacity. And so, for a long time, I never had the feeling or the idea that I could be harming anyone.

When the *coup d'état* against Hugo Chávez took place in Venezuela, I couldn't help wondering if we had had some indirect influence on it; first on its apparent initial success, then on its grotesque failure (there seems to have been a lack of resolve); and on its chaotic end. I watched the television intently in case General Ponderosa, or whatever his real name was, should suddenly appear, but I never saw him, perhaps he hadn't been part of it at all. Perhaps the coup had failed because Tupra had advised against any financial aid and support, who knows. With Tupra I couldn't remain entirely silent about it:

'Have you seen what's been going on in Venezuela?' I asked him one morning, as soon as I went into his office.

'Yes, I have,' he replied, in the same tone of voice with which he had confirmed to the Venezuelan civilian soldier that he did not have our telephone number, but we had his. It was his conclusive tone of voice, or perhaps I should say concluding. And when he noticed that I was hesitating as to whether or not to pursue the matter, he added: 'Anything else, Jack?'

'No, nothing else, Mr Tupra.'

No, they didn't usually tell me when I had been right and when I had been wrong.

'I might be going out on a limb here, but . . .' 'I could be wrong, but nevertheless . . .' That 'but' and that 'nevertheless' are the cracks that end up flinging all the doors wide open, and soon the actual verbal formulae we use betray our insolence: 'I bet you anything you like that he'd change sides as soon as things got even slightly difficult, and change back again as many times as he needed to, his biggest problem being that neither side would want him because he's such a manifest coward,' one says of a functionary face – gleaming bald head, smeared glasses – seen for the first time half an hour ago and whom one is observing now through the false window or false oval mirror in a state of mind that is a mixture of superiority and defencelessness (the defencelessness of believing that others are always out to deceive you, the superiority of looking while unseen, of seeing everything without risking one's own eyes).

'The woman is desperate for attention, she'd invent the craziest fantasies just to be noticed, she has a need to show off to anything that moves, in any situation, not just to people with whom it might be worth the effort and who might do her some good, but to the hairdresser and the greengrocer and even the cat. She isn't even capable of curbing her enthusiasm or selecting her audience: she just can't distinguish, she wouldn't be much use to anyone,' says Tupra of a famous actress – with beautiful long hair but a very tense chin, hard as stone; bewitched by her own vanity – on seeing her in a video, and we all know that he's right, that he is, as always, spot-on, although there isn't a shred of – how can I put it – credible judgement to support his assertions.

'The guy has principles and would definitely never succumb to a bribe, I'd stake my life on it. Or rather, it's not even a matter of principles, it's more that he aspires to so little and is so dismissive of everything that neither flattery nor reward would lead him to adopt views he didn't find persuasive or, at the very least, amusing. The only way you could get at him would be by threatening him, because he might be susceptible to fear, physical fear I mean, he's never been punched in his life, well, not since he left school. He would go to pieces at the first hint of pain. He would be completely taken aback. He would crumble at the first scratch, the first pinch. He could be useful in some cases, as long as he didn't have to run that kind of risk,' says Rendel of a pleasant, youthful-looking, fifty-something writer – with sharp, elfin features, a slow way of talking, a slight Hampshire accent, according to Mulryan, round-rimmed spectacles, an unaffected way of speaking – on seeing and hearing an interview filmed almost entirely in close-up, we didn't see his hands once; and it seems to us that Rendel is right, that the novelist is a valiant man in his attitudes and his words, but that he would flinch from the merest threat of violence because he cannot even imagine it in his daily reality: he is capable of talking about it, but only because he sees it as an abstraction. As in the videotape, he would have no hands with which to defend himself.

'I wouldn't even cross the street with this man, he might push me under the wheels of a car if the mood took him, in a fit of rage. He's impetuous and impatient, it's hard to understand how he can exercise authority over anyone, or how he's managed to build up a business, still less a prosperous one, let alone an empire. His natural bent is for mugging passers-by at dusk or beating the living daylights out of someone, a hired killer on the rampage. He's a bundle of nerves, he can't wait, doesn't listen, takes no interest in what other people tell him, can't bear to spend even five minutes alone, but not because he wants company, just an audience. He probably has a really nasty temper, too, it wouldn't take much to make him blow his top, and then there's his voice, he must spend all day and night bellowing at his employees, at his children, at his two ex-wives and his six lovers (or possibly seven, there's some doubt about that). It's a complete mystery how he ever came to be a businessman or the head of anything, apart perhaps from some Soho dive threatened with closure on a daily basis. The only possible explanation is that he must instil a great sense of panic in people, and his hyperactivity reaches such heights that some, at least, of his innumerable plans and sordid deals must inevitably turn out well: probably, and by sheer chance, the most profitable ones. He may also have a nose for it, although that doesn't really fit well with his general recklessness: since the former takes persistence and calm, and he doesn't know the meaning of the words: he just abandons anything that resists him or proves difficult, that's his way of gaining time. God knows what he'll get up to if he goes into politics, as he assures us he will. Apart from outrages and abuses, of course, aimed at the electorate, I mean, because he would insult any potential voters at the first hint of criticism, the slightest slip and he'd heap insults on them,' says Mulryan of a multimillionaire who can be seen smiling in almost every shot taken at various events, sporting, charitable and monarchical, about to climb into a hot-air balloon, at the Ascot races and the Epsom Derby, suitably and grotesquely attired for each, signing a contract with a record company, or with another American movie-cum-fairground company, at the University of Oxford in some exotic ceremony involving colourful robes (a one-off occasion perhaps, I certainly never saw anything like it), shaking the hand of the Prime Minister and of various secondary figures and that of some spouse ennobled precisely by his or her conjugal status, at premières, inaugurations, concerts, ballets, at vaguely aristocratic gatherings, encouraging talent in all the most eye-catching arts, those that bring with them audiences, performances and applause; and although he's always smiling and contented in the television report or documentary – a receding hairline that nevertheless fails to make his forehead appear any higher, instead it appears horizontal, elongated; very strong, invasive, almost equine teeth; an anomalous tan; a tempting suggestion of curls hovering above his collar and even slightly below it as a vestige of his plebeian roots; the right clothes for every occasion, but which always look usurped or even hired; his body imprisoned, toned and furious, as if at odds with itself – we all believe that Mulryan is quite right, and we have no difficulty imagining this wealthy man slapping members of his entourage (and, needless to say, bawling at his subordinates) as soon as he could be quite sure that he wasn't being filmed.

'That woman knows a lot or has seen a lot and has decided not to talk about it, I'm sure of that. Her problem or, more than that, her torment is that it is there before her all the time, the terrible things she has witnessed or that she knows about and her personal vow to say nothing. It's not as if she had one day made a resolution which had subsequently brought her peace, however dear that resolution cost her. It's not as if from then on she has been able to live with the acceptable tranquillity of at least knowing what she wants – or, rather, doesn't want – to happen; that she has been able to stow those facts or that knowledge away in one corner of her mind, to deaden them, and gradually give them the consistency and configuration of dreams, which is what allows many people to live with the memory of atrocities and disappointments: by doubting, at least, from time to time, that they ever existed; by blurring them, wrapping them in the smoke of the accumulated years, and thus devaluing them. On the contrary, this woman thinks about it constantly, intensely, not only about what happened and has been proved to have happened, but about the fact that she must or chooses to keep silent. It's not that she's tempted to go back on her word (she would only say this inwardly, to herself); it isn't that she feels the decision she took is permanently provisional, it isn't that she's considering reneging on that decision and spends sleepless nights going over and over it. I would say that it's irrevocable, indeed, if you pressed me, I'd say more than irrevocable, because it has nothing to do with a commitment made. It's always as if she had taken the decision only yesterday. As if she were under the troubling influence of something eternally new and that never grows old, when it's likely that now it's all very remote, both what happened and her initial desire that it would never become public knowledge, or not, at least, because of her. I'm not referring to events relating to her profession, although there will be some such events that are equally safe, but to her private life: events that affected her and affect her every day, or that wound and infect her and provoke a fever in her every night, when she goes to bed. "No one will find out anything about it from me, not from me," she must think all the time, as if those previous experiences were there pulsating beneath her skin. As if they were still the nucleus of her existence and as if they still required her maximum attention, they will be the first thing to greet her when she wakes, the last thing she says good night to when she falls asleep. Don't get me wrong, though, there's nothing obsessive about this, her daily life is light and energetic; she's very open, not embittered at all. It's something quite different: a kind of loyalty to her own story. Such a woman would be of great service to many people, she's a perfect receptacle for secrets and therefore perfect for administering or distributing them too, she's completely reliable in that respect, precisely because she remains alert all the time and because, for her, everything is always alive and present. However remote in time her secret becomes, it never grows dim, and it would be the same with any secrets transmitted. She doesn't miss a single detail. Once the roles have been distributed, she would never forget who knows what and who doesn't. And I'm sure she remembers every face and every name that has passed before her bench,' says the young Pérez Nuix of a female judge of a certain age and with a bright, placid face, whom we are observing together from our hiding-place while Tupra and Mulryan ask respectful, devious questions, ladies are always offered tea in the afternoon, if, given their position and poise, they really are ladies, but not the gentlemen, unless they're bigwigs or could be influential in a particular matter, at most a cigarette (although never of the Pharaonic variety), and, exceptionally, an aperitif or a beer if it's that time of day and things are dragging on (there's a minibar concealed amongst the bookshelves); and despite her serene appearance and jovial expression – the warm smile; the very white but healthy complexion; the quick, bright, albeit very pale blue eyes; the dark shadows under her eyes, so deep and so becoming she must have had them since childhood; her ready, generous laughter, with just a hint of politeness, which, while it in no way impedes spontaneity, banishes any suggestion of flattery, of which there is not a trace; her amused awareness that Tupra feels for her a degree of desire, despite the unpropitious age-difference (a theoretical desire perhaps, or else retrospective or imaginary), because he can still see the young woman she was, or can sense it, and this is seen in turn by the woman who is no longer young, and it pleases and rejuvenates her – when I listen to young Nuix everything she says and describes seems plausible, because I, too, can see in that judge something akin to the excitement or vitality which comes from knowing an important secret that you have sworn never to divulge.

Naturally, young Nuix does not talk like this while both of us are watching and taking notes in the compartment, not so fluently or precisely (I am ordering it and shaping it now, as we all do when we talk about something, as well as complementing it with her subsequent written report), instead she makes occasional remarks to me across the table, they cannot see or hear us, although they know where we are, posted here by Tupra himself. And when I listen to her, I remember – I remember it every time, not just when she's interpreting this judge, Judge Walton – the words that Wheeler attributed to Tupra that Sunday: 'He says that in time she'll be the best of the group, if he can hold on to her for long enough,' and each time I wonder if she isn't already the best, the most exacting and the most gifted, the one who takes the most risks and who sees more deeply than any of the five of us, young Pérez Nuix, with a Spanish father and English mother, brought up in London but as familiar as I am with her father's country (not for nothing has she spent every summer for the last twenty or so years in Spain), and completely bilingual, not like me, for me the language that always prevails is the one in which I first began to speak, just as Jacques will always be for me *the* name, because it is the one I first answered to and the one by which I was called by the person who most often called to me. Her smile, too, is warm, her laughter ready and generous, the smile and laughter of a young woman, and her eyes, too, are quick and lively, all the more for being dark brown and as yet unburdened by tenacious memories that will not go away. She must be about twenty-five, or perhaps two years older or one year younger, and when our eyes meet, across the table or in any other situation, I notice that Luisa and my children begin to fade, whereas the rest of the time they seem all too clear even though they're so far away, and even though children's faces change so much that they never have one fixed image; I realise that the image that is taking root or that predominates is the one in the most recent photos I brought with me to England, I carry them in my wallet like any good or bad father, and I look at them too. I notice also that, despite the difference in our ages, young Nuix does not rule me out; or perhaps I should use the conditional: I cannot rid myself of the idea that she has or has had some sexual bond with Tupra, although there is nothing to indicate this unequivocally, and they treat each other with deference and humour, and with a kind of reciprocal paternalism, perhaps that is the main indicator. (But I can't get rid of the idea, and I know that one does not compete with Tupra.) The idea that she doesn't or won't or wouldn't rule me out is something I see in her eyes, as I have in the eyes of other women over the last few years without once being mistaken – when you're young, you're more myopic and more astigmatic and more presbyopic, all at the same time – and I breathe it and hear it in the brief gathering of energy that takes place, out of shyness or some lurking embarrassment, before she comes over to talk to me, that is, beyond the initial greeting or the isolated question or answer, as if she had to gather momentum or take a run-up, or as if she mentally constructed the whole of her first sentence (which, oddly enough, is never short), as if she structured it and memorised the whole thing before pronouncing it. This is often what one does when speaking a foreign language, but when we are alone or in any private exchanges, this young woman and I, we always opt for Spanish, which is also her language.

And I was left in no doubt of this one morning when, in a situation in which she should, by rights, have been assailed by blushes, there was no sign at all of any lurking embarrassment. I had been given the keys to the building with no name, and, believing myself to be the first to arrive that morning on the floor we occupied (a bout of dawn insomnia had driven me out of the house to begin the day in earnest and to finish off a report I was writing), and believing therefore that I was the first to turn the key (the night-time bolts still in place), I was puzzled to hear noises and a gentle humming coming from one of the offices, the door of which I opened not violently exactly, but with verve and *élan*, with the vague idea of disconcerting the potential intruder, the early-rising spy or surreptitious burglar, and thus having the advantage if it came to a confrontation, although this seemed unlikely given the apparently tranquil humming. And then I saw her, young Nuix, standing by the desk, naked from the waist up and with a towel in the hand with which, just at that moment, she was drying one armpit, her arm raised. On her lower half, she was wearing a tight skirt, the skirt she had had on the day before, I always make a note of her clothes. I was so surprised by this vision (and yet, at the same time, not very surprised, perhaps not surprised at all: I knew it was a woman's voice doing the humming) that I did not do what I should have done, mutter a hurried apology and close the door, with me, of course, on the outside. It was only a matter of seconds, but I allowed those seconds to pass (one, two, three, four; and five) all the while looking at her with, I think, an expression that was part questioning, part appreciative and part falsely embarrassed (and therefore decidedly stupid), before saying 'Good morning' in an entirely neutral tone, that is, as if she was as fully dressed as I was, or almost, I still had my raincoat on. In a sense, I suppose, I behaved hypocritically as if nothing was amiss, and as if I had seen nothing; but I was helped in this – I would like to think – by the fact that young Nuix did exactly the same and also behaved as if nothing was wrong. For those few seconds in which I held the door open before withdrawing, she not only did not cover herself up, out of fear or modesty or, at the very least, surprise (she could easily have done so with the towel), she remained quite still, like a freeze-frame in a video, in exactly the same posture as when I had burst into the office, looking at me with a questioning but not remotely stupid expression, neither falsely nor truly embarrassed. All she did, though, was to cease her humming and her movement: she was rubbing herself dry with a towel, and she stopped doing that, the towel arrested at rib-height. And in that position she not only did not conceal her nakedness (which she didn't, not even as a reflex action), she kept her arm raised and thus allowed me to observe her armpit, and when a naked woman allows you to do that, uncovering one or both, it's as if she were offering up to you an additional nakedness. It was, of course, a clean, smooth and, I deduced, newly washed armpit, and, needless to say, shaved, without that awful bush of hair that some women insist on preserving nowadays as some strange protest against the traditional taste of men, or most men. 'Good morning,' she said in the same neutral tone. It was only a matter of seconds (five, six, seven, eight; and nine), but the calm and nonchalance with which we behaved during their passing reminded me of the time when my wife, Luisa, shortly after our son was born, stood stock-still half-way through getting undressed (her upper body bare, her breasts still swollen with milk, she was just about to go to bed) and answered some absurd questions I was asking her about our newborn child ('Do you think this child will always live with us, as long as he is a child or at least while he's still very young?'). She was getting undressed, in one hand she held the tights she had just removed, in the other the nightdress she was about to put on ('Of course he will, don't be so silly, who else would he live with?'; and she had added: 'As long as nothing happens to us, that is'), while young Nuix held in her hand the towel with which she did not even think of covering herself and, indeed, did not cover herself, and the other hand free and held up high, like a statue in antiquity. They were both half-naked ('What do you mean?' I had asked Luisa then), and the nakedness of one had nothing to do with that of the other (I mean as far as I was concerned, because clearly there was, objectively speaking, a resemblance): that of my wife was familiar to me and even customary, which doesn't mean I was indifferent to it, far from it, in fact, even in that fleeting, domestic moment, I glanced at her swollen breasts; but it was normal for us to go on talking as if it didn't matter, and not to interrupt our conversation because of it ('Nothing bad, I mean,' she had replied); that of my young work colleague was, on the other hand, new, unexpected, unprecedented, entirely unforeseen and even undeserved and, from my point of view, furtive, the product of a misunderstanding or of carelessness, and so I looked at her differently, not shamelessly or lasciviously but with an attention that sought both to discover and to memorise, with the apparently veiled eyes of the time we live in and that were always the norm in England, where we were living and where that mode of looking without looking and that way of not looking yet looking has been developed and honed to perfection, and from which I only ever saw one person almost escape or step free, and that was Tupra; and she allowed me to look without looking, she did nothing to prevent it, but neither was there shamelessness or exhibitionism in her eyes or in her attitude, and when she added something more, an explanation that was neither expected nor necessary, and which, despite being the first phrase she had addressed to me that day, did not appear to have been composed beforehand in her head ('I slept here, well, I didn't exactly sleep much, I spent the night wrestling with a particularly fiendish report'), her voice and her tone did not sound so very different from the tone and voice of the married existence I know so well. And so once the remaining seconds had elapsed (nine, ten, eleven and twelve: 'Oh, don't worry, I came in early to see if I can finish a report of my own,' I said in turn, not so much in order to explain myself, but more by way of a belated and implicit apology), I finally closed the door, with one resolute, almost hasty movement (I hadn't let go of the handle), and withdrew to my office, which was next door and which I shared with Rendel, she shared hers with Mulryan. Young Nuix belonged to a different generation, I told myself; I told myself that she probably spent the summers bare-breasted on the beaches and beside the swimming-pools of Spain, that she would be used to being seen like that and admired, her sense of modesty diminished. I also thought that we were compatriots and that when abroad that was almost the same as being related; it creates unusual complicities and solidarities and gives rise to baseless confidences, as well as to friendships and loves that would be unimaginable, almost aberrant, in the common country of origin (a friendship with De la Garza, Rafita, the great moron). But she was probably more English than Spanish, I mustn't forget that. Besides, I know very well that when a woman surprised in her nakedness makes no immediate attempt to cover herself up, even if only instinctively (unless, of course, she's a striptease artiste or something, and I've known a few in my time), it is because she does not rule out the person who has taken her by surprise and is now looking at her, and that goes for all living generations, or at least for the adults of those generations. It isn't that the woman feels attracted to that person or necessarily desires him, my theory would never entertain such ingenuous suppositions. It is simply that she does not rule him out, or does not exclude him, not entirely, and it is highly likely that it is only then that she finds out or realises, in that moment of being seen by someone and deciding not to cover herself up for him, always assuming, of course, that any decision is involved. Young Nuix's raised arm did not, in the end, remind me of the arm of a statue, at least not in my memory: instead I imagined her as if she were gripping the rail on a bus, or strap-hanging in a subway car. There she remained, still holding tight, her arm in the air, when I closed the door and ceased seeing both her arm and the smooth armpit that set off the rest. She must have put it down immediately afterwards. It lasted twelve seconds in all. I did not count them at the time, only afterwards, in memory.

At the time, I didn't quite know what was meant by certain frequently used expressions, which cropped up in both written and oral reports, and even in the spontaneous and apparently trivial comments exchanged while studying photos or videos or the flesh-and-blood people that Tupra had invited or, as was often the case, summoned, or even, it occurred to me, ordered to come. If we were commissioned to do this work by others, if we had no interests of our own and were merely giving our opinions, airing our views and making judgements, I assumed that the people we observed and who could be 'useful' or 'not useful', 'of great service' or 'of no service' (I myself quickly picked up these expressions, and grew accustomed to the concept without actually understanding it, practice makes up for so many things, as does unreflective habit), would be designated as such by the commissioners of the various tasks, depending on their specific needs and their particular investigations or problems, which must be more varied than I had imagined to begin with, when Wheeler spoke to me about the past or prehistory of the group, as he called it in order not to call it anything, lacking as it did a real name ('You won't find anything about this in any books,' he had warned me, 'don't even bother consulting them, you'll just waste your time and your patience').

I rarely knew the source or origin of each commission, and it was rarely alluded to, I tended to think that all of them or the great majority came from official, state, governmental or administrative authorities within Britain, or, on a few occasions (given the remote or repeated nationalities of the subjects under study), from their equivalents in friendly countries or in countries which, out of self-interest or circumstance, were their allies: I was surprised how many Australians, New Zealanders, Canadians, Egyptians, Saudis and Americans crossed our screens, especially the last. Nor could I really explain why some of these people were being submitted to our vigilance and judgement (because that was the predominant feeling, that we were watching and judging them), especially when we were not questioned afterwards regarding any particular area or subject or characteristic. That woman, Judge Walton, for example. Neither Tupra or Mulryan or Rendel asked me any specific questions about her after my turn on watch (although perhaps they did ask young Nuix, who had caught so much of her character), and I found it hard to imagine what possible point there could be in watching, interpreting, deciphering, un-ravelling or unmasking a woman as decent, intelligent and solid as she seemed to be. At other times, the type of question gave me some idea as to what was going on, as to what it was they were after, Tupra, Mulryan, Rendel, Nuix, or, more likely, what the superior or inferior authorities – the clients – were after, the people who contracted them and made use of them, that is, of us and our supposed gift, of our presumed abilities, or perhaps, merely, of our audacity, which was always on the increase, always growing.

As the weeks passed and then the months, I gradually broadened the spectrum of my responses, as well as my sheer bare-faced cheek.

'Do you think this woman is being unfaithful, even though she swears she's not and there's not a scrap of proof?' Mulryan asked me of a well-dressed woman with a slightly hooked nose who was there in her living-room denying any such infidelity to her husband, the two of them sitting on a sofa in front of the television, which was on at the time, and who were clearly being filmed by a hidden camera, possibly installed in the set by her very own spouse (a man with a broad face and a propensity for smiling, even when, as at that moment, this was entirely inappropriate), who had presumably come to us for advice, because he felt he could no longer distinguish her honest tones from her deceitful ones, custom and cohabitation do sometimes tend to level these things out, a certain lacklustre quality, a certain lethargy overtake dialogues and responses, and there comes a day when the important and the insignificant, the true and the false, all receive the same scant degree of emphasis.

'Yes, I think she is,' I replied. 'Her denial was too brazen, too eloquent, almost sarcastic. For all her gesticulating, his question didn't really take her by surprise. She wasn't offended by it either. She had been expecting this to happen for some time and had her response ready, had learned the words she was going to use almost by heart, had rehearsed precisely the tone and expression she would use when she spoke them. Not in front of the mirror, perhaps, but mentally. Her imagination was so imbued with it beforehand, all she had to do was to activate it. She was almost longing for the unpleasant moment to arrive.'

'You think. You think. Is that all, Jack? Or are you sure?' insisted Mulryan, ignoring what we all know: that no one can be sure of anything, unless they have acted or taken part or been a witness (and on many occasions, not even that: the drop of blood).

'I'm sure in so far as my sureness is based on what I see and perceive, on what you give me,' was my convoluted reply, a last attempt to protect my back slightly and not dive headfirst into further boldnesses. 'For example, she said she found his suspicions "hysterically funny". She wouldn't have used that adverb if she hadn't already considered, chosen, foreseen it. Nor would she if they really did strike her as funny. In that case, she wouldn't have used any adverb, or, at most, a more everyday one, like "terribly", less emphatic, less mocking. And if the accusation was false, she wouldn't have described it as "exhilarating", nor would she have lowered herself so much as to say how she, "little me", wished she could arouse the desires of other men. Few women, regardless of their age or physique, really and truly believe that they cannot still arouse someone's desire. I'm referring here to the wealthy, of course, to which class this lady apparently belongs. They might pretend that they believe it, they might complain in public so that others can contradict or reaffirm them, they might wonder to themselves and even doubt it in rare moments of depression or following a rejection. Rarely more than that. They soon recover from that kind of depression. They soon put the rejection down to a heart already taken, that usually provides them with a decorous, acceptable explanation.' – 'Nor Hell a fury, like a woman scorn'd,' I said to myself. And I thought: 'A bit of an exag-geration.' – 'And if they do one day believe it, they don't talk about it. Least of all to their partner.'

'But he believed her,' Mulryan objected or pointed out.

'Then he needs to be cured of his credulity,' I replied with more aplomb now. 'He can always choose to ignore our ver-dict, he can always tell us where to stick our verdict, assuming that the verdict is intended for him, assuming he's the one who commissioned it.' – By then, I knew that, during the sessions, there was no need to be overly careful with one's vocabulary. – 'But she's being unfaithful to him, I'll stake my life on it.' You always ended up putting your head on the block. Perhaps it was simply provoked pride, perhaps you really did see things more clearly as you talked; or convinced yourself that you did. Speaking is so dangerous. It isn't just that others can then no longer help but take account of what you've said. It's also that you yourself feel obliged to believe it, once it is there, floating in the air and not just in your head, where everything can still be ruled out. Once it has been heard and has gone on to form part of the knowledge of those other people, who can now make use of it and appropriate it, and even use it against us.

Or it could have been Tupra questioning me in his cosy

office, the morning after a celebrity supper I had been drafted into as a guest – 'An old Spanish friend of mine who's just flown in, a real artist, I couldn't possibly leave him all alone in his hotel room': 'Being an artist is the perfect passport nowadays,' he used to say, 'because it doesn't commit you to anything, you can be an artist in any field, be it interior design, footwear, the stock market, tiling or confectionery' – because a couple of my compatriots were also going to be there – the man was an artist in the world of finance, and the woman in the world of theatre – whom he wanted me to entertain, at the same time finding out a little about our host, while Tupra took care of the host himself and a few other major British players:

'Tell me, Jack, what did you think of our buffoon of a host last night, yes, that ridiculous singer, do you think he would be capable of killing someone? In some extreme situation, for example, if he felt really threatened? Or would he be simply incapable of it, would he be the sort who would just give in and allow himself to be knifed to death, rather than get his blow in first? Or, on the contrary, do you think he could kill, even in cold blood?'

I paused to think for a moment, I never now answered straight off 'I don't know; how could I possibly know that?', I never replied like that to any question, however strange or convoluted or fantastical or overly precise, not even one as arcane as that, after all, who knows who would be capable of killing, or when, and whether in hot or cold or lukewarm blood. And yet I always ventured some answer, trying to be honest, that is, trying to see something before actually saying it, and avoiding talking for talking's sake, or simply because I was expected to talk. I tried at least to place myself in the situation or the hypothesis thrown at me by every question asked by my superiors or my colleagues. And the strangest or most terrifying thing was that I always managed to see or glimpse something (I mean I didn't invent it, they weren't visions or mere cunning tales), and therefore was able to suggest something, that is doubtless the process by which audacity advances, and so much depends on practice, on pushing yourself. Most people are limited by their own lack of persistence, because they are lazy or too easily satisfied, and also because they are afraid. Most people will go only so far and then apply the brakes, they suddenly stop and sit down to recover from the fright or else drop asleep, which is why they always fall short. Someone has an idea and normally that one idea is enough, they pause, pleased with that first thought or discovery and do not continue thinking, or, if they're writing, do not continue writing more profoundly, they do not drive themselves onwards; they feel satisfied with that first fissure or not even that: with the first cut, with piercing a single layer of people and events, intentions and suspicions, truths and quackery, the times we live in are the enemy of inner dissatisfaction and, therefore, of constancy, they are organised so that everything quickly palls and our attention becomes frolicsome and erratic, distracted by the mere passing of a fly, people cannot bear sustained investigation or perseverance, to immerse themselves properly in something in order to find out about that something. The prolonged gaze, Tupra's gaze, the gaze that ends up affecting everything it gazes at, is not permitted. Nowadays, eyes that linger offend, which is why they have to hide behind curtains and binoculars and telephoto lenses and remote cameras, to spy from their thousands of screens.

In one respect – but only one – Tupra reminded me of my father, who never allowed us, my siblings and me, to be satisfied with what appeared to be a dialectical victory in our debates, or a success in explaining ourselves. 'What else,' he would say when we had assumed, exhausted, that an exposition or an argument was over. And if we replied: 'Nothing. That's it. Isn't that enough?', he would reply, to our momentary wild despair: 'Why, you haven't even started yet. Go on. Quickly, hurry, keep thinking. Having an idea, or identifying it, is something, but then again, once absorbed, it's almost nothing: it's like arriving at the first, most elementary level, which, it's true, is more than most people ever do. But the really interesting and difficult thing, the thing that can prove both truly worthwhile and very hard work, is to continue: to continue thinking and to continue looking beyond what is purely necessary, when you have the feeling that there is no more to think and no more to see, that the sequence is complete and that to continue would be a waste of time. In that wasted time lies the truly important, in the gratuitous and apparently superfluous, beyond the limit where you feel satisfied, or where you get tired or give up, often without even realising it. At the point where you might say to yourself there can't be anything else. So tell me, what else, what else occurs to you, what else can you bring to the argument, what else can you offer, what else have you got? Go on thinking, quickly now, don't stop, go on.'

Tupra did the same, by pointing out inadequacies, as he had ever since that first meeting with Soldier Bonanza, with his 'What else?', 'Explain that, will you,' 'Tell me what you think,' 'Why do you think that?', 'Go on,' 'Talk to me about those details,' 'Anything else?,' 'Is that all you noticed?' It was a gentle, measured tenacity, by which he nevertheless extracted everything you had thought or seen, even the dream or shadow of thoughts and images, what was not yet formulated or delineated and therefore not entirely thought or seen, but only sketched or intuited or still implicit, still unrecognisable and phantasmagoric, like the sculpture enclosed in the block of marble or the poems contained almost in their entirety by grammar books and dictionaries. He managed to make the illusory acquire speech and put on flesh. And find expression. Sometimes it felt to me like an act of faith on his part: faith in my abilities, in my perspicacity, in my supposed gift, as if he were sure that with just the right degree of insistence – guided by it, trained by it – I would always provide him at last with the drawing or the text, present him with the portrait he wanted from me, or needed.

Yes, that, more or less, was how it was, if the report I read about myself was authentic, and I had no reason to believe it wasn't. I came across it one morning while looking something up in one of the old filing-cabinets. What was not intended for everyone's eyes must have been kept and stored there rather than on computer, so insecure and unprotected. I saw my name, 'Deza, Jacques', and pulled out the file without even thinking about it. It was dated a couple of months after my first intervention (well, that's how I saw it), after my interpretation of Conscript Bonanza and the subsequent interrogation regarding my impressions of the man, and it wasn't really a proper report, just a few jottings, possibly handwritten – possibly made by Tupra himself – as a result of who knows what actions or interpretations on my part, although someone had clearly judged them of sufficient worth to be filed away and had had them transcribed on to a computer or typewriter – perhaps he had taken the trouble to do this himself. I read them quickly, then buried them again. No one had ever told me not to consult those old files, but I had the distinct feeling that it would be best if I was not found reading things that had been written about me and which I had not been shown. It was a brief report, a few impressionistic notes really, not at all systematic or organised, a bit confused and contradictory, almost indecisive. This, more or less, is what it said:

It's as if he didn't know himself very well. He doesn't think much about himself, although he believes that he does (albeit without great conviction). He doesn't see himself, doesn't know himself, or, rather, he doesn't delve into or investigate himself. Yes, that's it: it isn't that he doesn't know himself, merely that this is a kind of knowledge that doesn't interest him and which he therefore barely cultivates. He doesn't examine himself, he would see this as a waste of time. Perhaps it doesn't interest him because it's all water under the bridge; he has little curiosity about himself. He just takes himself for granted, or assumes he knows himself. But people change. He doesn't bother recording or analysing his changes, he's not up to date with them. He's introspective. And yet the more he appears to be looking in, the more he is, in fact, looking out. He's only interested in the external, in others, and that is why he sees so clearly. But his interest in people has nothing to do with wanting to intervene in their lives or to influence them, nor with any utilitarian aim. He may not care very much what happens to anyone. Not that he wouldn't regret or celebrate what happened, he's a caring person, not indifferent to others, but always in a rather abstract way. Or perhaps it's just that he's very stoical, about other people's lives and his own. Things happen and he makes a mental note, not for any particular reason, usually without even feeling greatly concerned most of the time, still less implicated. Perhaps that is why he notices so many things. So few escape him that it's almost frightening to imagine what he must know, how much he sees and how much he knows. About me, about you, about her. He knows more about us than we ourselves do. About our characters I mean. Or, more than that, about what shaped us. With a knowledge to which we are not a party. He judges little. The oddest thing of all is that he makes no use of his knowledge. It's as if he were living a parallel theoretical life, or a future life that was awaiting its turn in the dressing-room. Waiting for its moment in another existence. And as if all the discoveries, perceptions, opinions and verifications ended up there. And not in his present, real existence. Even what does affect him, even his own experiences and disappointments seem to split into two parts, and one of the two is destined for that merely theoretical or future knowledge of his. Enriching it, nourishing it. Not, strangely enough, with a view to anything. Not at least to anything in this real life of his that does move forward. He makes no use of his knowledge, it's very odd. But he has it. And if he did one day make use of it, he would be someone to be feared. He'd be pretty unforgiving I think. Sometimes he seems to me to be a complete enigma. And sometimes I think he's an enigma to himself. Then I go back to the idea that he doesn't know himself very well. And that he doesn't pay much attention to himself because he's given up understanding himself. He considers himself a lost cause upon whom it would be pointless squandering thought. He knows he doesn't understand himself and that he never will. And so he doesn't waste his time trying to do so. I don't think he's dangerous. But he is to be feared.

To be honest, all this left me fairly cold, although it did make me think that somewhere there must be a proper file on me, with dates and information, verifiable facts and detailed characteristics, along with my conventional CV (or, who knows, my unconfessable one), and with rather less ethereal and unverifiable observations and descriptions. There must be files on all of us, it would have been strange if there weren't, and I promised myself that I would one day quietly seek them out, those on Rendel and young Nuix might be of interest to me, though not so much Mulryan's; and Tupra's, of course, assuming he had a file. Before closing the drawer, I rested my thumb on the upper edge of the files and riffled through a few of them, not too quickly, just out of curiosity, stopping occasionally at random. I came across some very famous entries: '*Bacon, Francis*', '*Blunt, Sir Anthony*', '*Caine, Sir Michael (Maurice Joseph Micklewhite)*', '*Clinton, William Jefferson "Bill"*', '*Coppola, Francis Ford*', '*Le Carré, John (David Cornwell)*', '*Richard, Keith (The Rolling Stones)*', '*Straw, Jack*' (the British Foreign Minister, formerly Home Secretary, the one who so shamelessly let Pinochet go, he was the person I needed information on that morning, about his improper past), '*Thatcher, Margaret Hilda, Baroness*'. Those were the files that my thumb stopped at, some were already dead. A lot of other names meant nothing, being unknown to me: '*Booth, Thomas*', '*Dearlove, Richard*', '*Marriott, Roger (Alan Dobson)*', '*Pirie-Gordon, Sarah Jane*', '*Ramsay, Margaret "Meta", Baroness*', '*Rennie, Sir John*', '*Skelton, Stanyhurst (Marius Kociejowski)*', '*Truman, Ronald*', '*West, Nigel (Rupert Allason)*', my gaze fell on them, how many people there were who called themselves by other names, and I have an excellent memory for names.

It was pleasing that, in such company, they should take so much trouble over me; that they should want to get to the bottom of me, that they should take notice. The thing I found most intriguing was the moment in the report when the writer or thinker, whoever it was, openly addressed another person, indicating that his impressions or conjectures were directed at someone in particular: 'About me, about you, about her', he said. 'He knows more about us than we ourselves do,' and, by a process of elimination, I thought that young Nuix must be 'her', although I couldn't be absolutely sure. But who was that 'you', who was that 'I'? There were various possibilities, but there was no way I could find out. Nor could I imagine who it was, therefore, who believed I should be feared, that too struck me as very odd, because I didn't myself believe it at the time. (Unless the 'I', 'you' and 'her' were metaphorical, hypothetical, interchangeable, as if the expression had been 'It's almost frightening to imagine what he knows, how much he sees and how much he knows. About Tom, Dick or Harry.') Needless to say these notes were unsigned, like all the others in the file, or at least those in that drawer. They seemed to have been written rapidly, judging from the brief time I dared to spend looking at them, when my thumb lingered over some: the notes on me were as vague and speculative as were those devoted to ex-President Clinton or to Mrs Thatcher, which I glanced through quickly.

'Yes, I think he could,' I replied, having given a few seconds' thought to Tupra's questions regarding the host of that celebrity supper (the host was himself a singer-celebrity, I'll call him Dick Dearlove, one of the unknown or unlikely names I had seen in the file, and who, I learned, was a very high-ranking, very important civil servant in some ministry or other, I had only read a couple of lines about him, but with a surname like that he should really have been a great idol of the masses treading the boards of a thousand stages, like our ex-dentist singer-host). 'In a dangerous situation, he would, of course, get his blow in first, if he had the chance. Or even beforehand, I mean before the risk to his own life was imminent and certain. The mere suggestion of a grave threat would turn him into a man of excess, render him almost uncontrollable. He would, I believe, be quick to react violently. Or, rather, he would anticipate that violence: I don't know if the saying exists in English, but in Spanish we say that he who gives first gives twice. But that wouldn't be the reason, he wouldn't react in a calculating fashion, or out of bravery, or even out of nerves or, strictly speaking, panic. He's so pleased with his own biography and with the life he leads, so astonished and proud of what he has achieved and continues to achieve (he can't as yet see it ending), his fairy-tale is turning out so picture-perfect that he couldn't bear for it all to be destroyed in a matter of seconds, prematurely, by mistake and through bad luck, through recklessness or some unfortunate encounter. It's the idea he couldn't bear. Let's say burglars got into his house, ready for anything; or if he was mugged in the street; no, he wouldn't ever walk down a street. Let's say his car broke down while he was driving through a really rough area, that it conked out late one night as he was returning from his country house, alone at the wheel or accompanied by a bodyguard, he probably always has at least one with him, he wouldn't go a hundred yards without some protection. And that the moment they stepped out they were surrounded by a large, aggressive, armed gang, a band of desperadoes against whom two men could do nothing, especially when one of them was accustomed only to being flattered and pampered and to a complete absence of nasty surprises.'

'They would immediately call for help on their cell phones or would already have done so on the car phone, to the police or whoever,' Tupra said, interrupting me. It amused me the ease with which he joined in or participated in my fantasies. I think he rather enjoyed listening to me.

'Let's say that the car phone died at the same time as the car did, and that their other phones were out of range, or had been taken off them before they had time to use them. I don't know about in England, but in Spain that's the very first thing criminals steal, they go for your cell phone first and then your wallet, and that's why all muggers, even the really pathetic ones still clutching a needle in one trembling hand, all have cell phones. You won't see a single pickpocket in Madrid, or even a beggar, who hasn't got his own cell phone.'

'Really,' said Tupra, tempted to smile. He was familiar with my exaggerations, and did not really disapprove of them.

'Yes, really. Just go to Madrid and you'll see that I'm right. Well, in that situation, if Dearlove was carrying a knife, or even a pistol (he'd be quite capable of owning one, licence and all), he would probably start shooting or lashing out without even trying to negotiate and without gauging the precise nature of the threat, the degree of the desperadoes' desperation or hatred, they might well turn out to be admirers of his who, when they recognise him, would end up asking for his autograph, it could happen, you can't overestimate his popularity. He's a huge star in Spain as well, especially, as you may or may not know, in the Basque Country.'

'I can imagine. Nowadays any buffoon is guaranteed universal acclaim,' said Tupra. 'Go on.' At the time, he used to call me Jack, although I still called him Mr Tupra.

'What Dearlove could not bear,' obviously I didn't call him Dearlove, but by his real name, 'is that his life should end like that; in short, he would find the manner of his death almost more unbearable than death itself. He would, of course, be terrified to see his successful existence truncated and to lose his life, as would anyone, even if that life had been a failure; what's more, I don't, as I said, believe him to be a brave man, he would be terribly afraid. What most horrifies Dearlove, though, as it does other show-business people (although they may not know it), is that the end of his story should be such that it overshadows and darkens the life he's lived and accumulated up until now, eclipsing it, almost erasing and cancelling out the rest and, in the end, becoming the only fact that counts and will be recounted. If he were capable of killing (and I believe he is), that would be the reason, narrative disgust, if I can put it like that. You see, Mr Tupra, if someone like him were killed by a group of criminals in Clapham or Brixton, or, even more conspicuously, if he was lynched, that kind of death would create such a scandal, it would so shock the world, that it would be brought up every time his name was mentioned, on every occasion and in every circumstance, even if they were talking about him for some other reason, because of his contribution to the popular music of his time or to the history and heyday of buffoons, or because of the vast fortune he amassed with his voice or as one of the more worrying examples of mass hysteria. It would make no difference, they would still always mention the tale of how he was lynched in Brixton due to some awful misunderstanding, or in Clapham one fateful night along with his best bodyguard, or at the hands of a few unspeakably cruel felons from Streatham. A time would come, indeed, when that would be all that was remembered of him. Mothers would even use it to scold their children with when they strayed into the wilder parts of town or into other dodgy areas: "Just you remember what happened to Dick Dearlove, and he was famous and had a bodyguard with him." A real posthumous curse, for someone like him I mean.'

Tupra, who was smiling broadly now, improved on this by saying: 'Remember Dickie Dearlove, darlin', and 'ow they did 'im in,' adopting a cockney accent (or possibly a half-educated South London accent, I can't really tell the difference) and putting on a mother's voice. 'Good grief, I'm sure he could never in his life imagine a more sordid epitaph for himself. Not even in his most humiliating nightmares. What else, though, go on.'

'I don't know if such a phobia has ever been recorded, or if it has a rather less pedantic name than the one I gave it. Dearlove himself, of course, would never use such terms. He wouldn't even understand what I was talking about, I might as well be speaking Greek. And yet that is what it is: narrative horror or disgust; a dread of having his story ruined by the ending, wrecked for ever, destroyed, of its complete ruination by a finale too spectacular for the world's taste and hateful to himself; of the irreparable damage done to his story, of a stain so powerful and voracious that it would spread and spread until it had, retrospectively, wiped out everything else. Dearlove would be capable of killing in order to avoid such a fate. Or such an aesthetic, dramaturgical or narrative doom, as you prefer. I'm sure he would be capable of killing for that reason. At least so I believe.' When I finished, I would sometimes retreat a little, shrink back, not that it made any difference, I had spoken, I had said my piece.

'You'll all end up like Dick Dearlove, every one of you,' said Tupra, pursuing his imitation for a while longer, laughing briefly and wagging an admonitory finger. Then he added: 'The only thing is, Jack, that someone like him would never drive through Clapham or Brixton, either to enter the city or leave it.'

'All right, but he could get lost, take the wrong freeway exit and end up there high and dry, couldn't he? It does happen. I saw something similar in a film called *Grand Canyon*, have you seen it?'

'I don't go to the movies much, unless obliged to by my work. I used to, when I was young. But I'm afraid you haven't quite grasped the economic level of these people, Jack. For short trips Dearlove probably travels around in a helicopter. And for longer trips he uses his private jet, with an entourage that would make the queen's look positively puny.' He fell silent for a moment, as if recalling a journey made in just such a private plane. Tupra was always very scornful of Dearlove and similar figures, but the fact is that he mixed on occasions with quite a few of them, from the worlds of television, fashion, pop music and the movies, and whenever I had seen him with them, he had always appeared to treat them with easy sympathy and trust. Sometimes I wondered if these contacts, difficult to achieve for most people, were provided from on high, as part of his job and to make his work easier. Naturally, I never knew exactly what his job was. On the other hand, he never seemed uncomfortable in the company of even the most frivolous of celebrities. It could just be part of his training, of his trade, it didn't necessarily mean he enjoyed it. The truth is that he never seemed uncomfortable in any social situation, with the brainy or the serious, with the pretentious or the idiotic, with the marginalised or with the simple, he was clearly a man who adapted to whatever was required of him. Then he returned to the subject: 'Tell me, do you think he would be capable of killing in any other circumstance, apart from one in which he saw that his life might not only be in danger, but also, according to you . . . called into question? You may be right, he might well be horrified to think that his end could prove ugly, inappropriate, onerous, humiliating, sarcastic, turbulent, dirty . . .'

'I don't know,' I replied, slightly put out by his realistic rigour, and I immediately regretted having spoken those words, the words most guaranteed to disappoint in that building, or the most despised. I quickly covered them up. 'That seems to me the principal motive, but I suppose it wouldn't be necessary for his life to be in danger, if, as I believe, he is, in a sense, more concerned with his history, with the story of his life than with that life itself. Although he is probably unaware of this. That priority has, I believe, less to do with any future or present biographers than with his need to retell the story to himself every day, to live with it. I'm not sure if I'm making myself clear.'

'No, not entirely, Jack. Be more precise, please. Try a bit harder. Don't get yourself in such a tangle.'

Such comments spurred me on, a slight infantilism on my part, from which I've never managed to free myself and probably never will.

'He likes his image, he likes his story as a whole, even the odontological phase; he never loses sight of it, never forgets it.' I was trying to be more precise. 'He always has in his mind his entire trajectory: his past as well as his future. He sees himself as a story, whose ending he must take care of, but whose development he must not neglect either. It isn't that he will allow no upsets or weaknesses or stains in his story, he's not that naïve.

However, these must be of a kind that do not stand out too stridently, that do not inevitably leap out at him (a horrible protuberance, a lump) when, each morning, he looks at himself in the mirror and thinks about "Dick Dearlove" as a whole, as an idea, or as if he were the title of a novel or a film, which has, moreover, already achieved the status of a classic. It has nothing to do with morality or with shame, that's not it, indeed most people find it easy enough to look themselves in the face, they always find excuses for their own excesses, or deny that they are excesses; bad consciences and selfless regret have no place in our times, I'm speaking of something else. He sees himself from outside, almost exclusively from outside, he has no difficulty admiring himself. And perhaps the first thing he says when he wakes up is something like: "Goodness, it wasn't a dream: I am Dick Dearlove, no less, and I have the privilege of talking and living with that legend on a daily basis." This isn't really so very rare, whether you leave the word "legend" in or take it out. It has been known for writers who have won the Nobel prize to spend what remains of their life thinking all the time: "I'm a Nobel prizewinner, I won the Nobel Prize, and, my, how I shone in Stockholm," sometimes even saying this out loud, they've been overheard doing so by their anxious loved ones. But I know quite a lot of other people of no objective significance or fame, who, nevertheless, perceive themselves in just such a way, or similarly, and who watch their life as if they were at the theatre. A permanent theatre, of course, repetitive and monotonous *ad nauseam*, which does not scant on detail or on even two seconds of tedium. But those people are the most benevolent and easily pleased of spectators, not for nothing are they also the author, actor and protagonist of their respective dramatic works (dramatic is just a manner of speaking). This form of living and seeing oneself has become fact on the Internet. I understand that some people even earn money showing every soporific, wretched moment of their existences, endlessly filmed by a fixed camera. The astonishing, intellectually sick, seriously unhealthy thing is that there are people willing to watch this, and who even pay to do so; I mean spectators who are not also the authors, actors and protagonists, whose behaviour is not entirely anomalous or even incomprehensible.'

'Come on, Iago, please: get to the point. I get lost in your digressions. When do you think Dearlove would be most likely to bump someone off?'

Tupra was, of course, perfectly capable of following my digressions, he never got lost, even if he wasn't much interested in what he was hearing, although I don't think he did get bored with me, you can tell when you've got the attention of the people listening to you, not for nothing was I a teacher, although those classes are now moving further and further away in time. He would sometimes call me Iago, the classical form of my name, when he wanted to annoy me or force me to concentrate. He knew that Wheeler referred to me as Jacobo and probably didn't dare attempt the pronunciation, and so he placed my name somewhere half-way along the road, in familiar Shakespearean mode, possibly with some mocking undertone, I couldn't rule that out. Of course Tupra could follow me, but he would sometimes pretend that the traditional aversion to the speculative and theoretical, inherent in the education and mind of the English, prevented him from accompanying me very far on my digressions. He was not only following everything, he was recording it, filing it away, retaining it. And he was quite capable of appropriating it for himself.

'Sorry, Mr Tupra, I didn't mean to get diverted,' I said; I was still well behaved then. 'Well, they say that Dearlove is bisexual, or pentasexual, or pansexual, I don't know, but very highly sexed anyway, sex-mad, they hint at it all the time in the press. And last night he did seem rather overexcited when he slipped on his green gown and insisted on sorting out Mrs Thompson's tooth decay. Although he would doubtless have preferred to be rooting around in her young son's mouth. It was a shame for Dr

Dearlove, I suppose, that the boy refused to oblige, however sweetly he insisted. They also say that he's very fond of . . . of the newly pubescent, shall we say.'

'They do say that,' replied Tupra gravely, but barely bothering to conceal the fact that he found all this highly amusing. 'And?'

'Well, supposing a minor, male or female, it doesn't matter, laid a trap for him. If my information is correct, he happily allows these rumours to spread, as long as they are only that, rumours. I imagine it's not a bad way of airing them: by ignoring them, by not even admitting their existence with denials and lawsuits and complaints. As I understand it, he has never said a word about his sexual predilections. Besides, everyone knows he's been married, twice, admittedly both marriages were childless, but that, nevertheless, is what he holds on to, officially at least.'

'More or less. I don't know much about that aspect of his life.'

'Anyway, suppose a minor, male or female, slipped a sleeping-pill into his drink. While they were at it, both of them stark naked. Suppose the minor takes some photos of him while he's off in limbo, the boy or the girl also gets in on the shot, of course, puts the camera on automatic and takes charge of the stage direction, with our ex-dentist a limp rag-doll in his or her hands. Let's say, however, that the pill doesn't prove strong enough for the titanic Dr Dearlove: that an inner sense of alarm helps him pull himself together. So that he either doesn't fall very deeply asleep or else wakes up early. With one eye half-open he sees what's happening. With a quarter of his conscious mind he takes in the situation, or with even only a tenth part of it. It's not that he's puritanical in his attitudes or public declarations, that would lose him fans; he's quite daring, really, although he's careful never to go too far, he defends the legalisation of drugs, responsible euthanasia, the kind of cause that won't lose him any fans. But the appearance of such photos in the press belongs to an entirely different sphere, as would his knifing by thugs from Brixton, Clapham or Streatham. Exactly the same, I think you'll agree. Even though in one situation he would be the vile, despicable offender and in the other the poor, pitiful, much-mourned victim. As regards the effect on his narrative, they're not so very different, both are protuberances. In this case it wouldn't be an ending, the kiss of sleep and the photos I mean, but it would be an episode that would always have a place in his history, that could never be avoided in the story or in the idea of Dick Dearlove. And given the way the public feels about child abuse, it could lead to prison and an embarrassing trial. And even if he was absolved afterwards, the accusation alone and its reverberations, the images seen and repeated thousands of times, the scandal and the grave suspicions that will have lasted for months, could also end up as a warning used by mothers to their adolescent offspring: "Mind who you mix with, dear, you might end up with a Dick Dearlove." That's the trouble with being so famous: lose concentration for a moment and you could become the subject of a ballad.'

'You're very well informed about the buffoon. Even about his opinions; very impressive,' said Tupra wryly.

'As I say, he's almost as much of a superstar in Spain as he is here. He's given loads of concerts there. It would be hard not to know about him.'

'I always had the impression that the Basques were a very austere people, in the present context I mean,' he added, genuinely surprised. He never missed anything or forgot anything.

'Austere? Well, that depends. There's no shortage of buffoons either. The leader sets the tone, you know. Like in Lombardy. Or anywhere else in Italy for that matter. Not to mention Venezuela; remember our friend Bonanza.'

'Well, we're not far behind,' he said, and that shocked me a little, for no reason really: I didn't know exactly who Tupra worked for (that is, who we worked for), I only had Wheeler's hints to go on and my own unreflective deductions. 'The kiss of sleep you called it.'

'Yes, that's how the trick is known in Spain, it's used mainly as a ruse to strip the sleeping person's house of all its valuables. That's what the media call it.'

'H'm, the kiss of sleep, not bad.' He liked the name. 'So what would happen with Dearlove. He wakes with a kiss, and only half an eye open. And then what?'

'Something outrageous, anything. That's what I was coming to. He could also kill in a situation like that, I mean, that's just a possible example, there would be others. Narrative horror, disgust. That's what drives him mad, I'm sure of it, what obsesses him. I've known other people with the same aversion, or awareness, and they weren't even famous, fame is not a deciding factor, there are many individuals who experience their life as if it were the material for some detailed report, and they inhabit that life pending its hypothetical or future plot. They don't give it much thought, it's just a way of experiencing things, companionable, in a way, as if there were always spectators or permanent witnesses, even of their most trivial goings-on and during the dullest of times. Perhaps it's a substitute for the old idea of the omnipresence of God, who saw every second of each of our lives, it was very flattering in a way, very comforting despite the implicit element of threat and punishment, and three or four generations aren't enough for Man to accept that his gruelling existence goes on without anyone ever observing or watching it, without anyone judging it or disapproving of it. And in truth there is always someone: a listener, a reader, a spectator, a witness, who can also double up as simultaneous narrator and actor: the individuals tell their stories to themselves, to each his own, they are the ones who peer in and look at and notice things on a daily basis, from the outside in a way; or, rather, from a false outside, from a generalised narcissism, sometimes known as "consciousness". That's why so few people can withstand mockery, humiliation, ridicule, the rush of blood to the face, a snub, that least of all.

Dearlove cannot abide that feeling of repugnance, that anxiety, he cannot cope with that vertigo, and when he succumbs to those feelings, when the fit is upon him, then he no longer thinks. When he half-opens his eye and realises what is going on, it probably won't even occur to him to try and acquire the photos, to offer more for them than any tabloid newspaper would ever pay, to reach an agreement with the boy or the girl, to negotiate, to bribe, to deceive, to hire their services forever. His fortune, if he has both a plane and a helicopter, would allow him to buy them ten thousand, a hundred thousand times over, in body, in bondage and in soul.'

'But he wouldn't do that, you say. What would he do, then? According to you, what would he do next?'

'The same as he would with the knife-wielding thugs from Brixton, I think. He would misjudge things. He would throw caution to the wind. He would try to kill them, he *would* kill them. He would kill the minor, male or female, whom he had taken to his house that night. A heavy ashtray kills, it shatters the skull. A jug, a paperweight, a letter-opener, anything can kill, not to mention the swords and spears with which he has adorned that wall in his living-room, the long wall next to the dining-room where we had supper; I imagine you noticed them last night.'

'I did,' said Tupra. 'It might not have been my first time there, you know.'

'No, of course. Yes, it figures that Dearlove would be a devotee of the medieval, of things Celtic and semi-magical. Of fantasy chic. This is what I imagine would happen: despite still feeling very groggy from the pill he was given, or perhaps precisely because he is still groggy, he draws strength from the terrible fright he has had and staggers over to that wall; he accepts as clear, established fact that this terrible narrative protuberance will live with him forever because of these images treacherously taken of him, and, in his mental fog, this is what permits or empowers him to be angry and immoderate. And so he takes down one of those spears and with it pierces the chest of the girl or boy and destroys the flesh he had earlier desired, without thinking about the consequences, not at that moment. At such times, men like him do not see, they do not see what only three minutes later will become obvious to them: that it is less difficult to get rid of a few photos than it is to get rid of a corpse, less arduous to cover someone's mouth than to clean up their many pints of spilt blood. I've known men like that, men who were nobody and yet who had that same immense fear of their own history, of what might be told and what, therefore, they might tell too. Of their blotted, ugly history. But, I insist, the determining factor always comes from outside, from some-thing external: all this has little to do with shame, regret, remorse, self-hatred, although these might make a fleeting appearance at some point. These individuals only feel obliged to give a true account of their acts or omissions, good or bad, brave, contemptible, cowardly or generous, if other people (the majority, that is) know about them, and those acts or omissions are thus incorporated into what is known about them, that is, into their official portraits. It isn't really a matter of conscience, but of performance, of mirrors. One can easily cast doubt on what is not reflected in mirrors, and believe that it was all illusory, wrap it up in a mist of diffuse or faulty memory and decide finally that it didn't happen and that there is no memory of it, because there can be no memory of what did not take place. Then it will no longer torment them: some people have an extraordinary ability to convince themselves that what happened didn't happen and that what didn't exist did. For Dick Dearlove, the worst thing, the unbearable thing, would not be bumping off a mugger or a deceitful adolescent, but that people might find out, that the fact would remain attached (so to speak) to his file. Even in the midst of his confusion at the moment of the homicide, he perhaps knows that it might, albeit with enormous difficulty, be possible to conceal it. Not, on the other hand, his own death at the hands of savages, or photos of him naked with a young boy or a nymphette, once they have been printed and universally admired.' – I stopped for a moment. I thought, as I always did at the end of my interpretations or reports, that I had gone too far. And that I had again got caught up in digressions. It also occurred to me that I probably wasn't telling Tupra anything he didn't know already. He doubtless knew the score about such individuals, perhaps even as regards Dearlove, from previous visits, or, who knows, from plane journeys made together (Tupra as part of Dearlove's entourage, mingling with the other guests, the supervisors, the newly pubescent and the bodyguards). Perhaps he was not so much learning from what I was telling him as studying me. 'I've known men like that, Mr Tupra, of all ages, everywhere,' I added, as if apologising. 'You have too, I'm sure. We both have.'

'Cigarette, Jack?' he said. And he offered me one of the Pharaonic variety from his flashy red packet. It was a gesture of appreciation, at least that was how I understood it.

And I thought, or kept thinking: 'I've known Comendador, for example. Since forever.'

On that stubbornly rainy night in London, I decided to experiment by stopping suddenly, by coming to an abrupt halt without any warning in order to find out whether or not that light, almost imperceptible sound was coming from me, tis, tis, tis, whether it was the soft steps of a dog or the rustle of my raincoat as I walked briskly along, the shaking of my umbrella or the skulking step of some dubious character who did not come near and did not reveal himself, but who, nevertheless, persisted in following me – or accompanying me in parallel, at a distance of a few yards – if he should finally make up his mind, he still had time to think about it before I reached my house and opened the door and, before going in, furled my umbrella and shook it hard (a few more drops to add to the improvised lakes and miniature streams of the city streets), and then closed the door rapidly behind me, impatient to be upstairs, in my temporary home which was becoming ever more like a refuge and ever more mine, so that now it almost soothed me to go up the stairs and shut myself in and from my third-floor apartment – safe from questions and answers, from talk – to contemplate the square, with its murmuring trees in the middle, which seemed to accompany every meek surrender and rebellion of the mind; and the lights of the families or the other single people opposite (my fellows), the elegant hotel always lit up and lively, like a silent stage or like the pan shot in a film that never changed and never ended, the vast office blocks in repose now and guarded, from a cabin, by a night security guard who yawns as he listens to his radio, his cap pushed back on his head, the peak raised, and, in the darkness, the zigzagging, fugitive beggars who emerge to do their rummaging, and whose stiff clothes seem to emanate ashes, or perhaps it's just accumulated dust; and, of course, my dancing neighbour (who is so unconcerned about the world it cheers one to see him) and his occasional dancing partners, recently I had seen him launch boldly into the *sirtaki*, good grief, he looked poofy, not gay exactly, but something else – like an exquisitely dressed swank, a dummy, a honeyed, vainglorious rogue – the term has nothing to do now with the actual carnal preferences of the person thus described, I, at least, would make that distinction, and there is no more ridiculous dance for a man to dance alone than the Greek *sirtaki*, with the possible exception of the Basque *aurresku*, which, fortunately, my neighbour would not know.

So I experimented two or three times, I stopped suddenly without warning, and on those three occasions the sound of cautious or semi-aerial steps, the whirr of crickets, the swishing sound or whatever it was – like the crazy trot of an old wall clock, which also resembles the footsteps of a dog – took longer than usual to stop, I could hear it when I was already standing still and when I could not possibly be emitting any involuntary or uncontrolled sound. I did not turn my head when I made this experiment, to look behind or to the sides, as I did when I was walking steadily along, resting the umbrella on my shoulder, almost as one would with a sunshade when out for a stroll, as if I wanted above all to protect the back of my neck, to protect it from the wind and the water and from the possible looks of other people and from imaginary bullets that would have pierced both (the back of my neck and the umbrella), you think such absurd things when you have to walk a longish distance alone and at night, feeling as if you were being followed even though you can't actually see anyone following you. During the final stretch there were occasional grassy areas to the left and right, I took a short-cut through a small local park, so perhaps those unseen steps were made on the grass. I waited until I had left that barely lit park behind me and was already very close to home. I had only another two blocks to go and another square to cross when I tried again, and this time I did turn round when I stopped and then I saw them, two white figures at a distance that would not normally have allowed me to hear panting or footsteps. The dog was white and the woman, the person, was, like me, wearing a light-coloured raincoat. I thought, from the first, that she was a woman, and she was, because, after only a second or a sliver of doubt, I took an immediate fancy to her legs, when I saw that they were covered not by dark trousers, but by black, knee-high boots (with no heels, or only very low heels) which delineated or accentuated the curve of her strong calves. Her face was still hidden by her umbrella, she had both hands occupied, she was holding the dog's leash in one, the dog, somewhat hopelessly and possibly wearily, kept tugging on the leash, the creature had no protection at all, it must have been drenched, the rain doubtless continued to weigh on it however violently it shook itself each time they paused (for when they did, the rain didn't stop falling on the dog), and they were pausing then, because the two figures had also stopped, with a slight but inevitable delay after me or my very abrupt halt. I stood for a few, but not too few, seconds looking at them. The woman didn't seem to mind being seen, I mean she could just be someone who, despite the wild weather, had decided to take her dog for a walk, and she wouldn't have to explain herself to me were I to ask her to. It could just be a coincidence: sometimes you do find yourself following the same route as another pedestrian for many long minutes, even if your route is not a direct one, and sometimes you can start to feel annoyed by this, for no reason, it's merely a longing for that coincidence to end, to cease, because it seems somehow like a bad omen, or simply because it irritates you, so much so that you even go out of your way and make an unnecessary detour just to separate yourself from and to leave behind that insistent parallel being.

There was between the two of us, or, rather, between them and me, a distance of some two hundred or more yards, far enough for me to have to shout or to retrace my steps if I was going to speak to her, to ask a question of that human figure, who was clearly a young woman, her boots were waterproof, supple, shiny and close-fitting, they were not just any old rainboots, they had been chosen, studied, were possibly expensive, flattering, maybe by a well-known designer. I stared at them, she had not uncovered her face, at no point did she raise the umbrella covering it and did not, therefore, return my gaze, but neither was she troubled because a man was standing watching her from not very far away, at night and in all that rain. She crouched down, the skirts of her raincoat fell open when she did so and I could see part of her thigh, she patted and stroked the dog's back, probably spoke softly to him, then stood up again and the skirts of her raincoat closed once more over that glimpse of flesh, she did not move, did not set off in any direction, it occurred to me then that she might be in need of help, lost in an area she did not know, or a young blind woman out with her guide dog, or a foreigner who did not know the language, or a prostitute so hard up she could not miss even one night-time excursion, or was wondering whether or not to ask me for money, help, advice, something. Not because I was me, but because I was the only parallel being there. I had the feeling that any meeting was impossible, and, at the same time, that it would be a shame if it did not take place and that it would be better if it did not. The feeling was one of pity, whether for myself or for her, I don't know, certainly not for us both, because one of us would have come off worse – I thought – and the other would have benefited, that is usually how it is with such street encounters.

Many years before, in this same country, when I was teaching at Oxford, I had been followed off and on by a man with a three-legged dog, one of its back legs neatly amputated, and subsequently, without prior warning, he had visited my house, his name was Alan Marriott, he was rather lame in his left leg (although it was still intact) and he was a bibliomaniac who had learned of my own bookish interests, which coincided in part with his, from the second-hand booksellers I used to frequent there. The dog was a terrier, he'll be dead by now, poor thing, they do not last as long as we do. The young woman's dog seemed to me, from a distance, to be a pointer and still had all its four legs, which I found strangely cheering, in contrast with the crippled dog, I suppose, who came suddenly to mind in that night of eternal rain. 'But I don't want anything of anyone,' I thought, 'nor do I expect anything of anyone, and I'm in a hurry to get out of this rain and reach home, and forget all about the interpretations of this long day which doesn't end or which won't end until I'm safe up there on my third floor. Let her come to me if she wants something from me or if she's following me. That's her problem. She must have a reason, assuming she was following me or still is, it can't be in order *not* to talk to me.' I turned and hurried on to my destination, but I couldn't help listening out during the rest of my walk to see if I could or couldn't hear that tis tis tis which was, as it turned out, the sound of a dog and its eighteen toes, or perhaps of those long boots with such low heels that they glided over the asphalt without even striking it, without making a sound.

I reached my door, turned the key and opened it, and only then did I furl my umbrella and shake it so that it didn't drip too much indoors, and once upstairs, I immediately took the umbrella into the kitchen, leaving my raincoat there to dry as well, and then I went impatiently over to the window and scanned the square, but I saw neither the young woman nor the pointer, even though I had heard their weightless noise until the end, accompanying me as far as the door downstairs, or so I thought. I looked up and across at my dancing neighbour, who had often before had a calming effect on me. There he was, of course, he was unlikely to be out in that awful weather, and he had a visitor too, the black or mulatto woman with whom he sometimes danced: judging from their movements and posture and rhythm I was sure they were immersed in some pseudo-Gaelic dance, feet frantically flailing, but going nowhere (the feet keeping strictly to a point on which they insist and stamp and stamp again, an area no bigger than a house brick or, lest we exaggerate, a floor tile), while the arms are held, inert and very stiff, close to the body, it was likely, I thought, that the dancing couple would be listening to the music of one of those demented shows put on by that idol of the islands, Michael Flatley, who stamps his feet like a man possessed, they re-issue his old videos with remarkable frequency, maybe he's retired now and rations his appearances so as to make his furious boundings about the stage seem even more exceptional. Whether dancing alone or in company, my neighbour always seemed so happy that I sometimes felt tempted to imitate him, after all, that's something we can all do, dance alone at home when we think no one is looking. But you can never be sure that no one is looking or listening, we're not always aware of being watched, or followed.

Having one leg missing, the bibliomaniac Marriott's poor terrier would only have had fourteen toes, I thought. Perhaps I had remembered the dog because its image was forever associated with that of a young woman who also used to wear high boots, a gypsy flower-seller, who used to set up her stall opposite my house in Oxford, on the other side of the long street known there as St Giles'. Her name was Jane, and, despite her extreme youth, she was married; she usually wore jeans and a leather jacket; I would sometimes exchange a few words with her, and Alan Marriott had stopped at her stall to buy some flowers before ringing my doorbell on the morning or afternoon that he visited me, on one of those Sundays 'in exile from the infinite' (I quoted to myself). He and I had just been talking about the Welsh writer Arthur Machen (one of his favourites) and about the literature of horror or terror which the latter had cultivated to the great delight of Borges and of very few others, although I remember that Marriott had not heard of Borges. And suddenly he had given me an illustration of horror through a hypothesis involving his dog with its three legs and intelligent face and the flower-seller in the high boots. 'Horror depends in large measure on the association of ideas,' he had said. 'On the conjunction of ideas. On a capacity for bringing them together.' He spoke in short phrases and hardly used conjunctions at all, making minimal, but very deep, marked pauses, as if he held his breath while they lasted. As if his speech too were slightly lame. 'You might never see the horror implicit in associating two ideas, the horror implicit in each of those ideas, and thus never in your whole life recognise the horror they contain. But you could live immersed in that horror if you were unfortunate enough always to make the right associations. For example, that girl opposite your house who sells flowers,' he had said, pointing at the window with one very taut index finger, one of those fingers which, although clean, seems to be impregnated with whatever it spends its days touching, however frequently the owner of the finger may wash it: I've seen such fingers on coalmen and butchers and house painters and even greengrocers (on coalmen during my childhood); his fingers were impregnated with book dust, which always clings so and which is the reason I wore gloves when I went rummaging around second-hand bookshops, but, then again, the chalk I used when I was teaching had already started to stick. 'There's nothing terrifying about her, she doesn't in herself inspire horror. On the contrary. She's very attractive. She's nice and friendly. She stroked the dog. I bought these carnations from her.' He produced them from his raincoat pocket, into which he had carelessly crammed them, as if they were pencils or a handkerchief. There were only two, they were almost squashed. 'But she could inspire horror. The idea of that girl in association with another idea could. Don't you think so? We don't yet know the nature of that missing idea, of the idea required to inspire us with horror. Her horrifying other half.

But it must exist. It does. It's simply a question of it appearing. It may also never appear. Who knows, it could turn out to be my dog.' He pointed downwards with his vertical finger, the terrier had lain down at his feet, it wasn't raining that day, there was no danger of it dirtying the sitting-room, it didn't deserve to be exiled to the kitchen on the ground floor (his index finger covered in invisible dust). 'The girl and my dog,' he repeated, and again pointed first at the window (as if the flower-seller were a ghost and had her face pressed to the glass, it was the window on the second floor, that pyramidal house had three, I slept on the top floor and worked in that living-room) and then at the dog, his finger always very erect and rigid. 'The girl with her long, chestnut hair, her high boots and her long, firm legs and my dog with his one leg missing.' I remember that he then touched the dog's stump affectionately or tentatively as if it might still hurt him, the dog was dozing. 'The fact that my dog goes everywhere with me is normal. It's necessary. It's odd if you like. I mean the two of us going around together. But there's nothing horrific about it. But if she went around with my dog. That might be horrific. The dog *is* missing a leg. I'm the only one who remembers him when he had four legs. My personal memory doesn't count. It's of no importance in the eyes of other people. In her eyes. In your eyes. In the eyes of other dogs. Now it's as if my dog had always had one leg missing. If it had been her dog, it would certainly never have lost its leg in a stupid argument after a football match.' Marriott had told me the story already, I had asked him: some drunken Oxford United fans, late at night at Didcot Station, the lame man beaten and held down by several of them, the dog, not as yet lame, placed on the railway line so that it would be killed by a through train. They had let it go, they had drawn back, frightened, at the last moment, the dog had rolled over, it was lucky in a way ('You can't imagine the amount of blood he lost'). 'That's an accident. An occupational hazard for a dog with a lame master. But if it had been her dog, perhaps it would have lost its leg some other way. The dog is still missing a leg. There must be some other reason, then. Something far worse. Not just an accident. You could hardly imagine that girl getting involved in a fight. Perhaps the dog would have lost its leg *because* of her.' He emphasised the word 'because'. 'Perhaps the only explanation of why this dog should have lost its leg, if it were her dog, would be that she had cut it off. How else could a dog who was so well looked after, cared for and loved by that nice, attractive flower-seller have lost its leg? It's a horrible idea, that girl cutting off my dog's leg; seeing it with her own eyes; being a witness to it.' Alan Marriott's words had sounded slightly indignant, indignant at the girl's behaviour. He had broken off then, as if he had conjured up too vivid an image with his own terrible hypothesis and had indeed seen the horrific couple. As if he had seen the couple through my window – 'with the eyes of the mind,' I quoted to myself. He seemed to have unnerved himself, to have frightened himself. 'Let's change the subject,' he said. And although I urged him to continue – 'No, go on, you were on the point of inventing a story' – he was not prepared to go on thinking about it, or imagining it: 'No, forget it. It's a poor example,' he had said firmly. 'As you wish,' I had said, and then we had passed on to something else. There would have been no way of persuading him to continue his fantasy, I knew this immediately, not once he had alarmed himself by it. Perhaps he had horrified himself. He must have been shocked by his own mind.

A dog and a young woman in high boots. That rainy night was in fact the first time I had seen this conjunction, this image, with my own eyes; but my memory had already recorded or made the sinister association many years before, in this same country which was not mine, when I was still not married and had no children. (This present time of mine was beginning to resemble that other time; I had no wife or children, although I relied on them and sent them money and missed them every day, at some moment of each day.) The flower-seller Jane used to wear her jeans tucked into her boots, almost musketeer-fashion. The woman hidden behind her umbrella was wearing a skirt, I had glimpsed one thigh. It was doubtless because of that invisible precedent, that imagined image transmitted to me once by the lame bibliophile, that I had felt so relieved to find that the nocturnal white pointer had all its four legs, I had counted them one by one even though I had seen them anyway at a glance. But I had wanted to make quite sure (an instance of reflex superstition, I realised) that he and his mistress did not form some horrific couple already dreamed up by someone else.

That was what I was paid to do in the building with no name. I ceaselessly made associations, rather than interpretations or decipherings or analyses, or, rather, those merely came afterwards, as a rather feeble consequence. Wheeler had more or less announced this to me that Sunday in Oxford, in his garden or during lunch: there is no such thing as two identical people, nor has there ever been, we know that; but nor is there anyone who is not related in some way to someone else who has traversed the world, who does not have what Wheeler called affinities with someone else. There is no one who has no ties, there never has been, no links of fate or character, which, anyway, comes to the same thing (I was paraphrasing Wheeler freely), except perhaps for the very first men, if they really did exist before all others rather than many of them springing up in many places simultaneously. You see two very different people and see them, moreover, separated by centuries from your own life, so much so that, by the time the second one appears, the first has been forgotten for all those centuries, just as I had stored away the anaesthetised image of that horrific couple dreamed up by Alan Marriott. They are people who differ in age, sex, education, beliefs, mentality, temperament, affections; they might speak different languages, come from countries far, far away from each other, have entirely contrary biographies and not share a single experience, not a single parallel hour in their long, respective pasts, not a single comparable one. You meet a very young woman, with her ambition so untouched and intact that you cannot yet tell if she has any ambition or not, I remember Wheeler saying. Her shyness makes her hermetic, so much so that you're not sure if her very shyness is not merely a pretence, a timid mask. She is the daughter of a Spanish couple you know and whom you visit, the parents force her to say hello, to join in, at least for a while, to have supper with the guest and with them. The young woman does not want to be known or even seen, she is there against her will, feigning indifference and coolness, waiting for the world – which she feels owes her a debt – to take an interest in her, to court her, seek her out and even offer her reparation, but feeling vastly bored if the friend of her parents (whom she does not consider to be part of the world: she has, by association, excluded him) displays an insistent curiosity in her, watches her with friendly concern, flatters her and draws her out. She is a slightly offended sphinx, or perhaps she is frightened, or vulnerable and uncertain, or deceitful, an impostor. She's impossible to fathom, she wants people to take notice of her and, at the same time, sees this as interference, she can't bear to be noticed by someone who doesn't count, someone who, according to her perceptions and criteria, has no right to notice her. She isn't and cannot be unpleasant, she doesn't go quite that far, besides, no one with a pretty, blushing face ever is, but it is impossible to imagine what lies behind the helmet of her extreme youth, it is as if she wore the visor lowered so that all one could see of her eyes were her eyelashes. The immature and the unfinished are the most unfathomable of things, like the four lines of a drawing, dashed off and left incomplete, which do not even allow you to speculate on the figure they aspired to be or were on the way to becoming. And yet something nearly always does emerge, says Wheeler. Rarely do you meet a person about whom you remain forever in the dark, rarely – by dint of sheer persistence on our part – does a figure fail to emerge, however blurred or tenuous, and however different from what you were expecting, remote, defined, or out of keeping with those few initial lines, even incongruous. You become accustomed to the darkness of each face or person or past or history or life, you begin, after unflagging scrutiny of the shadows, to be able to make something out, the gloom lifts and you grasp something, discern something: the discouragement abates then or else invades and wraps around us, depending on whether we wanted to see something or to see nothing, depending upon which characteristics, which affinities we find in which person, or whether these are merely our own marks, our own memories. Anyone who wants to see nearly always does end up seeing something, imagine, then, what a person committed to seeing could achieve, or someone who makes a career out of it, like you and like me, you think you haven't begun, but you began a long time ago, you just haven't yet been paid to do it, but now you will be, very soon; it's the way you live anyway. There are so few of us who have the courage and the patience to keep looking that we get well paid for it ('Go on. Quickly, hurry, keep thinking and keep looking beyond the purely necessary, even when you have the feeling that there is no more, no more to think, that it's all been thought, that there's no more to see, that it's all been seen'), to examine in depth what appears to be as smooth, opaque and black as a field of heraldic sable, a compact darkness. Yet one suddenly catches a gesture, an intonation, a flicker, a hesitation, a laugh, a tic, an oblique look, it can be anything, even something very trivial. You hear or see something, whatever it might be, in the young daughter of the couple you are friendly with, you see something that you recognise and associate with something else, that you heard or saw in someone, I think, while Wheeler continues his explanation. You see in the girl the same conceited, cruel, neurotic expression, the identical expression, that you saw so often in a much older man, almost elderly, a magazine publisher with whom you worked for far too long, even a single day would have been too much. They are, in principle, unrelated,

This play by G. R. Rainier, which illustrates how careless talk, however innocent it may seem at the time, might be pieced together by the enemy and give away a vital secret, will be broadcast again tonight at 10.0.

no one would have made the connection, it's ridiculous. There is no resemblance, nor, of course, any family relationship. The man had grey, almost bouffant hair, the young woman's is a glossy, dark brown mane; his flesh sags, his face grows visibly more haggard every day, her flesh is so firm and exultant that, beside her, her parents seem one-dimensional (as do you, probably, but you cannot see yourself), as if she were the only person in the room who had any volume, or as if only she had been carved in relief; his eyes were small and treacherous, greedy and malicious despite the smiles that frequented his wide-set teeth – which looked as if they had never been polished or buffed (or as if the enamel had worn away, so that they resembled the tiny, grubby teeth of a saw) – in the hope of making the whole more cordial (and he deceived many, even me for a while, or perhaps I merely averted my gaze from what I saw, that is what the world does constantly, and you cannot always separate yourself from the world), whereas her eyes are large and elusive and grave and seem to covet nothing, her lips do not bestow smiles on those who do not, from her miserly point of view, deserve it, and she doesn't mind appearing sullen (she's not as yet interested in seducing anyone with flattery), and the rare glimpse you get of her teeth is a radiant benediction. No, they are entirely unrelated, that devious owner and publisher of magazines, that boastful and unpleasant older man, so insecure about his acquisitions and so conscious of his monetary and intellectual thefts that he would do his best to crush, if he could, those from whom he pilfered; no, nothing connects them, he and this girl on whom one would say the curtain has not yet gone up, who is still all potentiality and enigma, a ready-prepared canvas on which only a few tentative brushstrokes have fallen, a few experiments with colour. And yet. In the end, at the last, it is only when your persistence finally runs out that you see, with a clear, disinterested bitterness, that flash, the expression or even the look of that man whom she does not resemble and whom she does not know (thus ruling out any idea of mimesis). It isn't just a matter of superimposing their two faces, so different, so opposed – that would be a visual aberration, an ocular absurdity. No, it's an association, a recognition, an affinity grasped. (A horrific couple.) It's the same flicker of irritation or the same demanding look, doubtless provoked by different causes or following such divergent trajectories that his is already declining and hers is barely starting. Or perhaps there is no cause in either case and the trajectories count for little, the flicker or the look do not have their origins in a setback or in a piece of good luck, nor in what events might bring. In the businessman, such expressions were already deeply rooted, permanently resident in his ruddy drinker's complexion threaded with broken veins, whilst in the young girl they are only a momentary temptation, a mist perhaps, something that could yet be reversible and which, at this precise moment, is of no importance. And yet, once you've noticed that link, you know. You know what she is like in one aspect, and that there can be no emendation in that crucial aspect: it will go hard for anyone who thwarts her and equally hard for those who try to please her ('Some people are simply impossible, and the only sensible thing to do is to remove yourself from their presence and keep them at a distance, to cease to exist for them'). That look and that expression indicate something which you discerned and noted from the very first moment, but without making the link with that old, immensely arrogant petty thief, without noticing that the young woman shares that characteristic with him, or reproduces it (she doesn't even know him, yet she has produced an exact copy). Both feel, or perhaps judge, that the world is in their debt; that anything good which comes their way is merely their due – what else; they therefore know nothing of contentment or gratitude; they appreciate none of the favours done to them or the clemency with which they are treated; they see such things as evidence of respect, and respect they see as evidence of the weakness and fear of the person who had the cane in his hand, but chose not to beat them. They are quite simply insufferable, people who never learn, certainly not from their mistakes. They always feel that they are the creditors of the world, even though they spend their whole lives affronting and despoiling it, via any of the world's innumerable offspring who happen to stray into their line of fire. And if, given her age, the girl had not yet been able to shoot down many of these, I was quite sure that, swiftly and with great precocity, she would soon make up for the intolerably long waiting time that indolent physical growth imposes on the very determined. When you recognise that conceited, cruel, complex-ridden expression — which always presages anger — when you make that unhappy link, that is, when you cease to be curious about the young woman, or to look on her with sympathy, or to flatter her with the captivating questions of an adult. And she, who previously found those attentions so hard to bear and who spurned them because of the person they came from — a friend of her parents, so boring, so old — now finds it still harder to bear the withdrawal of that deferential behaviour. Which is why she bolts her dessert, gets up from the table and leaves the room without saying goodbye. She has suffered, she has collected and stored away yet another insult.

At other times, fortunately, it's quite the opposite: what you see or identify or associate is something so longed for and beloved that you immediately grow calm, Wheeler tells me. You hear the timbre and the familiar diction of the woman you're speaking to, to whom you have just been introduced. You hear her easy laugh with nostalgic pleasure, or, more than that, with distant emotion. You remember, you listen, you remember: why, of course, yes, I recognise that liking for parties, that infectious good humour, that rapid dissipation of all mists, that invitation to enjoy yourself, that spirit which quickly grows bored with its own sadness and does whatever it can to lighten or truncate the doses that life metes out to her as it does to everyone else, to her too, she doesn't get off scot-free. But neither does she surrender or yield, defenceless, and as soon as she sees that she can survive the burden, she straightens up a little and tries to shake it off, as far away as possible from her frail shoulders. Not in order to suppress sorrow, as if it had never existed, she doesn't wash her hands of it or wriggle out of it, she doesn't irresponsibly forget; but she knows that she can only watch over that sadness if she keeps it in perspective, at a distance, that she might then be able to understand it. And in that middle-aged woman you see an unmistakable affinity with a young woman who is gone forever, with your own wife – Valerie, Val, almost all that remains is the memory of her name, but now, vital, living traces of her appear again, in that other voice and face – the wife who died young and could never even have dreamed of reaching this great age, nor, of course, of giving birth to a child or possibly even fantasising about one, she died too young to imagine herself a mother, almost too soon to imagine herself married to Peter Wheeler, or Peter Rylands, too young either to imagine herself married, let alone actually being married. She had dreamy, diaphanous eyes and very happy, affectionately ironic lips. She joked a lot, she never lost her youthful ways, she never had the chance. Once, with those same lips, she told me why she loved me: 'Because I like to see you reading the newspaper while I'm having my breakfast, that's all. I can read in your face the mood in which the world has got out of bed this morning and the mood in which you have got out of bed too, since you are the world's main representative in my life. And by far its most visible representative too.' Those words return unexpectedly, when you hear that identical timbre and diction, and see that oh so comparable smile. And you know at once that this mature woman to whom you have just been introduced can be trusted absolutely. You know that she will do you no harm, or not at least without warning you first.

A FEW
CARELESS WORDS
MAY END IN THIS—

Many lives were lost in the last war through careless talk
Be on your guard ! Don't discuss movements of ships or troops.

*Keep mum
she's not so dumb!*

CARELESS TALK COSTS LIVES

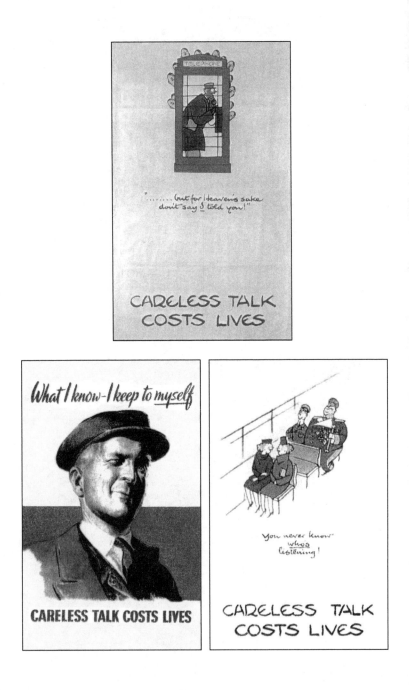

'This ability or gift was very useful during the war, indeed, in time of war it always proves invaluable, which is why the powers-that-be of the day did their best to organise and channel it, they combed the population for it, because they quickly came to realise how very few people had that gift or faculty, possibly even fewer then than now, war has an incredibly distorting effect on people's perceptions, half the people see ghosts and witches everywhere and the other half merely perfect their habitual tendency to see nothing at all, and do their best not even to see that. But it was the war that brought it to the forefront, ideas only surface when we need them, even the very simplest of ideas,' Wheeler had murmured to me in the garden, while we strolled slowly along by the river, waiting for lunch. 'It's just a shame that the idea didn't come up a few months earlier, who knows, Val, my wife Valerie, might not have died. But unfortunately, by the time someone had thought of it, she was already dead. I'm not sure who it was, Menzies or Ve-Ve Vivian, or Cowgill or Hollis or even Philby (I don't think it was Jack Curry, no, I'd rule him out), they were all vying with each other to be the most inventive, they've always prided themselves on that in MI5 and MI6, they kept a watchful eye on what their colleagues did, even ended up spying on each other, it probably still happens. It's likely that it was Churchill himself who had the idea, he was the brightest and boldest of the lot, the least afraid of ridicule. Not that it matters. It's impossible ever to know the true paternity of these things, and no one cares, apart from the candidates claiming to have given birth to that brief diversion from dusty death in our now distant yesterdays,' said Wheeler, adapting Shakespeare's famous words with a touch of bitter humour, 'everyone tells their story and no one believes a word of it or pays the slightest attention. Whatever the truth of the matter, it all started with the campaign against careless talk, have you heard of that?' It rang a bell that expression, literally '*charla despreocupada*' or '*negligente*' or '*descuidada*' or '*conversación imprudente*', it was difficult to find a satisfactory and exact translation, I related it to what in Spanish we term '*hablar a la ligera*', although it isn't quite that either, or '*cotilleo*' or '*chismorreo*' or '*habladurías*'. I shook my head: I didn't, at any rate, know of a campaign by that name. Nor, at the time, did I know any of the names that Wheeler had trotted out, apart from that of Churchill, of course, and of Kim Philby (that other foreign or bogus Englishman, born in India and the son of an explorer and orientalist who was, in turn, a native of Ceylon and who, in his forties, converted to Islam), who had also been in Spain during the Civil War as the *Times* correspondent on the side of the insurrectionists, but apparently under orders (from the Soviets, not the British) to take advantage of his proximity to assassinate Franco (he failed, of course, and didn't even try very hard: now for that he really should have been punished). Only later did I learn that they had all been civil servants or spies with grave responsibilities, just as it also took me a while to discover, for example (I'm not going to pretend to any God-given knowledge) that the first surname mentioned by Wheeler was written Menzies, even though he pronounced it as 'Mingiss'. 'You haven't, eh?' Wheeler went on, at the same time opening his folder and rummaging around in it. 'It began during the war, they plastered the whole country with posters, notices and illustrated examples, with radio and press announcements, using drawings by Eric Fraser and many others, Eric Kennington, Wilkinson, Beggarstaff (I've got a few of them here, see?), when we were all convinced and obsessed by the idea that England, Scotland and Wales were infested with Nazi spies, many of them as British as anyone else by birth, education and interests, people who had been bought, fanatical people under a spell, treacherous people, sick, infected people. Everyone distrusted everyone else, especially once the campaign started, with very uneven results in practice (we were, after all, fighting an invincible foe), but it was quite effective mentally or psychologically: people were suspicious of their neighbour, their relative, their teacher, their colleague, the shopkeeper, the doctor, their wife, their husband, and many took advantage of such easy, widespread suspicions, perfectly understandable given the climate at the time, to get rid of a hated spouse. You might not be able to prove that you were living with a German undercover agent or infiltrator, but mere insuperable doubt was enough of an obstacle to prevent you remaining by the side of the supposed monster you had detected, in other words, it provided sufficient grounds for divorce. How could you share a pillow, night after night, with someone about whom you harboured such very grave doubts, with someone so fearsome that he or she would not hesitate to kill you if they suspected they had been unmasked or were under threat? That was what people thought enemy spies were like, whether young or old, male or female, British or foreign, they were all ruthless individuals, with no scruples, no limits, always ready to inflict the greatest possible harm, direct or indirect, on the rearguard or at the front, on group morale or on military equipment, on the civilian population or the troops, it didn't matter. And that wasn't an entirely wrong-headed idea either. People exaggerated their fears in order not entirely to believe in them, to conclude, after all, that nothing could possibly be as malign as they imagined, it's something we all do, deliberately, but apparently unconsciously, thinking the worst, in ridiculous, paranoid fashion, imagining the most gruesome things merely to end up dismissing them in our heart of hearts: at the end of that process, that awful mental journey, shall we say, we always

CARELESS TALK COSTS LIVES

CENSORED!

In peace-time railways could explain
When fog or ice held up your train

But now the country's waging war
To tell you why's against the law.

The censor says you must not know
When there's been a fall of snow

That's because it would be news
The Germans could not fail to use—

So think of this, if it's your fate
To have to meet a train that's late,

Railways aren't allowed to say
What delayed the trains to-day.

MINISTRY OF HEALTH

Stop!
Think twice before making
any Trunk calls.

tell ourselves: oh, it won't be that bad. The funny or dismal fact is that the truth usually is just as bad, if not worse. In my experience and to my knowledge, reality often matches the most cruel of presentiments, and even, sometimes, surpasses them, that is, it provides a precise match for those ideas rejected at the very height or peak of fear, for ideas that were ultimately dismissed as the crazed, immoderate nightmares of anxiety and the imagination. Numerous Nazi agents on British soil did, of course, kill anyone they had to, anyone who posed the slightest threat to them, as did our agents in occupied Europe, ours being mainly but not exclusively members of the SOE. In time of peace it's impossible to understand or to know what war is like, it really is inconceivable, it's not even possible to remember the wars one has actually experienced, those that happened and happened right here, even wars in which one took part; just as in time of war it's impossible to remember or to conceive of peace. People don't realise to what extent the one negates the other, how one state suppresses, repels and excludes the other from our memory and drives it out of our imagination and our thoughts (like pain and pleasure when they are no longer present), or, at most, converts it into something fictitious, you have the feeling that you've never really known or experienced what is, at any given moment, absent; and when absent, always assuming that it existed before, it doesn't function in the same way, it doesn't resemble the past or whatever else is now gone, it's more like a novel or a film. It becomes unreal, a lie. And as regards war, it just seems unbelievable to us, all that waste.' I was tempted to ask Wheeler if he too had killed, in MI6 (a bag of meat, a bloodstain), perhaps in the Caribbean, or in West Africa, or in South-East Asia; or before that, in Spain. But he did not allow time for that temptation to become fact, because he barely paused before adding: 'We find it unutterably hard to believe it afterwards, as soon as war is over; the moment we're faced by defeat or victory, especially victory. They're like watertight compartments, the state of peace and the state of war.

Such a waste.' And then he immediately returned to what he had mentioned earlier: 'Look at this, have you ever seen this before?'

Wheeler took out of his file a yellowing newspaper cutting showing a drawing on which the first thing that leapt out at you was the large swastika in the middle, like a hairy spider, and the web that the spider had woven, which wrapped around or, rather, trapped inside it a number of scenes. '*Information to the Enemy,*' it said in large letters, the title of a play presumably, to judge by the small print at the bottom, which said: 'This play by G. R. Rainier, which illustrates how careless talk, however innocent it may seem at the time, might be pieced together by the enemy and give away a vital secret, will be broadcast again tonight at 10:00.' There were four scenes: three men talking in a pub over a game of darts, the man lurking behind them must be the spy, given that he has a hooked nose, an artist's long hair and prissy beard, and is wearing what appears to be a monocle; a soldier is sitting on a train talking to a blonde lady, she must be the spy, not just by a process of elimination, but also given her elegant appearance; two couples are talking in the street, one composed of two men and the other of a man and a woman: the respective spies must be the man in the bow tie and the man in the scarf, although here it wasn't quite so clear (but it seemed to me that they were the ones doing the listening); lastly, a pilot is welcomed home, doubtless by his parents, and alongside them stands a young woman in apron and cap: she is clearly the spy, since she is young, an employee and an intruder. In addition, at the top and the bottom, there was a plane, the one at the top positioned very close to a mysterious van (possibly just a front) with the words 'Laundry' painted on its side.

'No, I haven't,' I said, and after carefully studying the drawing by Eric Fraser, I turned the cutting over, as I always do with old cuttings. *Radio Times*, May 2, 1941. It appeared to be part of the schedule for that week, for the BBC, I assumed, which, at the time, broadcast only radio. The complete title of this didactic play by Mr Rainier (his name sounded more German than English, or perhaps he was a Monégasque) was, I saw, *Fifth Column: Information to the Enemy*. That expression, 'fifth column', had originated, I believe, in my city, in Madrid, which was besieged for three years by Franco and his troops and his German aviators and his Moroccan guards, and infested by his own fifth columnists, we swiftly exported both terms to other languages and other places: in May 1941, it had been a mere twenty-five months since some of us had met with defeat and others with victory, my parents were amongst the former, as was I when I was born (there are more losses amongst the vanquished and those losses last longer). Included in that radio schedule of sixty long years ago (one's eyes are always drawn to words in one's own language) was a performance by 'Don Felipe and the Cuban Caballeros, with Dorothe Morrow', they were due to be on for half an hour before the close of programming at eleven o'clock: 'Time, Big Ben: Close down'. Where would they be now, Don Felipe and the Cuban Caballeros and the inappropriately named Dorothe Morrow, presumably the vocalist? Where would they be, whether alive or dead? Who knows if they would have managed to perform that night or if they would have been prevented from doing so by a Luftwaffe bombing raid, planned and directed by fifth columnists and informers and spies from our territory. Who knows if they even survived that day.

'What about this? And this? Look at this, and this, and this.' Wheeler continued to take drawings from his file, in colour now and not originals this time, but cut out of magazines or possibly books, or else postcards and playing-cards from the Imperial War Museum in Lambeth Road and from other institutions, they must sell them now as nostalgic souvenirs or as curios, there was a whole pack of cards illustrated with them, it's odd how the useful and even essential things in one's own life become ornaments and archaeology when that life is still not yet over, I thought of Wheeler's life and thought too that I would one day see, in catalogues and in exhibitions, objects and newspapers and photographs and books whose actual creation or taking or writing I had witnessed, if I lived long enough or not even necessarily that long, everything becomes remote so quickly. That museum, the Imperial War Museum, was very close to the headquarters or head office of MI6, that is, the Secret Intelligence Service or SIS, in Vauxhall Cross, which was far from being architecturally secret, it verged, rather, on the flamboyant, on the prominent rather than the discreet, a ziggurat, a lighthouse; and it was very close to the building with no name to which I went every morning over what seemed to me a long period, even though I didn't know then that it would be for me another place of work, of which I've already had quite a few.

'Do you collect them, Peter?' I asked as I studied them. We sat for a moment on the chairs Wheeler had in his garden, they were protected by canvas or waterproof covers and arranged around a small table, he got the chairs out in early spring and took them in again in late autumn, when the days began to grow shorter, but he and Mrs Berry kept them covered up depending on what the day was like, on most days, in fact; the weather is always so changeable in England; that's why they have the expression 'as changeable as the weather', which they apply, for example, to very fickle people. We sat down directly on the canvas covers, the colour of pale gabardine, they were perfectly dry, a pause so that we could more easily sort out and arrange the drawings on the table, which was also covered, the tables and chairs disguised as modern sculptures, or tethered ghosts. There had been similar furniture in Rylands's garden, I recalled, in his nearby garden beside this same river.

'Yes, more or less, there are some things that one wants to remember as clearly as possible. Although it's more Mrs Berry who collects them, she's interested too and she goes to London more often than I do. You never think to keep the unimportant things when they occur in your own time, when they exist naturally, you think of them as easily available and assume they always will be. Later, they become real rarities, and before you know it, they're relics, you just have to see the silly things they sell at auctions nowadays, simply because they're not made any more and can't be found. There are collections of picture cards from forty years ago which fetch the most exorbitant prices, and the people who bid for them like mad things are usually the same ones who collected them as children and who, as young adults, threw them out or gave them away, who knows, perhaps, after a long journey, after the albums have passed through many hands, they're buying back the ones they themselves once collected and filed with such childish perseverance. It's a curse, the present, it allows us to see and appreciate almost nothing. Whoever decided that we should live in the present played a very nasty trick on us,' said Wheeler jokingly, and then showed me the drawings, his index finger trembled slightly: 'Look, you can see now what they were recommending. It's odd, isn't it, especially seen from a modern perspective, in these voracious, unrestrained times, so incapable of not asking questions or of keeping silent.'

One showed a warship sinking on the high seas in the middle of the night, doubtless having been hit by a torpedo, the sky is full of smoke and the glow of flames, and a few survivors are rowing away from it in a boat, though, like any crew member or shipwreck victim, without turning their backs on it, their gaze fixed on the disaster from which they have only half-escaped. 'A few careless words may end in this,' said the caption of what must have been a poster, or perhaps an advertisement from a magazine; and in smaller print: 'Many lives were lost in the last war through careless talk. Be on your guard! Don't discuss movements of ships or troops.' The 'last war' was the 1914–18 war, of which Wheeler retained direct, childhood memories, when he was still called Rylands.

Another depicted a more worldly scene: an attractive woman

lounges in an armchair (necklace, evening dress, corsage, long, painted fingernails) and stares coolly and mockingly ahead while she is encircled and courted and fawned upon by three officers at a party, each holding a cigarette and a drink, they are presumably regaling her with tales of recent escapades or announcing imminent exploits in order to impress her, or else talking amongst themselves, unconcerned that the woman might be listening to them. The caption says: 'Keep mum, she's not so dumb!' (in Spanish: '*Chitón, ella no es tan tonta!*', although in English there is a play on the word 'dumb' which means both 'silent' and 'stupid', and which also rhymes with 'mum'). In red letters underneath is the main campaign slogan: 'Careless talk costs lives.'

Another was even more explicit and didactic, and warned of the possible chain of communication, unwitting and uncontrollable, to which the spoken word is always vulnerable, and here the spy – male or female – is not there at the start, listening, but waiting at the end. The drawing was divided into four parts, two with a red background and two with a white background. The picture at top left showed a sailor talking to a young blonde woman (his girlfriend, his sister, perhaps a friend) whom he has no reason to distrust, on the contrary, she listens with disinterested interest (that is, she is more interested in him than in what he reveals to her or tells her), and gazes at him admiringly, almost spellbound. Underneath, in capital letters, is the word 'TELLING'. The next picture, top right, shows the same young blonde woman chatting to a female friend with brown hair drawn up on top of her head and who is listening with a look of amazement on her face, but her interest seems less disinterested: she is, at the very least, savouring in advance the prospect of passing on this tidbit of news; she may not be ill-intentioned, but simply gossipy, one of those people who enjoy retailing and acquiring any hot news to show how well-informed they are and thus surprising others with how much they know about everything. Underneath, in lower-case letters, is printed: 'a friend may'. The picture at bottom left shows the woman with the brown hair telling what she has heard to another female friend, this woman has black hair parted in the middle and arranged in a kind of low bun, she has cold, almond-shaped eyes and an interested expression on her face, an expression which, this time, is entirely self-interested, for as she is listening, she is thinking of the next person she will speak to, and to whom she will give not just a snippet of news, but some very valuable information. Underneath, again in lower case, is printed: 'mean telling'. Lastly, the picture bottom right showed the third woman, the one with the black hair – her eyes malevolently closed – almost whispering into the ear of a fair-haired man with shifty eyes and very hard features, doubtless a ruthless Nazi whose next step will not be to tell someone else, but to act, to take measures that will probably result in the deaths of many men, including that of the guilty and innocent sailor. Underneath, the letters were once more printed in upper case, 'THE ENEMY', and so the whole message was 'TELLING a friend may mean telling THE ENEMY', the principal message being the one conveyed by those capital letters set against the red background. I couldn't help smiling to myself and noticing the careful gradation of the three women: the 'good' one was blonde with shortish hair and wore a simple, modest white bow around her neck; the 'frivolous' or 'silly' one wore her brown hair swept up and had a necklace on (she was more of a coquette); the 'bad' one, the spy, had black hair arranged rather more elaborately, and around her neck she was wearing a kind of black choker with a lustrous, greenish-coloured brooch in the middle, and she was also the only one to wear earrings (she was doubtless a proper *femme fatale*). Many of my female compatriots, amongst them my mother, would, I thought, have received a very bad press in England at that time.

Another drawing showed an infantryman looking straight out at us: a middle-aged man (a veteran) with a cigarette between his lips and the forefinger of his left hand resting on his temple underneath his helmet, recommending us to 'Keep it under your hat', an idiom that translates into Spanish as '*De esto, ni palabra*' or '*De esto no sueltes prenda*' or perhaps in purer and slightly more antiquated Spanish: '*Guárdatelo para tu coleto*'. And at the top, in red letters, ''Ware spies!'

'Were these intended mainly for the forces, these posters?' I asked Wheeler.

'Yes, but not solely,' he replied with a slight tremor in his voice. 'That's the most interesting thing, the message wasn't intended just for soldiers, who knew more and so needed to take more care and be more discreet, but for everyone, including civilians. Look at these.' And he removed from his file a few other examples which were, indeed, not addressed to the military alone, but to the whole population.

Some were cartoons. One showed a man talking on the phone inside one of those red public telephone boxes that you occasionally still see in England: according to the caption, he was saying '. . . but for heaven's sake, don't say *I* told you!', while around the walls and roof of the booth appear the cloned faces of fourteen or fifteen small Hitlers. Another showed two ladies sitting on the Underground, and one was saying to the other: 'You never know *who's* listening!' A couple of seats behind them sit two uniformed Nazi bigwigs, one thin, the other fat and heavily bemedalled, the former also resembled Hitler. In another poster, based perhaps on a photograph, an ordinary man wearing tie, raincoat and cap (possibly a Cockney) seemed to wink at the viewer and say: 'What I know – I keep to *myself*.' There were others intended to persuade children and, by imitation, to inculcate in them the importance of keeping silent ('Be like Dad, Keep Mum!'), or purely typographical official warnings with no illustration ('Thousands of lives were lost in the last war through valuable information being revealed to the enemy through careless talk. Be on your guard!'), which must have filled the noticeboards and pinboards of offices and schools and pubs and factories, as well as streets, walls, the insides of trains and buses, railway and Underground stations. Others explained, in verse, why censorship was being imposed on apparently innocuous information which, in time of peace, would have been issued without any difficulty, which would, indeed, have been mandatory, for example, the reasons for a train being delayed or stopping or arriving very late: 'In peace-time railways could explain/When fog or ice held up your train/But now the country's waging war/To tell you why's against the law . . ./That's because it would be *news*/The Germans could not fail to *use* . . .' (a display of consideration and public spirit, explaining to the population why it was not possible to explain). And there were still more posters addressed to the members of the armed forces, whose carelessness could place everyone, as well, of course, as themselves, in greatest danger. A soldier in a helmet and with a telephone for a body warned: 'Stop! Think twice before making any trunk calls.' Or a uniformed man and woman with only feet and head visible behind a blue screen that concealed their respective ranks and was emblazoned, in white letters, with the word 'CENSORED'; the young man and woman were standing with the lighted ends of their cigarettes pressed together, one was giving the other a light and thus joining their lips, albeit with the interposition of tobacco and fire (smoking wasn't frowned upon or persecuted then, so things weren't all bad), but, they were warned: 'Your units must not be disclosed!' Most of the posters insisted, however, on the fundamental campaign slogan: 'Careless talk costs lives', '*Las conversaciones imprudentes cuestan vidas*'. Although another not entirely un-faithful translation might be: '*se cobran vidas*'.

'I have a vague recollection that during our Civil War there were similar warnings against fifth columnists, but I'm not sure, can you remember, Peter?' I asked. 'There's a slogan going round in my head along the lines of "The enemy has a thousand ears", but I may be inventing it, I'm not sure, on the other hand, I haven't any images stored away, any equivalents to the kind of thing you've shown me, I can't remember ever having seen them reproduced.' I really didn't know, but it wasn't impossible that this was another initiative we had exported. Or perhaps I was getting it confused in my memory with the defamatory poster against the POUM in the spring of 1937, a face stamped with a swastika appearing from beneath a mask bearing the hammer and sickle; Nin had been the victim of the half-justified paranoia that made people see Franco's spies and collaborators on every corner, or, rather, his enemies had made use of that paranoia to accuse him of treachery and espionage. He was accused of having informed, of having talked, and that, paradoxically, is what his torturers could never force him to do. He remained silent and did not save himself, he kept his mouth shut, he did not blab, he did not say a word, in short, 'he kept mum', what he knew he kept to himself or under his hat, or perhaps he said nothing because the accusations were all false, he would have had to invent some tall tales and stories in order to acknowledge and support them, to admit that he was the 'Trojan horse' as that poetic 'lover of the truth' and 'worthy Don Quixote' later described him in that 'lamp-light glow' of a voice which so bewitched Trapp-Tello, such a very slanderous voice.

'Last night I told you that before the war against Germany I had been briefly involved in yours, and I usually express myself with great precision, Jacobo. As I believe I am now. That means, I did not spend much time in Spain. I was just passing through,' Wheeler replied, and I noticed a slight touch of impatience in his voice, as if he were rather put out that I should, at that precise moment, want to drag in another war and another time, however closely related it was to his war and however close in time it might have been. 'But anyway, although I couldn't swear to it, I can't remember having seen such a thing in your country, I haven't read or heard anything about it either. If I'm not mistaken, though, there were posters, a campaign against fifth columnists; the populations of Madrid and Barcelona and possibly Valencia were urged to hunt them down and unmask them, to drag them out of the sewers and kill them, and it was the same on the other side: they were urged to track down and destroy intriguers, not that there would have been many left in an area full of talkative father-confessors, but that was what was asked of them. Obviously, they told people to keep their eyes open and to watch the rearguard, as they also did rather timidly, I believe, during the First World War, here and in France. But I don't think there was ever a campaign like this one against "careless talk", in which they not only put civilians on guard against possible spies, but recommended silence as the norm: people were prevailed upon not to speak, they were ordered, indeed exhorted, to keep silent. Suddenly people were made to see their own language as an invisible enemy, uncontrollable, unexpected and unpredictable, as the worst, most murderous and most fearful of enemies, like a terrible weapon which you, or anyone, could activate and set off without ever knowing when it might unleash a bullet, or if it would be transformed into torpedoes that would sink one of our battleships in the middle of the ocean thousands of miles away, or into bombs from a Junkers that would strike with deadly accuracy at our neighbourhoods and our houses, or fall on those military targets that most needed to be safeguarded and defended, on the most secret and most camouflaged and most vital of targets. I don't know if you quite realise what it meant, Jacobo: people were warned against using their main form of communication; they were made to distrust the very activity in which people most naturally indulge and always have indulged, without reserve, at all times and in all places, not just in this country and at that particular time; it made an enemy of what most defines and unites us: talking, telling, saying, commenting, gossiping, passing on information, criticising, exchanging news, tattle-taling, defaming, slandering and spreading rumours, describing and relating events, keeping up to date and putting others in the picture, and, of course, joking and lying. That is the wheel that moves the world, Jacobo, more than anything else; that is the engine of life, the one that never becomes exhausted and never stops, that is its life's breath. And suddenly people were asked to turn it off, that engine, to stop it breathing. They were asked to give up the thing they most love, that is most indispensable to them, the thing we all live for and which everyone, without exception, can enjoy and make use of, both poor and rich, uneducated and educated, old and young, the sick and the healthy, soldiers and civilians. If there's one thing that they do or we do which is not a strict physio-logical necessity, if there is one thing that is truly common to all beings endowed with free will, it is talking, Jacobo. The fatal word. The curse of the word. Talking and talking, without stopping, that is the one thing for which no one ever lacks ammunition. Grammatical, syntactical and lexical skills matter little, oratorial gifts still less, and pronunciation, diction, accent, euphony, rhythm even less. The wisest man in the world will talk with greater order, appropriateness and precision, and perhaps to his listeners' greater advantage, or, rather, only to the advantage of those listeners who resemble him or want to resemble him. But he will not talk any more fluently than the semi-literate housewife who talks non-stop all day and who only stops at night because sleep and her sore, much-abused throat finally get the better of her. The most widely travelled man in the world will be able to tell endless marvellous and delightful stories, innumerable anecdotes about adventures in outlandish, remote, exotic and dangerous places. But he will not necessarily talk with any more confidence than the rough innkeeper who has never been further than his own bar and has only ever seen the twenty streets and two or three squares that make up his obscure village. The most inspired poet or the most zigzagging of narrators will be able to invent and recite on demand a stream of hypnotic words that will sound like music, so much so that those listening will not worry overmuch about the meaning, or, rather, they will capture the meaning effortlessly and without having to think about it before grasping or absorbing it, the process will be entirely simultaneous, although afterwards, when the music has stopped, those listeners might be quite incapable of repeating or summarising it, incapable possibly of continuing to understand what a moment ago they understood so well while they were rocked by the rhythm and while the enchantment lasted, resting as lightly upon the mind as upon the ear, each as permeable as the other. But those poets and narrators will not necessarily speak with more assurance or ease than the ignorant office worker, repetitive and dull, who believes himself to be full of "*donaire*" and "*gracia*", a tedious fixture in all the offices of the world, regardless of latitude or climate, even in the offices of interpreters and spies . . .'

Wheeler stopped for a moment, more than anything – it seemed to me – to catch his breath. He had said the words '*donaire*' and '*gracia*' in Spanish, possibly paraphrasing Cervantes's words taken from somewhere other than *Don Quixote*, an unusual occurrence, but perfectly possible in his case. I could not resist trying to find out, and so I took advantage of his pause to quote slowly, little by little, almost syllable by syllable, as if casually or as if not quite daring to say it, murmuring:

'*Adiós, gracias; adiós, donaires; adiós, regocijados amigos; que yo me voy muriendo . . .*'

Farewell, wit; farewell, charm; farewell, dear, delightful friends; for I am dying . . .

I could not complete the quotation. Perhaps Wheeler did not like to be reminded of that last phrase out loud, often the old do not even want to hear so much as a mention of such things, of their death, perhaps because they are beginning to see it as something likely or plausible and not dreamed or fictitious. No, I don't believe it, I can't be sure, but no one sees their own end like that, not even the very old or the very ill or those under threat and in constant danger. We, the others, are the ones who begin to see it in them. He ignored me and went on. He pretended not to notice what I had recited in my own language, and so I never knew if it had been a coincidence or if he had, in fact, been alluding to Cervantes's joyful farewell.

'Sometimes people say of someone that he lacks conversation. That's ridiculous. A cultivated person, the Prime Minister (well, all right, let's call him mentally adroit) might say it of someone who is not at all cultivated, for example, his barber. What the former is actually saying is that he doesn't care about and is hugely bored by anything the latter has to say. Doubtless almost as bored as the barber is by everything the Prime Minister comes out with while he's having his hair cut, it's always a difficult chunk of time to fill, like journeys in elevators, especially if the scant head of hair requires all manner of primping if it's to look half-way presentable and not too much like an uprooted carrot. But the barber will certainly not lack conversation, he may have even more to say than the rather obtuse minister, who is more concerned with the progress of his country in the abstract and, more concretely, with the progress of his career. It seems to me that people who know absolutely nothing, people who have never consciously paused to think for a moment about anything, who do not have a single idea of their own or anyone else's really, nevertheless talk untiringly, unceasingly, without the slightest inhibition or self-consciousness. This is not just the case with people without training or education; there are far more astonishing cases than that of these rustics: you have only to see a group of rich loudmouths or idiotic snobs, most of them with PhDs from Cambridge or from us, and you wonder what the devil they can find to talk about amongst themselves after the first hour of exchanging greetings and telling each other the four miserable scraps of news that everyone knows about anyway because it's common gossip, or bringing each other up to date on their usual two bits of twaddle and three pieces of villainy (I've always wondered what such people can find to talk about at those lavish receptions, which are cram-packed with them). One imagines that they must often have to resort to saying nothing and to loudly clearing their throats, that they must have to suffer embarrassingly long pauses and endure witty comments about the rain and the clouds as well as the awkward silences characteristic of dead time at its most defunct and even stillborn, given their absolute lack of ideas, amusing remarks, knowledge and the necessary inspiration to recount anything, of ingenuity and dialogue and even monologue: of intelligence and substance. And yet that isn't the case. One doesn't know why or how or about what, but the fact is that they spend the hours and the days chatting endlessly, brutishly, spend whole evenings engaged in chit-chat, without once closing their mouths, even snatching the word from each other's lips, all intent on monopolising it. It's both a mystery and not a mystery. Speaking, far more than thinking, is something that everyone has within his or her grasp (I'm talking, of course, about things volitive, not merely organic or physiological); it's something which is shared and has always been shared by the bad and the good, by victims and their executioners, by the cruel and the compassionate, the sincere and the mendacious, by the not very bright and the extremely stupid, by slaves and their masters, by the gods and mankind. They all have it, imbeciles, brutes, merciless sadists, murderers, tyrants, savages, simpletons, and even the mad. And precisely because it is the one thing that makes us all equal we have spent centuries creating for ourselves all kinds of tiny differences, in pronunciation, diction, intonation, vocabulary, phonetics and semantics, all in order to feel that our group alone is in possession of a mode of speech unknown to others, of a password for initiates only. It is not only a matter for what used to be called the upper classes, eager to distinguish themselves from and scornful of everyone else; those known as the lower classes have done the same, they have proved no less scornful, and thus have forged their own jargons, their own ciphers, the secret or encrypted languages that allowed them to recognise each other and to exclude the enemy, that is, the learned and the powerful and the refined, and to prevent them from understanding, at least in part, what their members were saying, just as criminals invent their own argot and the persecuted their codes. Within the confines of the same language, their entirely artificial aim is to be *not* understood or at least only partially; it's an attempt to obscure, to conceal, and, with this end in mind, they seek out strange derivations and fanciful variants, defective and highly arbitrary metaphors, tangential or oblique meanings that can be separated off from the common norm, they even coin new and unnecessary substitute words, to undo what was said and to mask what was communicated. The reason being that what makes language intelligible is the habitual and the given. Moreover, that language, or tongue, is almost all that some people have and give and receive: the poorest, the most humble, the disinherited, the illiterate, the captive, the unhappy, the subjugated; the marginalised and the deformed, like that Shakespearean king of ours, Richard III, who did so well out of his persuasive gift of the gab. That's the one thing you can't take away from them, speech or language, perhaps the one thing they have learned and know, they use it to address their children or their lovers, to joke, to love, to defend themselves, to suffer, console and pray, to unburden themselves, to implore, persuade, save and convince; with it they also poison, instigate, hate, perjure, insult, curse and betray, corrupt, condemn and avenge themselves. Almost everyone has it, both the king and his vassals, the priest and his congregation, the marshal and his soldiers. That is why sacred language exists, a language that does not belong to everyone, a language intended not for men, but for the gods. People forget, however, that, according to our old and possibly now moribund beliefs, both God and the gods talk and listen too (what are prayers but sentences, words, syllables), and, in the end, that sacred language is deciphered and learned too, all codes are susceptible to eventual decoding, sooner or later, no secret can be a secret eternally.' Wheeler stopped again, very briefly, again to catch his breath. He placed one hand on the pictures we had laid out on the table, an instinctive gesture, as if he wanted to prevent them being carried off by a non-existent gust of wind, or perhaps merely to caress them. It wasn't cold, the sun was very high, pale, lazy; it was pleasantly cool. 'Language so binds and assimilates us that the powerful have always had to find non-verbal signs and insignia and symbols in order to be obeyed and in order to differentiate themselves. Do you remember that scene in Shakespeare when, on the eve of battle, the king wraps himself in a borrowed cloak and goes and sits down in the camp with three soldiers, pretending to be just another combatant, ready for battle, and unable to sleep through what's left of the night or through the few remaining hours before dawn? He speaks to them, he presents himself as a friend, he talks to them, and when he does, the four seem similar, he more logical and educated, they rougher and more intuitive, but they understand each other perfectly, they are on the same plane of comprehension and speech and nothing gets in the way of that exchange of opinions and impressions and even fears, two of them even quarrel and almost come to blows, the king who is not the king and a subject who is not, at that moment, a subject. They talk for quite a while, and the king knows that, as they speak, they become equal, that, at least for as long as the dialogue lasts, they are the same. Which is why, when he is left alone, thinking about what he has heard, he tells us what the difference is, he murmurs in his soliloquy what it is that really distinguishes him from them. Do you remember that scene, Jacobo?'

I too placed my hand on the drawings, as if I feared a breeze.

'No, Peter,' I said. 'What king is that?'

But Wheeler did not reply to my question, he went on, instead, to quote out loud, and this time I was in no doubt that he was quoting, for very few writers other than Shakespeare would ever have written 'great greatness' (and so many teachers and critics in my country now would have crucified him for doing so).

"'What infinite heart's ease must kings neglect that private men enjoy! And what have kings that privates have not too, save ceremony, save general ceremony?" That is what the king says when he's alone, and a little further on he reproaches ceremony for singling him out: "Oh ceremony! Show me but thy worth!" And he goes on to challenge it: "O! be sick, great greatness, and bid thy ceremony give thee cure!" What does it actually achieve, if it achieves anything? And later still, the king dares to envy the wretched slave who labours in the sun all day but then sleeps deeply "with a body fill'd and vacant mind" and "never sees horrid night, the child of hell" and who "follows so the ever-running year with profitable labour to his grave". And the king concludes with the obligatory exaggeration of all those monologues that no one else hears on the stage and which are heard only off-stage, in the auditorium: "And, but for ceremony, such a wretch, winding up days with toil and nights with sleep, had the fore-hand and vantage of a king."' That is more or less what Wheeler said and quoted, then he added: 'Kings of old were shameless creatures, but at least Shakespeare's kings did not entirely deceive themselves: they knew their hands were stained with blood and they did not forget how they came to wear the crown, apart from murders and betrayals and plots (perhaps they were too human). Ceremony, Jacobo, that's all. Changing, limitless, general ceremony. As well as secrecy, mystery, inscrutability, silence. But never speaking, never talking, never using words, however exquisite or captivating they might be. Because that, deep down, is within the grasp of any beggar, any outcast, any poor wretch, any one of the dispossessed. In that regard, they only differ from the king in the insignificant and ameliorable matter of perfection and degree.'

'What infinite heart's ease must kings neglect that private men enjoy!' were the words quoted by Sir Peter Wheeler, as I found out later, when I located and recognised the texts. And he recited word for word the whole of the rest of the soliloquy, for that kind of memory he preserved intact.

'But it's not within the reach of the very young,' I commented, 'or the dumb or those whose tongues have been cut out or to whom the word is simply not given or permitted, there's been a lot of that in history, and, as I understand it, there are Islamic countries in which women still do not have that right. As far as I understand it, and if my memory serves me right, that was the case with the Taliban in Afghanistan.'

'No, Jacobo, you're wrong: the young are merely waiting, their inability is purely transitory; I imagine they are preparing themselves from that very first yell when they're born, and they make themselves understood very early on: they use other means, but they are still *saying* things. As for the dumb and those with no tongue, and those denied voice and word, they are exceptions, anomalies, punishments, coercions, outrages, but never the norm, and, as such, they do not count. Besides, that is not enough in itself to render that norm null and void or even to contradict it. Those thus afflicted resort to other sign systems, to non-verbal codes which they quickly establish, and you may rest assured that what they are doing is neither more nor less than talking. They are soon telling and transmitting again, like everyone else; even if it's in writing or through signs and without uttering a sound; they are still *saying* even if they are doing so silently.' Wheeler stopped talking and looked up at the sky, as if, having spoken of silence, he wanted to immerse himself for a moment in the eloquent silence he had evoked. The whitish, indifferent sun lit up his eyes, and to me they looked like glass marbles flecked with colour in which the dominant shade was dark red. 'Earlier, I said that speaking, language, is something we all share, even victims and their executioners, masters and their slaves, men and their gods, you have only to read the Bible and Homer or, of course, in Spanish, St Teresa of Ávila and St John of the Cross. But some people cease to share it, how can I put it, they do not possess it, and they are neither dumb nor very young.' He looked down for a second, and still had his eyes fixed on the grass, or perhaps beyond that, on the earth beneath the grass, or beyond that, on the invisible earth beneath the earth, then added after a brief pause: 'The only ones who do not share a common language, Jacobo, are the living and the dead.'

'It seems to me that time is the only dimension they share and in which they can communicate, the only dimension they have in common and that unites them.' That quotation, or perhaps paraphrase, came into my mind, and I felt I had to say it out loud at once, or at least mumble it to myself.

But Wheeler was, I thought, gradually coming to the end of his digression. In fact, he always knew precisely where he was, and what seemed in him random or involuntary, a consequence of distraction or of age or of a somewhat confused perception of time, of his digressive and discursive tendencies, was always calculated, measured and controlled, and formed part of his machinations and of trajectories he had already drawn up and planned. I told myself that it would not be long now before he returned to the subject of 'careless talk' and the posters, indeed, he was once more looking at them intently, where they lay on the waterproof canvas cover as if they were cards in a game of patience, we, too, were sitting on the protective covers, and their folds gave to that simulacrum of an old man and to me, too, I suppose, a slightly Roman look, made us look, perhaps, vaguely like senators taking the air, our feet almost engulfed by the skirts of some very long, exaggerated tunics. Anyway, he either didn't hear me or preferred to ignore me, or simply didn't notice the words I had said, which were not mine but another's, the words of a dead man when he was still alive.

'But it wasn't always so,' he continued with his own

thoughts. 'Throughout the centuries, they too shared speech and language, at least in the imaginations of the living, that is, of the future dead. Not just the talkative ghosts and loquacious phantoms, the chatty spirits and garrulous spectres present in almost all traditions. It was also assumed that they would, quite naturally, talk and speak and tell tales in the other world. In that same scene from Shakespeare, for example, before the king gives his soliloquy, one of the soldiers with whom he speaks says that the king will have a hard time of it should the cause of the war prove to have been a bad one: "When all those legs and arms and heads, chopped off in a battle," he says, "shall join together at the latter day, and cry all, 'We died at such a place.'" You see, that was what they believed, not only that the dead would speak and even protest, but that their scattered, separated heads and limbs would protest as well, once reunited to present themselves for judgement with due decorum.'

'We died at such a place.' That was what Wheeler had said in his language, and in my own language I completed the Cervantes quotation to myself, the one he had not allowed me to finish and which also bore witness to that same belief: 'Farewell, wit; farewell, charm; farewell, dear, delightful friends; for I am dying, and hope to see you soon, happily installed in the other life.' That was what Cervantes hoped for, I thought, no complaints and no accusations, no reproaches, no settling of accounts or demands for compensation for all his earthly troubles and grievances, of which he had known not a few. Not even a final judgement, which is what the unbeliever most misses. Instead, a renewed encounter with wit and charm, with his dear, delightful friends, who would also find contentment in the next life. That is the only thing from which he takes his leave, the only thing he would wish to preserve in the eternity for which he is bound. I had often heard my father speak of that written farewell, which is not as famous as it deserves to be, it can be found in a book which almost no one reads and which may, nevertheless, be greater than all the others, greater even than *Don Quixote*. I would have liked to remind Wheeler of the whole quotation, but I did not dare to insist or to cause him to deviate from his path. Instead, I accompanied him along the way, saying:

'The very idea of a Final Judgement meant that, according to common expectations, that would be what people would mostly be doing after death: telling everyone's story, then talking, relating, describing, arguing, refuting, appealing and, in the end, hearing sentence. Besides, a trial on such a monumental scale, the trial on a single day of everyone who had ever lived on Earth, Egyptian pharaohs rubbing shoulders with modern-day business executives and taxi-drivers, Roman emperors with modern-day beggars and gangsters and astronauts and bullfighters. Imagine the noise, Peter, the entire history of the world with all its individual cases transformed into a madhouse. And the more remote and ancient dead would get fed up with waiting, with counting the uncountable time that would elapse before their Judgement, doubtless furious about the literally infinite delay. They who had remained silent and alone for millions of centuries, waiting for the last person to die and for no one else to be left alive. That belief condemned us all to a very long silence. There you have a true example of "the whips and scorns of time", "the law's delay",' and this time I was the one to quote from his poet. 'And according to that belief, the very first man ever to die would, right now, still be counting the hours of his silent solitude, those that had passed and those still to come; and if I were him, I would be selfishly longing for the world to end once and for all and for there finally to be nothing.'

Wheeler smiled. Something in what I had said, or perhaps more than one thing, had amused him.

'Exactly,' he replied. 'A silence *sine die*: that would be the best-case scenario, assuming one's faith was unshakeable. But there is, of course, the aggravating factor that, by then, during the Second World War, hardly anyone believed in that parliament or justification or final report by each individual at the end of time, and it was hard to think that the heads and limbs which, night after night, were being shattered by the bombs raining down on those cities could ever one day be reunited in order to cry out at some later date: "We died at such a place"; and it was little consolation that the causes were just, and it mattered still less if they were or weren't good, when the main cause of all the dying and killing became instead mere survival, one's own or that of those one loved. It probably hadn't been much believed before that either, perhaps not since the First World War, which was no less ghastly for the world that watched it and which is also my world, don't forget, as is this world that contains both you and me today, or is perhaps merely dragging us along with it. Atrocities make men into unbelievers, at least in their innermost consciousness and feelings, even if, out of some superstitious reflex reaction, or some other reaction based on a mixture of tradition and surrender, they decide to pretend the opposite and gather together in churches to sing hymns in order to feel closer and to instil themselves not so much with courage as with integrity and resignation, just as soldiers used to sing as they advanced, almost defenceless, bayonets fixed, mostly in order to anaesthetise themselves a little with their cries before the impact or the blow or being hurled into the air, in order to numb thoughts that had been wounded long before the flesh ever was, and to silence the various sounds made by death as it prowled around on the look-out for easy prey. I know this, I've seen it in the field. But it isn't only the acts of savagery, the cruelties, those one has suffered and those one has oneself committed, all in the cause of survival, which is as just as it is unjust. It is also the stubbornness of the facts: the fact that no one has ever come to talk to us after they have died, despite all the efforts of spiritualists, visionaries, phantasmophiles, miraculists and even our present-day unbelieving believers, who, even though their belief is only residual and habitual, can be counted in their millions; long experience has forced us to recognise over the centuries, perhaps only in our heart of hearts and possibly without ever actually admitting as much to ourselves, that the only people who have no language and never speak or tell or say anything are the dead.' Peter stopped and looked down again, and added at once, without looking up: 'And that includes us, of course, when we join their ranks. But only then and not before.'

He remained like that, staring at the grass. He seemed to be waiting for me to make some comment or to ask some question. But I didn't know which, which of those two things he wanted and for which one he was silently asking me, or if he really needed either. And so the only thing that occurred to me was to whisper in my own language, a language in which the words had not originally been written, but the only one in which I knew them:

'It is strange to inhabit the earth no longer. Strange no longer to be what one was . . .and to abandon even one's own name. Strange no longer to desire one's desires. And being dead is such hard work.'

Fortunately, I suppose, Wheeler ignored this too.

'Yes, they only talk to us in our dreams,' he went on, as if my unattended half-verses had, none the less, triggered some reaction. 'And we hear them so clearly, and their presence is so vivid, that, as long as sleep lasts, these people with whom we can never exchange a word or a look when awake, or make any contact, seem to be the very people who are, in fact, telling us things and listening to us and even cheering our spirits with their longed-for laughter, identical to the laughter we knew when they were alive on this earth: it's exactly the same, that laughter; we recognise it unhesitatingly. It really is very strange; if pressed, I would say inexplicable, it is one of the few intact mysteries left to us. One thing is certain, though, at least for rationalists like you and like me, and as Toby was and Tupra still is, those voices and their new voices are inside us, not somewhere outside. They are in our imagination and in our memory. Let's put it like this: it is our memory imagining, and not, for once, only remembering, or, rather, doing so in impure, motley fashion. They are in *our* dreams, the dead; we are the ones dreaming them, our sleeping consciousness brings them to us and no one else can hear them. It is more like an impersonation' (a word that translates into Spanish as a mixture of *encarnación*, *suplantación* and *personificación*) 'than a supposed visitation or warning from beyond the grave. Such a mechanism is not unknown to us, when we're awake I mean. Sometimes you love someone so much that it's very easy to see the world through their eyes and to feel what that other person feels, in so far as it's possible to understand another person's feelings. To foresee that person, to anticipate them. Literally, to put yourself in their place. That's why the expression exists, very few expressions in a language exist in vain. And if we do that when we're awake, then it's hardly surprising that these fusions or conversions or juxtapositions, metamorphoses almost, should occur while we're asleep. Do you know that sonnet by Milton? Milton had been blind for some time when he wrote it, but he dreamed one night of his dead wife Catherine, and he saw and heard her perfectly in that dimension, that of the dream, which so welcomes and withstands the poetic narrative. And in that dimension he recovered his vision threefold: his own, as faculty and sense; the impossible image of his wife, for neither he nor anyone else could still see her in the present, she had been erased from the earth; and, above all, her face and figure, which, in him, were not even remembered but imagined, new and never seen before, because he had never seen her in life other than with his mind and with his touch, she was his second wife and he was already blind when they married. And as he leaned forwards to embrace her in the dream, "I wak'd, she fled, and day brought back my night", that's how it ends. With the dead you always return to night and to hearing only their silence and to never receiving a reply. No, they never talk, they are the only

347

ones; and they are also the majority, if we count all those who have passed through the world and left it behind. Although they all doubtless talked when they were here.' Wheeler touched the drawings again, tapped them with his index finger, pointing at them vehemently as if they were more than they were. 'Do you realise what this meant, Jacobo? They were asking people to be silent, to sew up their lips, to keep their mouths tight shut, to abstain from all careless talk and even from talk that might not seem careless. They filled everyone with fear, even children. Fear of themselves and of betraying themselves, and, of course, fear of other people, even the person one most loved, the person who was closest and most trusted. So, when you think about it, what they were asking with these slogans was not just that people should renounce the air, but that by doing so, they should become assimilated with the dead. And this at a time when each day brought us news of so many new dead, those on the infinite fronts scattered around half the globe, or those you could see in your own neighbourhood, in your own street, victims of the night-time bombing raids, when anyone might be the next. Weren't those deaths enough? Wasn't it enough, that definitive and irreversible silence imposed on so many without those of us still alive having to imitate them and fall silent before our time? How could they ask that of a whole country or of anyone, even of an isolated individual? If you look at these posters (and there were more), you'll see that no one, however insignificant, was excluded. What interesting or dangerous information, for example, could those two ladies travelling on the Underground be harbouring, they're probably talking about their hats or about the most innocuous details of their daily lives. Ah, but their husband or brother or son might have been called up, that was the norm, and although their men, already forewarned, would not have told them much, they might know something of importance that could be used, how can I put it, without their even knowing that they knew it or unaware of its importance. Everyone could know something, even the most misanthropic beggar to whom nobody speaks, not just in time of war but never, and even though the majority aren't aware of the precious nature of what they know. And the less conscious one is, the more dangerous one becomes. It may seem like an exaggeration, but everyone is capable of unleashing calamities, disasters, crimes, tragic misunderstandings and acts of revenge merely by speaking, innocently and freely. It is always possible and even easy to let the cat out of the bag or, as you say in Spanish, *irse de la lengua*, what a lovely expression, at once so broad and so precise, covering both the intentional and the involuntary nature of the action.' And Wheeler, of course, said that lovely expression, *irse de la lengua*, in Spanish. 'Whatever the era or the circumstances, no one is safe from that. And never forget: everything has its moment to be believed, however unlikely or anodyne, however incredible or stupid.'

Wheeler looked up again, as if he had heard before I did what I heard immediately afterwards, but only after a few seconds, the noise of an engine in the air and that of a propeller too, perhaps he had got used to picking up the slightest sound or aerial vibration during the war or during his wars, before it was even audible, I suppose it's also possible to learn to have a presentiment of a presentiment. Then a helicopter appeared, flying low over the trees, an odd sight in the Oxford sky, still more so at a weekend, on one of those Sundays in exile from the infinite, perhaps some academic ceremony was being held that required the presence of the Prime Minister or some other high-ranking official or someone else from the crowded monarchical ladder (the Duke and Duchess of Kent seem to be in a dozen places at once, with, it's said, supernatural help) and about which we knew nothing, Wheeler had been retired for so long now that, with each year that passed, the university authorities were more and more inclined to forget to invite him to their solemn feasts. British premiers have traditionally shown a kind of homing instinct for our university, although, during my time as a teacher there, I still remember how we members of the congregation denied a doctorate *honoris causa*, by a majority vote, to the modest Mrs Thatcher (the rancorous Margaret Hilda) when she was still only Mrs and not Baroness or Lady. She was an Oxford graduate and was in power at the time, but that didn't help her much. I had a temporary right to vote and it was with great excitement and pleasure that I gave my vote to the nay-saying majority. The woman took the snub badly, and later appeared to exact her revenge by imposing restrictions and laws prejudicial to Oxford University and to others too, but she was the first Prime Minister to whom such a degree had been denied, for it had been awarded to all or almost all her predecessors, with barely any opposition, a mere formality, or, shall we say, graciously.

The noise of the blades immediately became unbearable, Peter clapped his hands over his ears and at the same time screwed up his eyes hard, as if the clatter – a giant rattle – hurt his eyes too, and thus he could not prevent the drawings from being blown about in the turbulence. He didn't even see this happen. I tried to hold down those I could with my hands, but only very few. The helicopter started making passes overhead, as if we were the object of its vigilance, perhaps it amused the pilot to see this frightened old man and to watch his companion chasing after some elusive bits of paper that were heading in the direction of the river. I had to hurl myself flat on the grass (not just once or twice either) to rescue the more graspable papers before they fell into the water, while the helicopter circled overhead with what I perceived, possibly erroneously, to be mockery, as I hurled myself this way and that. Then it moved off and disappeared in a matter of seconds, just as it had come. A few drawings were still flying about, especially the newspaper cuttings, which were the lightest, I feared that Fraser's '*Information to the Enemy*' might not only crumble like a papyrus (it was over sixty years old that bit of paper), but also get a soaking. I was still chasing after various of these when I saw that

Wheeler had finally opened his eyes as well as his ears, and – with his hands free again – was now raising one arm to his forehead – or it may have been his wrist to his temple – as if he were in pain or were checking to see if he had a fever, or perhaps it was a gesture of horror. And I saw that he had stretched out his other arm, pointing with his forefinger just as he had the previous night when he couldn't find the word he wanted and I had to guess or work out what it was. I would have assumed that this was the same thing again, this momentary aphasia, had it not been preceded by the helicopter flying over and by Peter's contrived deafness and blindness while the blades thundered above us, I had seen him, how can I put it, defenceless and helpless, and possibly overcome. I went fearfully over to him, I abandoned the bits of paper for the moment, abandoned my hunt for the remaining rebellious items.

'Peter, are you feeling ill, is something wrong?' He shook his head and continued pointing with a look of alarm on his face at the banks of the peaceful Cherwell, I didn't need approximations this time: 'The cartoon?' I asked, and he nodded at once even though I think I may have used the wrong term, it was the original cutting that was worrying him, he had only become aware of the danger when he opened his eyes after his initial fright or his lightning realisation, not before; and so off I went again, I ran, leapt, fell, caught it, closing my fingers on it, still intact, on the very edge of the gently flowing stream, I must have looked like one of those fielders in cricket who hurl themselves to the ground, in that quintessentially English game about which I understand nothing, or else a goalkeeper in a football match performing a full-length save, in that no longer so quintessentially English game which I understand perfectly. The air had grown still again, I picked up another two or three bits of paper from the ground, they were all safe, none had been lost, none had got wet, a few were merely slightly crumpled. 'Here you are, Peter, I think they're all here, and they hardly seem to be damaged at all,' I said, smoothing some of them out. But Wheeler was still unable to speak, and he pointed at me repeatedly with his finger as if at an heir or at an addressee, and I understood that these drawings were for me, that he was giving them to me. He opened the file and I began putting the drawings back, apart from the one by Fraser, the one that was not a reproduction but an original cutting, because he raised his forefinger again to stop me as I was about to put it back with the others, then immediately touched his own chest with his thumb. 'No, not that one, that's for me,' said the gesture. 'You're keeping this one?' I asked, trying to help him out. He nodded, I set it aside. It was strange that he should suddenly have been left speechless, just when he had been talking about the few or the many – depending on how one looked at it – who were also speechless. The previous night, when he had been unable to come out with the word 'cushion', he had explained afterwards, when he had recovered his voice or his fluency: 'It happens from time to time. It only lasts a moment, it's like a sudden withdrawal of my will.' And it was then that he had used that rather recondite word, although less so in English than in Spanish: 'It's like a warning, a kind of prescience . . .' without actually completing the sentence, not even when I had urged him to do so shortly afterwards; to which he had replied: 'Don't ask a question to which you already know the answer, Jacobo, it's not your style.' Prescience means a knowledge of future events, or knowing beforehand exactly what will happen. I don't know if such a thing exists, but sometimes we also give a name to what does not exist, and that is where uncertainty begins. I had no doubts now as to how that sentence should end, I had wondered about it and had guessed at it the previous evening, now I knew the answer even though he had not told me: 'It's like a warning, a kind of prescience, a foreknowledge of what it's like to be dead.' And he could perhaps have added: 'It's not being able to talk, even though you want to. Except that you don't want to, your will has withdrawn. There is no wanting and no not wanting, both have gone.' I looked back at the house, Mrs Berry had opened a window on the ground floor and was waving to us. Perhaps she had looked out as soon as she heard the racket made by that predatory helicopter and had, without our realising it, seen me haring around and diving to the ground. I raised my voice to ask: 'Time for lunch?' and accompanied my cry with the rather absurd gesture of one hand held at mouth level, like someone twirling spaghetti round a fork. I don't think she heard me, but she understood. She said 'No' with her hand and then used it to indicate waiting, as if to say: 'No, not yet,' and then pointed at Peter with a gesture of disquiet or uncertainty, 'Is he all right?', was the translation. I nodded several times to reassure her. She raised both hands at once, as if she were being held up at gunpoint, 'Good,' then closed the window and disappeared inside. Wheeler recovered his voice:

'Yes, I'll keep that one, but I can get you a copy if you like,' he said, meaning the drawing by Fraser. 'You can have the others, I've got several copies, or else reproductions of them in books; I have a few other originals too. I particularly like the spider-cum-swastika. Wretched helicopter,' he added without a pause and with a hint of annoyance, 'What on earth was it up to, hanging around a studious area like this? I hope they don't come back again to ruffle our hair; by the way, have you got a comb on you? You Latins usually do.' Wheeler's hair was indeed like the furious foam on the crest of a wave, and mine had clearly become tangled. 'What did Mrs Berry want?' he said, again without a pause. He had gone back to referring to her as he did in company. He was regaining his composure and that must have helped him; or perhaps it was just force of habit in him to dissemble. 'Was she calling us in for lunch already?' He looked at his watch without actually looking at it, he was trying to get over his shock with no need for any remarks from me, although he knew I wasn't going to let him off that easily.

'No, it's not ready yet. I imagine she was frightened by the noise, she wouldn't have known what it was,' I replied, and added, in turn, without a pause: 'You lost your voice again, Peter. Last night, you told me it only happened occasionally. But that's twice now in one weekend.'

'Bah,' he replied evasively, 'it was just a coincidence, bad luck, that damn helicopter. They're absolutely deafening, it sounded almost like an old Sikorsky H-5, the noise alone used to be enough to provoke panic. Besides, I've been talking a lot, I talk far too much when you're here, and then I suffer the consequences, I'm not really used to it any more. You let me ramble on, you pretend to be interested and I'm very grateful to you for that, but you should interrupt me more, make me get to the point. I suppose I've been a bit alone here in Oxford lately, and with Mrs Berry there's nothing more to be said, of what can be said between us, I mean, or of what she might want to talk about. I don't have that many visitors, you know. A lot of people have died, others went to America when they retired and live there like parasites, I didn't want to do that, they just lounge around, getting as much sun as possible, they even go so far as to wear bermuda shorts, they get hooked, via television, on that football they play over there, all padding and helmets, they worry about their digestion and eat nothing but broccoli, they prowl around the library and whatever campus it is that they've landed up in, and allow their departments to exhibit them now and then like prestigious foreign mummies or the wrinkled trophies of some vaguely heroic times that nobody there knows anything about. In short, they're like antiques, most depressing. Besides, I like talking to you. The English shy away from anything that isn't either anecdote, fact, event or ironic gloss or comment; they don't like speculation, they find reasoning superfluous: and that's precisely what I most enjoy. Yes, I like talking to you very much. You should come down more often, especially as you're so alone there in London. Although perhaps soon you'll be much less alone. I still have a proposal to put to you, and I ask you, please, to accept it without giving it too much thought or asking me too many questions. You can't really waste time that you already consider to be wasted, these periods of sentimental convalescence can be filled up with anything, the content doesn't really matter, whatever happens by and helps to push them along will do, one tends, I think I'm right in saying, not to be too choosy. Afterwards, it's hard even to remember those times or what one did while they lasted, as if everything had been permissible then, and one can always cite disorientation and pain as justification; it's as if those times had never existed and as if, in their place, there was a blank. They're free of responsibilities too, "I wasn't myself at the time, you know." Oh, yes, pain has always been our best alibi, the one that best exonerates us of every action. It has always been man's best alibi, I mean, the best alibi for humankind, for both individuals and nations.'

He said all this quite casually, but I couldn't help but feel a twinge of excitement and another of pride, I had always thought that I amused him and that he liked me, and that perhaps I flattered him a little, that he found me easy to be with, but never more than that. He always had a lot to say and to discuss, although he was very sparing with the former; his conversation taught me, instructed me and provided me with new ideas or else renewed ideas that I already had; in short, he captivated me. I don't think I offered him much in return, apart from company and an attentive ear, the look of interest on my face was real not fake. Rylands had bequeathed him to me and, more than that, had turned out to be his brother. Perhaps Peter regarded me with benevolent, affectionate eyes because he, too, saw me partly as a bequest from Toby, although I could never be a substitute for him, as Wheeler was for me. I wasn't old enough, I lacked the shared past, the acuteness, the knowledge, the mystery. I felt slightly embarrassed, I didn't know what to say, so I removed from my inside jacket pocket the Latin comb he had asked me for.

'Here you are, Peter,' I said. 'One small comb.' He looked at it for a second, disconcerted, he had forgotten that he still needed it. Then he gingerly took it from me, held it up to the light (it was clean) and recomposed his hair as best he could, it's not easy without a mirror and with only a small comb. He tamed the top, but not the sides, the aeronautical wind had blown them forward and they were rebelliously invading his temples, giving him a still more Roman air. 'Allow me,' I said. He trustingly handed me the comb, and with three or four rapid movements I smoothed the sides of his hair too. I hoped Mrs Berry wasn't watching us, she would have taken me for a mad, frustrated barber.

'You'd better comb your hair too,' said Wheeler, regarding my head critically, almost with distaste, as if I had a parrot perched on top of it. 'I don't know how you managed it, but you've got grass stains all over you. And you hadn't even noticed.' He indicated the front of my pale shirt, revealing that he didn't make the connection between the two or three smudges of green and my rescue of his drawings. What with the party the night before, my subsequent studies and the glasses of wine, the lack of sleep, the very rapid shave I had given myself and my recent vicissitudes al fresco, I must have looked like a beggar down to his last penny or a disgraced criminal fallen on very hard times. My jacket and trousers were crumpled from rolling around on the grass. 'Honestly,' said Wheeler, 'you're just like a child.' He was probably pulling my leg, and that cheered him up too. I ran my fingers over the small comb (a mechanical gesture) and then disentangled my hair, by touch alone. When I had finished, I turned to him for his opinion:

'How do I look?' I said, theatrically displaying my two profiles.

'You'll pass,' he said, after casting a condescending eye over me, like a superior officer making a cursory inspection of a soldier's head. And then he returned to where he had been just before the aerial attack, he never lost the thread unless he wanted to. Despite the many detours, meanderings, diversions, he always concluded his trajectories. 'So what happened with that campaign?' he asked rhetorically. 'Well, overall, naturally enough, it failed. A failure to which it was irremissibly condemned from the start. Well, it served some purpose, obviously, quite a good purpose really: people became aware of the dangers of talking too much, something that had never even occurred to most of them. It doubtless had an effect on many in the armed forces and that was the main thing, since they would be the best-informed and the most vulnerable to the consequences of verbal excess or carelessness. And the leaders, both political and military, were, of course, very careful indeed. There was an increased tendency to communicate in code, or else through *doubles entendres* and semantic transpositions, using improvised or rough-and-ready synecdoches and metalepses, and this happened spontaneously throughout the population, depending on the individual's talents and abilities. The idea that someone, anyone, could be listening with hostile intent was created and implanted. You could say (and this, in itself, was both unusual and admirable) that people became fully and collectively aware, however temporarily, of what was depicted in that sequence of scenes that begins with the sailor talking to the young woman: the fact that our words, once uttered, are beyond our control. They, more than anything, cease to belong to us, far more so than our actions which, in a way, good or bad, stay inside ourselves, and cannot be appropriated by anyone else, except in flagrant cases of usurpation or imposture, which, however tardily, can always be denounced, aborted, undone or unmasked.' Wheeler used the Spanish verb '*desfacer*' for 'undone'. He had also used the Spanish '*como estaba mandado*' and '*de andar por casa*' for 'naturally enough' and 'rough-and-ready' – he liked to show off both his colloquial and his bookish Spanish, as he did with his Portuguese and French, I suppose, those were the three languages he knew best, and possibly others, he certainly, to my knowledge, had a smattering of

Hindi, German and Russian. 'Nothing surrenders itself so completely as the word. One pronounces words and immediately lets them go and gives possession, or, rather, usufruct, to the person who hears them. That person may agree with them, to start with, which is not necessarily pleasing because in a sense, by doing so, he or she takes them over; the person may refute them, which is equally unpleasing; more than that, he or she can, in turn, transmit them limitlessly, acknowledging their source or making them theirs depending on their mood, depending on how decent they are or on whether or not they want to ruin or betray us, depending on the circumstances; not only that, they can elaborate on them, improve on them or mar them, distort them, slant them, quote them out of context, change their tone, alter their emphasis and thus easily give them a different and even a contrary meaning to the one they had on our lips, or when we conceived them. And they can, of course, repeat them exactly, verbatim. This was what people most feared during the war, which is why many people tried to speak obliquely, metaphorically or nebulously, with deliberate vagueness or even resorting to secret languages. Many learned to say things without really saying them, and became accustomed to that.'

'Something of the sort happened during Franco's dictatorship in Spain, to get around the censorship laws,' I said; Wheeler had, after all, invited me to interrupt him more often. 'Many people started talking and writing in a symbolic, allusive, parabolic or abstract way. You had to make yourself understood within the deliberate obscurity of what you were saying. A complete nonsense: camouflaging yourself, concealing yourself and yet, nevertheless, wanting to be recognised and wanting the most diffuse, cryptic and confused of messages to be picked up and understood. People have no patience for the hard work involved in deciphering codes. It lasted far too long, and at one point it looked as if it wasn't just a passing phase either, but was here to stay. Some people never managed to lose the habit afterwards, and that was when they fell silent.'

Wheeler listened to me, and it occurred to me that if he took me up on what I had said, he might get diverted once more from his trajectory. Now, however, he seemed resolved to continue along that path, albeit at his own measured pace:

'Many learned to say things without really saying them,' he repeated, 'but what almost no one learned to do was to say nothing, to keep silent, which is what was being asked of them and what was needed. It was normal, it's only natural: it's an impossible thing for most ordinary mortals, believe me, it's asking too much of them, it goes against their very essence, that's why the campaign was always doomed to more than partial failure. It was tantamount to saying to people: "Right, not only do you have to put up with all the shortages, the hardships and the rationing, endure enemy bombing raids – never knowing, despite the wailing sirens, who might not wake up tomorrow or tonight – see your homes set on fire or reduced in an instant to rubble after the explosion and the noise, and sit buried for hours in deep shelters so as not to be burned in streets that still seem just the same, and suffer the loss of husbands and sons or, at the very least, their absence and the constant torment of anxiety over their daily survival or death, to climb into planes and, while you do battle with the air, to be machine-gunned by the enemy, who do everything possible to bring you down, to be sunk and go under, in distant, flaming waters, in submarines and destroyers and warships, and suffocate or be burned alive inside a tank, and parachute out over occupied territory only to come under artillery fire or be set upon by dogs if you do manage to land safely, and be blown to pieces if you have the bad but very possible luck to be hit by a shell or a grenade, and then face torture and the executioner if you're caught on your mission in forbidden territory wearing civilian clothes, or engage in hand-to-hand combat at the front with bayonets fixed, in fields, in woods, in jungles, in swamps, in arctic and in desert conditions, and blithely blow off the head of the boy who peers out at you wearing the hated helmet and uniform, and not know, day or night, whether or not you will lose this war, a war which may turn out, in the end, to have served only to make of you forgotten corpses or the perpetual prisoners or slaves of your conquerors, and put up with extreme cold and hunger and thirst and distress and, above all, fear, fear and more fear, a continual terror to which you will eventually become habituated even though you have already spent several years like this and that eventual state of habituation has not yet arrived . . ." Yes,' added Peter, coming to an abrupt halt, making a minimal pause and then taking a long breath, 'it was like saying to people: "As well as all this, you must keep silent too. You must not speak any more, or tell stories or jokes, or ask, still less answer questions, not of your wife, not of your husband, not of your children, not of your father and definitely not of your mother, your brother or your best friend. And as for your beloved . . . don't even whisper in your beloved's ear, not a word, no truths or sweet nothings or lies, don't say goodbye to her, don't even give her the consolation of voice and word, don't leave as a souvenir even the murmur of the last false promises we always make when we say goodbye."' Wheeler stopped and became suddenly abstracted, banging his knuckles on his chin, a few soft taps, as if he were remembering, I thought, as if he had experienced this too, withholding the truly important words from his beloved, the words that cry out to be heard and to be said, the words that are so easily forgotten afterwards and become confused with other words or are repeated to other people with identical lightness and with just the same joy, but which, at each last moment, seem so necessary, even though they may only be sweet nothings, extravagant and therefore somewhat insincere, that's the least important thing, at each last moment. 'That's how it was, or pretty much. Not put so crudely, not in those terms. But that's how it was understood by many, that's how it was understood and accepted by the most pessimistic and demoralised, by the very frightened and the very despondent and the already defeated, and in time of war they make up the majority. In time of uncertain wars, that is, those which, quite rightly, people fear might be lost at any moment and which are always hanging by a thread, day after day and night after night, over long, eternal years, wars that really are a matter of life and death, of total extermination or battered, besmirched survival. The most recent ones don't fall into that category, the wars in Afghanistan or Kosovo or the Gulf, or the Falklands War, what a joke. Or the Malvinas, if you prefer, oh, you should have seen how pathetically worked up people became, in front of their television sets I mean, I found it all very upsetting. In today's wars, the euphoric abound, smugly following the wars from their armchairs. Euphorically, of course. The great fools. The criminals. Oh, I don't know. But then, it was just too much to ask, don't you think? To expect people to put up with all that and then to keep silent about the very thing tormenting them, without letting up even for an hour. The innumerable dead had been quite silent enough.'

'And did you yourself keep silent?' I asked. 'Did the campaign affect you?'

'Of course. It affected me, as it did most people. In theory, you see, a lot of people took the recommendations absolutely literally. And not only in theory, but in the collective memory too. Overall, I'd say it was, inevitably, a failure, but if you ask other people who lived through that period or who've heard about it first hand, or if you look up references to "careless talk" in certain books, whether historical or sociological or that mixture of both which is now pretentiously known as microhistory, you'll find that the accepted version, and even genuine personal recollections of the time, all affirm and believe that the campaign was a great success. And it's not that they're consciously lying or have come to some common agreement on the subject or that they're all quite mistaken, it's just that the real impact of something like that is barely verifiable or measurable (how can we possibly know how many catastrophes were unleashed by careless talk or how many avoided by secrecy?), and when wars are won (particularly a war in which all the odds are stacked against you), it's easy, almost unavoidable really, to think, in retrospect, that every effort made was selfless and vital and heroic, and that each and every one contributed to the victory. We had such a bad time and were so consumed by uncertainty, let us at least tell ourselves the tale that most lightens our mourning and compensates us for our sufferings. Oh, I'm sure there were millions of well-intentioned British people who took the warnings and the slogans very seriously indeed, and believed themselves to be scrupulously applying them in practice: that's what they believed in their consciences, and some actually did comply, especially, as I said, the troops and the politicians and the civil servants and the diplomats. As, of course, did I, but this involved no particular merit on my part: bear in mind that between 1942 and 1946 I was only in England for very short periods of time, when I was home on leave or on some specific mission which rarely detained me here for very long, my main base was miles away, my postings far too variable. As you saw in *Who's Who*, I ended up in the most diverse places during those years, and in jobs that already entailed or required secrecy, discretion, caution, pretence, deceit, betrayal if necessary (in the line of duty), and, needless to say, silence. I had an advantage, it cost me nothing to observe that last stricture to the letter. More than that, perhaps because I was on a constant state of alert wherever I was posted, I was more aware of what was happening to people generally, here at home, in the rearguard. The campaign was also a tremendous temptation, in a way, for the entire population: as immense as it was disregarded, as irresistible as it was unconscious, as unforeseen as it was sybilline.'

'What are you talking about, Peter? I don't understand.'

'The citizens of any nation, Jacobo, the vast majority, normally have nothing of any real value to tell anyone. If you stop each night to think about what has been told or recounted to you during the day by the many or few people with whom you have spoken (their degree of culture and knowledge is irrelevant), you will see how rare it is ever to hear anything of real value or interest or discernment, leaving to one side details and matters of a merely practical nature, but including, of course, on the other hand, everything that has reached you via the newspaper, the television or the radio (it's different if you've read it in a book, although that depends on the book). Almost everything that everyone says and communicates is humbug or padding, superfluous, commonplace, dull, interchangeable and trite, however much we feel it to be "ours" and however much people "feel the need to express themselves", to use the appallingly "*cursi*" phrase of the day. It would have made not a jot of difference if the millions of opinions, feelings, ideas, facts and news that are expressed and recounted in the world had never been expressed at all.' (Needless to say, Wheeler resorted to my language for that word '*cursi*', which has no exact equivalent in any other, but which here would mean something like 'corny'.) '"*Hablando se entiende la gente*", you often say in Spanish. "Talk things over and sort things out". "It's good to talk," people say in various situations and contexts. All it needed was for psychologists and the like to put that absurd notion into the heads of talkers for the latter to give even freer rein to what has always been their natural tendency. Talking is not in itself either good or bad, and as for people sorting things out by talking to each other, well, talking is just as much a source of conflict and misunderstanding as it is of harmony and understanding, of injustice and reparation, of war and armistice, as much a source of crimes and betrayals as it is of loyalties and loves, of condemnations and salvations, of insults and rages as it is of consolations and mollifications. Talking is probably the biggest waste of time amongst the population as a whole, regardless of age, sex, class, wealth or knowledge, it is wastage *par excellence*. Almost no one has anything to say that their potential listeners might consider to be of any real value, worth listening to, let alone bought, I mean no one pays for something that is normally free, apart from in a few very exceptional cases, and yet sometimes you're obliged to. Strangely, though, and despite everything, the majority continues to talk endlessly and every day. It's astonishing, Jacobo, when you stop to think: men and women are constantly explaining and recounting, as well as explaining themselves to themselves *ad nauseam*, looking for someone to listen to them or imposing their diatribes on others if they can, fathers on children, teachers on pupils, parish priests on parishioners, husbands on wives and wives on husbands, commanding officers on troops and bosses on subalterns, politicians on their supporters and even on the nation as a whole, television on its viewers, writers on their readers and even singers on their adolescent fans, who pay them the still greater tribute of chanting the choruses of their songs. Patients impose their diatribes on their psychiatrists too, except that here the nature of the relationship is revealing, it's a very clear transaction: the listener charges, the speaker pays. He who talks most pays most.' (These last words were again in Spanish: '*Desembolsa quien raja, se retrata quien larga*' – I thought of a woman friend of mine in Madrid, Dr García Mallo, a very wise psychiatrist: I would advise her to increase her fees without the slightest twinge of conscience.) 'That is an exemplary relationship, and it would, in fact, be the most appropriate relationship for all occasions. For there's a real shortage of people willing to listen, there are never many, mainly because there are infinitely more who aspire to be in the other man's trench, that is, to be the ones doing the talking and, therefore, being listened to. In fact, if you think about it, a permanent and universal struggle is being waged to grab the floor: in any crowded place, private or public, there are dozens if not hundreds of irrepressible voices fighting to prevail or to cut in, and the desideratum of each voice would be to rise above all the others and silence them: and that, within tolerable limits, is what they try to do. It could be a street or a market or Parliament, the only difference is that, in the end, they agree to take turns and those waiting are forced to pretend to be listening; it could be in a pub or at a tea-party in a stately home, only the intensity and the tempo vary, in the latter one moves very slowly, one dissembles a little in order to gain confidence before holding forth as if in a tavern, albeit with the volume turned down. Gather four people round a table and very soon at least two of them will be competing to call the tune. I did well to become a teacher: for many years I enjoyed, unimpeded, the enormous privilege of not being interrupted by anyone, or, at least, not without my prior consent. And I still enjoy that privilege in my books and articles. That is the illusion of all writers, the belief that people open our books and read them from start to finish, holding their breath and barely pausing. It is and always has been, believe me, I know from my own experience and from that of others, you, as far as I know, have so far escaped, you have no idea how wise you have been not to be tempted by writing. For that is the illusory idea of all novelists, who publish their various immense tomes full of adventures and endless reflections, like Cervantes in Spain, like Balzac, Tolstoy, Proust, and the author of that tedious quartet about Alexandria that was once all the rage, or Oxford's own Tolkien (who really *was* born in South Africa), the number of times I passed him in Merton College or saw him with Clive Lewis, enjoying a drink of an evening at The Eagle and Child, and not one of us had an inkling of the fate that awaited his three eccentric volumes, he even less than us, his highly sceptical colleagues; it's an illusion shared by poets too, who pack so much into those deceptively short lines, like Rilke and Eliot, or before them, Whitman and Milton, and, before them, your own great poet, Manrique; it's shared by playwrights who aim to keep an audience in their seats for four or more hours, as Shakespeare himself did in *Hamlet* and *Henry IV*: of course, at the time, a lot of the audience would have been standing and would have quite happily strolled in and out of the theatre as many times as they wished; it's shared by all those chroniclers and diarists and memorialists like Saint-Simon, Casanova, El Inca Garcilaso and Bernal Díaz or our own illustrious Pepys, who never tire of furiously filling up those sheets with ink; it's shared by such essayists as the incomparable Montaigne or me (not, I can assure you, that I'm comparing myself with him), who ingenuously imagine, while we write, that someone will have the miraculous degree of patience required to swallow everything we want to tell them about Henry the Navigator, it's madness, isn't it, I mean, my latest book about him is nearly five hundred pages long, it's rank discourtesy, an abuse really. Have you read it yet, by the way?'

'No, Peter, I haven't, you must forgive me, I'm truly sorry. I find it very hard to concentrate on reading at the moment,' I replied, and I wasn't lying. 'But when I do read it, don't worry, I'll be sure to read the whole thing from start to finish, holding my breath and barely pausing,' I added, smiling, and in a tone of gentle, affectionate fun, and he reciprocated with a slight smile, with that rapid glance of his, with those eyes so much younger than the rest of him. And then I asked: 'Anyway, what temptation? I mean the one that the campaign against careless talk brought with it. You were telling me about that, weren't you, or were about to?'

'Ah, yes. Good, I like it when you do as you're told and keep me on a tight rein.' And there was a mocking quality about his reply too. 'No one realised at first, but the temptation was very simple and hardly surprising really: you see, this same population who normally never had anything of vital interest to tell anyone were suddenly informed that their tongue, their chatter and their natural verbosity could constitute a danger, they were urged to watch what they talked about and to keep an eye on where, when and with whom they talked; they were warned that almost anyone could be either a Nazi spy or someone in their pay listening in to what they said, as illustrated by the cartoon of the two housewives travelling on the Underground or the men playing darts. And this was tantamount to saying to the people: "You probably won't notice, but important, crucial information could occasionally emerge from your lips, and it would be best, therefore, if it was never uttered at all, in any circumstance. You probably won't recognise it, but amongst the rubbish that pours daily from your mouths, there could be something of value, of immense value to the enemy. Contrary to the normal state of affairs, that is, other people's general lack of interest in whatever you insist on telling them or explaining to them, it is likely that, amongst you now, there could be ears that would be more than happy to pay you all the attention in the world, and even to draw you out. In fact, there definitely are: a lot of German parachutists have been landing in Britain lately, and they are all well prepared, specially trained to deceive us, they know our language as well as if they were natives of Manchester, Cardiff or Edinburgh, and they know our customs too, because quite a few of them have lived here in the past or are half-English, on their mother's or their father's side, although now they have opted for the worse of their two bloods. They land or disembark bereft of all scruples, but amply provided with arms and perfectly forged documents, or, if not, their accomplices here will soon obtain them for them, many of these accomplices are our genuine compatriots, as British as our grandparents, and these traitors are hanging on your every word, to see what they can pick up and transmit to their butchering bosses, to see if we let something slip. So be very careful: the fate of our air force, our navy, our army, our prisoners and our spies could depend on your irresponsible chit-chat or on your loyal silence. The fate of this war, which has already cost us so much blood, toil, tears and sweat"' (and Wheeler quoted the words in their correct order, without forgetting 'toil', as people always do) '"may lie not perhaps in your hands, but definitely in your tongue. And it would be unforgivable if we were to lose the war because of a slip on your part, because of an entirely avoidable act of imprudence, because one of us was incapable of biting or holding his tongue." That is how people saw the situation, the country plagued with Nazi agents all with ears cocked, ready to eavesdrop' (a rather difficult word to translate into Spanish) 'not just in London and in the big cities but in the smaller ones too and in villages, not to mention on the coast and even in the fields. The few anti-Nazi Germans and Austrians who had sought refuge here years before, after the rise to power of Hitler, had a pretty awful time of it, I knew Wittgenstein, for example, who had spent half his life in Cambridge, I met the great actor Anton Walbrook and the writer Pressburger and those magnificent scholars at the Warburg Institute of Art: Wind, Wittkower, Gombrich, Saxl, and Pevsner too, some of whose oldest neighbours suddenly began to distrust them, poor things, they were British citizens and probably had a keener interest than anyone in seeing Nazism defeated. It was at this time that they first brought in an official identity card, against our tradition and our preference, to make things a little more difficult for any would-be German infiltrators. But people weren't used to carrying such a document and kept losing it, and there was such generalised hostility to it that, around 1951 or 1952, the card in question was suppressed in order to quell the discontent provoked by its obligatory nature. According to Tupra, there is talk in government circles of imposing something similar, along with other inquisitorial measures, these mediocrities who rule over us in such a totalitarian spirit and who have more or less been given *carte blanche* to do so by the Twin Towers massacre. I hope they don't get their way. They can insist all they want, but we are not truly at war now, not a war of constant uncertainty and pain. And although there are only a few of us left who played an active part in the Second World War, for us it's insulting, an out-and-out mockery, what these pusillanimous, authoritarian fools want to do and impose on us in the name of security, that prehistoric pretext. We didn't fight those who wanted to control each and every aspect of our lives only to see our grandchildren come along and slyly but very precisely fulfil the crazed fantasies of the very enemies we vanquished. Oh, I don't know . . . but then, whatever happens, I won't be here much longer to see it, fortunately.' And Wheeler looked down at the grass again while he muttered these superfluous phrases, or perhaps he was looking at the various cigarette ends I had been scattering on the ground and stubbing out with my shoe. This time, however, he immediately took up the thread on his own: 'So what was the effect of telling all this to the citizens of the time? They found themselves in a strange, almost paradoxical situation: they might possibly be in possession of valuable information, but most of them had no idea whether or not it really was or, if it was, what the devil that information could be; they had no idea either who in their world would find it of value, which close friends or acquaintances or, indeed, anyone else, which meant that no one could ever be discounted as a potential danger; they knew, lastly, that if these two eternally unverifiable factors or elements should occur – that is, their unconscious possession of some piece of valuable information and the proximity of a concealed enemy who might extract it from them or happen to overhear it' (here he used another verb in the same semantic area – 'overhear' – which, again, has no exact equivalent in my language), 'that conjunction could be of enormous significance and could have calamitous results. The idea that what one says, speaks, comments upon, mentions or recounts could be of importance and cause harm and be coveted by others, even if only by the Devil and all his hosts, is irresistible to most people; and, consequently, two opposing, contradictory and conflicting tendencies came together and coexisted in them: the first meant keeping silent about everything all the time, even the most anodyne and innocuous of facts, in order to ward off any threat as well as any feeling of guilt, or any sense of having fallen into some horrific error; the second entailed telling and talking about absolutely everything in front of everyone everywhere (whatever one knew or had heard, most of it trivia, froth, nothing), in order to have a taste of adventure, or its ghost, to feel a *frisson* of danger, as well as the new and unfamiliar thrill of one's own importance. What's the point of having something valuable if you don't parade and exhibit and rub it in people's faces, or of having something covetable if you can't feel other people's covetousness or at least the possibility and the risk that they might snatch it from you, or of having a secret if, at some point, you don't reveal or betray it. Only then can you get the true measure of its enormity and its prestige. Sooner or later, you get tired of thinking to yourself: "Ah, if they only knew, ah, if he ever found out, oh, if she knew what I know." And sooner or later, the moment comes to produce it, to get rid of it, to surrender it, even if it's only once and to only one person, it happens to us all sooner or later. But since the citizens (with some exceptions) were incapable of distinguishing gold from mere trinkets, many would, with a pleasurable shudder of excitement, place everything they had on the counter or the table, attracted by the thought that they might have before them some evil spy, at the same time, crossing their fingers and praying to heaven that they didn't, and that there wouldn't be anyone either who could pass it on, their confusing or impetuous story I mean. And nothing could be more thrilling than that some more responsible, upright compatriot should tell them off and reproach them for being so flippant, because that was an almost unmistakable sign to the speaker that he had entered the forbidden territory of the serious, the meaningful and the weighty where he had never before set foot. That state of fearful excitement, of laying oneself open to harm and simultaneously exposing the whole nation to harm as well, is illustrated by that cartoon of a man phoning from a public call-box besieged by little Führers, and by the third, rather than the second, scene of the sequence that begins with the sailor and his girlfriend, that's them to a T. Most people, whether intelligent or stupid, respectful or inconsiderate, vitriolic or kindly, resemble, to a greater or lesser extent, that young woman with her brown hair caught up on top of her head: generally speaking, they listen with amazement and glee, even if they're being told something really terrible, because (and this is the reason why, briefly and occasionally, they deign to pay attention, because they can already imagine themselves retelling it) it's overlaid with the anticipated pleasure of themselves passing on the news, even if it's repugnant, horrifying, or brings with it awful sorrow, or provokes in others the very reaction being provoked in them now. Basically, all that interests us and matters to us is what we share, pass on, transmit. We always want to feel part of a chain, we are, how can I put it, the victims and agents of an inexhaustible contagion. And that is the greatest contagion, the one that is within the grasp of everyone, the one brought to us by words, this plague of talking from which I, too, suffer, well, you can see what happens, how I launch off once you let go of the rope. All credit, then, to anyone who has ever refused to follow this predominant inclination. And even more credit to anyone who was brutally interrogated and who, nevertheless, said nothing, gave nothing away. Even if their life depended on it, and they lost their life.'

I heard the sound of the piano coming from the house, background music to the river and the trees, to the garden and to Wheeler's voice. A Mozart sonata perhaps, or it could be by one of the Bachs, Johann Christian, one of Mozart's teachers and the poor, brilliant son of the genius, he lived in England for many years and is known there as 'the London Bach' and his music is often remembered and performed, an English German like those who worked at the Warburg Institute and like that admirable Viennese actor who was known first as Adolf Wohlbrück, and who also abandoned his name, and like Commodore Mountbatten, who was originally Battenberg, bogus Britons all of them, not even Tolkien was free of that. (Like my colleague, Rendel, who was an Austrian Englishman.) Mrs Berry must have finished all her chores and was amusing herself until it was time to call us in for lunch. She and Wheeler both played; she played with great energy, but I had rarely seen or heard him playing at all, I remembered one occasion when he wanted to introduce me to a song entitled *Lillabullero* or *Lilliburlero* or something rather Spanish-sounding like that, the piano was not in the living-room, but upstairs, in an otherwise empty room, there was nothing you could do there except sit down at the instrument. Maybe it was the contrast of the present cheerful music with his own mournful words, but

Wheeler seemed suddenly very tired, he raised one hand to his forehead and allowed the full weight of his head to fall on his hand, his elbow resting on the table with its full-skirted canvas cover. 'And so the centuries pass,' I thought, while I waited for him to go on or else put an end to the conversation, I feared he might opt for the latter, he had become too conscious that he was lecturing, and I saw him close his eyes as if they were stinging, although they were hidden by the fingers resting on his forehead. 'And so the centuries pass and nothing ever yields or ends, everything infects everything else, nothing releases us. And that "everything" slides like snow from the shoulders, slippery and docile, except that this snow travels through time and beyond us, and may never stop.'

'Andreu Nin lost his life,' I said at last, my improvised studies of the long previous night still floating in my head. 'Andrés Nin,' I said, when I noticed Wheeler's confusion, which I noticed despite the fact that he had still not moved, and remained motionless and apparently drained. 'He didn't talk, he didn't answer, he gave no names, he said nothing. Nin, I mean, while they were torturing him. It cost him his life, although they would probably have taken his life anyway.' But Wheeler still did not understand or perhaps he simply did not want any more bifurcations.

'What?' he managed to ask, and I saw that he was opening his eyes, saw a gleam of stupefaction, as if he thought I had gone mad, what's that got to do with anything. His mind was too far from Madrid and Barcelona in the spring of 1937, maybe what he had experienced in Spain, whatever it was, had dwindled in importance compared with what came afterwards, from the late summer of 1939 to the spring of 1945, or possibly even later in his case. And so I tried to return to the country we were in, to Oxford, to London (sometimes I forgot that he was well over eighty; or, rather, I forgot all the time, and only occasionally remembered):

'So the campaign was counterproductive, then?' I said.

He slowly uncovered his face and I saw that he was looking refreshed again, it was extraordinary how he recovered or recomposed himself after those moments of low spirits or of weariness or inability to speak, it was usually interest – his scheming mind, or the desire to say or hear something, something more – that revived him. Or else humour, a flash of irony, charm, wit.

'Not exactly,' he replied, slightly screwing up his eyes, as if they were still stinging. 'It would be both facile and unfair to say that. There was very little malice in people, not really, not even amongst the most indiscreet and boastful of blockheads.' And this last word he said in Spanish, '*botarates*', sometimes you could tell that he hadn't visited my country for quite some time, because you never hear that word there now, or, for obvious reasons, other similar words: after all, when a society consists largely of imbeciles, halfwits, blockheads and oafs there is no point in anyone calling anyone else names. 'And there were others, too, who remained silent as the grave. I'm not referring to the dead, but to certain scrupulous, strong-willed, tenacious people with a keen sense of duty, who unhesitatingly sealed their lips, even though no one would ever know of their obedient response or congratulate them on it. There were many such people, although perhaps not that many, it was a very difficult order to carry out, almost absurd really, "Don't speak, not a murmur, not a whisper, nothing, because they can read your lips, so forget your language."' ('Keep quiet, then save yourself', was what crossed my mind and, also, just for a second, I wondered whether my Uncle Alfonso would have talked or kept silent, we would never know.) 'The reason I say that the campaign failed overall is not because people were not prepared to comply, the majority were; and it served a purpose, it served to give us a general awareness that we were not alone, but had as many companions as actors in a theatre; and that beyond the spotlights, in the penumbra, in the shadows or the darkness, we had a packed and very attentive audience, each member of which was endowed with an excellent memory, however invisible, unrecognisable and scattered that audience might be, and was made up of spies, eavesdroppers' (again that word which is so difficult to translate into Spanish), 'fifth columnists, informers and professional decoders; that each word of ours they heard could prove fatal to our cause, just as those we stole from the enemy were vital to us. But at the same time, this campaign – and this was where it was bound to fail despite its indisputable benefits and successes – increased, inevitably and incredibly, the numbers of the verbally incontinent, the out-and-out blabbermouths. And although many people who had previously always talked freely and unconcernedly did learn, as one of these cartoons recommends, to think twice before speaking, there were many others who had always tended to be silent or, at least, laconic, inhibited or taciturn, not out of choice or prudence, but because they felt that anything they might say or tell would be dull, unworthy of anyone's interest and utterly inconsequential, but now they found themselves unable to resist the temptation of feeling dangerous and reprehensible, a threat, and thus deserving attention, to feel, in a way, that they were the protagonists of their own small world, even though, for the most part, that protagonism was mad, unreal, illusory, fictitious, mere wishful thinking. Whatever the reason, they began to talk nineteen to the dozen; to give themselves airs and pretend they were in the know, and anyone who pretends that usually ends up trying to be genuinely in the know, within their capabilities, of course, and thus becomes yet another entirely gratuitous spy. And whether they succeed or not, it is also true to say that everyone knows something, even when they don't know that they do, even when they imagine that they know absolutely nothing. But even the shyest and most solitary of men who merely grunts at his landlady if he should happen to meet her during the day, even the scattiest or most obtuse of women with barely an ounce of intellect, and even the least curious or sociable and most self-absorbed child in the kingdom, all know something, because words, that fierce contagion, spread without any need for help, they overcome all obstacles and proliferate and penetrate more, much more, unspeakably more than you, or indeed anyone, could ever imagine. All it takes is a sharp, detective's ear and a malicious, associative mind to capture and make the most of that something and to express it. The people in charge of the campaign were aware of this, that all of us know some effects and some causes, however unconnected. As I said, what valuable information could those two ladies on the Underground possibly know, or that very ordinary man in the cap, saying: "What I know — I keep to *myself*"? And yet the campaign was also directed at them, at people like them, trying to persuade them to forget their language. A vain endeavour, don't you think, trying to encompass everyone? And a pretty pointless task given that a partial result was no use at all.'

Wheeler stopped and indicated my pack of cigarettes. I held it out to him, offered him a cigarette, and immediately lit it for him. He took a few puffs and looked with bemusement at the lighted end, thinking perhaps that it had not taken, doubtless unaccustomed to the feeble, insipid cigarettes I usually smoke.

'And what did you have to do with all that?' I finally asked.

'Nothing. With that, nothing at all, or, rather, I was just one of many, albeit in a privileged position. As I told you, for most of that time, I was in far less uncomfortable places than London, something that still weighs on my conscience. But I *was* involved in what the campaign indirectly brought with it: the formation of that group. When MI6 and MI5 realised what was tending all too frequently to happen, what we would nowadays call the collateral effect, which, indeed, ran counter to the initiative, it occurred to someone that we should take advantage of that, or at least turn it a little in our favour, place it at our service. Someone, whoever it was (Menzies, Vivian, Hollis or even Churchill himself, it doesn't matter), saw that just by listening attentively and allowing people who wanted to talk and wanted to be heard (sometimes not even that much was necessary), and observing them with a mixture of shrewdness, deductive ability, interpretative boldness and a talent for making associations, that is, with precisely the skills that we assumed and even conceded in the German experts who were infiltrating us and in the hidden pro-Nazis who were on our territory from the start – just by doing all this, we could get to the depths or the bottom, almost to the essence of people; to find out what they would and wouldn't be capable of doing and how far they could be trusted, their characteristics and qualities, their defects and limitations, if they were by nature strong or fragile, corruptible or incorruptible, cowardly or intrepid, treacherous or loyal, impervious or susceptible to flattery, egotistical or generous, arrogant or servile, hypocritical or candid, resolute or hesitant, argumentative or docile, cruel or compassionate, everything, anything, everything. One could also find out beforehand who would be capable of killing in cold blood or who would submit to being killed, should that prove necessary or were they ordered to do so, although the latter is always the most difficult thing to be sure of in anyone; who would turn tail and who would go forward, however insane such a decision might seem; who would betray, who would support, who would fall silent, who would fall in love, who would feel envious or jealous, who would abandon us to the elements and who would always cover us. Who would sell us down the river; and who would do so dearly or cheaply. It might be that the people who rarely spoke would have nothing very grave or interesting to say, but they always ended up revealing almost everything about themselves, even if they were pretending. That is what they discovered. That is what continues to happen today, and that is what we know.'

'But people aren't all of a piece,' I said. 'It all depends on the circumstances, on what happens to turn up, people can change, they can get worse or better or stay the same. My father always says that if we hadn't gone through a war like our Civil War, most of the people who acted despicably during the War or afterwards, once it was over, would probably have led perfectly respectable lives, or lives, at least, that were relatively un-besmirched; and they would never have found out what they were capable of, fortunately for them and for their victims. My father, as you know, was one of the latter.'

'No, people aren't all of a piece, Jacobo, and your father is right. And no one is ever always this way or that, which of us hasn't seen some alarming or unexpected streak appear in someone we love (and then your whole world collapses); you must always remain alert and never imagine that anything is definitive; although there are some things on which there is no going back. And yet, and yet . . . it is also true that, right from the start, we see much more in others and in ourselves, much more than we think we do. As I said before, the biggest problem is that we don't usually want to see, we don't dare to. Almost no one really dares to look, still less to confess or tell themselves what they really see, because often it isn't very pleasant what one observes or glimpses with that undeluded gaze, with that profound gaze which, not content with penetrating every layer, keeps going beyond even the very last one. That, generally speaking, is how it is, both as regards others and oneself; and most people, in order to go on living with a degree of calm and confidence, need to delude themselves and to be slightly optimistic, and that's something I can understand, and something which, throughout the many days of my life, I have missed greatly, that calm and that confidence: it's harsh and unpleasant having to live in that knowledge and expecting nothing else. But that was precisely what the group suggested or proposed, finding out just what individuals, independent of their circumstances, would be capable of and thus being able to know today what face they would wear tomorrow, if I can put it like that: to know right now what their face would be like tomorrow; and, to use your or your father's words, to try and ascertain if a respectable life would have been respectable anyway or was only on loan to them because no opportunity to tarnish that life had yet presented itself, no serious threat of some indelible stain.' ('I still haven't asked him about the bloodstain,' I thought suddenly, 'the stain I cleaned up last night from the top of the stairs'; but I immediately realised that this was not the moment, nor could I now see the stain so very clearly in my mind.) 'But that is knowable, because men carry their probabilities in their veins, and it's only a matter of time, temptation and circumstance before these, at last, lead those probabilities to their realisation. So it is knowable. You can get it wrong, of course, but more often than not you get it right. Besides, it still provides you with some sort of basis to work on, even though the main cornerstone is always something of a gamble.' ('He's right about that,' I thought, 'if another Civil War ever broke out in Spain, I have a pretty good idea who would come and shoot me – I cross my fingers and touch wood, or touch iron as the Italians say; I know who wouldn't think twice before putting a bullet in my brain, just as they did with my Uncle Alfonso. Too many friends have destroyed the trust I placed in them, and when someone is disloyal to you, they never forgive you for their having failed you; and – at least in my country – the greater the betrayal, the greater the offence committed by the betrayed, the greater the traitor's sense of grievance. When it comes to enemies, they are perhaps the one thing of which there has never been any shortage there, almost all us have a few.') 'What proved unexpectedly difficult was finding people who were able to see, interpret and apply that gaze with sufficient dispassion and serenity, without flailing blindly, or even half-blindly, about.' (Wheeler kept resorting more and more frequently to Spanish words and expressions, he doubtless enjoyed making these lightning visits to a language that he had few opportunities to speak any more.) 'Even then it was a rare gift, and it soon became clear that such people were far rarer than one might at first have thought, when the group was thrown together or created in that impromptu, ad hoc fashion, their initial, urgent mission (it later changed direction or broadened out) was to uncover, while the war still raged, not just spies and informers but also possible spies and informers of our own (I mean men and women who might be suitable for that purpose), as well as people who would prove easy or propitiatory prey for the former, the chatterboxes who could not resist temptation and who always showed an imprudent predisposition for talk; and that applied as much to our territory as to other places in the rearguard or places that were neutral, for there were spies and informers and dupes and blabbermouths everywhere, even, I can assure you, in Kingston, by which I mean Kingston, Jamaica, not Kingston-upon-Hull or Kingston-upon-Thames. And in Havana too, of course.' ('So the Caribbean meant Cuba and Jamaica,' I stopped to think for a moment, unable to avoid consciously registering the fact. 'What would they have sent Peter there to do?') 'At the time, an awful lot of British people had developed an inquisitorial spirit or a paranoid mentality or both, and their suspicious nature drove them to denounce almost anything that moved, to see Nazis in the mirror before realising they were looking at their own reflection, and so they were no use at all. Then there were the great distracted masses, who tend to see little and observe nothing and to distinguish still less, who seem to be permanently wearing tight earflaps over their ears and a blindfold over their eyes, or, at best, a mask with eye-slits that were very narrow or virtually stitched shut. Then there were the impetuous and the frivolous and the gung-ho, who were so eager to be involved in something useful and important (not all of them, poor things, were ill-intentioned), they would gaily come out with the first bit of nonsense that popped into their heads, so having them passing judgement was like throwing a dice, since their opinions lacked all validity and foundation. Then there were the many who, exactly as happens now, had a real aversion, no, more than that, a terror of the arbitrariness and possible unfairness of their own views: the sort who prefer never to declare themselves, hamstrung by responsibility and by their invincible fear of making a mistake, the ones who anxiously asked themselves when confronted by a face: "And what if this man whom I believe to be honest turns out to be an enemy agent, and my incompetence leads to my own death and that of my compatriots?" "And what if this woman whom I consider to be suspicious and devious turns out to be entirely harmless and my hasty judgement leads to her ruin?" They couldn't even point us in the right direction. So, foolish though it may seem, it immediately became apparent that there wasn't much to choose from, not, at least, with any confidence. It was necessary to comb the country for recruits as quickly as possible, there were no more than twenty or twenty-five here in England, plus a few others where we happened to be, and we joined when we came back. Most were from the Secret Services, from the Army, a few from the former OIC, which you've probably never heard of,' Wheeler caught my blank look, 'the navy's Operational Intelligence Centre, there weren't many of them, but they were very good, possibly the best; and, of course, from our universities: they always turn to the studious and the sedentary when it comes to difficult, delicate tasks. It's almost unimaginable the debt they owe us since the war, which is when they first began using us seriously, and they should have respected Blunt's immunity and their pact until the day he died, even until Judgement Day' ('We died at such a place,' I thought or quoted to myself), 'even if only out of gratitude and deference to the profession. Obviously we all had to get used to the job, and work to improve, refine and hone our gaze and attune our listening, practice is the only way to sharpen any sense, or gift, which comes to the same thing. We never had a name, they never called us anything, not during the war or afterwards. You can only convincingly deny or conceal the existence of something if it doesn't have a name; that's why you'll find nothing in books, not even in the really thoroughly researched ones, at most, hints, conjectures, intuitions, the odd isolated case, loose ends. It was better like that: we even wrote reports on the trustworthiness of the top brass, Guy Liddell, Sir

David Petrie, Sir Stewart Menzies himself, and I think someone drew up a report on Churchill based on newsreels and which was, therefore, not entirely to be trusted. In a way, we placed ourselves above them all, it was an experiment in audacity. Of course, they never found out about our excesses, it was semi-clandestine. That's why it seems a grave mistake on Tupra's part, this tendency of his to speak in private (only amongst ourselves I trust, but that already constitutes a risk) of "interpreters of people" or "translators of lives" or "anticipators of histories" and suchlike; rather smugly too, given that he's in charge and is therefore including himself among them. Names, nicknames, sobriquets, aliases, euphemisms are quickly taken up and, before you know it, they've stuck, you find yourself always referring to things or people in the same way, and that soon becomes the name they're known by. And then there's no getting rid of it, or forgetting it.' ('And yet so many of us abandon even our own name.')

Wheeler fell silent then and glanced at his watch, and this time he did register the position of the hands; then he looked back at the house, Mrs Berry's piano-playing was still providing us with an accompaniment.

'Shall I go and see how lunch is coming on, Peter?' I suggested. 'We might be running a bit late. My fault.'

'No, the music is reaching the end now, there's just a very brief *minuetto* to come. She'll call us at five minutes to, it's only twelve minutes to at the moment. I know this piece.'

I was tempted to ask him what the piece was, but I wanted him to answer another question, and opportunities vanish so quickly:

'Am I to understand, Peter, that what you call "the group" is still active, and that Mr Tupra is in charge?'

'We'll talk more about that in a minute, because I want you to do me a favour in that regard. It would be a good thing for you too, I think; in fact, I phoned Tupra this morning, while you were still asleep, to tell him that you had shown great perspicacity in the test, about him and Beryl I mean. But, yes, I suppose you could say that; although it's changed so much I barely recognise it. It's difficult to be sure that anything or, for that matter, anyone, has remained unchanged. As far as I can tell, these anonymous duties and activities have evolved a lot, and are required for very different purposes. I imagine they've gone downhill, like everything else: that's just a realistic supposition, I don't say that in order to criticise or blame anyone. I simply don't know. Look at me: am I the same as I was then? Can I, for example, be the man who married a very young girl who has stayed forever young and who has not accompanied me on one single day of my long old age? Doesn't that possibility, that idea, that apparent truth, doesn't it seem totally incongruous, for example, with the man I've been since? Or with the acts I committed later, when she was no longer there to witness them? Or even, simply, with the way I look now? She was so very young, you see, how can I possibly be the same man?'

Wheeler again raised one hand to his forehead, but not this time out of sudden exhaustion or fright, his gesture was a thoughtful one, as if he were intrigued by his own questions. And then I tried to get him to answer another question, although it was perhaps absurd to do so at that precise moment, when lunch with Mrs Berry was only a matter of minutes away. Although, had he chosen to respond, he probably wouldn't have minded answering the question in her presence, for she would know the whole story.

'How did your wife die, Peter? I've never known. I've never asked you. You've never told me.'

Wheeler removed his hand from his forehead and looked at me, red-faced, not from surprise or annoyance, but with his eyes alert.

'Why do you ask me that now?' he said.

'Well,' I replied, smiling, 'perhaps so that you won't one day reproach me for never having shown any interest, for never having asked you about it before, as you did last night when I finally found out about your part in our War. That's why I'm asking now.'

Wheeler suppressed a smile, immediately erasing the temptation. He raised his hand to his chin and made the same sound that Toby Rylands used to make when he was considering how best to answer:

'H'm,' that was the sound. 'H'm', the sound of Oxford. Then he spoke: 'It's not because you're worried about Luisa, is it, and that you suddenly thought the worst and saw yourself reflected in me? Is that it? You're not afraid you might end up widowed rather than divorced, are you? Be careful with such apprehensions. Distance invokes many ghosts. Loneliness does too. And ignorance even more.'

This disconcerted me slightly, it could be a cunning ploy on Wheeler's part to avoid the question, a swift change of direction. But I wasn't going to let him go. I nevertheless paused to think. He was, unwittingly, quite right, at least in part, and I didn't see why he shouldn't know that, for he so enjoyed his own perspicacity:

'Yes, I am a bit worried. And about the children, too, of course. I haven't really had much news of them since I've been here, and even less of Luisa. There's a kind of opacity, even though we talk to each other fairly frequently. I don't know who she's seeing, or not seeing, who comes in and who goes out, it's a kind of process of creeping ignorance, of her and her replacement world, or perhaps that world is still in flux. The truth is I no longer know what's going on in my own house, I have no images any more. It's as if the old images had grown dimmer and get darker every day. But that isn't why I asked you, Peter, it was because you mentioned her – Valerie, I mean.' And I dared to pronounce that name, so private that I had never even heard it until that morning. I had a sense of sacrilege on my lips. 'What did she die of?'

Then Wheeler stopped playing. I saw him tense his jaw, I

noticed him clenching his teeth, lining up top teeth with bottom teeth, like someone summoning up enough composure so that his voice won't break when he speaks again.

'Ah . . .' he said. 'Do you mind if I tell you another day. If that's all right.' He seemed to be asking me a favour, every word was painful.

I did not insist. It occurred to me to whistle the melody I had just heard on the piano, a particularly catchy tune, to see if I could dissipate the mists that had suddenly wrapped about him. But I still had to answer him, silence here was not a reply.

'Of course,' I said. 'Tell me about it when you want to, and if you don't want to tell me, don't.'

Then I began my whistling. I know how infectious whistling is, and so it turned out: Wheeler immediately joined in, probably without even thinking about it; no wonder he knew the piece by heart, he probably played it too. Then he suddenly stopped short and said:

'One shouldn't really ever tell anyone anything.'

Wheeler said this standing up, as soon as he got to his feet, and I immediately followed suit. He grasped my elbow, held on to me to recover his strength. Mrs Berry was waving to us from the window. The music had stopped, and now all that could be heard was our whistling, thin and out of time, as we turned our backs on the river and walked up to the house.

It was still raining and I had not yet grown tired of watching it from my window overlooking the square, it was a steady, comfortable rain, so strong and sustained that it alone seemed to light up the night with its continuous threads like flexible metal bars or endless spears, it was as if it were driving out the night forever and discounting the possibility of any other weather ever appearing in the sky, or even the possibility of its own absence, just like peace when there is peace and like war when war is all that exists. My dancing neighbour opposite had performed a few ridiculous square dances with his partner, such anodyne moves and measured steps after the machine-gun fire of those Gaelic feet, and both had put on cowboy hats for this disappointing end-of-the-party dance, the mad or very fortunate fools. They had just turned out the lights and, given the rain, the mulatto woman would surely be staying the night, but before I could sit thinking warmly of her for a while, I had to be sure, and so for a few minutes, I looked down, beyond the trees and the statue, I watched the square in the unlikely event that she would emerge and leave. And it was then that I saw the two figures coming towards my front door, the woman and the dog, she with her umbrella covering her, and the dog, uncovered, wandering here and there – tis tis tis. As they approached the front of the building, they almost entirely disappeared from my field of vision, by the time they stopped at the door, they were immediately below me, and I could see only a fragment of the cupola of the open umbrella. The bell rang, the downstairs bell. I again looked vainly out for a second, with the window open, leaning out, bending over (my neck and back got wet), before going to pick up the entry-phone: everything except that fragment of curved cloth remained outside my perpendicular line of sight. I picked up the phone. 'Yes?' I said in English, a literal translation from my own language in which I had been thinking, and it was in Spanish that the other person spoke to me: *'Jaime, soy yo,'* – 'Jaime, it's me' – said a female voice. 'Can you open the door, please? I know it's a bit late, but I must talk to you. It'll only take a moment.'

The kind of people who, on the phone or at the door, say simply 'It's me' and don't even bother to give their name are those who forget that 'me' is never anyone, but they are also those who are quite sure of occupying a great deal or a fair part of the thoughts of the person they're looking for. Or else they have no doubt that they will be recognised with no need to say more – who else would it be – from the first word and the first moment. And the woman with the dog was right about this, even if only unconsciously and without having stopped to think about it. Because I did recognise her voice, and I opened the front door for her from upstairs without wondering why she was entering my house that night and coming upstairs to speak to me.

July, 2002